TROLL

DAVE FITZGERALD

Published in the United States and Canada by Whisk(e)y Tit: www.whiskeytit.com. If you wish to use or reproduce all or part of this book for any means, please let the author and publisher know. You're pretty much required to, legally.

ISBN 978-1-952600-32-6

Cover art: *The Painter's Studio*, Gustave Courbet.

For Jeanette,
Who believed in this book before I'd written a word,
Who believed in me before I believed in myself,
You are the best one.

"I dreamt I had entered the body of a hog,
that I could not easily get out again,
and that I was wallowing in the filthiest slime.
Was it a kind of reward?
My dearest wish had been granted;
I no longer belonged to mankind."

— Comte de Lautréamont, *Les Chants de Maldoror*

SEASON 1

Pilot

The day wakes you like a toothy blowjob, your turgid pee-boner scraping rough against yesterday's jeans. You swat at your alarm clock - the equivalent of a Cold War air raid siren - while bayonets of light stick you repeatedly through the slats of your jaundiced blinds. Your feet, numbed into ectothermic hibernation during the night, fail you upon impact, and you slump sideways onto a pile of dirty clothes. From your prone position there you see the wide, blue lagoon eyes of Zooey Deschanel studying you intently via the cover of a trampled *Us Weekly* you nicked from the staff lounge. Hair blown out into perfectly manicured disarray; mouth invitingly agape; hands pressed against face - *Home Alone*-style - almost as if she too were being harassed by the relentless screech of morning.

Unable to reach the snooze from the floor, you grab the fraying power cord and yank it hard from its coverless socket. Sparks fly across the splotchy brown carpet and you jump up instinctively - hotfooting left to right, your feet prickly pears attached at the ankles - scanning for stray embers while your blood meanders back into your extremities. Once assured your house won't burn down around you mid-bowel-movement, you flick a bit of fossilized crust from your eye, wipe your nose on your bare wrist, and shuffle off to mount your morning assault on the bathroom.

You step over a morass of dirty towels on your way to the toilet, rank and saturated from sopping up an overflow. Your boxers are so threadbare you don't even bother pulling them down, as your dick is already lolling out of its own accord, and you farted through the seams in back long ago. Your urine feels *serrated*, and as shit starts falling out your ass like *hot dogfood from a rusty can*, you reach for a small notebook atop the tank.

Several Christmases ago, you participated in a White Elephant gift swap at your office and came away the proud owner of *What is Your Poop Telling You?* - a somewhat juvenile guide to bristol health. Though you barely scanned the book's "scientific" portion, you found in its blank journal pages an unlikely artistic opportunity. You described every smell like a master sommelier and every shape like a bright-eyed museum docent. When you ran out of room, you bought a new journal. And then another. And another. You're up to 37 now; a veritable Encyclopedia Shittanica of meticulously omnibused odes to your stool.

Upon standing, a few more involuntary drops of piss leak onto your feet a la *gasoline from a recently discharged Texaco nozzle*. Glimpsing your bloodshot eyes in the mirror, you briefly consider a shower before hefting your foot up for a cursory sink rinse instead.

Your attention to hygiene is close to laughable. You bathe only when you've accumulated a noticeable film, deodorize only when you can actually smell yourself, and brush your teeth only when they start to hurt (a task which reliably makes your ill-defined bicep sore before you reach your back molars). Your razor makes but rare cameo appearances, usually after your beard has already overgrown your neck and invaded the softer allopatrics of your chest hair. All-in-all, you maintain your physical appearance with an eye toward remaining inconspicuous, and with your foot now ostensibly clean, you get dressed and list toward the kitchen, still slowed by the invisible manacles of poor circulation.

You hate coffee and never drink it. The alertness it causes. That chemical compulsion to interact with the world. Coffee is for people who bike to work and banter with the receptionist. You're more inclined toward eyes-down power-walking and sidelong ogles of said receptionist's cleavage. You opt for a cold, sweaty slice of pizza

- onions and veiny bacon - leftover from... well, no more than a week ago. It's hard to be exact as your fridge is a thicket of takeout containers congealed in sticky soda, spicy mustard, soy sauce, and sriracha. The smell mutates daily between sickly sweet and necrotic, and it rouses your senses with an olfactory bitchslap no Colombian dark roast could ever muster.

Your breakfast conquered, you slake your Arakeen-dry mouth with a swig of flat Mountain Dew, flop onto the musty grey couch in your adjoining living room, and turn on the TV.

Nancy Grace berates a black woman for her lack of parenting acumen; a grandmother drops a Plinko ball on *The Price is Right*; Montlick and his Associates urge you to join a questionable class action suit; Tony and Angela argue over who is, in fact, "the boss"; a smartly-groomed Pekinese executes a backflip; a still-obviously-bald man explains the life-changing wonders of a spray-on hair system; Matlock bangs his fist on his desk; smooth jazz plays over a weather map; and so on.

You settle on *SportsCenter* and take a vertiginous hit off the half-smoked bowl of weed on your coffee table - a yin-yang of green kief and black soot that the you of yesterday thoughtfully paid forward to the you of today - a zen-minded gift.

The first hit of the day is always the best. An anesthetic fog pours upward, filling your head like an inverted basin. You exhale a puffy, aeolian cloud and watch it wheel and twist through a sunbeam, morphing through a hundred Rorschach abstractions in a handful of seconds before disappearing into the ceiling.

The straight world might snicker - call you pothead, stoner, burnout, and any number of other uncreative derogatories - and they wouldn't be wrong - but given a choice, the word you prefer is dendrophile. You're just a guy who loves trees, and the idea you might have a more diagnosable problem than that is pure social construct. You don't have a problem. You haven't had a problem in years. They have problems. Endless, ceaseless mountains of problems. What you have, is the solution.

The score ticker at the bottom of your overcrowded, ADHD screen cycles back to the top of the order as four jutting, clacking, impossibly square jaws argue vociferously about HGH. You don't care. In this moment, you don't even understand why *they* care. Or why anyone cares. About anything. Your legs are greaves. Your arms are gauntlets. Your chest a toasty warm cuirass; your head a hotbox stechhelm. On the outside, nothing can touch you, and inside...

[You are crushed green velvet, wall-to-wall.]

Sensing the time, you float to the coatrack, don your ratty brown hoodie, and empty a roll of toilet paper, two coffee mugs, and a stapler from your messenger bag before finally apprehending your rickety, off-brand shuffle and prized, noise-cancelling headphones (one of the only non-smokable things for which you've ever paid top dollar).

Your skull abuzz, you set off for work to the crepuscular skreeks and sozzled yawps of Young Thug's "Beast," your steps falling into syncopated time. You scan the world at Dutch angles, endlessly distracted by amorphous shadows; neon OPEN signs nictitating themselves awake; gnarly trees cracking their knuckles; photons contorting oil stains into brilliant pools of spectrum. The only thing that wrests your attention is the occasional bystander flicking his Bic. That Pavlovian fshht cuts through your playlist every time, by way of some unnamed sixth sense, not unlike the feeling you get when you know a television is on in a room even before you see its lazuli glow. That thrum. That energy.

Sometimes it's the Golden Pantry attendant who offers you a grim, silent wave during his 7:30 smoke break. Other times it's the Tiddlywink Café hostess, stealing a moment of nicotine bliss amidst the morning latte rush. Usually it's at least two or three working girls (strippers by night, hookers by later that night). Carmen, Lacey, Melody, Scheherazade. You see them often on these walks - you beginning countless shifts just as they end them - but find them profoundly intimidating and unapproach- able, even while grasping that approachability is their stock-in-trade.

Unable to resist any longer, you light up. Cigarettes are a stopgap for you - a way to kill time, both in the short- and long-term. They provide a disapproved-of, but socially tolerated respite from any moment of which you'd just as soon not be a part. When you're smoking a cigarette, you're not doing anything else. They don't make you happy, per se, but you still find them preferable to breathing fresh air.

You drag and exhale, the smoke extending your frozen breath another two feet in front of your face. A kind of tunnel vision sets in as you press onward, eyeing the orange tip of your carcinogenic friend like a divining rod. Without warning, your ankle slips under a stray crabapple, and you pitch forward onto your knees, half-swallowing your butt. Ash singes your uvula, inducing a hack-n-slash coughing fit.

This unfortunate sequence of events brings your reality into focus much quicker than you'd like, and you seriously consider calling in sick right there just so you can walk the two-and-a-half blocks home and resuscitate your fast-fading high. Before you can get purchase on your embarrassingly last-gen cellphone however, a voluptuous shadow falls across your path.

"You got a light?" asks the shadow as your eyes make their way up its owner's *Wizard of Oz* hourglass frame a tad slower than appropriate, eventually landing on the impatient, paprika-freckled face of Melody.

"I'm sorry?" you ask – batting away your headphones – still browsing her redonkulus body while trying not to stare at any one part too long.

"A light?"

"Um, sure."

Diving back into your pants for anything that might make her happy, you produce a powder blue lighter, and after a few impotent clicks engage her long Marlboro 100. She rolls her eyes at your forced chivalry, tossing a salty "thanks" over her shoulder as she ducks past. Bolstered by this exchange, you decide to save your sick days and brave the rest of your commute, spending the next several blocks uncomfortably suppressing a hard-on and entertaining a mild curiosity as to her price breakdowns.

Having reached the outskirts of what constitutes "downtown" in your growth-stunted city, you begin evasive maneuvers for dodging the gaggles of alley folk that congregate there to harass the morning foot traffic. You weave around meters and bike racks, sidle between cars parked parallel, and frogger crosswalks at every opportunity, all in the name of not helping those less fortunate. You avoid eye contact at all costs, as these wraiths will traipse after you for blocks on end – spinning tales of their cancer-riddled spleens or their 9-year-old daughters turning tricks down by the docks – swearing to baby Jesus that a dollar from you could make all the difference. You never offer anyone more than a muted "sorry man" or "not today," but they just keep shaking their styrofoam cups at the heavens and asking and asking and *asking*.

You see two of the more aggressive regulars zeroing in on a woman in a navy pantsuit – one making labradoodle eyes while the other paws at her handbag – and wonder if it's in any way your responsibility to intervene. Instead, you sprint past this potentially dangerous scene-in-progress to the comparably safer confines of the park ahead.

The only such annoyances you regularly encounter here, amidst murmuring water features and Marienbad topiaries, are the Women in Black: three middle-aged gals - one of whom appears to speak only Farsi - who've been "occupying" the park's Northern gate since around the time we cacked Bin Laden. For months, none of them made a peep. Their mouths covered by burqa-lite attire, they moved only to pass a hand-lettered sign: **"WOMEN IN BLACK: A Silent Protest for World Peace."**

Over time, however, the burqas gave way to black sweater sets and matronly dresses (once you even saw two of them agitatedly send the third one home to change after she showed up in a black Josh Groban t-shirt), the sign was lazily propped against the cobblestone outer wall, and the group devolved into little more than a daily gab-sesh. They'll still clam up if they see anyone coming, but you've overheard them more than once discussing not plans for boycotts or demonstrations, but rather *American Idol* preferences and tips on glazing a ham. They'd begun with the absolute barest minimum qualifications for activism, and found even that to be too much effort. *How*, you wonder sarcastically as you hustle past, *have they not yet effected world peace?*

Episode 2

Your office resides in a seven-story tower the squalid grey of three-day-old snow. Home to a bevy of startups, the surrounding business complex somehow always feels muddied and damp even during the most skeletal stretches of Summer. But now, on the rainy cusp of Autumn, it's the fucking Somme. Blurry exhaust fumes produce tiny fata morganae as your fellow workers cut their engines and venture out into the same chilly environs through which you've been trudging for the past half-hour (no job of yours is going to dock you $40 a month for a fucking parking permit), swaddled in Burberry scarves and puffy North Face vests all for the treacherous 20 feet separating their cars from their cubicles.

"Hey!" squeaks Jennica, the dingbat front-desk secretary, as you push through the revolving door and cross the menstrual-pink marble lobby. You try to skate by with a wave and a grimace, but she is undeterred.

"How was your weekend!?" she asks.

"Fine."

"Do anything fun?"

"Not really."

"Oh, that's too bad. Me and my friend Kiffany went to the new J-Law movie. You guys at GRUNDL should write about it. It's super-cute. I loled so hard I spilled my Coke Zero."

"I'm sure someone will get to it," you say with a caustic chuckle.

She laughs along with you, either oblivious or immune to your contempt, before adding, "You should really smile more."

"Excuse me?"

"It's just... you have a nice smile is all. You should show it off."

"Yeah? And why's that?"

"Well... you know... it never hurts to smile. It takes less muscles than frowning."

"Fewer," you reply before you can stop yourself.

"What?"

"Fewer. It takes fewer muscles."

"Oh. Ok. It takes fewer muscles. It's less work. That's all I was saying."

"Yeah, well, I'm trying to get more exercise, so..."

She stares at you bewildered, as though you were the actual hunter who shot her actual mother.

"Oh! Gotta run!" you blurt, making a dash for a closing elevator.

Safely inside, you discover it was your co-worker Bradley who provided your timely egress.

Bradley covers the mainstream box office beat – everything from Michael Bay's flying robot clusterfucks to any-and-all ongoing efforts to convince the world Katherine Heigl is likeable – with the same true-believer devotion you reserve for the phantasmagorias of David Lynch or the gutsy, formalist experiments of Werner Herzog. He's an earnest fan of popcorn fare. Populist to a fault. It's kind of sweet, in a way, but makes him almost unbearable to talk to for longer than an elevator ride. Around the office he's known for assigning unimaginative, overly familiar nicknames (Marsha in HR is "Marshmallow"; Rick in ad sales is "Rickus Maximus"; etc.). This, for you, has meant being called "Sweats" at least once a day for the past six years because, on your first day at GRUNDL, amidst a furnacine heatwave, you arrived so dripping in your own salty excretions that multiple people lost their footing walking through the lobby behind you.

"Morning Sweats," offers Bradley.

"Morning."

"You catch the *Simpsons* premiere? They're about to hit 600 episodes. Pretty crazy."

"I'll bet."

"Lotta stuff went down. Some big surprises."

"Yeah?"

"Yeah!"

"Bart still ridin' that skateboard?"

"Um... yeah."

"Lisa still playin' that sax?"

"Well sure, but..."

"Everybody still yellow?"

"...yeah. They're still yellow."

"Ok then."

The elevator reaches the 4th floor, and you sidle through the doors before they're even fully open. You've seen every episode of *The Simpsons*, and are well aware of the sexacentennial milestone to which Bradley was referring, but you can no longer bring yourself to discuss it, or even claim it in public.

Though it began as brilliant, ruthless satire, *The Simpsons* has squidged under its own success, now resembling nothing so much as a jar of etiolated apricots preserved in sticky-sweet sentimentality. Once a broad, artistic vision committed to lampooning the workaday life and the nuclear family, it's now just another paean to the supposed virtues of same. Any worthwhile social commentary was left in the rearview over a decade ago, but not before turning its fans into junkies, so addicted to the comfortable, confectionary delights of Springfield, Wherever-The-Fuck that, 600 episodes in, they still can't let go. Viewers who tuned in for black bile on that storied pilot night in 1989 now guzzle viscous, syrupy pablum and long for the same simpler time they once rejected as saccharine fantasy.

You know this, all too well, and yet you are one of them.

For while *The Simpsons* may be a grotesque ouroboros of a series, as a pathological slave to completism, you've stubbornly sulked along for the ride, whistling "Mr. Plow" past the graveyard as it keeps munching away at its own rotting, sucrotic tail. It's not your fault. To abandon the show now would be like going toe-to-toe with Tyson for 28 rounds only to throw in the blood-soaked towel in the 29th. Also, it's ostensibly part of your job; staying up on pop culture, even as its "pop" wanes to nil. That's what you tell yourself anyway, every Sunday at 8:00 PM. Surely, the end must be nigh. Surely, soon, you'll be free. But until then, Lord how you hate the fucking *Simpsons*.

You'd worked a series of odd jobs before settling in at GRUNDL. You delivered newspapers for a while, enjoying existence in the inky gulf between *The Late Late Show* and *Good Morning*

America. Alone in your van, zipping along deserted streets, observing that mysterious class of people that hangs out at 24-hour gas stations despite not owning cars, you learned the rusty quirks of every 50-cent paper box in town. Sure, you subsisted mainly on peanut butter and ramen back then – but you wrote. Oh, how you wrote. Pages and pages. Tomes. Sagas. Curled up in the tiniest, cheapest, most womb-like apartment imaginable – smoking, reading, writing, watching, and smoking some more – you wrote to your heart's content, never more than a bong rip away from inspiration.

Once the 24-hour news cycle brought print circulation to a resounding, "STOP THE PRESSES" halt, you took a job at a big-box bookstore, reluctantly hawking *New York Times* bestsellers and cut-rate E-readers for a buck-and-a-half above minimum wage. You worked a little more, and wrote a little less, but started submitting your proudest attempts in hopes of publication. You got cable, and Netflix, and maybe a little more comfortable than you should have. Even then, you knew it couldn't last. You were living in an age, after all, when the main reason people came to bookstores was to live-tweet the newest *Twilight* installment, and the only things separating you from Amazon were fake smiles and an in-store coffee shop. Inevitably, soon enough, people started to realize they could make coffee at home.

After that, you spent some time at a second-run movie palace - the kind of beloved, opulent institution you once thought artistically-inclined people in an academic town would keep open in perpetuity, despite more convenient alternatives popping up in their Google autocompletions every day. Drowning in many directions by then - in debt, in a weed habit that had grown problematic (to put it kindly), in preformatted rejection letters (when they came), in silence (when they didn't), and worst of all, in the increasingly real possibility that you were simply too ordinary to ever achieve your dreams - you committed hard to the place.

You learned to make espresso and run a 35mm projector; to deal with vendors and balance the books. You worked your way up to management, put a downpayment on a house, and started chipping away at your student loans. You made a few friends, and even had some decent arguments (including one about Terrence Malick you definitively lost, which tend to be your favorite kind). You grew to take a measure of pride in the modest bastion of cinephilia you'd fostered. But ultimately, it too proved a walking dead medium.

A 3D IMAX megalith sprouted up down the road. The streaming boom echoed through the hills. Attention spans shrunk, costs grew, and eventually you just couldn't make it all work anymore. You screened a beautiful print of *The Last Picture Show* the night the place closed, afterwards weeping openly in front of the six patrons who showed up to watch it with you. In a final ignominy, the building was sold, gutted, and turned into an Apple store. There's a Redbox out front now.

And just like that, your overextended youth came to a close, with your having failed to in any way justify its lasting as long as it did. It seems impossibly naïve now, but on some level you'd always felt if you could just be near the written word - that if you read, and watched, and learned enough - stayed close enough - consumed enough - that someday you'd figure out how to contribute. To be a part of it. You thought if you championed art long enough, someday art would champion you. But as of that night, you hadn't written anything in two years, and in the meantime had seen every artform you'd ever loved pulled under by the unrelenting swell of the information age, and swept out into a vast, anonymous sea of content. Your Smaug's hoard of cultural capital was reduced, in pitiless short order, to chump change.

And so, when the opportunity to monetize yourself came along, you'd already fallen far enough to resignedly faceplant into it. GRUNDL offered as good a salary as you'd ever made, passable health insurance, and in its own banal, dispiriting way, the chance to be creative. You'd already absorbed more entertainment than anyone else you'd ever met. You'd danced the Madison with Godard and pushed paper with Jim and Pam. You'd smelled the napalm with Francis Ford and were well aware as to who killed Laura Palmer. You'd fought demons with Buffy and Angel, entered the void with Gaspar Noé, and spent many, many a weekend at Bernie's. And here was a place that had use for all of you; a patsy, willing to subsidize your worst habits; a job that literally paid you to watch shit.

Suckling at a bottle of Vanilla Coke, you browse the morning's news. Lady Gaga looks to be "going country"; Edward Albee died; Hawks center Dwight Howard was hospitalized with extreme dehydration; Bill Clinton's slated to appear on *The Daily Show* (likely damage control for Hillary's "basket of deplorables" fiasco); the One Direction breakup is looking more permanent by the day; Jay McInerney has a new book out; a Kardashian is rumored to have gotten butt implants - it doesn't matter which one; *Bones* is finally getting canceled; and so on.

Uninspired, you decide to draw on your encounter with Bradley, tapping out the header `Top 10 TV Shows That Lasted Way Too Long` and locking in *The Simpsons* at #1.

The keys to a successful GRUNDL post are accessibility, brevity, and controversy (insert *Glengarry Glen Ross* joke here). Find a listicle-ready topic about which even the most cretinous simpleton will have some opinions, write no more than five sentences per entry, and throw in a few picks that will leave at least half your readership inordinately pissed off. This one practically writes itself. You take easy shots at *The X-Files* and *Grey's Anatomy*, infuriate two volatilely stupid demographics by including *Entourage* and *Sex and the City*, put the execrable *Two and a Half Men* at #2, indefensibly ahead of *The Simpsons*, and voila: clickbait.

Pleased, you head off toward the men's room for your second morning deuce. So close you're practically already unzipping, however, the door suddenly swings outward and you find yourself face-to-face with Arthur, a sun-deprived carapace of a human being who absolutely lives for reality TV. Everything you hate about GRUNDL is everything Arthur loves. His "Top 10 Hottest Hoarders" was the site's most-read piece last year. He can name every Duggar in chronological order, and he had the foresight to home-record *Mr. Personality*, *The Swan*, and *Buckwild* for posterity. You would kill Arthur under the right circumstances. If you were diagnosed with a terminal disease tomorrow, for example, you'd come to work in a rented tux, hand Arthur a rose, and then promptly beat him to death with a three-hole-punch while reciting every inane fact about *The Bachelor* he's ever lodged unbidden in your limbic mind.

"Hey" he mumbles, blocking the doorway. "You hear there's gonna be a *Real Housewives of Ferguson, Missouri*? Seems like they're kinda scraping bottom, but I guess with the riots and everything it could be..."

"That's great Arthur."

"Right!? It's crazy. They're actually putting Michael Brown's aunt and the Police Chief's wife in a house together. I'm not saying I won't watch. I'll definitely watch. But it seems kind of..."

Arthur pauses as though for effect, but after a moment you realize he just doesn't know what word he wants to use.

"What Arthur? What does it seem kind of? Cheap? Exploitative? Disgusting? What?!"

"Oh… I was gonna say dangerous. I know it's been a few years, but they've still gotta really hate each other, right? Could make for some killer catfights."

You feel another salvo of invective racing up your throat, but having known Arthur a long time, you tamp it down.

"…Yeah man. Crazy stuff. You mind if I get around you here? I'm about to piss my pants."

"Oh, sure. Sorry."

Like the appeased guardian of some medieval bridge, he steps aside, and you loose a string of modally discordant Dr. Seuss farts as you head toward the commodes.

After a few spritzes of carbonated urine, proceedings quickly deteriorate into a *carnival taffy pull* as a long, sticky rope of feces spirals out of your asshole. You imagine *tiny spelunkers* climbing down what feels like a foot-and-a-half of continuous line to explore the cavernous sinkhole below, and smile as you pinch it off and send them plummeting to their deaths. Though much of the end product has already disappeared into the plumbing, you're convinced this might be *a personal record for length*, and record your observations in your travel notebook, applying more artistic muscle and craft than you will to anything else you do here today.

You obtain a vending machine lunch from the breakroom, where you also pocket a couple of spoons someone left in the sink, and spend the next hour browsing other, better versions of your site. Just as you're finishing a Vulture article about the Kierkegaardian undertones of *It's Always Sunny in Philadelphia*, you feel the internal tug of chemical dependency lacing its fingers through your ribcage, and you move to steal a cigarette on the 5th floor terrace. But alas, your boss Barry's office sits unavoidably between your desk and the elevators.

"Hey! Can I see you for a minute?" he brays, and your shoulders slump forward to tow you inside.

"What's up?"

"Well, it's this article you posted yesterday."

"Which one?"

"You know which one."

"Sir. I really don't."

"Yes. You do. 'Top 10 Hottest *Game of Thrones* Rape Scenes'? Remember?!"

"Oh... that one."

"Yes. That one. You miserable fuck. How did you get this past editing!?"

"I don't know Sir. I was pretty surprised too - I mostly wrote it as a joke - but no one ever sent it back for revisions so I just figured it passed muster."

"No one ever saw it. It just went straight onto the site. Do you have any idea how many calls I've gotten today? How many pissed off college dykes have tweeted about this shit? Not to mention our advertisers. It's a goddamn nightmare!"

"So, you weren't personally offended then Sir?"

"What?! No, I wasn't personally offended! Jesus! It's the fucking internet! It'll be over in a week like anything else. What pisses me off is you took that week - my fucking week - and turned it to shit. My QB just tore his goddamned ACL! I'm trying to make a playoff push with fucking backups, and now, on top of all that, you've served me up a goddamned shit week!"

"I don't think the playoffs start until January Sir."

"Fuck you. You know goddamned well I'm talking about my Fantasy team asshole. I hope one of those big Dothraki motherfuckers comes to your house and rapes you. That'd be number one on my list every time."

"Sir," you reply, maddeningly calm, "I don't know what happened here, but I swear I sent the article through the usual channels. Maybe one of the editors is lying?"

"Why would anyone risk their job for your stupid fucking article?"

"Maybe they thought it was funny?"

Barry stares broadswords at you.

"Get out."

"Sir?"

"I swear to God. Get the fuck out of my office!"

"Am... am I fired sir?"

"If it was up to me you would be. But the owners say any traffic is good traffic, and traffic is way up. We took it down hours ago, but people are still looking for it, and bitching about it."

"Well, that's something I guess."

"Yeah. You won Twitter for about fifteen minutes. Congratufuckinglations. Meanwhile, I'm the one who has to deal with it. No quarterback and a goddamned week of shit."

"I'm sorry Sir. Maybe it won't be so bad. And as for your team, maybe you could get a new quarterback before the weekend? I hear that Tom Brady cat is pretty good. Is he available?"

Barry reaches for a coffee mug inscribed with the phrase "Write Drunk, Edit Sober," and draws back his beefy, trebuchet forearm, but before he can launch, you smartly take his advice and get the fuck out of his office.

Upstairs, a droopy ficus awaits you, already littered with scores of discarded butts. You light up and take a long, enervating drag.

Of course you uploaded the story. It was easy. You recruited some underpaid nerd from a failing Radio Shack to build you a backdoor years ago. It wasn't the first time you've pulled something like this, and it won't be the last. Hits will go up. The advertisers will be happy. Barry's fantasy team will bounce back. Everything will stay its course. You can't fight the internet. For good or ill, it's in charge of us. Not the other way around.

The most irritating thing about that whole encounter wasn't the yelling or the cursing. It was how much that asshole cares about Fantasy Football. Much like yourself, Barry uses the site to underwrite his addictions, covering sports with a monotoned, DVOA-obsessed style that drones right off the page. The actual players are tertiary at best – toy figurines for him to painstakingly select and display to his college buddies, most of whom don't take their annual league half as seriously as he does. They all moved on to impressive jobs, Lombardi Trophy wives and kids in Pop Warner, while he sits behind a desk, staring at stats and shepherding through acres of writing that barely rises to the level of adware. And all he really cares about in this sad, scrivenerian existence is Fantasy fucking Football.

It makes you kind of sick, and so, when Barry waltzed into work last Monday crowing about his team - which features two players currently accused of domestic violence, and another who beat a sexual assault charge last year - you decided to have a little fun. You never expected to make any kind of point with him, and even with the waves of angry broads buffeting his extension, you still don't. But you turned his week to shit, and that feels like reason enough.

Deciding to throw him a bone - you return to your desk and start working on `Top 10 Blockbusters You Never Noticed Were Wildly Sexist`, realizing quickly that your biggest challenge will be not limiting yourself to Disney cartoons. *Sleeping Beauty* and *Cinderella* - basic bitches who while away their days worrying about fashion and beauty rest - seem too easy. Their only real sin is not being proactive. The true offenders, IYHO, are *Snow White*, whose only demonstrable qualities are having good skin and being willing to service seven midgets on the daily until a handsome man comes along to rescue her; *Pocahontas*, a real-life 13-year-old turned jaw-droppingly pneumatic Warpaint-Barbie who betrays her entire tribe for a handsome man with whom she can barely converse; and worst of all, *The Little Mermaid*, who literally gives up her literal voice in exchange for a handsome man and a vagina with which to please him.

From there, the rout is on. You pick apart *Back to the Future*, a film you love but have been mildly put off by ever since realizing that present-day George and Lorraine McFly are essentially friends with Biff, Lorraine's one-time attempted rapist. You tack on a few much-loved rom-coms – your *You've Got Mail*s, your *Maid in Manhattan*s – and throw in some high-profile arthouse imports (how entire generations of women failed to notice that *Lola rennt* is just a super-fit gal cleaning up her loser boyfriend's messes, or that *Amélie* is the prototype for every manic pixie dream girl they now despise, is truly beyond you). You fill in the gaps via Bette Davis's and Goldie Hawn's IMDB pages, toss off an obnoxious reference to the Bechdel Test, and there you have it: another day at GRUNDL in the books.

Neither this piece, nor the one for which it's theoretically atoning, means much of anything to you in the old grand scheme, and if Barry were hipper to the way the online world works, he'd see this is your greatest value. Idealism is played out. Caring may draw eyeballs, but not caring keeps them coming back. Everyone really is a critic now. They don't want you to tell them why you're right. They want to tell you why you're wrong. Your power is in giving them that. In feeding it, every day. In not believing what you just wrote. In not knowing what you might write next.

Episode 3

Goodbye Cruel World

Cursived on a foxed scrap of paper, these words rest impotently in your pocket at all times. You have no intention of killing yourself. You've never made so much as a "cry for help" attempt. But you often wonder how a Christian deity might judge such things. If a "cry for help" isn't answered, and its executor dies when all he wanted was some morsel of attention from a self-involved world, does he still tumble to Hell, or is he given a celestial hall pass? Does God judge intentions, or results? The Bible says he knows our hearts, but this is difficult to comprehend. We are fragile ecosystems all – constantly outthinking ourselves – and while our final thoughts may exist solely between us and our preferred demiurge, you doubt anyone's ever jumped off the Empire State Building only to revel in the brilliance of his decision all the way down.

Whatever the answers, you carry this 17-character cliché with you wherever you go because you don't want anyone taking the blame (or the credit, as the case may be) for whatever absurd way you do end up meeting your cardiomniscient maker. You try to transgress every day - to pick at the threads in the fabric of society. You like to think you're challenging people, but you don't know sometimes. You might just be an asshole. And no matter how you end up dying, or who finds your body, you want them to know it was your fucking idea.

You can't really say what got into you the day you wrote that failsafe message. You were having a lousy one, to be sure, but nothing that should've inspired you to throw yourself in front of a speeding sportscar. It was less a wanting to end it all than a general indifference as to whether or not it ended. A minute - a moment really - where you genuinely could've gone either way.

So, when you saw a black Boxster skid onto your street and start accelerating through a school zone like it was responding to the fucking Bat Signal, you decided to teach its undoubtedly insufferable occupant a lesson. You remember standing at the crosswalk, staring him down, giving him every opportunity to slow his roll. You could see the Country Club parking pass hanging from his rearview; the Lacoste alligator snapping at his nipple; the diamond-studded Bluetooth earpiece he was chortling into. Flashing. Catching the light.

Again, you don't really know what got into you, but when he got within about twenty feet, you just went for it, stepping into his path with utter disregard for the consequences. You watched as he swerved left, jumped the opposite curb, nearly sledged a Middle School marquee advertising a forthcoming production of *Grease*, toothpasted a wholly unprepared chipmunk's innards out of its eye sockets, kachunked back down to the asphalt, and sped off – class-ringed middle finger thrust through his moonroof.

To this day you can't say if you wanted him to hit you or not. You just knew you wanted to hit him, even if you had to fly through his windshield to do it. In the months that followed, you honed the rulebook for your newly devised hastilude, and perfected a full-body stutter-step that could derail a freight train. You figured if you were going to put yourself in harm's way just to stick it to the occasional reckless roadster, you might as well minimize your risk. You were still indifferent, but you were indifferent with purpose. Thus, the note.

Your town is a daedalian drainpipe maze of half-finished subdivisions, dashed-off apartment complexes, decrepit government housing, and extended-stay hotels, surrounded by a churning hive of megastores, megachurches, megabanks, and megagyms. The area's defining feature is a preponderance of Shoney's restaurants, an eatery that's largely gone the way of the undercooked buffalo burger everywhere else. Filling in the cracks are Ca$h-4-Gold exchanges, drive-thru liquor lockers, title pawns and strip malls – the sarcomal connective tissue of our thrashing, dying whale of a country.

A behemoth state university keeps the lights on in this Olympic-sized cesspool, and as such, cheap options are all anyone wants, be they students, dropouts, aimless grads, under-nourished hipster "creatives" (to call them starving artists would be an insult to both starving people, and artists), or those who guest-lecture and adjunct-profess with misguided sincerity the archaic ideals that foster all of the above. Everyone warned you when you decided to take a year off after college (theoretically to write, but in actuality to smoke hella weed and masturbate four times a day): "You have to get out of this town the second you graduate, or else you'll never leave."

Ten years removed from your last day of matriculation (though still five away from your last student loan payment), every one of those everyones has been proven fatidic in their foretelling of your dead-end future. Your folly is inescapable. No matter what route you take home, you're guaranteed to see a University bus whizz by or glimpse one of the crumbling dormitories you used to call home - teeming, iniquitous high-rises after J.G. Ballard's own heart.

You remember those walls fondly enough, but their loft-bed-hopping denizens seem unknowably alien to you now, speaking in acronyms and interfacing indefinitely with their smartphones. For all their collective promise, you feel a kind of freedom when they pass you on the street, snapping posterity selfies midstride, refusing for even a moment to let the universe forget they exist. They present as hostage to one another - in constant negotiations for proof of life. Their feet are on the ground, but their heads are in the cloud. You don't envy them. Not really. You may not be young anymore, but youth ain't what it used to be.

Your flip-phone is a point of pride under these dystopian conditions. You harbor no illusions as to your own complicity in the internet panopticon. You're as bad as anyone - and probably way, way worse - but thanks to some combination of sanctimony, luddism, and gut-level fear, you long ago drew the line at carrying the whole of the world's knowledge around in your pocket. You know yourself well enough to know this level of accessibility could only lead you to a ruinous end. It would simply be too much.

Enjoying the impossibly clever, near-artisanal turns of King Gheedora's "Anti-Matter," you hang a left and stroll past a row of smallish, "historic" homes, each marked with some tragic signifier of municipal decay: a criss-crossed brick portico rendered nearly opaque, so gummed are its rectangular pores with cobwebbing and wasp nests; a shotgun shack slimed by sophomoric art majors in Barneyesque purple-and-green; a tin-roof porch bathed in sawdust, and littered with enough old-school power tools to suggest Leatherfaced horrors inside; and finally an empty corner lot housing half a tractor and a ratty orange couch reminiscent of the *Friends* title sequence, sewn together by thorny clinging vines.

Upon reaching an intersection, you spy a decapitated Yield sign across the way, and take a furtive look around while you light a cigarette. You're about to cross when an eggplant SUV full of sorority cuntlets comes roaring up the road, just begging for a game of chicken. You imagine their gas-guzzling bratmobile sailing into a double barrel roll and bursting into screams and flames. Honestly, nothing would make you happier. Whatever the outcome, it would be worth it. You would consider a life prison sentence a wash. You tense as they close the gap, and with inches to spare, make a microexpressive feint at their grill.

Nothing. Not even a flicker of taillights. If you'd actually stepped to them, you'd be dead right now. Simple as that.

A little shaken, you take a drag and let your eyes follow their PRYNCZZ vanity plate all the way to the next intersection, at which point a thin, be-bangled wrist does reach out and offer a wave, though it feels more dismissive than apologetic, and you're not sure it's even for you as a 20-something in jorts and a screen-printed tank-top featuring the cast of *Full House* has strolled up beside you. He waves back at them, lowers his heart-shaped sunglasses, and offers you a sympathetic "bitches, man" before asking to bum a smoke. You truly hate this town.

After you ensure no one else is coming, you cross to where the Yield sign lays sunning itself in the utility strip, tuck it under your arm, and dip down a one-way street lined with high privet.

You started stealing shortly after the incident with the Porsche, and you've never really gotten tired of it. Your home and yard are artfully arranged landfills. Shrines to neglect. You have enough bicycles to outfit the Tour de France, and enough patio furniture to furnish the Biltmore. You have garbage cans of every size, layered inside one another like Matryoshka dolls. You've never shoplifted - not so much as a Twix or a disposable lighter - but when it comes to public property, or willfully unguarded private property, you tend to feel that people get what they deserve. You take things others take for granted. It's rare anyone notices or cares, but the kind of people who do care, well, they *really* care.

Think about it. How often do you hear about little inconveniences being the tipping points for violence? "She took the last muffin." "He cut me off in traffic." "I couldn't stand one more second of that laugh/that voice/that look/that face." More than politics, or religion; sex, or art - these are the things that truly piss us off. The things that make us hop on Facebook and Twitter and type, in all seriousness, "Fuck My Life." And that's what you hope to exploit through all your inane mischief. Your greatest wish is that somewhere, someday, someone embarks on a cross-country, natural-born-killing spree because you stole the toilet paper from the stall he happened to shit in that morning.

Once, shortly after you first started this particular strain of IRL trolling, a construction worker chased you with an Allen wrench for the better part of a mile after you gathered up a quartet of traffic cones he'd arranged in a civic rondo around a fresh patch of concrete (and this was a man who did not look like he'd run a mile at a stretch in his entire life). After gaining enough distance to pull it off, you turned and placed the cones around yourself in a protective square. Drenched in sweat, hard-hat askew, blunt steel raised high over his head, he pulled up just short of a collision, blinked once, twice, and then proceeded to vomit up the most insane, terrifying peals of laughter you've ever heard. He absolutely lost it. He laughed until he doubled over, his pugilistic, pulled pork breath battering your nostrils. He was still laughing when you inched away, cone-less, but content that you'd somehow changed his entire outlook on life.

Incidents like this, however, are few and far between. Most of the time, you abscond with a wire-frame sign for a long-concluded political campaign, or pocket an ashtray from some bar's outdoor seating, or palm office supplies from virtually everywhere you go (you have three highlighters and a ream of printer paper from GRUNDL in your possession at this very moment). Your cabinets house platoons of salt and pepper shakers, arsenals of ketchup and mustard bottles, and enough Sweet-n-Low packets to wallpaper your kitchen. Your guest bathroom is essentially a toilet-paper closet, stocked by your local Subway, McDonalds, Chick-fil-A, and Taco Bell. Your garage is lined with plastic crates (pallets of which can be found behind any grocery or liquor store) stacked three-high and packed to the brim with lightbulbs, batteries, bar soap, and ink pens. One might describe your overall décor as something like "world's shittiest doomsday prepper."

Likewise, if you ever find yourself bored with your isolationist job and antisocial lifestyle, your front lawn has gathered enough orphaned rakes, hoes, shovels, sheers, saws, picks, and axes to start a landscaping business from scratch. Ditto a sporting goods store, as your backyard is an athletic orgy of balls foot-, base-, basket-, golf-, tennis-, volley-, and soccer-, as well as frisbees, pucks, bats, sticks, skates, helmets, and gloves. Inflatable kiddie pools help contain all this purloined youth, but you still have to watch every step lest you trip on some ill-gotten piece of someone else's pudgy, privileged childhood.

Your house is a bit of a monstrosity - both visually and spiritually - with the kind of low-concept layout that tends to arise when a 9-year-old is given an instructionless, jumbo-assorted bucket of Legos. A converted duplex, its central divider was destroyed one night when the owner/landlord/dextral resident, having had it up to here with his sinistral renters' nightly screaming matches (not to mention their equally boisterous makeup sex), lit into it with a sledgehammer and handed them eviction papers right through the wall.

Opting afterwards to just lean into the damage and create an open floorplan, his subsequent DIY remodel begat a host of problems. The overhead light fixtures for the now-conjoined living rooms were struck impotent, and the ceiling gained a Damoclean sag. He turned one of the kitchens into a spacious laundry room (it floods if you do more than one load a week). He nailgunned a splintery pinewood deck onto the back (it collapsed last year under a mountain of stolen firewood). And he stuck the aforementioned garage onto the side, essentially with putty (it remains inaccessible except via a hand-cranked, corrugated steel rolling door).

There was one feature, however, which towered above all these systemic inconveniences and, for you, made the place an unbeatable bargain: an 8-foot-high, knotless, crackless, weather-sealed fence of sturdy, red cedar surrounding the entire estate in priceless privacy. The only thing our dear old man-crone paid to have done professionally, it was arguably the house's lone selling point, but it sold you. *I like the dark*, you remember thinking, *and I don't do that much laundry anyway*. Being behind that fence gave you the warm fuzzies. You knew in an instant. This was home.

Ironically, it was the fence that proved the poor hermit's undoing when his beloved pitbull turned on him at the ripe old age of 91. Unable to escape, the great, foaming beast made chew toys of his achilles tendons, and needless to say, by the time EMTs were able to reach him his fence had more than proven its worth.

The house stayed on the market for months – becoming notoriously unsaleable – and you ultimately snatched it up at a little over half the asking price, feeling remorse for neither the deceased (own pitbulls at your own dumbass risk) nor his son, who scrawled every signature with a sigh of relief, thrilled to pass his inherited burden on to you.

You dial in your six-digit padlock code, which you change every three months, always using the birthdate of a different jazz musician (Mal Waldron til New Year's), drop the Yield sign atop a messily burgeoning pile of stolen traffic sigils, and relock yourself safely inside.

Only now, ensconced in this sacred space, does your real life begin. Only here are you free.

Episode 4

You realized a long time ago that you like TV more than most people. Now, this is not to say that you like TV more than most people like TV (though that is also almost certainly true), but rather, that you like watching TV more than you like most people.

Between your work computer and your home screens, you spend nearly two-thirds of every day in communion with the digital world. You are Cypher. You may have accepted the red pill, once upon a time, but you've been looking for a way back to the blue ever since. You're not just aware of the Matrix. You believe in the Matrix. Evangelically. Sure, the little playlets you enact outside your various hard drives and streaming services change from time to time, but your inner life is plotted to perfection. Fuck Zion. The Matrix is real, and Neo can blow you in bullet time.

Your house winces as you step onto the conestoga hardwood, shut the door, and quickly exfiltrate yourself from your clothes, loosing a cavernous, dubstep belch in the direction of the great Irene Jacob (who, already looking chilly in your original, French-language poster for

Krysztof Kieślowski's *Rouge*, appears to shiver a bit as she flutters away from the wall).

You consider her place one of honor, as nearly every other inch of vertical real estate is occupied by a chockablock *Tetris* grid of second-hand shelving. Squat, dorm bookcases sit atop low console units which buttress teetering, particle-board towers whose upper floors are stabilized by homemade, cut-to-fit 2x4 shelves, with knockoff IKEA cubes filling the odd nook and cranny - all in service of keeping somewhat organized your perpetually, isotropically expanding media library.

At last inventory your shelving plexus housed around 4,000 DVDs (all of which you've watched), 3,000 LPs (about half of which you've listened to), and nearly 5,000 books (maybe a tenth of which you've read). (Maybe). Woody Allen to Robert Zemeckis. Cannonball Adderley to John Zorn. Douglas Adams to Howard Zinn. Yours is a methodical kind of madness.

Entertainment functions like any other drug, and for your woefully average, American upbringing, that meant getting hooked young on Disney and *Star Wars* - your first fixes amidst a childhood spent rabidly suckling at the boob-tube. Middle school brought the candy cigarettes of *SNL, Monty Python,* and *MST3K* (and your first real cigarette by way of a secrecy-sworn, sleepover screening of *Porky's*), before you dove headlong into a morbidly curious teenagerhood of shotgunning Natty Lights with Stallone and Schwarzenegger, and deadening your senses with ditch-weed and Jay and Silent Bob. By college, you'd graduated to the hard stuff - downing stiff double-shots of *The Shield* and *The Sopranos* - taking epic bong rips of Greenaway, snorting Kubrick by the kilo, and shooting Bergman directly into your eyeballs.

You've always been this way. All highs point somewhere higher, and all depths lead somewhere lower - the promise of ecstasy and depravity, in equal measure, forever just around the next bend; the next album; the next film; the next hit. In essence, your whole life is a Wikihole. If you'd ever had the balls to try smack or meth, you'd surely be long dead by now. The more you know...

The entire, shoddy apparatus shudders under your heavy footsteps as you lovingly run your hand along all three walls of stringently abecedarian spines before heading to the couch and flipping on the fourth.

With ESPN blathering in the background, you turn your attentions to Blaze Pascal, the diminutive glass pipe you emptied this morning.

The art of packing a bowl is subtle and underappreciated. Though not as sexy as the joint, or its gluttonous cousin the blunt, the bowl prizes economy above all. Finely attuned to your own tolerances, you craft every hit with mathematic precision and conveyor belt uniformity, twisting three pea-sized nugs between the tar-stained teeth of your grinder with the dispassionate brutality of an iron maiden.

Grinding your weed provides for a more even, controlled burn, and allows you to dole out prescription hits with Hippocratic discretion (you've even adopted the practice of dividing each new sack into a color-coded, two-week pill planner). The brass screen is over a week old – you'll need to change it soon – but for today the smoke still flows freely between its ash-crusted apertures, and upwards into your skull.

[You are a honey-baked ham.]

While the first hit of the day is always the best, the first hit of the evening is never far behind. Embracing you with the tenderness of a doting, naked-beneath-her-apron housewife, it stills your fidgety digits and demands your lips' attentions again and again until you both collapse, sated and spent, and sink into the magic hour. Where the first hit of the day is your suit of armor, the first hit of the evening is your silk pajamas. Where the first hit of the day is your espresso shot, the first hit of the evening is your glass of oak-aged red. Regardless of whatever came before it, in a single moment, it makes absolutely everything ok again.

Suddenly, your dim hovel is rendered a symphony of cleanly wonder, as if transformed by a wave of the *Fantasia* sorcerer's wand. What seemed, mere hours ago, like the wholesale contents of a Waffle House kitchen *Akira*-ing their way out of your rancid refrigerator, is now a delectable smorgasbord of dinner options to rival the feasts of Heliogabalus. What often feels like a desultory, Kansas-monochrome life, is plunged into Oz-ian technicolor, with nothing ahead but miles of yellow-brick road and only the occasionalest of commercial interruptions.

And so you begin your nightly journey, up the dial, and into the ether.

Roger Federer smacks an ace across some poor sap's schnozz; a well-coiffed African American woman warns of a sexual predator; Ross, Chandler, and Phoebe sip syndicated coffee; a couple examine a brownstone with an overzealous realtor; Devry University offers you a sad fresh start; an *NCISCSISVU* agent makes an off-color pun on the word "stiff"; a Honda vehicle is declared both luxurious and affordable; an edited-for-tv Samuel L. Jackson demands his "mutual-fundin' money!"; a model nearly jiggles out of her demi-cup as she gorges on a Western bacon cheeseburger (you pause momentarily); a nervous man misses a *Jeopardy* question; smooth jazz plays over a weather map; and so on.

You circle back to the *Friends* rerun, as you've been working your way haphazardly through the series for something like the 10th time and have come to find the vocal rhythms and telegraphed punchlines as soothing as steady rain or ocean waves. You know them all by heart, but still chuckle at every suave "how you doin'?" or exasperated "I know!", and while you tell yourself you're doing research for a long-gestating polemic, in your heart you still want to love the *Friends* more than you want to hate them. Theirs is a near-perfect fantasy – the kind that never seems too far-fetched until you really start to think about it. No matter how cynical you become, they will always be "there for you."

You finish off your bowl with a coffle of quick, sequential puffs, and hold them in until you cough up thick, frayed ropes of hemp. Finally tranquilized, you shamble to the bathroom to pop out a few compact, *rock-tumbler poops*, and stroll through the kitchen to retrieve a mucosal Styrofoam container of Mongolian beef and a family-size bag of Cheetos. As you return to the couch, your gently drifting mind notes a striking resemblance between Chester and the outlaw tobacco mascot Joe Camel, and you wonder if he'll someday meet the same societally-mandated, excommunicatory fate. They're both essentially cartoon drug dealers after all, luring kids into their deviant vans with purred promises of tinted glass "cool."

Your couch sits only a few feet from your TV – close enough to letterbox your peripheral vision and dive in like Captain N. Tonight, however, the pot-addled senses have their own ideas, and as you overtake your pile of cold Chinese food your interest in the *Friends* is waning fast – their beat-perfect badinage dissolving into white noise with a slight Long Island accent. Pausing to fellate Cheeto dust off your fingers, you catch a glimpse of your own bowed reflection in the dead, grey screen of the wood-console Magnavox atop which your working unit sits (a remnant of your childhood; the first box you ever watched), and are struck by a familiar, paranoid notion you've held since long before you were a permatoasted hophead: that people behave... *differently*, when you're not around.

You've always imagined yourself to be a kind of social antimatter; that any conversation you wander into is immediately dampened or quelled until you excuse yourself again. You suspect – no, don't sugarcoat it, *you believe* – that *real* people who *really* care about each other in *real* life are every bit as codepedently conjoined as the Gellers, Greens, Bings, Buffays, and Tribbianis group-hugging onscreen; that they sit around hip coffee shops and impossibly unaffordable apartments discussing their personal lives ad-overcaffeinated-nauseam until all issues are resolved and all emotional ties affirmed. You're positive that these oversharing thinktank conversations take place – that there are groups of people who spend all their time effectively helping one another regress toward the socially-acceptable mean – and you're just as positive that you've simply never been invited.

As the *Friends* give way to a string of noisy commercials, you start flipping channels again, climbing into the three-digit jungle canopy of niche cable. You pass snippets of exotic flora and fauna: decade-old *Queer Eye* episodes; Canadian curling semifinals; Senators debating in real time whether to declare August 12th "National Take

Your Gun to Work Day." Beyond that is a wasteland of condescendingly specified radio channels - Jazz Moods, Urban Beatz, Latin Fire - a note or two from each blipping and bleeding into the next like some maniacally microsampled Matthew Herbert track until finally, after minutes of rhythmic clicking, you're deposited into a calm, bluescreen ocean of premium movie and sports channels to which you do not currently subscribe. You'll see nothing but lapis for the next 400 stops, but you click on, allowing silent, creeping dread to take hold.

For people who smoke marijuana in responsible measure, paranoia is something of a winky cliché. They talk about how it makes them wonder if no one else in the room likes them, or think every exterior noise is the cops coming to batter their door down. They joke about it, like the munchies or tie-dye or reggae, but they've likely never approached the kind of ingrained, paranoiac sensibility prolonged THC consumption can forge in an otherwise reasonable mind. As an all-day-every-day adherent to the greenfold path, you do not wonder if other people like you or not. You take as a given that they don't.

You revel in the knowledge that you're smarter than literally everyone you encounter in your day-to-day life, but also acknowledge that bumptious thought's half-empty obverse – that your day-to-day life is literally filled with idiots. Your coworkers take pride in their shallow work, forwarding their every unthink-piece to their families and friends for fear no one else will read it before it's cast to the winds of disposable content. They see themselves as writers by simple virtue of the fact that they write words, and those words are published by persons other than themselves. This infinitesimal remove and light dusting of validation are enough for them to feel their place in the zeitgeist is secure.

An outside observer might see you as doing much the same, but you rarely allow yourself to utter the words "I'm a writer" in mixed company, instead answering questions about your job with self-deprecating jokes about plagiarism and prostitution. Sure, you've written plenty – short stories, one-act plays, half of two novels, even some poetry – and mailed it off everywhere from the Iowa Writer's Workshop to *Cracked* Magazine, but you don't believe you've earned the right to call yourself a writer. Not yet.

Rejection takes a toll. You'd never in your life felt like you needed someone to tell you you were talented, until sixty-or-so publications of varying quality bluntly suggested that maybe you weren't. It's been years since you wrote a word that mattered to you. Why bother? We're talking about a reading populace that's collectively decided YA is a genre rather than an age-specific comprehension level, and that only even *tried* to crack a Faulkner after Oprah recommended it. What reward even awaits true literary talent today? Total audience numbers that likely wouldn't get within shouting distance of your "Top 10 Sluttiest Rap Videos Parental Control Software Doesn't Block" article. 46,000 views and counting. That's the world you write for now.

It's vindicating - and on some base, simian level, even exciting - to generate that kind of traffic - to have your finger on the throbbing pulse, however briefly. But it doesn't make you a writer. Not in your book.

Truth be told, if your work for GRUNDL was your proudest accomplishment, you'd likely be too stupid to know you should kill yourself. Your coworkers seethe with jealousy - you're certain of that. Everything they do, you do ironically. Everything they experience as a life well-lived, you endure as misanthropic performance art, banging out better copy in minutes than they can write in hours and feeling nothing but pulpy toothache and self-loathing. Even if they don't hate you back, they definitely should. Inside, you are venomous and vile. What are *they* trying to prove?

The lambent sea of non-subscriber blue seems deep now, and sentient enough to challenge you to a game of chess; the subtle, sinister difference between an undertow and a riptide.

On nights like this, your coworkers are only the tip of the proverbial berg, and you can easily slide deep into overwhelming fears that every compatriot you've ever known was, in fact, a paid agent of some malfeasant, backroom power broker to whom you are unwittingly beholden. Whether the church, the state, the 1%, or just your meddlesome parents, you imagine you are, and have always been, so unlikeable that, somewhere along the way your elected leaders, or a manipulative member of the idle rich, or dear old Mom and Dad, negotiated handsome salaries and drew up triplicate contracts ensuring that you would occasionally encounter other people who at least *appeared* to enjoy your miserable company.

You've lain awake many a night parsing past conversations, sniffing out the evidence to prove your every erstwhile friend false. And even if they weren't, you can't believe any of them actually understood or appreciated you, much less loved you for your true nature, as you know that true nature to be a bottomless pit of self-doubt and egomania; self-righteousness and despair. Anyone who knew you - *really knew you* - would carjack their grandmother to get away, and anyone who didn't would have to have ulterior motivations ten times rottener than your own.

You live now as a virtual recluse; a hypodermic needle in a haystack. Everyone bails on this go-nowhere town eventually - who wouldn't choose to go *somewhere*, given the opportunity? - and even those who tried to keep in touch, you turned on at some point or another - certain they could only be driven by self-interest or amusement or pity - time and again encouraging them to stop calling - stop texting - stop DMing and poking and @ing, and just leave you the fuck alone. It turns your stomach even now, thinking of all those so-called "friends" who dared presume your *need* for them.

You're in it now. The dark, vampire squid-infested benthos. Where the blue fades to black.

From here, your disconnect with humanity can magnify to an even greater scale, cornering you into suspicions that your whole existence is nothing more than a *Truman Show*-aping entertainment - a conspiratorial joke on which every Earthly viewer is in, except you, the viewerest of all.

Your mind sheepshanks and killick hitches into a Gordian nightmare of backstabbings and betrayals until you are no longer convinced you have even the smallest measure of control over your life's course. You envision legions of actors, directors, cameramen and sound techs stealthily choreographing your every waking moment; armies of propsmasters, carpenters, plumbers and electricians fabricating every locale you visit mere hours before you arrive - tirelessly creating the world piecemeal as you derive need for it. Your every decision prefigured by forces beyond your ken, you find yourself wishing, even begging for it to be true; for it to be true that everything is a fiction, so little sense do the facts make.

This far out, paranoia is no longer something you can reasonably call a side effect of your lifestyle. The word itself retains only the most tenuous and abstruse of meanings, connoting a misguided mania for which your very capacity to grasp all but disappears. In these moments, you don't understand yourself as a paranoid person anymore. You're simply at peace with the lie.

Thankfully, you hit dry land back at Channel 0001, and though a histrionic hairpiece is reporting an e-coli outbreak at your local Dairy Queen, you feel nothing but regularly scheduled relief. By the time you return to the *Friends* a few channels up, you barely even remember what you were thinking about.

"Relax please" you say in perfect unison with Phoebe, snickering both at her delivery of the line, and your eidetic recall of same. It's a strange phenomenon, the clarity with which you retain such details. You can recount every episode of *Seinfeld* and *Breaking Bad* as though you'd lived them, but things like bills, or e-mails, or where you set down that eggroll a few seconds ago, are often lost to the murky bongwaters of your short-term memory.

A third episode of *Friends* is starting, and a glance at The Guide reveals five more to come, plus another two-hour block seven channels up after that. These mini-marathons air on a nightly basis, and though you have access to all ten seasons in your DVD library, and streaming on Netflix, part of you enjoys the old-fashioned experience of watching only the ones made available by the good people at TBS or Nickelodeon, or whoever - erectile dysfunction commercials and all.

Much like listening to the radio has become a credibility signifier for Gen-Xers, watching old-school, broadcast television has developed a patina of retro cool to your mind (though maybe not to anyone else's). Today's youth could never understand the excitement you once felt in the molasses-drip hours leading up to a new installment of your favorite series. The waiting. The anticipation. The complete lack of any information that might qualify as a "spoiler." These are things of the past now.

These days, everyone can watch whatever they want, whenever they want, and then hop online to react to whatever they've just watched as soon as they're done watching. It's brought a disproportionately introverted segment of society closer together, made us all smarter with regards to interpretation and comprehension, and instilled in us a collective desire for better, more challenging programming across the board. And yet, you feel something's been lost in our ultra-consumerist efforts to have – and you're paraphrasing a number of well-known soft-trolls here, including Chuck Klosterman and Louis CK – "everything, all the time, right now, forever." Why did we assume reaching that mountaintop would make us happy, and what are we supposed to do if it ultimately doesn't? Go outside? Climb real mountains? Please.

You smoke another couple fat bowls and idly decimate the rest of the Cheetos as three episodes stretch into eleven. You are intensely, irretrievably baked now - your body a formless, flattened non-entity chameleoning into your couch cushions; your head a billowing hot-air balloon drifting toward the troposphere. Even the *Friends* become strange and incomprehensible to you - like an odd word repeated aloud until it's rendered meaningless - their faces aging and rearranging; their conversations taking on double, and triple layers of deep, philosophical meaning.

When a person smokes as much weed as you do, they grow accustomed to such low-level mental chicanery. Visual and auditory hallucinations are fairly common - though not in a formicatory, afterschool special kind of way so much as a "hey, was that a bug over there? Nah. It wasn't. Or was it? I dunno. Whatever" kind of way. Likewise, if you stay up smoking into the Leprechaun hours, you can develop a sort of fixed cataract mirage - like a fly in your aqueous humor, or a smudge on the contact lenses you know perfectly well you're not wearing. This is generally a sign it's time to start thinking about sleep.

That said, your phosphenes can play Laser Floyd all night when fueled with enough sativa, and left to their own devices, your ears can betray you as well as your eyes. Falling asleep in front of the TV is often necessary, as silence tends to hiss and crackle with the stressful, subterranean energy of Ornette Coleman vinyl. Even on nights when you long for quiet, the best you can usually hope for is familiar noise.

As is often the case, Monica's, Rachel's, and Phoebe's nipples are all hard as Everlasting Gobstoppers and poking through their haute 90's blouses like Chilean miners trying to pickaxe their way to sunlight (in your zombaked state you feel you've tapped into your third eye for the sole purpose of staring at all six simultaneously). Before long, your hand is creeping toward your gradually inflating member as though you were a nervous teenager subtly trying to make a move on yourself, and you decide to wander back to your bedroom and continue this unexpected pop-up party on the small screen.

Episode 5

You rifle through your dresser for a well-loved sock.

Sports and porn are the only unscripted entertainments you watch anymore. You like to think of it as keeping tabs on the best both sexes have to offer. Jumpshots and cumshots – your last few, strained tethers to reality.

And make no mistake, these girls are the best. Of all the women fucking in the world, these are the select few who've taken it upon themselves to become expert. They are practiced. They have their 10,000 hours. This is their craft, and you sit – splay-legged and jacking – in awe of them.

Opening your laptop and its bookmarked harem, you decide to ease into things with the gentle, girl-on-girl oeuvre of Lily.

Lily is a Ming Vase under tallow moonlight; a soft-focus lotus in a pool of impressionist cerulean. She is a ripe breast cupped through a jersey t-shirt, and a pert bottom hugged by white cotton panties. Her every partner a pupil, drawn out through tussling, kittenish play. Her every choice a nurturing, animal instinct. Her every movement an ancient, sacred rite. Nips at napes, lobes, and navels; lips pressed against scrunched noses; fingertips traversing tummies and milky thighs. Breaths catch. Bodies quiver and bloom. Her tongue activates in others a near-bioluminescent glow.

Lily waves you into the labyrinthine world of internet porn with a coy, beckoning finger, and perusing the next page you notice a screencap of Kaci, a rubenesque starlet with whom you've grown increasingly enamored of late.

Kaci is a fucking remora. She doesn't just suck cock; she vacuum seals it. Her Clara Bowe DSLs form a perfect, 360° "O" and her eyes fix ever upward in grudging gratitude. Manmade concepts of length and girth are immaterial to her. Her embouchure expands with the rhythms of the spheres. Whether chipmunking curious schlongs into her rosy cheeks, deepthroat gagging until her jugular bulges and her irises roll, or just letting mouthfuls of satisfied "MMMMMs" escape the corners of her jampacked maw, she makes sure you know: she doesn't just love this; she craves it. Among blowjob queens, she is an Empress - and you her loyalest subject.

Disappointingly, Kaci's co-star switches the game up and gets to work eating her ragdoll pussy, but below you notice a hyperlink to Lexi -

an adorable strumpet of whom you're rather fond in a creepy, paternalistic way.

Lexi loves to play dress-up, and scrolling down reveals a Tri-Delt Halloween Party's-worth of coquettish costumery. Making her rounds in a bunny-white minidress, the vermillion X between Nurse Lexi's sculpted, silicone CC's practically begs her patients for their loads. Suffering through detention, Catholic Schoolgirl Lexi's idle fingers work their devilish way up beneath her tartan skirtfolds. Bent over a Xerox machine, her pencil skirt pinstripes bunching into right angles, Secretary Lexi's boss plows her from behind in one-third of a three-piece suit. Lexi is a chameleon – the kind of pornstar who absolutely believes she'll be an actress someday – and as Cowgirl Lexi lays across a haybale squealing "fuhth me, fuhth me, fuhth me" around a mouthful of her own sopping wet panties, well... you're hard-pressed to bet against her.

Alas, Lexi's a bit girlish for your tastes, often playing the jailbait lallation card despite being in her mid-to-late twenties. After a few more virtual quick-changes, you jump to a pumpkin-bottomed beauty named Alexis.

Alexis has an ass like an under-inflated beachball, which she readily presents to a lens that can barely contain it. Striated with cellulitic stretchmarks, it suggests the same sucking, grasping, squelching quality as the Sarlac pit monster, and it's easy to imagine her using it to pick up the morning paper or a danish accidentally dropped on the kitchen floor. Swallowing up her g-string between its ruddy cheeks, Alexis's gluteus maximalus seems to have a mind of its own - not unlike the mighty brontosaurus, with its separate brains for head and tail - and as she gives it a firm, corporal smack, you could swear you see its faultline asscrack almost smile - smug with anticipation.

Though a first-rate novelty, as a breast man, Alexis can only hold your attention for so long - especially with a zaftig pop-up GIF named Lucie massaging its tits in the corner of your screen.

Unlike Alexis, Lucie keeps all her junk in the glove compartment. With vacant, wide-set eyes, and the kind of naturally pneumatic, *Liberty Leading the People* breasts men of the Greatest Generation went to war for, she resembles nothing quite so much as a submissive, E-cupped Precious Moments figurine. Scrolling through a field of POV dicks prairie-dogging her doughy mounds, you happen upon an embonpoint double-BJ she filmed with the similarly-proportioned Carmella, and as they bunch their two whimpering faces and four jiggling breasts into a sweet, fleshy melon patch and receive their gift - contented as sisters catching Christmas snowflakes on their outstretched tongues - you too expel a hydrant jet of pressurized jism into the toe of your spooge sock.

You close your eyes, your entire body basking in a warm, sticky glow. But upon looking back at your screen, you are repulsed, not just by pornography, but by all women, by the very idea of sex, and by their foul complicity in it. Cold drops of cum slide down your inner thigh and you shiver with shame as you pull a pair of pajama pants on over your soggy, shriveled unit.

Δ

After a urethra-cleansing, acid-wash piss punctuated by several inquisitive, upward-inflected farts whose pungency makes you crave McDonald's french fries, you return to your computer for your eighth consecutive hour of uninterrupted screen time.

You like to hit dating sites right after you've blown your load. You don't waste time on anyone whose profile crackles with Wodehousian wit, or who's plastered their page with ducklipped, yoga-panted, glamour-selfies. These are the grand illusions of the online dating world. Workaholic careerists looking to pencil in a pregnancy? Ab-sculpting former Prom Queens digging for gold? These are not the women who want to fuck you. You are pyrite with low motility. Tempting as they might be, pursuing them is little more than chasing shadows in the dark web.

By the same token, having just emptied your cakebag also gifts you a certain level of erotically disenthused discernment. Much like going to the grocery on an empty stomach, one should never shop the robust pages of OKcupid in "Anything that moves" mode, as one will absolutely find something that does (however slowly). For every aspiring Lena Dunham and Cara Delevingne, there are fifty agoraphobic hags lying in wait, ready to call you an Uber and have you delivered to their spider-veined lairs like so much online-ordered Papa Johns. They set traps with frontierswoman cunning, posting untagged photos full of hotter friends and listing bro-bait interests like "microbrewing" and "Pac-12 football" - their every message appended with a thirstily winking emoticon; their every "i" dotted with a tiny, hope-filled heart.

Your goal then, in this Goldilocksian endeavor, is to find those middling girls willing to do you juuuuuuust right; to enlist some sort of happily compliant sex slave or low-maintenance, off-site concubine, eager to live her life on call to your moody, whimsical dick.

It's not that you don't believe in love - quite the opposite in fact. If anything, you believe too much - in the perfect, life-altering, neverending storybook love espoused by every piece of popular literature, music, film, and television that's been hucked at humanity for the past 100 years. You believe in it to such a specific and willfully naïve degree that you'll absolutely never find it. You couldn't possibly. And even if you did, you couldn't help but fuck it up. You've waited too long now. Built it up too much in your mind. It's a sunk cost you refuse to see as fallacy; an ideal you'll cling to forever, despite overwhelming evidence against your hopeless case.

And so, in the meantime, what you're looking for is someone to be in thrall to you - to come when you call, cum when you tell her to, and go. Someone who worships your cock like a heretic disciple of Baal, but couldn't care less where you went to elementary school or what you consider to be your favorite color. Someone who'll drop whatever she's doing to come give you a sloppy, sleep aid blowjob, but doesn't mind driving herself home so you can get back to watching fucking TV and not have to share your fucking stash. Is that so much to ask?

Tinder might seem the obvious choice here, but the format is overwhelmingly stacked against you. Even the most basic mombods in the game are fending off dicks on a daily basis now, swiping left on human men as mindlessly as they'd flip through a Pottery Barn catalog. The app makes them too confident; gives them too much power. They're in thrall to no one but themselves.

Besides which, even if you did get laid a little more - and it would only be a little - the volume of rejection that accompanies a Tinder account is, you're quite sure, more than your softshell ego could endure. It's been said that when it comes to sex, men are afraid women will laugh at them, and women are afraid men will hit them, and there's nothing more frightening than the silence of every woman on the internet laughing at you, far, far out of reach. You want the kind of girl who only laughs nervously, after you explain your jokes to her. The kind who maybe wants you to hit her a little.

The best indicator a gal runs free-and-easy after this particular fashion is palpably low self-interest: lone, smirking photographs flipping off their photographers; exculpatory complaints about friends who "forced me to sign up for this stupid thing in the first place"; standard bio questions like "What do you do for a living?" and "What do you do for fun?" proffered one-word answers like "work" and "drink." This is your sought-after vibe. Less, in these cases, is quantifiably more. It takes very little effort after all, to type the phrase "down for whatever," and even less to mean it.

When stalking this disenchanted, quietly surrendering prey, it's important to have a sense of what most men consider average, and also to remember that most men have absurdly high, *Maxim*-and-Brazzers-inflated standards. If then, the collective self-esteem of all women were treated as a bubble, a la the housing market, then something like 95% of men think they work for JP Morgan. Scratch that. 95% of men think they *are* JP Morgan. Blame their cooing, coddling mothers.

With this in mind, you operate in the mold of a hard-target-searching Tommy Lee Jones hunting down undervalued, underappreciated, undersexed would-be-sluts (every sorority house, coffee house, halfway house, and Waffle House). While delusional day-traders pass up perfectly good properties with a subprime scoff, you knife through the statuesque tens and the beached zeros and cut right to the soft, fight-breast-cancer-pink middle - fours, fives, and sixes - that magical place where high demand and low expectations sometimes meet for a nooner.

(Ok. Maybe you don't really understand the financial crisis, but you do understand women are more susceptible to fluctuations in the market than men. They're open to doubt and nuance; to booms and busts; and to the possibility that maybe, just maybe, at this particular time, on this particular day, they don't deserve any better than you).

Your finger moves like a menacing dorsal fin, skimming twenty some-odd profiles before hitting on the chummy, chubby face of Melissa. Under favorite books she lists both **The Girls Guide to Hunting and Fishing**, and **Lolita**, providing the subtlest suggestion of a wanton sensibility. She **cuts hair** at the local **mall**, an unmistakable sign of a life gone off course, and she enjoys **reading, baking,** and **hanging out with friends**. You stare at her picture, imagining her spread-eagled in a sunshine-yellow cheerleading uniform, stretching herself almost punitively around a prizewinning, State Fair cucumber, before deciding she's too fat and moving on.

After a dozen more nonstarters you stumble onto Karen, a **phlebotomist** with a hollow-woman face reminiscent of Shelley Duvall at her most terrorized. Karen looks like she's been through the wringer, only to find the wringer was where she liked it and circle back around. Her favorite movie is **All About Lily Chou-Chou,** and under interests she's listed only **"drugs," "death,"** and **"Princess Diana conspiracy theories."** You admire her aesthetic, but can't imagine her expressing enthusiasm about much of anything, up to and including your dick. You take a pass.

Next up is a lanky, dishwater lass named April whose profile pic appears to be an unusually flattering mugshot. Though she's written a fair amount about her heroine's work at a **battered women's shelter,** under "Hobbies" and "Favorite Movies" she's typed the same sparse response: **"Coffee and Cigarettes."** She's more intensely interesting-looking than she is pretty – like a polychromatic skyline you know to be the result of toxic factory fumes – but you're drawn to her hardscrabble disdain. About to inform her that you too enjoy the films of Jim Jarmusch, however, you notice she has a **5-year-old son** and frantically click for the hills.

Miles of pages later, you're pleasantly surprised by a promiscuous haiku of words and images named Claire. Cross-armed and glaring at a crowded Christmas party, her picture defiantly returns your gaze - a dark, waifish raincloud amidst a candied pinesap orgy of red and green polyblend. Oozing concentrated sarcasm, she claims to like **"romantic, candlelit handjobs,"** **"cuddling by warm housefires,"** and **"long walks off short piers."** Incongruously, under "Favorite Movies" she's named **"Sleeping Beauty and Romance,"** but you suspect this too may be a smart-alecky MacGuffin.

As she's not currently online, you leave a quippy message about catching a **"sexually deviant art film"** at this **"cute little place I know,"** and continue the search.

Feeling less picky by the minute, you scan the deets of a girl named Patricia while wishing she had bigger tits. Nothing about her page seems uncommonly forward, but you read on, forgiving even her five-sentenced love of **jogging** as it's helped her maintain a lithe, spandex-appropriate figure. You're talking yourself into her - envisioning her shaving her salt-blonde pussy in a sunken tub - when you notice through droopy eyes that she's identified as an **Evangelical Christian**. Gross.

You're experiencing full-body flaccidity. You're down for the sperm count. Your dog won't hunt. You take another hit off Blaze Pascal, but your brain turns it away at the gate with an erratically flashing "No Vacancy" sign. You need sleep, and are preparing to resign yourself to a fruitless logoff when...

"**Hi!**" says a reasonably cute chat box named **Emma_Lee12495**. "**You're up late!**"

Utterly bushwhacked, you scramble to mount a verbal counteroffensive, but your brain can muster only a scalar, qwertyesque holding pattern. With zero time for opposition research, you throw out all your predatory protocols and just blindly type "**Hi**" back before flanking over to recon her intel.

Emma Lee is, at a glance, distressingly generic. What do you do for a living? "**Student.**" What do you do for fun? "**Movies. Hiking. Hanging out with friends.**" Favorite books: "**Harry Potter. Twilight. Hunger Games.**" Favorite movies: "**RomComs. Marvel. Pixar.**" Favorite music: "**Coldplay. Drake. Adele.**" She is, however, right on the Maginot line between full-figured and fat, and has beautiful, bulbous breasts - the kind that tend to bulge with soft, blue veins when squeezed around a pistoning cock. You love those blue veins.

"**I was about to get ready for bed when I found your profile**" she continues. "**I figured anyone on this late must be looking for trouble.**"

"I guess you could say that" you reply while stroking yourself through your softpants. **"Can't say I've ever met trouble that self-identified before though. Why should I believe you?"**

You scroll through her pictures, and sure enough, see a faint smidgeon of blue descending into the neckline of a low-cut green dress like the Amazon. Semi-rigid and delirious from exhaustion, you recklessly follow it toward the heart of darkness.

"Well..." she types, her ellipsis a tantalizing breadcrumb trail leading toward... what? High-vocabulary cybersex? A hastily Skyped striptease? Dare you hope even, an inquiry, as to the fastest route she might take to your aching, importunate member? Your yawning eyes project hallucinatory images of her cum-slathered mouth, and your bloodshot ears echo with her slurped thankyous. Whatever comes after this nymphomaniacal threeway of punctuation, you're certain it will be the evening's photo finish moneyshot.

The reality of the situation proves something of a letdown.

"I dunno. No one's ever asked me that before. I was just trying to be flirty. Sorry."

Horrified, but far too deep into Colonialist fantasy to swim back against the current, you rush to salvage the conversation.

"**No worries. I was just being flirty too**" you reply. "**You just seemed so confident, I thought I should play along. I hope I didn't skeeve you out.**"

"**Not at all!**" she answers with the broadest-smiling of all the emoji. "**Guess I should work on my game before I go starting things I can't finish!**"

In walking back her provocative demeanor, she's revealed herself to be more-than-willing, but perhaps less-than-able, with regards to hookup negotiations. And so you decide to help her along - to reach out, take her by the hand, and lead it gently down your pants. There's no easier mark than a girl who wants to be sexy but doesn't know how.

"**Well I hope you don't mind me saying so, but from the way you're working that green dress, I'd argue you've got game to spare...**" you type, drawing her in with a suggestive ellipsis of your own. "**I've definitely started something you could finish.**"

[You are a duck blind,
drenched in Axe Body Spray.]

"**Oh my!**" she responds, this time with a winking emoji. "**And I thought I was trouble!**"

You raise your fists like you just summited the *Rocky* steps. Triumphant Bill Conti trumpets herald your victory. You've got her. You've fucking got her.

"**LOL!**" you lie. "**What can I say? You're really hot. I'd love to take you out sometime. No expectations, of course.**"

"**Aww. That's really nice. You're cute too.**" she responds, now blowing you an emoji kiss.

"**Are you free this weekend?**" you ask, already stockpiling negs in the back of your mind.

"**I'm actually out of town.**" she writes (though with a frowny face, for whatever that's worth). "**I won't be back for a few weeks.**"

"**Oh**" you write back, refusing to couch your disappointment in the forgiving cushions of emoji-speak. It's better for you if she genuinely feels bad.

"**Think you can manage til then?**" she asks, positively dripping implied availability.

You let her dangle while you hopscotch back to your porn site and rabidly accost yourself to a Czech stewardess as she enrolls both her pussy and her gaping, bleached asshole in the prestigious, Soviet Bloc chapter of the Mile High

Club – electric blue boob vein heaving throughout. Battering your dick until it dry-heaves a stringy second load that rubber-cements your right hand into sticky uselessness, you then navigate back to Emma Lee with your left, and awkwardly hunt-and-peck the words **"Sure! Can't Wait!"**

Episode 6

Only a day into October and already munching on candy corn, you find yourself lying splendor-in-the-grass-high in a Saturday afternoon sunbeam, your mind bathed in Thomas Kincaid light. It's amazing how, for all its deleterious effects on users' short-term memories, cannabis can also act as a kind of brain colander, or perhaps a drain-snake for decrepit neural pathways, gently sieving out detritus and plunging pipes until it unearths a singular moment from the past and renders it so clearly that you not only remember, but *feel* whatever it was you had felt anew. Listing drowsily between fantasy and memory, you trawl back through the halcyon days of your higher education - in particular, a sociological experiment you encountered along your campus's Liberal Arts corridor - that which has stayed with you longer than any scribble of Baudelaire or Baudrillard you ever read...

Δ

The premise was simple. Two sophomore boys - the student gazette would later identify them only as Greg and Sam - posted up at high-traffic sidewalk intersections on the Northeast quad just before the daily hubbub of the 12:15 class change. As lectures came to a close, and their Jansporting, walk-and-texting peers scurried out of the brickwork - heads down in willful defiance of the present, fingers tapping out poorly punctuated plans for the future - this sociodynamic duo began talking to strangers:

"Killer smile buddy!"

"You're crushing it today!"

"Dope shades bro!"

"Your hair looks amazing!"

"You're cooler than the other side of the pillow!"

And so on.

They were a wellspring of inert positivity - their smiles could've disarmed bombs - and anyone who walked within a five-foot radius received some unmistakably earnest testimony to his or her observable best self. They offered no explanations. They affixed no amendments. They just kept at it - as inoffensive as calisthenic cat posters; as trite as Tony Robbins tracts; as forgettable as fortune cookies. They sought only to brighten everyone's day.

The sole variable at play: Sam was draped in a sandwich board which read in bold, 200-point Helvetica font: **FREE COMPLIMENTS!** (and below, in commanding, KJV-red: Line Up Here!) while Greg wore only jeans and a t-shirt.

Standing about two football fields apart, they ensured none of their hundredsfold pool of unwitting subjects would get wise to the surreptitious human trials in which they were participating until they'd already done so sans waivers. You, however, had the good fortune to happen by both of these aspiring Habermases (Habers-mas?) early on, and having been suspiciously told twice in the span of a few minutes that you had "excellent posture," you doubled back to a central location – a beloved beech tree encircled by kissin' benches – and Zacchaeused up to observe over the thickening pedestrian crush.

Responses to Greg were spotty at first – a "thanks" here; a "shut up" there – but as more and more heads started popping up – unfixing their gazes from sidewalks and screens – he became increasingly inundated by sarcastic retorts and brashly lowered shoulders. Shoes he endorsed turned to tread on his heels. Biceps he applauded became turnstiles of harassment. A diapason of agitation was billowing up around the poor kid's towhead. Nobody could figure out what his deal was, and nobody gave a shit.

Even in your younger and more vulnerable years, this was pretty much what you expected.

Yours was a generation raised on self-aware irony; on multiplatinum "alternative" music and multimillion dollar "independent" films; on a polarized politics scored chiefly in talking points and gaffes; on end-times environmentalism and low-income expectations; on divorce statistics and early-onset-atheism and a near-militaristic sense of self-regard. To their minds, a man – and a peer no less – on the street corner, offering words of encouragement with no ulterior motive, was as implausible as any grizzled, granite-toothed doomsday prophet proclaiming himself the second coming of Christ. It just didn't track.

Meanwhile, at the other end of the mall, Sam was seeing a line form, and intrigued, you de-treed to go eavesdrop, crenelated by viburnums and a well-worn copy of Ken Kesey's *Sometimes a Great Notion*.

"This is such a nice idea!" one girl said to another.

"It's, like, so simple and honest," chirped a third.

"Yeah, I wonder what he's selling," cracked a skeptical wannabeatnik, to strikingly swift admonishment.

"He's just being nice!"

"Don't be a jerk!"

"If you can't see how cool this is, I feel sorry for you."

Banished to the back of the line to reassess his game, the handsome hipster's ouster allowed a decidedly schlubbier kid to shuffle forward and offer an opportunistic toast to this trio of Ugg-booted Valkyries.

"I just have to say, I couldn't agree with you more" he announced to none of them in particular. "I think we could all stand to be a little kinder to strangers."

The girls agreed with sagacious nods.

"Heck" he added with a glance at their retreating victim, "that guy probably needs it more than any of us."

At this the girls tittered and demurred, and in moments, he had all three of their numbers. Behind your paperback shield, your jaw fell like Newton's apple.

Sam's queue of disciples grew fast – thirty, forty, fifty – and the good vibes radiated down the line in a life-affirming game of telephone. Winklevossian bros who would've laughed Sam off the court and out the gym any other day were reddening his palms with stinging high-fives. Women who would've hit Sam over the head with a barstool before accepting a drink from him were kissing his cheeks and draping themselves across his undefined deltoids.

And what's more, people started talking *to each other*. You saw a band of husky D&D enthusiasts explaining the finer points of spellcraft to the school's star third baseman. You witnessed a friendly exchange on marijuana legalization between a Phishhead and a Young Republican. You overheard a terminally shy girl from your Shakespeare class accept an invitation to try out for University Improv.

Small talk grew large. Hugs broke out. The whole world sang an Up With People tune. With five words in two colors, Sam had created a human conveyor belt of validation and acceptance; a perpetual-motion machine of encomium. You had to hand it to him. It was fucking magical.

A little nauseous, you picked your way back across the lawn, certain this atmospheric anomaly wouldn't last the hour. Sam may have put some love in the air, but Greg could see which way the wind was blowing.

You returned to find him, not un-impressively, still offering innocuous pep to whoever might hear it. But he looked rough. His jeans half-camouflaged by grass stains and red clay, he'd clearly been jostled off his New Balance more than once while you were spying on his better-delineated half, and with the class-change mob now at full capacity, he was – as an NFL announcer might put it – absorbing a lot of contact.

This culminated in two popped-collar behemoths engaging in some impromptu recess bullying, shoving Greg back and forth between their American Gladiator pecs like a blonde medicine ball. In so doing, they inadvertently became the organizing principle his side of the experiment so badly needed (though in stark contrast to Sam's, it was less a line, and more a *Fight Club*-style "ring of pain" into which his subjects organized themselves. People are unpredictable that way).

But Greg stuck to his guns, firing off round after round of positive reinforcements even as his stumbling pirouettes robbed him of the ability to aim. Amidst a Howitzer hail of laughter, he stood strong on his one square yard of concrete, and refused to die.

In the end, one of his hastily flung bouquets – "Beautiful form!" – landed fatefully between a statuesque female jogger, and her equally marble-hewn boyfriend, bringing the latter to a curl-route halt.

"The fuck did you just say to her!?!" demanded the boyfriend - a rippling lion of a man encased in jet-black Under Armour.

Greg's jughead assailants practically put their hands up in surrender as they eased back into the crowd, so menacing was this advancing Beastmaster, but Greg - to whom you must here give all the credit in the world despite what you personally consider to be his abject stupidity - just kept showering his onlookers with goodwill, even whilst they cheered his imminent receipt of a new asshole.

"Awesome hat!"

"You look like a million bucks!"

"Whatever you're doing, it's working! Keep it up!"

"Hey dipshit! I asked you a fuckin' question!" roared the boyfriend, his Cleganian frame effectively blotting out the sun. "What'd you just say to her?!"

The supposedly-injured party, for her part, watched from a distance, a mudflap silhouette in black lycra so form-fitting you had to assume it was part of her genetic code; a sweat-wicking epidermis she shed and regrew every few weeks like some rare species of stupid-hot rattlesnake. She looked bored.

"I..."

"What?!" interrupted the boyfriend, likely just using this time to decide which part of Greg to eat first.

"I was…"

"Spit it out bitch!"

"I was just complimenting her form," was the combination of words Greg landed on – a miscalculation on par with "Let them eat cake" and "We'll be greeted as liberators."

"Her form? What the fuck does that mean!? Why are you even looking at her fucking form motherfucker!?!?"

"Nonononono" Greg sputtered, stepping back only to be body-checked by an impenetrable wall of Philistines, lustily braying for a Goliath grudge match 5,000 years in the making. "Her form, like, as a runner. Yours too actually. You know… just being friendly."

With this final attempt at appeasement, Greg watched the boyfriend's eyebrows knit into a crinkly inchworm of bewilderment, which slowly hellbent downward into a sharp, skull-splitting V of rage.

"So now you like my form too!? You wanna get friendly with me!?!?"

Greg was fucked. You recall surveying the landscape behind you for a viable exit strategy in case this controlled bloodletting escalated into

Grand Guignol, and seeing that Sam's line had grown so long as to have nearly merged with Greg's savage scrum (indeed, as the commotion reached a boiling point, the tail-end broke off to join the fray like so many kids playing crack the whip). Sure enough, by the time you turned back around, Greg was taking a grand piano haymaker cleanly to the temple.

He crumpled, and the crowd went wild - a miasma of fist pounds, chest bumps, recalcitrantly ponied side bets, and more than a few belligerent cries of "Are you not entertained!?!" that apparently missed the entire point of their source material. Greg, from his prostrate position, offered a final, selfless "Nice kicks" to someone's sneakers before a fierce, button-combo kick to the ribs shut him up for good.

Sadly, that was pretty much it. The brutalist boyfriend flexed a Kruschevian self-clasping handshake, ensuring his place in GIF lore, but one flip of his consort's bouncy curls and he broadjumped to her side.

"Can we go now?" she asked.

"Sure baby," he said.

The multitudes parted at the turn of her hips, and they were off, instantly regaining the -

you must say – truly beautiful form that had gotten them noticed in the first place.

No greater riot materialized. Day-drunk on Molotov cocktails and pipebomb dreams, the howling phalanx that encircled Greg soon couldn't wait to fan out and scatter AWOL, and you watched, fascinated, as scores of perspiration-soaked bodies unstuck from one another like shamefaced Pillsbury pull-apart rolls.

Once it seemed safe, you helped Greg to his feet and shepherded him toward one of the benches. In the distance, you could make out Sam's congregation, dwindled to twenty-five or so as classes resumed. After lighting a cigarette, you broke the silence.

"I know what you guys were doing."

Greg sniffled, but remained stoic.

"You both gave me the same compliment."

Still nothing.

"You said I had good posture."

". . ."

You continued your insufflations at a leisurely pace while Greg collected himself, gargling the smoke and letting it float out of your mouth on its own schedule. Clutching at his purpling left side, he eventually angled back onto his feet to start covering the two-football-fields-worth of ground between him and his tousled, lipstick-smeared colleague. You weren't expecting anything more from this bit part you'd played in his short, dark afternoon of the soul, but after a few steps, he looked back and offered these despondent parting words:

"You're a really good person."

Δ

You saw the writing on the Facebook wall that day. While you had no idea what Greg's and Sam's initial goals or ultimate conclusions were for their telling little project, the takeaway for you was simple: don't be a stranger.

People your age had become so embedded in their suspicion, and so defined by their irony, that they could no longer accept sincerity in even its purest, least adulterated form. *Everything* was something else to them. It *had* to be. Why *should* they trust anyone? What was in it for *them*? To wit, you'd just watched one guy spend the afternoon giving himself away, and getting absolutely destroyed for it, while a few-hundred yards down the road another guy was blatantly selling himself, and enjoying a virtual deification. For you, this was revelatory.

Up until that day, you'd been obdurately resistant to the inchoate universe unfurling under the umbrella-term "social media." You felt you were above it, and what's more, that you'd be rightly recognized as a noble iconoclast for refusing to conform. "Why join a friend site?" you'd ask with a dickish chuckle. "I barely like the friends I have now."

That night, however, you created a profile. With painstaking care, you curated a hyperlink museum of iconic jazz cats and underground mixtape MCs, Neuer Deutscher cinema and Sundancing micro-indies. You speed-reread dozens of your favorite books - Bukowski, Rand, Sartre, Easton Ellis - lifting quotes to illuminate your as-yet-unappreciated genius. Finally, you would be understood. Finally, people would see you the way you wanted to be seen. Asked to state your religious views, you wrote "God is dead." For political views you typed "Fuck the police." Where your picture was supposed to go, you imported a thumbnail of Warhol's checkerboard Che Guevara. *This* you thought, *this was your revolution!*

You could see, for the first time, the dawning of a new era; one in which everyone would be the star of their own screen, and everyone else would be reduced to supporting players. One in which it no longer mattered what you were like; only what you *said* you were like. One in which your depressed, desensitized, disenchanted generation - a generation of helicopter-parented children carried kicking and screaming into adulthood by the very strangers they were taught not to talk to - would finally work its way back around to a new kind of innocence. One in which it was safe to talk to strangers again, because no one would be a stranger anymore. Everyone would have a big, bold, Helvetica sign.

Episode 7

As a direct result of your remaining permanently pan-fried, you have a tendency toward magnifying even the most inconsequential interactions into exaggerated caricatures of significance; those which cast looming, Star Destroyer shadows across your Rachel-Leigh-Cooked brain until you can think of nothing else. Your entrapment of Emma Lee was a thing of beauty, and your intractably gutter-bound mind has been spinning 2 Live Crew songs on a nasty-ass loop ever since. Having reread and reparsed your conversation over a dozen times now, you're quite certain: you'll soon be laid.

While some might mistake such distraction for nascent infatuation, or even obsession, in actuality it has almost nothing to do with her. Pussy's the goal. She's just the goaltender. You've already mapped out a variety of directions in which you hope to steer the evening (though they all end with you smacking your sloppy rod against that ultramarine titty vein). You are Lionel Messi, thinking three moves ahead as you drive toward the net. She has no chance.

That said, when sex is on the horizon, your whole life fades to interminable intermission. All units of measurable time run blearily together like so many over-easy, surrealist stopwatches. Days stack into weeks, weeks flatten into months, months devour years, and you've nothing to mark any of it save the television through which you've dutifully slogged. You may well remember that you spent 9+ hours revisiting the third season of *Community*, another 8 immersed in Éric Rohmer's *Six Moral Tales*, and 13 more knocking out Carl Sagan's *Cosmos* (betwixt your weekly commitments to 15-or-so other currently-airing series), but as to which happened when, and in what order, you couldn't really say. Time is no longer a precious commodity to be "spent," but a bottomless expanse to be "filled" and a grueling endurance trial to be "passed." You've traded "now" for "next," and "all" for "more." You feel nothing but the screens in front of your face, and the waiting.

Your only respite comes when you make arrangements to visit your third-favorite weed dealer – a shady, low-wattage lout named Gander – after your first's voicemail informs you she'll be drafting off the Widespread Panic tour bus for the next month, and the second frenziedly explains that he's "drier than Steven Wright in a Swedish sauna." Though you prefer not to call upon Gander unless absolutely necessary, he offers to sell you a nip of his personal stash – asserting in the next breath that a 50% markup will be the cost of doing business amid a county-wide drought. No honor among heads.

In the past you've always met behind condemned fast-food franchises, or under the prison-yard spotlighting of mall parking lots while dropouts practice their ollies in the background. There you carry out the dubious pantomime of shaking hands, circling each other for the duration of a cigarette, shaking hands again, and speeding off toward opposite ends of the night.

Any cop worth his dress blues would recognize this playlet from a mile away, but Gander's outlaw delusions easily triple your own, and he's got at least one prior (he *claims* he was picked up for spraypainting a six-foot, bleach-white penis on the side of a daycare center where, he *claims*, he lost his virginity at age 12 when, he *claims*, a stacked, blonde Summer intern rode him like a mechanical bull smackdab in the middle of, he *claims*, a duck-duck-goose circle while, he *claims*, the other kids cheered him on before breaking into a helpfully rhythmic chorus of "Wheels on the Bus"). This was the third thing he told you about himself, after his name, and the strata of drugs he could acquire (always weed, sometimes coke, occasionally shrooms, and a laundry list of pills long enough to restage *Valley of the Dolls*).

You're skeptical, of all this, but he's never failed to come through, and when your first- and second-favorite dealers are every bit the blazed-and-confused mnemonic catastrophes that you are, it's nice to have a self-serious ace in the hole, even if he's a little more Rick Ross than Freeway Rick. Shit, who doesn't like Rick Ross?

This time, Gander's uncharacteristically insisted you come to his place – an aluminum trailer home that resembles a beached submarine, and on which he's been stubbornly paying week-to-week rent for nine years – insistent on unfettered mobility in order to "stay one step ahead of the man." Though he's always been cagey on the phone (he insists on codewords from day one. If you want weed, you ask to borrow his lawnmower. Coke is the snowblower. He owns neither of these items), you get the impression something's happened since you last spoke that's treed him even higher into the leafy heights of his California Redwood psychosis. This guy is the Julia Butterfly Hill of paranoia.

And that's the thing about Gander: he's basically adopted all the most incommodious aspects of being a legitimate drug kingpin as a kind of method posturing. You don't believe for a second anyone's after him, or that he'd possess the skills to elude them if they were, but he remains nostalgic for a level of romanticized criminality he has no real way of achieving. He speaks with the menace of a Tarantino character, but comes off about as menacing as a Tarantino interview. He wants to be Tony Montana, but mostly just logs a lot of *Grand Theft Auto* miles. He's playing Made-believe.

The tinker-toy beats of WC and the Maad Circle's "Homesick" make your minivan feel like a '64 Impala as you roll into his unpaved drive. Your tires instantly become chew toys for his dissevered Cerberus of rottweilers - Cheech, Butthead, and Kumar - and you observe a crush of smoke as he steps out after them, radiating off his compressed, fire-barrel frame as though he's just emerged from cold storage.

"What up bro?" he shouts while scanning the treeline for snipers.

"Not much" you reply, giving your handle a snap-back tug to ensure it did in fact lock.

"Come on in" he says, his minions trailing behind him, harmless as the make-way-for-ducklings.

Inside is a strangled confluence of puerile paraphernalia; like a Hot Topic took a shit in a

Bonnaroo port-a-potty. You count eight lava lamps (all a rich, erythrocytic red) giving the entire space a sinister, human trafficky vibe. A laptop displaying an offshore sportsbook site rests atop a 10-gallon terrarium housing three virulent-looking snakes - Beavis, Harold, and Chong, incidentally - that were definitely not purchased at pet stores. Every surface is wallpapered with movie posters (*Reservoir Dogs*, *Scarface, 2 Fast 2 Furious*, and three separate depictions of *The Boondock Saints*), music posters (Zeppelin, Korn, Marley, Eminem), and dated pinups (Pam Anderson, Carmen Electra, Jenny McCarthy, and a ceiling collage of scotch-taped *Playboy* centerfolds - mostly Miss Hawaiian Tropics and Girls of the Big 10). It's a Bayeux Tapestry of douchebaggery. The place looks warm, but feels uncompromisingly cold. There's not a book in sight.

He motions you over to a futon which is clearly also his bed, and hands you a giant, purple, plastic bong.

"Oh," you say, trying not to disingratiate yourself, "I actually wasn't planning on staying. I don't like driving high when I've got the shit in the car, ya know?"

He recoils without moving a muscle, staring you down like you just told him to run and get his fuckin' shinebox.

"You wearin' a wire?" he asks.

"Um... no?" you say, unsure if he's joking.

"You askin' me or tellin' me?" he asks, definitely not joking.

"Dude. I'm not wearing a wire. Chill."

"Don't tell me to chill. This is my fuckin' house. Don't tell me to chill."

"Ok. Sorry. I just meant, I'm clean is all."

"Then why won't you blaze with me?"

"I just said why."

"Seems like bullshit."

"I'm tellin' ya man."

"Nah. I don't buy it."

"Ok... how can I convince you?"

"Well, I'd say you've got two options. You can strip down and give us a little spin, ya know, the way your moms did last night, or you can be cool and hit this fuckin' bong. Either way, I'll know you're straight. Capisce?"

"You're serious?"

"Yeah. I'm fuckin' serious. Dealer's choice."

"But... but you're the dealer."

"Don't be a smartass."

Silently vowing to promote your fourth-favorite weed dealer, you stand, and begin unbuttoning your shirt. As your eyes adjust to the oppressive infrared, you spy the hand of a topless Sailor Jerry girl reaching out the sleeve of Gander's Metallica t-shirt (one of those craniocidal jobs from their 90's heyday) almost as if she's signaling for help in escaping his tiny, gym rat body. The things you notice.

"So, you don't wanna hang out then?" he asks as you approach your navel.

"I mean..."

"You'd seriously rather get naked than smoke a bowl with me?"

"I guess I thought I could leave my boxers on?" you answer nervously.

"So, you just wanna come over here - I haven't heard from you in *months* - and you wanna come over to my *fucking house*, buy a piece of my *personal stash*, in the middle of a *fucking drought*, and be on your *merry fucking way*?"

"Um..."

"That's what you want?"

"Well..."

"Alright man. I see how it is."

"Aw. C'mon dude."

"Whatever."

"No. I just..."

"You just?"

"I wasn't..."

"You weren't?"

"I..."

"You?"

Fast losing interest in this hostile game of shadow, Gander starts looking for his remote, all but saying aloud that you've squandered your chance. In the interest of recurrying favor, you cast about some too, only then spotting the Glock on the nightstand, hugged by a brown leather holster.

"Look man..."

"No, *you* look. I'm doin' you a fuckin' favor here. You haven't been around in forever. I know I'm not your main guy, but I thought we were at least fuckin' friendly. I thought we were cool. But whatever. Maybe not."

"I..."

"I've been goin' through some shit man. You don't even know. I've had some real fuckin' troubles. And it's not like I'm askin' you to do a drive-by with me here. I'm not callin' you for fuckin' bail money at three in the fuckin' morning. I just wanna smoke a fuckin' bowl. Is it really such a burden to sit here and smoke a bowl with me? Am I just like fucking trash to you?!"

"Dude! No! Of course not!"

"Well what then?!"

Somehow, despite the rounded nature of his home, he has you cornered.

"You know what? You're right. I'm being stupid. I drive stoned all the time. It's all good. Let's burn it down."

You reach for the enormous rig - a collapsed lung waiting to happen - but alas, even this proves too simple an outcome.

"Not so fast," he says. "You gotta earn it now."

Before you can respond to this unnerving turn of phrase, he shoves a different piece of hardware your way: the plastic Stratocaster commensurate with dueling him in *Guitar Hero*. You wonder if this could be the so-called "rock bottom" addicts are always going on about.

He selects Van Halen's noxious cover of "You Really Got Me" - but between the hemoglobin lighting and his apparent disinterest in adjusting the tint or contrast on his 32" Zenith, you have no hope of defeating him. You might as well be playing Jordan on his home court. You tap out a futile, no-wave assault of crushingly wrong notes while he flies through a pitch-perfect Eddie solo. More than doubling your score, he laughs a gloatacious, Nelson Muntz laugh and mimes smashing his axe over your head. You're uncomfortable, but also feel that if this is all he wanted, you don't particularly mind giving it to him.

"That was pathetic," he says.

"I know. Sorry. Haven't played in a while."

"It shows."

"Yeah," you agree, affecting glum defeatism. "You pwned me bro."

[You are a jackhammer at rock bottom.]

"Well," he says, "I don't know if you earned this, but you sure as Hell deserve it now."

He passes you the bong – a two-man operation which stands only about a foot shorter than him – and provides a gentlemanly spark while you inhale two hours-worth of cannabinoids in approximately eight seconds. Stifling a cough, you unleash a vast low-pressure system of smoke toward the ceiling, briefly providing his pornographic angels with some Sistine cloud cover. The room's harsh, 24-hour tanning bed ambiance falls away as your senses Feng Shui into their ideal flow state. With everything suddenly in its right place, you even sense you may somehow be needed here.

Gander queues up Dethklok's hyperthyroidic, speed-metal symphony

"Thunderhorse," and finding your eyes adapted and your button dexterity heightened after that double XL bong rip, you decide to take an interest.

"So what's been going on?" you ask, expertly wiggling your whammy bar. "You said you've been having a tough time?"

"It's cool," he says, tightening up at your newfound proficiency. "You don't wanna hear about my shit."

"Dude, I totally do. I'm sorry about before. I get weird when I don't have green. I'm not myself, ya know?"

"Yeah, I get it," he says, swapping his power chord stage presence for brow-mopping, Methenyesque concentration. "It's fine. Let's just play."

"Alright," you say, hanging ten on a gnarly swell of arpeggios. "Your call."

"Shut up!" he says, unleashing a drumfill of staccato "fucks" as he misses a power-up.

You're plastic guitar neck-and-neck. It's all down to the incendiary closing lick. You're on a virtuosic, 100+ note-perfect run. And yet, you know he needs this, not just more than you do, but in a way you never could. In a way you honestly can't even comprehend.

In a bit of kismet, Kumar breaks the competitive tension with a plea to be let outside, and while Gander hammers home the last few bars, you feign a slip-up and throw the match.

"BOOM!!!" he bellows, hopping onto his coffee table and kicking an empty Natty Light. "You got served bitch!"

"Bullshit. Your dog distracted me!"

"Whatever you gotta tell yourself bro."

"One more game?" you ask, heavily implying he would not beat you a third time.

"Nah. I'm bored with it now."

"What, are you scaaared?"

"No. I just don't wanna play anymore."

"Come oooooooooon."

"*I said no!*"

"Whoa. Sorry man. Just joshin'."

"It's fine... I... I'm just obviously better is all. What's the point, right?"

"Yeah. I guess you're right."

Though he doesn't formally ask you to leave, you're becoming concerned he's completely forgotten why you came over in the first place, and you sit in silence while he packs and empties a smaller bong in five ferociously sequential, bone-deep hits (a display of moto perpetuo flare that makes you want to go home and put on some Rahsaan Roland Kirk).

"You wanna talk about it man?" you ask, as he brutishly prunes another bud with his stubby, CHOOS/ELIFE-knuckle-tatted fingers.

"I dunno," he says, offering you the bowl. "It's a pretty fuckin' weird situation."

"Try me," you reply, enjoying a modest toke.

"Well... I guess it all started when I banged my aunt Sheila last month."

Whatever the gaseous equivalent of a spit-take is, that is what you do, coughing up smoke you were fairly certain was beyond the point of no respiratory return. "You did what now?"

"She's not my real aunt. Just my uncle's wife. But still."

"But still indeed," you say, carefully devoid of judgment. "So what happened?"

"It just got super weird man," he says, as though that somehow shouldn't be the case. "Like, she was there when I was born. She changed my fuckin' diapers. She took me to see Santa and shit 'cause my moms was... fuck, I dunno. Fuckin' somewhere else. Gettin' wet or dryin' out. The point is, this lady's always been there for me, and now... now we're fuckin' fucking."

"And your uncle's still in the picture?"

"Yeah. She says she's unhappy though. Has been for years. She showed up a few weeks ago just itchin' for a taste. Really jonesin'. So we did a couple bumps, had a couple beers, and before I know it, she's all over me. I won't say I was unwilling - I'd fuck an alligator with enough coke in me - but I was definitely surprised. She was nasty too, man. Really went for it. She's spry for 63."

"Wow," you say, scouring your lexicon for appropriate response words.

"You don't believe me?!" he asks, probably unable to feel anything but defensive as he explains this situation out loud for the first time. "Look!"

He holds up a picture of a UV-damaged, but otherwise reasonably well-preserved woman in a full-length black dress and sunhat. Still managing to come off a little slutty despite being well-covered, she cuts the figure of an uninvited, half-soused mistress looking to make trouble at a daytime funeral.

"So, what happened next?" you ask, hoping to sidestep any evaluation of Aunt Sheila's physical attractiveness he might want from you.

"Well," he says, roasting the third bowl and immediately packing a fourth, "we said right off the bat it couldn't happen again. But she just kept showing up, and, well, you know."

"Uh-huh."

"So after the seventh or eighth time, I was just like, I gotta put my foot down. Right? This is fuckin'... weird. Right? And it's making me feel... *weird*. Right? And I just, like, don't wanna *do* it anymore, ya know? So I tell her this, and she flips the fuck out. Says if I don't keep fuckin' her, she's gonna turn me in to the fuckin' cops."

"Dude."

"Right!?! And it's like, shit, this is my livelihood bro. She helped me get set up when I was like sixteen and shit. I'm a fuckin' juvenile delinquent over here. I didn't finish *high school*. I don't have any fuckin' *skills*. This is it for me, and she knows it. So, it's keep fuckin' my aunt, or go to fuckin' jail. It's un-fuckin'-believable."

"You're right about that," you say.

"So, last night I called her bluff. I reminded her the chances of findin' another dealer who'll sell coke to a fuckin' fiendin', racist old lady are pretty fuckin' slim, and I told her if I ended up in jail anytime soon I'd make sure my first call was to Uncle Teddy, and then she'd really be in the shit. I think I got through to her, but I'm still pretty freaked out."

"So is this what all that 'wearing a wire' stuff was about?"

"You can never be too careful man. This lady was like a mother to me. Can you imagine? If your moms was also your craziest customer, and your ex-girl? It's a mindfuck. She's in my fuckin' head. And on top of all that, I still really fuckin' miss her. She means a lot to me, ya know?"

"Well... if you still want me to strip, I'll do it – you've clearly been having a time of things – but let me assure you, I've never met your Aunt Sheila, and if I did, I think I'd run like Hell. She sounds like a real C-U-next-cuntsday."

"Hey! That's my fuckin' lady!"

"Sorry. Just trying to be supportive. Sounds like maybe you're still a little conflicted?"

"Yeah," he concedes, meekly kicking his coffee table. "I dunno. Let's fuckin' drop it."

"Whatever you want man. But for what it's worth, I say just do you. If you wanna bang your aunt, then bang your fuckin' aunt. Life is short."

"...You mean that?" he asks, tears threatening his mean mug facade. "You don't think it's weird?"

"Oh, it's definitely weird bro. No way around that. But who cares? I mean, shit, who's not fuckin' weird? Nobody I know. And lemme tell ya, the people who seem the most normal?

The most together? The least likely to, say, bang their coked-up, non-biological aunt on the sly? Those people are the weirdest of all. They go home at night, and they box up their kinks, and they stuff 'em in the top shelf of their fuckin' 100,000 threadcount linen closets, and they hang their hang-ups on the wall in a nice fuckin' frame. They watch *Modern Family* and *The Good Wife* and go to bed at a reasonable hour, and do it maaaybe once a week, missionary, with a little red wine for courage. They refuse to let themselves have the things that they want, and that, to me, is weirder than anything you just told me. That shit's fucking tragic. And that's not you man. You're the real fuckin' deal. You're livin' the fuckin' life. And life is fuckin' weird."

At a loss for words, Gander looks around as though to reconfirm that you're alone, and then quietly scooches over and laces you into a straitjacket hug, pinioning your arms to your sides.

"Thank you man," he sniffles into your shoulder. "I really needed to talk about that shit."

"It's all good," you say, straining against his muscle-milked Koala grip. "Happy to help."

"I know I seem like this hard, stone cold gangster and shit," he continues, "but I got feelins too, ya know? I got feelins, and she's the only one

I could ever talk to about 'em, and now shit's all fucked up. She's, like, my best friend and shit."

"Well," you say, politely choosing not to comment on his alleged hardness, stone coldness, and/or gangsterism, "maybe that's something you ought to hold on to then. I mean, fuck it, right?"

"Yeah" he says, wiping his eyes with the sockets of his t-shirt skull, "fuck it. I'ma call her tonight."

"Good for you. Fuckin' cheers."

"Fuck yeah!" he says, draining the fourth bowl.

"So," you ask, still hoping to escape with at least a smidgeon of what you came for before he smokes it all right in front of you, "you wanna get down to brass tacks?"

He cocks his head queerly to one side.

"The weed?" you ask.

"Oh!" he exclaims. "Yeah! Let's do it!"

You wait, tenterhooked, as he traverses his psychedelic Dia de los Muertos-themed area rug, unpadlocks his freezer, retrieves a small gun safe, punches in an R2-D2 monologue's-worth of digital beeps and boops, and returns with a vintage, tin lunchbox featuring no less than seven of the *Uncanny X-Men* in various action poses.

"What can I do for ya?" he asks, slowly opening the lid for maximum effect.

Inside is an Ikebana display that would shame the Hanging Gardens of Babylon. Widow whiter than a Bing Crosby Christmas. Kush purpler than a flying people eater. Dream bluer than Heisenberg meth, and enough Sour Diesel to keep every 18-wheeler in Alabama rollin' on. These are trees that would make Joyce Kilmer weep; bud so kind it'd give you a kidney. It's intoxicating; like viewing Eden through a keyhole.

"I've got coke too," he says, "but I already kinda stepped on it, so it's not the best. Also oxy, adderall, xannies, and a little 'cid."

"That's cool," you say. "Not really my bag these days."

"Word. Then take your pick. I'll sell you an eighth of anything you see here."

"Killer. You're a lifesaver. And you said it's gonna be a little extra right? I brought $75."

"Nah. That's alright. The regular $50's fine. Call it friend prices."

"You sure? I really don't mind. I know shit's scarce right now."

"Yeah, I'm sure. You did me a real solid today. I'd give it to you for free, but I gotta scare up some better coke before I call Sheila tonight. Women, right? You know how it is."

"Sure," you say, in fact having no idea how that particular situation might be.

Struggling against overchoice, you settle on a gorgeous Hawaiian hybrid labeled Pineapple Upside-Down Cake, drooling lustily as he weighs it out. This particular strain sheds like a Christmas tree in February, and in a final act of customer service, he carefully scrapes all the molted kief off his scale and into your baggie while you silently vow to promote him to your second-favorite weed dealer.

Δ

Outside Gander's molten mancave the entire world presents as sepia-toned, as though your very eyes were suddenly longing for a simpler time. Still higher than a Petronas penthouse suite, you back out with cautious deliberation, your hands choking the life out of the ten and two positions, your eyes a Williams sisters tennis match of unease.

The distance home is a scant 15 minutes, but between driving ten miles under the speed limit, hitting an Arby's drive-thru, and sitting three solid minutes at a Stop sign that just refused to turn green, you stretch that to 45. At one point you take four carefully-signaled left turns to evade a tailgating Ford Taurus you're convinced is an undercover K9 unit. Whether Gander believed you or not, your claim holds true: you absolutely hate driving high when you've got the shit in the car.

Once safely re-entrenched in your atheist's foxhole, you set about prepping to test your newly acquired wares. Wielding a paperclip with the precision of an archaeologist's micro-chisel, you unearth the basaltic screen from your pipe and commence to rigorously jabbing through the bowl, carb, and mouth, scoring incidental scrimshaw into weeks of tarry buildup, and occasionally dislodging a larger chunk like so much brain matter through the nostril of a mummified Pharaoh. After loosening as much soot and silt as you can, you flush with Isopropyl alcohol, sluice out an efflux of gloppy melancholia, and start again. Scrape, rinse, repeat.

You're not entirely sure why you said what you did back at Gander's. You certainly didn't believe everything you said. Life is not short, first of all. Life is long. Obscenely so. Anyone who says otherwise is either afflicted with hyperthymia, or legitimately retarded (in which case, life may well be short, so there's that). With enough creative license you could probably convince yourself you acted out of pragmatism: tell the poor bastard what he needs to hear, and maybe he'll hook you up. It'd be far from the worst thing you've ever done - it likely wouldn't even crack St. Peter's top 100 when the time came to account for yourself - if it were true.

But it wasn't.

The truth is, though you can't say you've ever given much thought to incest in the concrete (or whatever one might call this zero-calorie, semantic cognate. Diet Incest? Incest Lite?), you don't believe your advice was especially calculated or disingenuous or even wrong. The poor guy was clearly wrestling with a compendium of moral quodlibets that, in a vacuum, just didn't amount to much. All you did was point out, in the most exoteric of terms, that he is in the uniquely advantageous position of living in a vacuum.

What's more, you may have even stumbled onto some newfound respect for your pal Gander. This is a man who takes what he wants and answers to no one, racing full-tilt toward death like a *Supermarket Sweep* contestant, grabbing anything that looks good to him and leaving whatever else strewn pell-mell in his wake. You have to admit, you're kind of impressed, and maybe even a little jealous.

Sure, you push boundaries in your own high-minded and half-assed way, but Gander pushes boundaries in the name of forbidden, hedonistic love. He lives dangerously because he doesn't care, and in a farcically stupid way, you live dangerously (albeit less so) because you care too much. You consider your nihilism instructive. On some level, you still want to change the world. You could spend the rest of your life trying to not care as much as he doesn't. You imagine it must be nice.

Your first puff of the Hawaiian is ambrosial, shoving your brain toward lovely hypoxia. Your dick would be flabbergasted were it presented with a sexual opportunity right now, but in a few days... whatshername? Emily... or something. Will be back from... wherever... and you'll take a run at her.

For now though, it's back to the waiting, and with your last cognizant impulse, you find the remote, flump into your familiar couch divot, and compel the equine features of Jerry Seinfeld to materialize and recite a timely, timeless catchphrase.

"Hello, *Newman!*"

Episode 8

You arrive at the bar early – a nostalgic overreach of a place your internet quarry described as a "legit, old-school dive." Looking along the overcrowded walls, you spy a few things to like – a young Billy Dee Williams pimping Colt 45, a *Big Wednesday* poster improbably signed by Gary Busey, a busted cigarette machine repurposed as a Little Free Library – but as with nearly every college bar, this zeitgeisty sound and fury comes to signify next to nothing. For every genuinely interesting pop-cultural artifact, there's a life-sized Captain Morgan, or a framed football jersey, or an "ironic" Bigmouth Billy Bass just inches away, robbing the room of all authenticity.

You pull a copy of *Naked Lunch* from the Pall Mall slot, snag a booth beneath a cardboard Miller Highlife Girl astride a crescent moon, and revisit Burroughs's heroin-fragged, alien-ass-rape prose until a chirpy soprano slices in like an aggressive bookmark.

"Hi!" says the bookmark, drawing you away from the horrors of the Interzone. "I'm Emma Lee. Are you...?"

"Yep," you say. "That's me. How's it going?"

"Good!" she replies, taking a seat across from you. "I hope you're not getting any ideas from that book though. Not that I'm a prude or anything, but we just met."

She follows her joke with a very practiced giggle while you struggle to grasp that she's referring entirely to the word "naked" in the title, and not the myriad acts of sexual depravity described therein.

"Don't worry," you say. "Lunch is a long way off. How 'bout a drink?"

"Yes please!" she giggles again. "Can I get a pomtini? I know it sounds girly, but they make them really strong here."

"Sure," you reply, heading to the bar with an eyeroll so pronounced you appear to be peeking up the Highlife Girl's corrugated skirts.

You return with a $10.00 magenta concoction in an oversized martini glass - a quarter of your budget already blown - and a super-saver 24-oz. PBR for yourself.

"Here you are EmmaLee."

"Thanks! And not to make things awkward, but it's pronounced Emma Lee."

"...I think that's what I said."

"Oh. It sounded like you said Emily. Like Emily Dickinson. But it's actually two names. Emma. Lee."

"Uh, yeah. I know. We met online, remember? I saw it on your profile."

"Ok," she says, still feigning affrontment. "You said it kind of fast is all. I guess I'm just used to correcting people. Don't worry about it."

"I definitely won't," you reply, taking a passive-aggressively long pull from your beer. "So what do you do?"

"I thought you already knew everything from my profile," she says, still snippy.

"All it said was you were a student. Horticulture, right?"

"Yeah."

"So?"

"So what?"

"So, what do you *do*?"

"Um... I study plants?"

"I know what horticulture is. Jesus. I mean, do you have a job? Hobbies? Pets? Anything?"

"Oh!" she exclaims, seemingly more surprised by your interest than your increasingly aggravated tone. "Well, I don't really have a job right now. My parents say school is my job, so they help me with rent and clothes and stuff. As for hobbies, I love being outdoors. Me and my friends are in an intramural kickball league, and we go hiking and camping every once in a while.

I've been to Coachella the past few years too. Festivals are the best. Last year I saw Mumford and Sons, and they were soooo..."

Your ears refocus as the Wu-Tang Clan rappels down from the sound system - Shaolin style - via the classic Ghostface posse cut "9 Milli Bros." While Emma Lee waxes prosaic about the joys of arena folk, you find yourself already composing a mental Yelp review of her person. First off, she's decidedly heavier than she appeared in her pictures - surprise, surprise - and looks uncomfortable in her too-tight blouse. Furthermore, you're crestfallen to see she's dyed her mousy brown locks the yellowed blonde of an overripe banana, and ditched her fetching bangs in favor of a fussy milkmaid braid that reveals a Metalunan five-head. Lastly, you've zeroed in on a shrunken, greyish tooth in the upper-right quadrant of her smile - this relieving you of any-and-all interest in making her happy.

Add in the Smirnoff-and-hummingbird-nectar she made you buy, the entirely-too-rehearsed dustup about her name, and the fact that you fucking hate being outdoors, and the night's already over for you. And yet there you are, wondering if she'd let you snake your dick between her d-cups and pound them right out of the c-cup bra into which she has them so stubbornly crammed. You fade back in as she's gushingly comparing The Weeknd to Michael Jackson, having decided to put forth, at most, zero effort, and see what happens.

"Anyway," she says, drawing her list of musical mudstains to a close, "I hope that answers your question."

"Totally."

"So, what about you?" she asks.

"What about me?"

"What do you do?"

"Ah. Well, I work for a pop culture website, so I write a lot. And read. And watch shit. I'm not really into the whole outdoorsy thing like you are."

You say all of this with deep disinterest while crepitating your beer can to create an intentionally annoying, junkshop beat. She stares at the can, clearly wishing you'd stop.

"Do you like music?" she asks the can.

"Sure," you grin.

"Like what?" she asks through gritted teeth (this expression, you're pleased to notice, does not reveal the dead tooth).

"Oh, this and that. Stockhausen. Cecil Taylor. Throbbing Gristle. Tyler, the Creator. Whatever really."

"I don't know who those first three are," she says, downing her drink and balancing the tiny umbrella behind her ear, "but I looooove Tyler."

"Really?" you ask, pleasantly surprised. "But he's such a misogynist."

"A what?"

"A misogynist. He hates women."

"Ooooooh!" she says, laughing as though you've finally said something stupid enough to put her at ease (you wince at the cadaverous canine's reappearance). "I don't think that's true. He's just playing the bad boy. I actually met him once after a show. He was out by the merch table signing girls' boobs and stuff. I didn't want him to sign mine, but he let me take a selfie, which I thought was really sweet. So yeah, I know a lot of people hate him or whatever, but I just don't think he means all that stuff."

"You don't huh?" you ask, draining your beer.

"Nah. He's just trying to shock people. All those rap guys talk that way. It's just dirty fun. I actually think it's kinda hot."

"Is that right?"

"Yeah" she says, pinching her tongue between her teeth like a cockteasing gecko.

"Can I get you another drink?"

Δ

Back at the bar, you're taking stock of the situation a little more sociopathically than you're proud of. This girl is not choosy. She's not looking for Jiff. Any old store-brand peanut-butter will do. If you can keep slogging through her bootcamp personality, you might just find yourself tracking mud into an adult-sized princess bed later tonight.

This thought raises your weary member's lowered head, and when the bartendress leans over to take your money you have to fight the urge to plunge a single wrist-deep into her tube-top. She shoots you an optic bird like she knows exactly what you're thinking, and you're instantly reminded why you meet women almost exclusively online.

Your sex life is essentially dependent on shame – occasional bouts of initiative between extended dry spells most men would categorize as global heat death. It's not that you don't like sex, so much as that you don't like work, and sex is a lot of fucking work. Between the scores of Emma Lees out there you have to wade through to find anyone you'd actually want to bang multiple times, and the bonanza of free pornography available at the wave of your nondominant hand, well, a downy sock and a collagen-infused French maid just seems like a more economical use of your time. Wham, bam, thank you webcam.

You used to be a devoted stan for old-fashioned romance. But with every alleged milestone of postfeminism – every grey-rape mined for humor on *Girls* and every breathalized, jizz-dripping chart-topper from Lana Del Rey – you set another piece of your Lohengrin chivalry adrift.

For so many women of the 21st century, feminism just means being jaded enough to lower their expectations and contrarian enough to believe they like it that way. Romance is more intimate than sex. You can't just spring it on people. Nobody wants to be publicly serenaded, or chased down in an airport, or grabbed and kissed midsentence. Not really. Such love can only exist in two states: requited, and creepy as fuck; and having had it made abundantly clear to you which one you are, you adapted. You stopped trying to win their favor, and just started trying to win. Why play the white knight, you thought, when they've all already resigned themselves to blackguards?

You receive your drinks, deftly pocket a bottle-opener, and return to find your date invested in her iPhone.

"I've been reading some of your articles. You're really funny" she coos, flashing a moony smile.

All you can think about is painting that grey tooth white.

"Thanks," you say, annoyed at being cyber-stalked in real time.

"'Top 10 Most Unexpected Dicks' was awesome!" she continues. "LL Cool J in *Any Given Sunday* was actually the first penis I ever saw."

"You don't say?"

"Yeah. So, I guess you know a lot about movies huh?"

"I do ok."

"What's your favorite?"

"*Irréversible*," you say, without a trace of irony.

"What's that?"

"It's French. You should check it out."

"Oh cool! Is it like *Amélie*? I don't watch many foreign movies but I looooove *Amélie*."

"Yeah. Practically a sequel. Super cute."

"Awesome!"

[You are a rotten tomato.]

"So what about you?" you ask.

"Ummmm... I don't want to say. I'm embarrassed."

"There's nothing to be embarrassed about," you lie. "No judgment."

"It's not serious or important or anything. I'm sure you hate it."

"Don't assume things like that. You barely know me."

"Ok. Sorry."

"Just tell me."

"Well... I really love *You've Got Mail*. I used to watch it with my Mom when I was little. It just seemed like such a nice idea - two people falling in love without ever seeing each other. I mean, I'm a modern girl. You're not my first internet date, and I'm on Tinder too. I know how this stuff usually goes. But deep down, isn't that what we're all looking for? That... connection?"

You tense every muscle against laughter before replying with a near-flat affect. "Absolutely."

"Oh!" she says, relieved, "that's so nice to hear. It's such a girly movie, I feel silly for liking it, but it just makes me happy."

"Nothing wrong with that. What else do you like to watch?"

"You're really nice" she says, her expression softening into baby powder as she launches into a glowing review of *Hitch*.

You've come to realize that she's much younger than you thought, playing up her experience through an unabashedly forward online persona - a lamb in low-cut wolf's clothing. Five words - "you wanna get outta here?" - and you're positive you could be slithering around her various creases and folds within the hour. The level of validation she requires to let her guard down is heartbreaking. You want to tell her to run; to spare her the horror of who you really are. In all honesty, you want to sprint home, blaze up, and forget that horror yourself; maybe kick back with Joey and Chandler; enjoy some free porn.

You're crinkling your beer can again, though now it's just intentionless, nervous energy. You're afraid of yourself. There's an evil man lurking inside of you.

She doesn't deserve this, you think, having all but decided to ditch her when, unwilling to abide your atonal tympanics any longer, she grabs your hand, stifles your neurotic cadence, and swallows your bad idea with a kiss.

"You wanna get outta here?" she asks.

Δ

You accept Emma Lee's invitation, but "outta here" turns out not to mean her undoubtedly sparkly and stuffed-animal-filled one-bedroom apartment (or worse, dorm), but rather, another expertly curated "dive bar." That kiss left you spun for a minute, but by the time you see the Japanese lanterns and discarded license plates adorning your new locale, you've resolved to disabuse her of any notion she might have about giving it up to you tonight.

"So, I hope you don't mind," she says, insistently holding your hand as you pay another $10 in cover charges, "but I promised my friend Madison I'd come watch her sing tonight. Get another drink in me and I might do one too. Do you like karaoke?"

"I love karaoke!" you reply, the first thing you've said all night that isn't a lie.

"Awesome! I couldn't really tell if you were the type. Lots of guys think it's dumb, or they act like they do because they're embarrassed."

"Yeah. I don't really get embarrassed. What do you want to drink?"

"How 'bout a Screwdriver? I need to get my courage up."

"Sounds good," you agree, turning to a bartender who looks like he despises Karaoke, anyone who enjoys Karaoke, and the entire country of Japan for inventing Karaoke.

"Two Screwdrivers and two shots of Jameson," you shout, handing over a credit card you know to be dangerously close to overdraft.

"Oh… I don't usually do shots," Emma Lee says. "I'm already a little tipsy. I don't want to fall offstage!"

"Who said they were for you?"

"Oh," she says again, a little hurt, but clearly relieved.

"I need a lot of courage," you explain, turning back to retrieve the two citrus-filled glasses and their thimbeline kinder - a family portrait in orange and brown. You slug both shots before she even brings her glass to her lips, and she eyes you warily as you excuse yourself to the men's room - like she's seeing you for the first time.

Naturally, the stalls have all been relieved of their locks, with the middle commode papier macheted in soggy toilet tissue by some inebriated, wannabe Christo. You settle into the back-most vestibule, stray molecules of other men's urine sending unsanitary rivulets of cold up your tailbone. To your right, two chunky,

Magic Marker stick figures swordfight with disproportionately large penises. Starting to feel the Jameson, you close your eyes and concentrate on your pulsating asshole.

Things come piecemeal - small but fiery - and with every *sandpapery tubule* scraping out your *sunburned anal cavity* you curse your penchant for late-night ghost pepper salsa binges. As the *molten lavalanche* subsides, you're certain you've left the bowl a splattered abattoir, but instead are surprised to find a *Lilliputian army* of turdlets amassed beneath - a *nodular*, almost *artful formation*, like a *sea anemone* or a *nest of baby snakes*.

The capper to any bar bathroom experience, of course, is finding all means of cleaning oneself either broken or empty. A distended sac of fatty, pink soap hangs down from the dispenser like a prolapsed bladder, and you scrape a trail of liposuctiony slime off the wall to wash your hands while sizing yourself up in the pockmarked mirror.

Good God do you love Karaoke.

Karaoke is emotional bloodsport. Everyone's vulnerable. Everyone's brimming with as-yet-unconfirmed confidence. Almost everyone is three drinks in. It's a volatile fucking situation; a kind of groupthink Russian Roulette. People form a line, hold out their hearts in their largely untalented hands, and offer themselves up for schadenfreudian sacrifice. Everyone's an artist, and a critic; a star, and a hater; a post, and a comments section. For every would-be K-Clarks harboring smalltown dreams of American Idolization; for every Jägerbombed bro belting a Backstreet Boys ballad in hopes of landing some homesick freshman tail; for every overdressed, over-rehearsed, overwrought waiter with a showtune in his soul; for every detached, hipsterrific asshole full of joyless, arch mockery; for all of them, and so many more, you truly, madly, deeply love Karaoke.

Δ

"My friend's on!" Emma Lee squeals upon your return.

Reintroducing yourself to your now-watery screwdriver, you take one look at the ivory-blonde human yoga mat on stage, pouting through an Adele song like she's raising money for sexy hurricane victims, and your mind forms an instantaneous thought bubble: *"That girl is not your friend."*

"Isn't she great?" Emma Lee asks, now seeking even your vicarious approval.

"I guess," you shrug.

"You guess?! She sounds just like Adele!"

"I'll give you that," you agree.

"So what? You don't like Adele?" she asks with a level of incredulity usually reserved for Holocaust deniers.

"Eh. She's fine. Just kind of a ripoff artist."

"Ripoff!?! How can you say that!?! Who else even *sounds* like her!?!"

"Well, for starters" you say, "there's Dinah Washington, Roberta Flack, Dionne Warwick - all just absurdly better than her by the way. It's kind of insulting to even mention them. You could also get into Martha Reaves, Shirley Bassey, maybe even Dusty Springfield, and then, just in the past decade, there's Beth Orton, Joss Stone, KT Tunstall, Corinne Bailey Ray, Leona Lewis, Brittany Howard, Amy Winehouse, *obviously*, and, of course, your friend Madison. But whatever. She's fine."

Emma Lee looks at you like you just strangled a puppy with the American flag, reducing her screwdriver to pulp-flecked ice in two determined gulps. You're losing her, just as planned.

"Alright Mr. Music genius! What're you gonna sing then?"

"I think I'll let that be a surprise," you say, indicating you're going outside to smoke.

"Fine!" she says. "I'm gonna get another drink, and we'll see what meets your lofty standards!"

Δ

You've found a number of reliable methods for destabilizing karaoke nights over the years. On the day David Bowie died, you incited a mass exodus from a trendy, gender-bendy lounge-in-mourning with an egregiously lisped and offkey rendition of "Boys Keep Swinging." When Prince passed, you pulled the same trick in reverse, delivering a junk-thrusting, hip-swiveling, overtly sex-positive performance of "Let's Pretend We're Married" at a Christian singles mixer.

Another time, you walked into a bar full of ROTC guys giving their buddy a boozy sendoff to Afghanistan, and proceeded to yowl through Lee Greenwood's "Proud to be an American" in a falsetto that suggested your recent castration – something everyone there likely wanted to do to you by the time you screeched out a revised final chorus that referenced both waterboarding and *Loose Change*, and ended on a fortissimo *"God Fuck the U.S.A."* You ended up with a black eye and a couple bruised ribs, and count yourself lucky it wasn't any worse.

That is the trick though: to instigate violence without becoming the object of it. You're not really looking to fight people. You're not on some bullshit Tyler Durden trip. It's not about *you*. It's about creating an emotional clusterfuck. Bringing the vitriol of the internet into a real-world arena. Showing people what they're truly capable of, IRL.

You suck down the last noxious centimeter of your cigarette, along with a prickly skosh of the filter, and head back in, confiscating a half-drunk rum and Coke midstride as you beeline toward the Karaoke station and queue your selection.

The words "ImsorryifIwasweirdbefore" cascade out of Emma Lee's drunken mouth upon your return.

"I dont care if you dont like Adele" she persists. "I was just being grumpy. Im sure you know way more about music than I do. Ive never even heard of half those singers you said."

"It's cool," you say, taking a last, wistful ogle of that lusty blue vein.

"Maybe you could play sum stuff fer me later?" she slurs, making cordate eyes through pomtini goggles. "I have Spotify premium."

"Yeah, maybe... You gonna sing?"

"Im up next! I usually go fer more current stuff, but tonight I was in the mood for something a little... older" she says, repeatedly arching her eyebrows lest you miss her lascivious intent.

"K. I'm gonna hit the bar. Sing good."

"Ok," she says, woozily leaning in for another kiss as you stand, pretending not to notice.

You fork over your last fiver for a beer and turn around without tipping, just in time to watch Emma Lee shoot you an ostentatious wink, blow you a kiss, and fire a finger gun in your general direction, more or less simultaneously.

"This is fer the nicest guy I ever met on the innernets," she slurs over the opening beats of Christina Aguilera's "Genie in a Bottle." You see Madison bounce to the dancefloor, woooooooing all the way and drawing a pack of alpha males around her like so many prowling, creatine-soaked jackals. This was going to be easier than you thought.

Emma Lee sings like Miley Cyrus engaged with a sybian, pitching herself nearly a full octave below her natural speaking voice in an attempt at smoky allure. Watching her - palming perspiration stains down her thighs; licking her lips like they're covered in meaty barbecue sauce - it's what you imagine a roadside strip club might sound like around 2:30PM on a Tuesday (a vibe Madison happily obliges with an impromptu peepshow routine).

Despite their best efforts, your serenade closes to tepid applause. Madison slips her doffed tank-top back on over a lacy, Fredericks of Hollywood balconette, and they both stumble toward you.

"That was so fun!" Madison says, hugging Emma Lee. "You were super sexy. Those guys were all about it."

"Yeah," Emma Lee says, conflicted. "They seemed more like they were all about you. But yeah. Super fun."

"Oh come on! Don't be like that. You were totally hot! And look at that hair! I told you you were a blonde at heart! Don't you love it!?!"

"I guess..."

"You don't need those guys anyway" Madison continues. "You've obviously already bagged your cutie for the evening. I'm so totes jealy. Like seriously. Peanut-butter and jealy over here. That's me."

Emma Lee perks up at this, giggling and taking a presumptuous swig of your beer.

"I know right?! He's a total doll. I can't believe I met him online. What'd you think sweety?" she asks, assuming an unearned familiarity for Madison's benefit and begging you with her eyes not to hate her for it.

"Well," you say, reclaiming your bottle, "it was no Adele, but it was pretty solid."

Emma Lee seems to accept this as a small victory, playing it off with a fake laugh that gets quickly strangled by Madison's very real cackle.

"Yeah. We can't all sing like Madison," she winks, trying to ensnare you in an inside joke which you callously ignore.

"Do you like Adele?" Madison asks, putting a hand on your arm in an assertion of dominance that feels more like queen-bee habit than genuine sport.

"Who doesn't?"

"Are you gonna sing?" she asks, poking your chest with her other hand while Emma Lee looks on defenseless, caught between two people she desperately wants to please.

"I'm up next."

"Oh fun! What'd you pick?"

"That's for me to know..."

"Come oooon" she whines. "Just whisper in my ear. I promise I won't tell."

You effect for Madison a devilish smile. Girls this despicable are so easy to manipulate. They can't imagine a world where someone like you wouldn't do anything for a shot at their tight, honeypot twats, and so they never quite realize when they've ceded control of a situation. If you hadn't already committed to other plans, you might even turn on the charm and try to take this vajazzled gorgon home, if only to impress upon Emma Lee what a diabolical cunt she really is.

You lean in as though you're about to give her exactly what she wants; your lips grazing her earlobe; your mouth breathing warm, liquored air into her cochlea. But hearing your name called, you pull back without a sound.

"That's my cue," you say as Emma Lee exhales with relief.

"You jerk!" Madison squeals. "Can we at least get a hint?"

"Let's just say it's one of my favorites. I know we just met, but you're exactly the kind of girl I think about whenever it comes on."

"Oh, that's so sweet" she says, gobbling up your attentions like a svelte, spray-tanned Hungry-Hungry-Hippo. "And Emma Lee too, right?"

"Oh sure. We talked about music some earlier. She said she thinks songs like this are really sexy. I hope she likes it."

Emma Lee looks at you, utterly bewildered, and you finally offer her the rakish, honest-to-god wink she's been looking for all night.

Δ

If one of the primary appeals of listening to jazz is that it makes you feel better than everyone else, then you'd have to say listening to hip-hop makes you feel bigger than everyone else. Bolder. Hotter. Meaner. Like you could fuck any girl in this place - or three or four at once - and they'd thank you for the privilege. It's the music of dark twisted fantasy; of the phallus unbound; a direct route to truths about the male brain so ugly they can only be spoken in rhyme.

You seriously considered Slick Rick's "Treat Her Like a Prostitute," as recreating his poncey accent tends to elicit a simmering undercurrent of annoyance before you even get to the cockswagger lyrics about how all women are unrepentant, fellatious whores. It's something of a standby.

You're not a feminist. You're not a misogynist either, but you hate women who start sentences with "I'm not a feminist but..." The phrase is an idiotic copout, almost always rendered even more idiotic by whatever caveat follows it. It's not that you don't think women deserve equality (some arguably don't, but that's just as true of men) so much as that, other than a few National-tier bitchwhistle issues like equal pay and abortion rights, you feel like they more-or-less already have it. They've sacked the dating game like a bunch of damn Visigoths in no-clump mascara, racking up lost-time notches in their bra straps at an unprecedented, and frankly, unladylike rate. They hold all the cards on reproduction, turning the medical community into their personal, short-order semen cooks such that they may someday excise dicks from the equation altogether. They're winning the internet via the apocalyptic weaponization of social media – using generations of pumice stone-hewn, Lady BIC-sharpened interpersonal skills to catapult themselves aerodynamically past men's brutish, grunt-heavy brand of corporate climbing without so much as even learning to play golf. They're running fearlessly at night, running Fortune 500 companies, and running forgone conclusion campaigns for President. And yet, so many still swear they're not feminists. You get it, you guess. Why let anyone have your number if you don't have to? But if you're going to run around fucking with Debbie-in-Dallas impunity, while also maintaining that having a door held open for you is tantamount to acquaintance rape, then at least have the labes to own the movement that allows you that kind of posturing. So no, you're not a feminist. But any woman who says she's not is an idiot, and pretty much asking for it.

Your runner-up was Kurupt's "Ho's a Housewife." You've had success with it before, once evaporating an entire bachelorette party into a nimbus glitterbomb cloud of huffs, glares, and exasperated "I nevers." Furthermore, its healthy dosage of racial epithets and g-funk slang make it a much more dangerous option. You always edit the worst slurs out of your performances - you're subversive, not suicidal - but you definitely don't feel any moral compunction about dropping N-bombs if the moment feels right. Mostly, you just want the first time to be special.

You're not a racist, but you're heavy in the struggle for semiotic unity. You'll step to any fool spouting the term "reverse racism," as that only belies the exceptionalist belief that whiteness is the gold standard. Your fist is raised for a truer equality, in which all socially constructed signifiers are rendered meaningless via a cleansing bonfire of Kangol hats and Klan robes. And Lord knows, that change is gonna come. Just in your lifetime, black people have Killah-Beeswarmed the entertainment industry with the cutthroat efficiency of the Nat Turner rebellion. They have all the best singers, all the best dancers, all the best athletes, and all the best parties, and they have the whole of the millennial generation krumping around like lily-white hooligans, trying to join up *Soul Man*-style. America's first black president single-handedly made the nation's highest office so unfairly, undeniably, unimpeachably... *cool* (!) that it's hard to imagine a white guy this side of Marlon fucking Brando ever doing it justice again. In recent years, black culture has gone from a much feared and reviled bugaboo to an inundating tide of Moët and Alizé that even the Grandest of Imperial Wizards couldn't make disappear. It's fucking everywhere, and if any brother from another mother has earned the right to grip grain, sip lean, get crunk, and wild out, it's you. You were bumpin' 8Ball and MJG before anyone uttered the words "cultural appropriation." You can't be a racist. You don't give 3/5ths of a shit about *race*. But you are absolutely sick to death of all these fucking wiggers!

You step onstage, already hearing some gasps in recognition of your unflinchingly vile heel's anthem. You're not a sexist, or a racist, but you do believe we're living in a post-ism America, where white cops occasionally shoot unarmed black children, and strong men occasionally force themselves on weak, defenseless women, but where, by and large, anyone who truly desires power can find a way to get it.

Most Americans seem to agree that all the really important battles have already been fought, and that their side came out on top. Congress has made it clear they're largely done doing stuff – other than voting every few months to keep the lights on – and if we're honest, that's the way we like it. This isn't the product of a broken system; it's the end result of a fixed one. It's not gridlock; it's parity. Everybody's winning, and losing, in about as equal measure as is sustainable, and eventually the outliers will die of stress-related heart attacks and rage aneurysms and the whole of society will regress toward the mean. Evolution is just going along to get along. Rainbow-stripe your profile and bitch about guns on Facebook after any mass shooting with more than six fatalities, and you're a progressive. Refuse free healthcare and teach your kids to worship the great, bearded, grandfather-genie in the sky, and you're a conservative. Civilization is at a standstill because who has the fucking energy anymore? We enjoy sporadically playing at being incensed, but the truth is 99.9% of us just want to be left alone to watch Netflix and make excuses for why our impossibly unique and difficult circumstances won't allow for anything else. These are the people you want to reach.

You unholster the mic and shout "this is for my friends Madison and Emma Lee," who cringe as you point them out with all the subtlety of an "I'm With Stupid" t-shirt before bringing a towering middle finger against your fast-bulging crotch. You lock eyes with the crowd like a blazing sunset staring down a sea of lemmings; daring them to jump. -Isms don't make schisms. *You* make fucking schisms. You, Snoop, and Dre.

"Bitches ain't shit but hoes and tricks!!!"

Boos rain down faster than you've ever conjured them before. The first projectile bottle launches with a high, non-threatening arc that more suggests you get the fuck of stage than demands it, but the second comes from a contingent of burly African American fellows near the pool tables, and with decidedly more zip. Off to a fine start.

You roll through the first chorus on autopilot, dodging empties and observing the scene back at your table, where Madison is absolutely laying into a distraught Emma Lee, waving her arms around in some kind of irate, privileged-white-girl semaphore. All you can do is smile, dividing your attention between the latter's tumescent cleavage and the former's cresting whale-tail until she finishes her diatribe and marches it right out of the bar.

Rounding into verse three, you spy a beleaguered bartender edging around to unplug your bid for bedlam. Deciding it's now or never, you bark out the next available N-word in all its terrible, race-baiting glory, and ignite a chain reaction of barbarism better than you ever could have planned.

First, some Richie Cunningham-looking motherfucker sporting a high school letter jacket doubles over laughing at the bar, inviting one of the brothers by the pool tables to walk over and viciously kick his stool out from under him. Hitting his chin while falling, he gropes maniacally for support, coming up with a fistful of some poor girl's baby-pink taffeta mini, and inadvertently ripping it clean off. Trying to cover her Hello Kitty-print undies, the girl quickly abandons all pretense of modesty and gives her denuder a swift kick to the groin. Meanwhile, billiard balls start flying in every direction, and one gets short-hopped off the back of a strawberry-blonde's head. She slumps into her boyfriend's Popeye arms, and he deposits her in a booth before rampaging through the room like a crack-addled rhino, knocking over tables, chairs, and at least three other people in a blind quest to suplex whoever-the-fuck just beaned his best girl. Broken bottles are turning the floor into a no-man's land of glass, and just as the charging pachyderm seems about to overtake his prey (whose chosen defense is to assume a kind of standing fetal-position and piss himself), he slips out of his designer flip-flops and topples acrobatically onto his back, his lacerated foot ejaculating a perfume spray of blood into the face of a goth girl attempting to capture the fray on her iPhone. Their overlapping shrieks create a shrill dissonance only Meredith Monk could love, and the entire place descends into shitfaced free-for-all. A dart bullseyes a black-and-white Audrey Hepburn poster, lending a 3-dimensional quality to her long, Tiffany's-breakfast cigarette. Wild-pitched shot- and pint-glasses shell the liquor display behind the bar like a knock-em-over carnival game, sending a waterfall of spirits crashing from the top shelf down. The staff retreat to the back offices soaked in their own wares – their cuts and scrapes pre-sterilized by the downpour – and opportunistic alkies start absconding with whatever merchandise is still intact while the rest of the crowd makes for the door.

You stopped rapping five minutes ago, but everyone was too distracted to notice, and with the fire alarm already blaring, you're free to slip quietly out the emergency exit.

Emma Lee - potentially in medical shock - stands among the ruins, an unwitting angel of death, and you linger by the back door just long enough to watch her leave - glide, practically - out the front, emotionally devastated but physically unharmed.

Feelin' yourself, you can't help but wonder if you might be able to talk your way back into her control-top panties, even now. But you don't want to risk ending a great night on a note of failure. She's been through enough, and this is better than sex anyway. Your work - your glorious work here - is done.

Episode 9

Michael Jordan, the general consensus greatest basketball player of all time (you prefer Kobe, but almost entirely out of contrarianism), has famously and repeatedly had misattributed to him the following inspirational Wayne Gretzky quote: "You miss 100% of the shots you don't take." These words, however, while mathematically true, tell only half the story. A quick Google search reveals that Jordan's career shooting percentage clocks in at just under 50% (49.7 to be exact), which, while statistically disgusting, still serves as something of a technical foul against his logic. To wit, while the average Joe might indeed miss 100% of the shots he doesn't take, he could also spend a lifetime busting his ass - becoming the be-all, end-all, undisputed GOAT of whatever endeavor to which he's applied himself - and still wind up failing a little more than half the time. Personally, you've never liked these odds.

A life-sized window sticker MJ smiles at you now through the grease-smeared glass of a McDonalds (an apparently irremovable relic from the '97 championship season) where you sit five car-lengths back from the laryngectomous clown face waiting to take your order. Often drawn to the golden arches during weed-induced fugue states, you've studied this image many times.

Still on cloud nine a week after your karaoke attack - with Gander's high-grade hibiscus, and the Gulf Coast trunk muzak of Curren$y's "Briefcase" setting your mind adrift on a seabreeze - you close your eyes and wander through an Escherian landscape of tessellated chicken nuggets and Mobius french fries, back to where it all began...

Δ

Your much-hoped-for revolution had never come. Facebook did not change everything, no matter what Mark Zuckerberg or David Fincher would have you believe. It felt like it would though, for a time. People reconnected with the swingset sweethearts and treehouse compatriots of their youth. Divorcees found new avenues down which to backpedal their poorly chosen adventures. Altruistic clumps of enthusiasm flocculated into larger, more actively engaged social movements. Loneliness - Hell, the very idea of even *being alone* - seemed on the verge of obsolescence. How, after all, could anyone be lonely, when mere clicks away there was hard-coded reassurance for all to see that he had 300

Friends and counting; that some of them enjoyed the baby hedgehog video she posted; that others offered encouragement when he bemoaned being brined in gutter water by a bus he failed to catch; that still more remembered her birthday last month, even as her ski-lodged parents forgot until the belated following weekend. It was unimpeachable. Everyone was connected. Everyone was popular. Everyone was *in*. The incantatory hum of our increasingly speedy modems echoed across the land. No one was immune. Not even you.

ForDrapersOnly.wordpress.com was your first blog: a hyper-literate, detail-obsessed space for dissecting Matthew Weiner's television masterpiece *Mad Men*. You garnered a small but dedicated readership mocking up weekly creative for Sterling Cooper, and periodically made time for other highbrow heavyweights like *The Sopranos*, *Deadwood*, and *The Wire*. Your pageviews climbing weekly, you felt every bit the lucky-striking parvenu as Don Draper himself, regularly chatting with fellow superfans about everything from Joan's vintage dresses to Roger's preferred brand of scotch to secretly 'shipping the unsinkable Peggy Olson and the captious Pete Campbell. It was truly the "Golden Age of Television."

It soon became apparent, however. Nothing golden can stay.

The following year, you'd pen prolix eulogies for that same trio of HBO founding fathers as all came to bitter ends with mixed reviews – last gasps of the dying monoculture, soon replaced by pallid epigones like *True Blood* and *Boardwalk Empire*. Facebook's noble attempt at Brook *Farmville*-ing the world took little time in poisoning its own wells, slash-n-burning its pixelated crops, and reverting humanity to the feudal hierarchies into which we're so fond of tiering ourselves. Instead of communal E-topia, what materialized was an age in which everyone had a brand, but no one could afford to buy anything.

Friends became a commodity; the social currency by which we measured our inherent value. Those embryonic pods of mutual interest turned insular and sclerotic, circling the wagons around their precious opinions and drowning in their own Kool-Aid. Romantic love began its slow transformation into a retronym, its death knell sounded by the cognitive sciences and pushbutton pornography. Talk was cheap. Text was cheaper. Within a limitless incubator for interpersonal exploration, the line between dating and hiring an escort shrank such that the only real remaining difference was that dating, if properly negotiated, could be free.

And even all that maybe would've been fine, (maybe), if it weren't for the unchecked, unmitigated rise of anonymity; the Great-and-Terrible Oz-like power that came with our suddenly, and all-at-once, realizing we could say whatever we wanted, to whomever we wanted, with little fear of anyone peeking behind our firewall curtains. Somehow, we all agreed. The internet was to be a Kakistocracy. Join or die.

Your first taste of that power came during *Mad Men's* second season (Episode 8, if memory serves, kismetically titled "A Night to Remember") when you decided to abandon your longstanding commitment to spoiler alerts and post your latest article under the carelessly conspicuous title `A False Don: Betty Turns Mad Woman Over Draper's New Side-piece`, decorum be damned.

Little did you know that this belabored bit of punnery would spark your rebirth, in silico, as an information supervillain; a scrofulous, cross-platform spoilsport; an unrelenting, unrepentant, and wholly toxic troll.

Welcome to the Wild Fucking West.

"**WTF?!?!**" demanded **BigWhitman69**, throwing wide the chatroom doors like John Wayne silencing a saloon.

"**Can I help you?**" you typed.

"**I dunno. Are you a time traveler? Can you unspoil tonight's episode for me? Do you have that power?!**"

"**I'm not sure what you mean.**"

"**Well let me spell it out for you. I got home late from church because my wife was cleaning up after the dumbass potluck and my kids were playing capture the dumbass flag.**"

"**Sounds nice.**"

"**It fucking SUCKED! All I wanted was to come home, pour myself a highball, and kick back with the DVR, when what happens? I get a phone alert from your site. That's right. I have a phone alert for your dumbass *Mad Men* site.**"

"**Aww. That's really cool. Thanks man.**"

"**Fuck you asshole!**"

"**Whoa.**"

"**No. Seriously. Fuck you. I have a phone alert because I like your articles, but you've never ruined a major plot point in the fucking title before! FUCKING COCKSUCKER!!!**"

"**Dude, you need to calm down. As spoilers go, I'd say this barely qualifies. It's still a great episode. I was just trying to draw some fresh eyeballs, ya know? Build my readership?**"

"Build your readership!?!?! Who do you think you are, Roger Fucking Ebert!?!?! NO ONE CARES ABOUT YOUR SHITTY LITTLE SHITBLOG MOTHERFUCKER!!!"

You'd tried, up to this point, to maintain your composure – **BigWhitman69** was a well-known blowhard around these pages, but no one took him seriously, and his fervent enthusiasm helped him remain well-liked in spite of himself. That said, your decency in the face of his increasingly capslocked vitriol only served to spin him further out.

"Look man," you wrote, **"I'm sorry. I really am. But you need to get a grip. I'm trying to run a classy site here, about a classy show. So show a little class. I don't want to have to block you."**

"Block me? YOU'RE GONNA FUCKING BLOCK ME NOW SHITHEAD!?!?! I SWEAR TO CHRIST I WILL KILL YOUR PETS AND BURN YOUR FUCKING HOUSE DOWN!!! I WILL FUCK YOU IN THE ASS WITH A CURLING IRON!!!! DO! NOT! FUCK WITH ME!!!!!"

You could have blocked him right then. No one would've blamed you. Instead, for reasons you can't entirely explain, you fired back.

"Ok. You know what? That's enough. You're fucking pathetic dude. BigWhitman69? Seriously? What are you, twelve? I can't believe you found a woman willing to touch your flaccid babydick. I'll bet it's like a fun-size candy bar. I'll bet you jerk off

like you're playing the world's smallest violin. And that violin is playing the world's saddest song. And that song is dedicated to your world's tiniest dick."

A few commenters began peeking out from behind the upturned tables of your virtual watering hole, chipping in monosyllabic reinforcements like "**Snap!**" "**Damn!**" and "**Burn!**" You felt strong.

"**Yeah?**" he typed "**Well your Mom sure had a good time with it last night!**"

"**I'm sure you know a lot about pleasing moms since you're probably typing from yours' basement right now,**" you replied. "**In fact, based on your Facebook page,** *Howard Blankenship*, **I'm not convinced you even have a wife. Or kids. Did they bail, or did you make them up?**"

"**What the fuck?! How are you on my Facebook page!?!**"

"**About that. Maybe don't accept every single friend request you get. Seems kinda desperate. People might take advantage. I mean, you wouldn't want just anyone to know that while you're passing off mediocre fanfic about your "wife" and your "kids" as some semblance of your real life, what you're actually doing is sitting around in your tighty-whiteys while your clinically disappointed mother cooks you up some nice, juicy, after-church Tyson Chicken Nuggets and wonders what she could've done differently. I'm curious, do you sleep in the same bed? I'll bet you** do. I'll bet you're the little spoon. I'll bet sometimes, when you can't sleep, she gives you a reach-around and cries into your back, and when she dies – probably at one of the three jobs she works to support you while you sit at home browsing *Tomb Raider*-themed hentai – you'll be so helpless and alone you'll have to become a ward of the state. Does that sound about right?"

"**Jesus**" typed PeggyOlsonTwin67.

"**Holy shit**" typed 9VoltSlattery.

"**Of course, I'm assuming your dad's long gone,**" you continued, flames spilling out of your keyboard with the automated ease of a player piano.

"**How anyone could sire a loser like you and not see it as an agonizing reminder of his failures as a man... I mean, it must be unbearably emasculating is all, to watch helplessly as his son grows into a repulsive, thumb-sucking, Pampers-messing, garbage-island of a human being. A living manifestation of swamp-ass. My only real question is whether he pulled the old 'goin' out for a pack of smokes' trick, or just straight up killed himself. I honestly wouldn't blame him either way.**"

"**Dude**" typed MohawkMoProblems14

"**SHUT UP!**" typed BigWhitman69, dry-clicking his majuscule six-shooter. "**You don't know shit about me! I will find you and fuck you up! You're the one with the fucking TV blog! You're the fucking loser! Not me! Who cares that much about fucking *Mad Men* anyway!?!**"

"**Apparently, you do,**" you typed, in complete, emotionless control. "**But what's the real problem here Howard? Is the world a lonely place? Is life not everything you thought it would be? Are you a bitter, impotent, microphallic waste of space with nothing but a few unresolved TV plotlines standing between you and the persistent urge to deepthroat a Winchester? Because if so, let me make a suggestion: do it. Just fucking do it. Find a seller on Craigslist. Use the gun show loophole. Do what you have to do, and get it done. You'd be doing the world a huge fucking favor.**"

No one typed a word.

Crickets chirped outside your window.

A few minutes later, he signed off.

Your shirt collar dotted with pointillist perspiration; a partial erection bivouacking in your khakis; you remember feeling utterly invincible, and likewise, positively certain that your telephile patronship would applaud your heroics to a man.

"**That was messed up**" typed **HarryCrane-Kick83** after a protracted silence.

"**I know, right!?!**" you thrilled to reply. "**He was out of control!**"

"**No. What you did was messed up. Seriously, what's wrong with you?**"

"**Are you joking?**" you asked in disbelief. "**He's an asshole. And he threatened me! What was I supposed to do?!**"

"**Why didn't you just block him?**" asked **BettyDraperEyes**, a newish reader for whom you were nursing a small cybercrush. "**That was so mean.**"

"**But he started it!**"

"**But you're the moderator. You're supposed to be the adult in the room.**"

"**Yeah**" added **HammOnRye77**. "**He's obviously harmless. What you did was cruel.**"

"**So because I'm quicker on the draw, I'm somehow the badguy? You can't be serious!**"

"**You got on his Facebook though? Wtf? Have you secretly friended anyone else?**"

"**I feel naked**" typed **SallyForth22**.

"**That was really uncomfortable**" typed **WebCampbell84**.

"**And you did kinda spoil this week's episode**" typed **UgotJWN3D**. "**I was a little pissed myself.**"

"**I live with my parents right now**" added **FallingMan101**. "**I got laid off and lost my apartment. Think I should kill myself too asshole?**"

"**Of course not! But come on. That guy was the worst. That username was fucking** embarrassing. **We don't need people like that around here, right?"**

"**People like what?**" asked **BettyDraperEyes**.

"**People who are down on their luck?**" asked **HarryCraneKick83**.

"**People who need friends?**" asked **PeggyOlsonTwin67**.

"**People who like your writing?**" asked **WebCampbell84**.

"**People who are passionate about** *Mad Men***?**" asked **HammOnRye77**.

"**People like you?**" asked **BettyDraperEyes**.

Though you'd never seen their faces, you could feel their eyes on you; judging you; "S"ing their "H"es with unearned superiority; dragging you through the thoroughfare declaring you an unfriend of the people. You'd lost them.

"**You're all fucking crazy!**" you wrote as, one by one, they logged off, peppering you with a firing squad of glissandoing sign-out dings. "**uck every last one o you motheruckers!**" you wrote, typing so brutishly you displaced your F key - blocking them all the second they were gone. They were wrong. You were right. You'd never been more sure of anything in your life.

Δ

In the months that followed your syntactic shootout, you never once questioned your decision-making. You did, however, find yourself researching - somewhat obsessively for a time - a broad cross-section of historically (or at least, mathematically) "great" serial killers, taking particular interest in one William George Heirens.

Heirens, it came to light after his capture, committed his first murder, for all intents and purposes, by accident. This is not to say he wasn't a disturbed individual with some unsavory appetites (women's underwear, Nazi iconography), but simply that he wasn't aware of his true calling until right up to the moment when he stabbed an innocent girl in the neck with it. He even recalled trying to save her, only to be distracted by a flurry of spontaneous orgasms. Faced with such an (ahem) outcome, what else could he possibly do now? What else could even be expected of him? Before that day, no one could've accused him of anything more glamorous than misdemeanor panty-raiding and given him a slap on his handsome, sociopathic wrists. But after that day, by his own admission, he wanted nothing quite so much as to kill again.

Now you were no Bill Heirens - at least that's what you told yourself - but you did discover in short order that you'd acquired a taste for dispensing a certain brand of verbal vigilante justice. If presiding over the high-horsed cowherds of your prestige cable ranch made you feel like Wyatt Earp, then lighting out for the wide, campestral veldt of the internet at large turned you into The Man With No Screenname, riding around with a sawed-off shotgun wit and a saddlebag full of gleeful spoilers.

You tried to limit yourself to deserving marks at first: the unpleasable Yelpers, the sanctimonious wowsers, the erudite I-could've-written-thats. You picked fights. You got goats. You sought the worst in people and found it in abundance. Before long though, your criteria for who was deserving took a precipitous plunge. You grew impatient, roaming the badlands of Reddit and 4chan; lying in wait amidst the sagebrush for dicks and pussies to show their asses. Your pleasure, you realized, came not from executing some Manichaean code of comment section conduct, but from the simple act of sowing indiscriminate discord.

ForDrapersOnly fell into disrepair, soon cutting the figure of a condemned, Yoknapatawpha manse. You'd taken your shot; tried to build something. You took it as seriously as Kobe doin' work, and just like Kobe, the bastards tore you down anyway. You'd never be

MJ; never be the GOAT. Having lost all interest in sharing your lunatic love for meta-sitcoms and antihero dramas, you vowed instead to spoil them, for everyone.

You reclaimed your webspace as a repository for orgulous screeds against anything that was popular, and pro bono devil's advocacy for anything that wasn't, forever haranguing the masses for their collective intellectual incuriosity. You presaged catastrophic deaths and long-awaited couplings with a restive dedication, like some miscreant lovechild of Cassandra and Slenderman. You reveled in depriving others of the already flimsy joys of peak TV; in preventing them from escaping, for even a scant half-hour, the bleak monotony of their paycheck-to-paycheck lives. You loved the rage it inspired; the wrath it incurred. You fed on it; grew strong from it. You couldn't stop yourself. You were Belphegor in the flesh - a dark, slovenly edgelord slowly fusing with his fetid couch cushions.

After a year, you branched out from pop culture trolling and immersed yourself in the artificially-high-stakes world of politics, attacking people with real convictions and experiencing all the foamy-mouthed zeal that entails. The pro-lifers; the anti-vaxxers; the NRA crazies; the PETA nuts; The climate deniers; The Greenpeacers; the birthers; the truthers. With Gadsden fangs and Bald Eagle talons, they had a will to retaliation no television series could inspire. But nothing phased you. Your only allegiance was to truth. You'd say anything, so long as it was true. Politics was just another show you already knew the end to.

For what it's worth, BigWhitman69 never unfriended you, and by all social media accounts moved out of his mother's house shortly after your showdown – an outcome for which you couldn't help feeling somewhat responsible. It seemed like justification. People, you were more certain by the day, needed to hear what you had to say. You weren't a villain. You were a freer of minds.

Sooner than you would've guessed however, you came to terms with the fact that you didn't really believe in anything at all. That conflict was its own reward. Gussied up in the intellectual bodice-and-bustle of "making people think," you disabused yourself of social niceties like chivalry and white guilt, and began throwing bombs for the sheer, unadulterated fuck of it. You called Hillary the C-word. You called Obama the N-word. You invoked Adolph Hitler, Martin Luther King, Jesus, Muhammad, and Donald Trump on a near-daily basis. You mocked snowstorms as disproof of Global Warming. You interrupted Me Too Tweetups with GIFs of triggery bondage porn. You started #NoLivesMatter.

You didn't mean any of it. You didn't care enough to mean it. These words; these ideas; they were only tools to you. You'd reached apex predator status. Everyone else was just food.

Δ

"*WRCMTUMCDRNLDZ*WOODJULYKTU TRY*UN*EXTRVALYOOMIILTDAY?*"

"Hi!" you say as this garbled communique jolts you from your reverie. "I'm ordering for a bunch of people, so it's gonna be a lot. Is that ok?" you ask, knowing perfectly well such a decision is above an intercom lackey's paygrade.

"*GOHEDWTHYRORDR*" says the voice, sketching its staticky outline as female, African American, and pretty well over it.

"Ok. I need three Big Macs, five McDoubles, three ten-piece McNuggets, one filet-o-fish, twelve large fries, eight..."

"*WAYWAYWAYHOLUPAMINIT*" says the voice, suddenly alert. "*IGAHTREEBGMAX* *FIMCDUBBLS*ANNWHUTELS?*"

"Three ten-piece McNuggets," you repeat with exaggerated diction, "one filet-o-fish, twelve large fries, eight large Cokes, four large Sprites, and... are you guys doing the all-day breakfast thing?"

The voice is unresponsive for a full minute.

"Hello?!" you ask, affecting silver spoon impatience.

"*SER*ARYUSHERYUWOODENRATHR JSTCUMNSYDE?*"

"No! I have people waiting. You've already taken most of my order. I just want to add a few McMuffins and hashbrowns. *What* is so hard about this?"

"*...*HAUMINIMCUPHENZANASHROWNS?*" the voice sighs.

"Ummmmmmm... I guess three egg McMuffins, and five hashbrowns. Oh, and a Happy Meal for little Billy. Almost forgot."

Another full minute of silence.

"*WILTHATCUMPLEETCHRORDR?*"

"I believe so."

"*OKYRTRTLWILBSVNTYTOODOLERZ*AN THURDEFISINTS*"

"Jesus," you say, soaking the lord's name in disdain, "you guys sure are proud of this crap food huh?"

"*WOODULYKTUCANSLYORORDURSER?*"
the voice asks hopefully.

"No! Don't be ridiculous! Just get it right, and make sure you throw in plenty of napkins and ketchup. Think you can handle that?"

You could swear you hear a muffled "asshole" crackle through the speaker, but you let it go. She's in too deep now. All you have to do is wait for her to wave you through.

"*PAYATHEFURCEWINO*THAKEYOO*"

"Thank *you*" you reply, transitioning to a more conciliatory tone. "Sorry if I was rude just now. I'm having a rough day. It's nothing personal."

"*IZFYNESER*PLEEZDRYVAROWN*"

"I mean, you have a hard job in there. It's hot. It smells. You're overworked and underpaid. I read the papers. I know about the minimum wage strikes and stuff. I just want you to know I respect you. I really do. I'd hate to be in your shoes."

"...*THAKEYOOSER*PLEEZDRYVAROWN*"

"And this all-day breakfast thing? I mean, I read this article on *HuffPo* - that's a news website - that said it's just a nightmare. Twice the work. Equipment crammed everywhere. It's ridiculous!"

"…*(audible sigh)*… *YESSER*THAKE YOOSER*PLEEZDRYVAROWN*"

"I mean, for us, as a society, to decide this is something we need - for us to look at - and I mean no offense here - but for us to look at what's generally considered to be one of the worst jobs in America - the job our parents used when they wanted us to do our homework - you know, like, 'you kids better study. You don't want to end up working at McDonalds when you grow up' - for us to look at that job and say, hey, let's make that job worse - let's make that job shittier - because we need to eat fucking McGriddles at three in the afternoon? It's unconscionable!"

"*SER*"

"And what they pay you!? It's fucking degrading. It's not right. You're a person. You've probably got three or four kids at home you're trying to feed…"

"*SER!*"

"And bills. And health problems, I'm assuming. I mean, working at McDonalds is practically a health problem in and of itself…"

"*SER!!!*"

"And just because you're not a doctor, or a lawyer, or a quote unquote skilled laborer, or quote unquote contributing to society, and you didn't quote unquote graduate from high school doesn't mean..."

"IGRAJUATDFRUMHISKOOLASSHOLL!!! *DRYVETHAFUKAROWN!!!*"

[You are lovin' it.]

"Whoa. No need to get pissy ma'am. I'm on your side. You're the one who sounds like she's based on the novel *Push* by Sapphire. If you don't want people assuming things about you, maybe work on your fucking elocution. The rain in Spain. Unique New York. Shit like that. Jesus. Some people."

"*THAFUKDJUJUSSAYTAME!?!*"

"Sapphire? She's an author. Authors write books. Books are things you read. Well, maybe not you, but other people. Anyway, is my order ready? Should I drive around?"

You hear the fractured crunch of the headset being violently chucked at the floor.

Your ungainly order is surely close to complete, and even if it isn't, the woman behind the intercom has no recourse to cancel it. You can only guess at the tourbillion of profanities flying about inside as a result of your showstopping performance, but you've almost certainly ensured that every McItem you just

McOrdered will come garnished with a healthy dollop of McSpit, McPiss, or McPubes, up to and including your fake son's Happy Meal. Ah, little Billy. Such a troublemaker.

And at that, you swerve out of line just before reaching the pay window, press a middle finger to your driver's side glass, and slow-roll toward the exit. A slingshot filet-o-fish splatters against your back windshield in a fountain of ejaculatory tartar sauce – fired, you're nonplussed to see, not by a *Precious*-lookalike, but rather a middle-aged white woman. The world, it seems, is still capable of surprising you, and you merge anonymously into traffic, your appetite thoroughly satisfied.

Episode 10

"I'M GETTING MARRIEEEEEED!!!"

This is what you hear after knocking three Houellebecqs and a half-full Mr. Pibb off your nightstand while groggily groping for your phone. You recognize the affected, girlish squeal immediately, and your first instinct is to hang up, but unfortunately, she knows you all too well.

"Don't hang up you jerk! I know you're there, and I know you're thinking about hanging up, so just don't ok? I got this number from your parents. I know it's right. I'll call as many times as I have to."

You sigh; the deep, world-weary sigh of a Holocaust survivor being asked to recall his time in the camps.

"Hello, Artemis."

"HI!" she squeals again.

"Ok. It's six in the morning. Take it down a notch."

"Sorry! I'm just excited! I got engaged! Also I'm in Prague, so, time difference."

"Of course you are."

"What's that supposed to mean!?!"

"Nothing," you say, reminding yourself that antagonizing her only prolongs the conversation.

"Jesus!" she says, unconvinced, "I'd think you could just be happy for me! That for once you could just be fucking nice and say 'congrats Artemis' and leave it at that. We've known each other for how long? But noooooooo! Not you. Not Mr. Too-Cool-for-the-Fucking-Waldorf-School! You just have to be a jerk about everything, don't you? Don't you!?"

You sigh again.

"Well!?!" she demands, hands, you can only imagine, firmly on hips like some self-righteously posing Wonder Woman with a beret and an art history degree.

"..."

"Aren't you going to say *anything*!?!?"

"...Congrats Artemis."

"THANK YOU!"

"You're welcome."

"So?"

"So what?"

"Soooo? Aren't you going to ask me who it is? How it happened? When the wedding is? *Anything*!?

"Sure. Whatever. All of that."

"Well!" she starts, determined to stockade you into sounding board-dom, "his name is Eduardo - he used to be a Matador, but now he runs an animal rights nonprofit."

"Jesus. Way to have your cake and eat it too Artie."

"Shut up. He's a really good guy. And don't call me Artie. You know I hate that."

"My bad. So, Artemis's great, Boethian wheel of sexual fortune finally landed on dick once and for all huh? Just another college lesbian lost to the dustbin of herstory."

"Ugh. You're so heteronormative it just makes me sad for you. Things are much more fluid here on the continent. Everyone's so open. I swear, I don't even know how to relate to Americans anymore. Eduardo's absolutely ruined me."

"I'll bet."

"Don't be gross. We're post-sexual, if you must know. We've given ourselves over to one another completely. Nothing's off limits. We strive to embody all roles and satisfy all appetites. It's exhilarating. You have no idea."

"So, like, anal and stuff?"

"*Anyway,*" she continues, "we were at this big protest in Greece. There was some concern about the Kri-Kri - the Cretan mountain goat - what with the country going bankrupt and all, so he organized this benefit concert to raise money and awareness. He even got Yanni to headline."

"Yanni!? Are you fucking kidding me Artie?!"

"Asshole! What did I just ask you not to do!?"

"No, seriously," you cackle as you try to paint a mental pastoral. "I have to ask. What is the mood at a Yanni concert? Are people on drugs? Do they dance, or sway? Or do they just bring books and pillows and, like, fall asleep reading? But, you know, *Live*!?!"

"Are you done?"

"...I think so..." you say, wiping away a tear.

"You sure?"

"...Yeah."

"Ok then... So anyway, that's where he proposed."

You rupture into derisive laughter all over again, Artemis's chipmunked voice swearing at you in miniature as you clutch your phone to your chest.

"You are the absolute worst," she says upon your return. "I'm so happy, and so excited, and I just wanted to share this with you, *my oldest friend*, and it's just, like, stop it. Ok? Can you please stop? Can you just let me have this? Please?!"

"*Dare to Dream*," you reply with a snort.

"The absolute worst."

"Fine. I'm the worst. So what's the deal?" you ask, suddenly wanting nothing more than to drag the pertinent details out of her as quickly as possible. "Destination shindig I'm assuming? North of Italy? South of France? Middle of nowhere? Back of beyond? Probably won't be able to make it. Pretty broke these days. Starving artist and all. You understand."

"No, actually," she sulks, indignant. "We wanted to do it in Vienna. There's this abandoned amusement park..."

"Sure."

"...but Daddy can't leave work to fly out here, and even if he could, I'm sure most of our friends would balk at the price, so we're coming back to the States to do it at the Oxfordshire."

"Wow," you say, genuinely surprised.

"I know, right!? It's going to be so fun! Daddy rented out the entire club. It cost a fortune, but he said it's my special day, and I deserve to feel like a Princess."

"Just not a Princess of Vienna."

"Fuck you."

"Just keepin' it real."

"*Anyway!*" she continues, "we'll have a Jewish-Catholic hybrid ceremony..."

"How very *Goodfellas* of you."

"...and then it's off to Amsterdam for the honeymoon."

"Amsterdam!? Shit Artie, bury the lede why don't you!?"

"Don't call me..."

"I mean fuck," you interject, "I'd give anything to go to Amsterdam. That's so fucking cool. You're gonna have access to the best fucking drugs in the world. Probably plenty of 'post-sexual' folks for you crazy kids to play with too. I don't mind telling you, I'm actually jealous. I mean, if I was getting married I'd probably wanna stay fucked up for a week too, but jeez. I didn't think you had it in you."

"Um... yeah," she says, measuring the pros and cons of continuing this phone call - if not your entire friendship. "It's not really like that."

"What do you mean?"

"I mean we're not going to do drugs and party. We're actually going to be doing some community organizing. Maybe staging some protests."

"WHAT!?!"

"Yeah. There's so much energy pollution from leaky neon and old, inefficient bulbs. Eduardo says it's a prime grassroots opportunity. We think a lot of the working girls will like it too.

God knows all that red lighting isn't doing anybody any favors."

"IT'S CALLED THE RED LIGHT DISTRICT!"

"Yeah, but it doesn't have to be, right? Wouldn't some nice CFLs or LEDs be just as good? Everyone looks better in softer lighting. And it's cost effective. Our hope is that, with the right people on board and the right changes getting implemented, maybe someday it'll be known as the first *Green* Light District."

"So…" you say, your lip actually quivering, "you're not even gonna get high? Like, at all? Not even once?"

"I just don't know when we'd have the time."

"…Well, I gotta hand it to you Artie," you say, this time using the detested nickname 100% on purpose, "only you could make a week in Amsterdam sound so fucking boring. At least try to carve out a little time for some post-sex, ok? It is your honeymoon."

"I'll be sure and do that," she says, audibly blowing her Lhasa Opso bangs out of her eyes. Having exhausted each other into a stalemate of diehard old habits, you both just want this to be over.

"So, it's December 29th," she says, picking up the thread and trying to Ariadne herself out of the conversation, "and I want you to fucking be there, ok?"

"…"

"OK!?!"

"… fine."

"Good. Ok. So how are you? Anything new? Are you still writing? I think it was a screenplay last time?"

"You know. Here and there. Fits and starts."

"That's great. Can't wait to read it."

"Uh-huh."

"So what else? How's the site? What is it again? Grumble? Grackle? Gargamel?"

"GRUNDL."

"Right. So it's good then?"

"Sure. Fine."

"And your folks?"

"Fine I guess."

"Any special ladies in your life?"

You sigh for the third and final time – the ragged, hopeless sigh of an ISIS insurgent who long ago gave up any useful information he had, but remains rotting in Guantanamo, black metal and stress positions assaulting his sleep-deprived brain.

"I've gotta get to work," you say. "Time difference. Remember?"

"Oh, right. Ok. Well, I guess I'll see you in a couple of months. December 29th. Don't forg…"

You end the call and plod glumly to the bathroom.

Arranging yourself atop the toilet - elbows-to-knees, face-in-hands - the classic posture of the man in shambles - little rips and toots of methane eke their way out around what feels like a pile of wooden alphabet blocks crammed haphazardly into your colon. You push harder, but it's all corners. Then you remember: the party-sized can of mixed nuts - deftly extracted from the donation bin for the GRUNDL Fall food drive, and polished off last night in that mindless, hand-to-mouth way that often accompanies stony analgesia. This is likely to be a protracted battle, fought on multiple fronts - mind over fecal matter. Deciding to fall back and regroup, you wave a thin white flag across your buttonhole and head for the living room.

You seek distraction in routine, turning on the TV and sticking to your punctilious bowl-packing criteria. But nothing helps. Artemis always wrecks you. How that vacuous, preening show-cat of a woman - that bog of pretension - that human selfie stick - ever managed to find artistic success - and in *fucking Europe* - while you toil away in the good old U.S. of Anonymity with twice her talent and a fraction of her income is just... fuck! She's not even interesting! She's barely Pinteresting! She's just... so... fucking... "AUGH!" You actually unleash this Charlie Brown wail of frustration before inhaling a crackling wave of suffocants. But alas, today these are kite-eating trees.

You brew yourself a rare cup of coffee to combat your rectal clog, and annihilate your first cigarette before you're even past your front gate. While nothing's really changed since you took this same walk 24 hours prior, everything seems just a little bit worse. Yesterday's sunny briskness has solidified into today's overcast chill, and you smoke ambidextrously to give both your hands equal pocket time. The homeless are huddled together in alcoves and under awnings in mottled heaps of secondhand fabric. The park is empty save the Women in Black, whose cold weather balaclavas reduce them to three pairs of watchful, illuminati eyes.

Your MP3 player dies as you reach your building, choked out amidst the thorny verbal briarpatch of Company Flow's "Population Control," but you keep your headphones on as pretense to ignore Jennica's pep-squad "Good Morning!" and shrug past a confrontational "What's eating you?" from Cynthia - the office gossip, and a woman you once described as an adult undergarment taken human form.

Cynthia writes primarily about celebrity couplings, infidelities, and disintegrations. She's a nulliparous revealer of baby bumps, a pear-shaped appraiser of bikini bodies, and both rugose judge and xanny-poppin' jury as regards plastic surgeries, rehab stints, and anything else that, in a civilized society, would be considered nobody else's fucking business.

Likewise, when Barry picked up a shiner courtesy of his nephew's little league umpire (*I heard he dropped him like a sack of potatoes*), when Mandy in accounting cried all day over her husband and his private oboe instructor (*How did she not see that coming?!*), and when you engaged in a regrettable New Year's hookup with a former coworker (*She told me he came like THAT!*), Cynthia made sure these things hit the front page too. An armchair paparazzo, it's all just capital to her. Bradley calls her Cyn City. You call her Cunthia in certain circles.

You head straight to the men's room, but remain stymied. Your shit is straight-up breech. You pop by the staff lounge and slug two of Marsha's Activia yogurts like Jell-O shots before pouring yourself a second cup of coffee and spitefully pocketing a fistful of Splendas. Your unaccustomed nervous system resents being flooded with this much caffeine, but short of taking actual laxatives, you don't know what else to do. Full of entropic, negative energy - your every thought filtered through Artemis's adenoidal, expat condescension - you return to your cubicle to parse the news for click fodder.

The Simpsons hit 600 episodes; "Grab 'em by the pussy" is trending hard; Andrzej Wajda died; Durant and Westbrook are beefing again; Jimmy Fallon was spotted checking in at a detox clinic; Kathy Ireland was spotted protesting at an abortion clinic; Bob Dylan was awarded the Nobel Prize in Literature for some reason; Roman Polanski's facing extradition to Poland; A Kardashian was robbed at gunpoint in Paris - it doesn't matter which one; *One Day at a Time* is getting the reboot treatment; and so on.

Inspired by Polanski, and your dyspeptic attitude toward your half-Jewish friend - *the fucking Green Light District!?* – you open up a fresh, pure, lilywhite Word document, type `It Wasn't That Bad: 10 Times Holocaust Movies Went Too Far`, and proceed to eviscerate as melodramatic apocrypha a scene from *The Pianist* in which a woman asphyxiates her crying infant to keep from being discovered by the

Schutzstaffel. Your hands shake with nefarious glee and breakfast blend stimulants as you effectively call bullshit on a master director/ notorious kid-diddler's entire tragic youth.

A lousy childhood is not a free pass to rape children. I don't care how many of your other options got Mansoned, you think, cracking your knuckles like a leather-gloved cyber-Eichmann. *The Holocaust is so played out anyway. It's the Beatles of genocide. We get it. It was a big deal. But it's enough already. People are being slaughtered in Africa every day.*

Before you know it, you're mowing down *Life is Beautiful* like a strafing Richthofen, spraying Mauser fire across a pair of stagey Anne Franks, and raining down Luftwaffe devastation on *The Grey Zone*, *Sophie's Choice*, and *Schindler's List*. You're about to start firebombing *The Sound of Music* into Dresdenesque smithereens when you hear a coworker on your six and rush to shield your work from view.

Suddenly a little more cognizant of what you've been doing this past half-hour, your countenance droops under its own avoirdupois. Even if you wholeheartedly believed every frothing, despotic word you've just written - and you're altogether certain you don't - you'd never get this past editing. Hell, this is the kind of thing you could get fired just for *reading*, let alone writing. No amount of web traffic would save you this time.

On some level you feel your point about WWII oversaturation is fair - that Nigeria, or Syria, or the Sudan, would all be worthier recipients of the big-screen treatment than any as-yet-unfilmed Holocaust ephemera - but you employ a personal system of checks and balances in these matters, (believe it or not), and as much as you might like to, you simply can't justify trolling six million Jews just to troll your ugly American friend and one shitheel pedophile. You mash the delete key like Himmler hitting the gas, watch every last word scroll off to the showers, and head up to the terrace for a smoke.

The ideal of free speech has taken a very strange turn in the 21st century. For every protected protestation of "I have a dream" and "nothing to lose but our chains" there's now an equally free "kill the Jews" or, more recently, "build the wall" counterprotesting across the street. The ugly thoughts we once segregated from our public personae have wormed their way out of us, pupating quietly online before bursting forth in an obstreperous Human Centipede of social media newsfeeds and the idiots who rely on them for sustenance. All willfully ass-backward hate speech is free speech. The state-sanctioned propaganda that fuels it is free speech. Quantifiable lies are free speech. Mythomania is free speech. You may not be allowed to yell fire in a crowded theater, but you can sure as Hell capslock it in a crowded SubReddit. "The Holocaust never happened!" "9/11 was an inside job!" "Sandy Hook was a false flag!" "The World is flat!" If someone has the right to say it, you have the right to believe it. For many, the very idea of objective truth is now equated with oppression and tyranny.

Not that you mind, per se. It certainly makes your job easier. But you do wonder sometimes, looking out from this terrace for reassurance in that barely perceptible bowing of the horizon, where and how it ends. Or if it even can. If it's maybe already too late.

As you spark up a dromedary compatriot, a poster from your 11th grade History class italicizes your mental chyron:

First they came for the Jews, but I didn't stand up because I wasn't a Jew.

Then they came for the blacks, but I didn't stand up because I wasn't black.

Then they came for the gays, but I didn't stand up because I wasn't gay.

Then, when they finally came for me, there was no one left to stand up.

You considered this little bit of sloganeering often during high school between doodling dongs on your desk and scanning your female classmates for panty-lines - wondering what you would've done had you lived through such Hellish times. How you would have comported yourself. What kind of man you might have been. But try as you might, you always imagined things going a little differently:

First they came for the Jews, but I didn't stand up because I wasn't a Jew.

Then they came for the blacks, but I didn't stand up because I wasn't black.

Then they came for the gays, but I didn't stand up because I wasn't gay.

Then, when they finally came for me, I was all like "Hey bros, that was awesome! Who's next? Mexicans? Arabs? Asians? I mean, I know the Japs have been cool and all, but come on? Let's be real. No? Ok then what about women? Seriously, can we please do something about all these women? Well, at least the ugly ones, amiright? Or what about kids? Kids are super annoying. Yeah, let's do kids next!"

You smile as you light another cigarette. Yes, no matter how many times you read this provocative thought experiment, all it ever did was remind you that "they" would never come for "you"; that your demographic power was overwhelmingly consolidated; your piece of the pie cut too large for anyone else to eat without keeling over from stomach perforations. Winner, winner, chicken dinner. You're not a white supremacist - you've never been impressed enough with yourself or your pigmentation for that kind of capital-P "Pride" - but you are a white pragmatist, and when it comes to staring down Nazi Stormtroopers at the gate, the difference is mostly semantic.

You spend the rest of the day trying hard not to focus on your ardently impacted mineshaft, banging out publishable pop garbage at an Olympic trial pace ...And Chill?: Top 10 Netflix Offerings that are Basically Porn; We Don't Love Dem Hoes: Top 10 Gucci Mane Tracks to Get Over Your Ex; Not That There's Anything Wrong With That: Top 10 Most Homophobic Shows of the 90s; In Memoriam: Top 10 Celebrity Deaths to Hope for Next Year; Pitch Perfect Angles: 10 Times You Could Almost See Anna Kendrick's Boobs; Skit Row: 10 Worst SNL Cast Members Ever (always a reliable fomenter of comment thread violence); You Up?: 10 More Netflix Offerings that are Basically

`Porn` (surprisingly fertile ground); and `Hothouse Jazz: Top 10 Most 🔥 Recordings of Dizzy Gillespie's "A Night in Tunisia"` (you doubt editing will even read this one, but if you trick it out with Emoji and Trojan Horse it in with all the stuff about ladyparts, someone might post it by accident).

You submit two, bank the rest, don your empty headphones and head for the exit, bobbing a dumbshow of musical enjoyment as you pass Cunthia on your way out. Now there's a Nazi sympathizer if you've ever met one. A woman after the Fuhrer's own heart. She'd prod her own mother onto the cattle car for a gold star from the in-crowd.

Δ

Hoping some exercise might help churn through your duricrusted constipation, you turn down an undeveloped stretch of road lined with milkweed and embowered by tall pines.

You walk almost a mile without a single car passing (though you do observe a logging truck, a horse trailer, a surprisingly roadworthy industrial tractor, and a small house being relocated in two pieces). You consider challenging a couple of these vehicles to one of your parlous blinking contests, but ultimately think better of it. Men who haul felled timber and crated broncos across county lines are generally not the kind of men who blink, and even cut in half, the house always wins.

Instead, you fix your eyes on the woods, hoping to spot a rustle of wildlife amid the brindle of browns, greens, and approaching dusk. While not exactly the great outdoors, this is as back to nature as you've been in some time. The ambient drone of cicadas and treefrogs is growing immersive, with nest-bound Phoebes and Nuthatches providing occasional, contrapuntal flairs out of the wash, and as the sun descends, you find your splenetic funk tapering off a bit.

So what if Artemis is getting married (*to a fucking matador, ugh*)? So what if she gets to flounce around Europe blurbing back alley pinochle games and plates of paella for the travel blognoscente? So what if she wants to encase Amsterdam in a kale-and-quinoa-fueled Biodome. So what?! You're above it. You've always been above her shit. She's a sentient Q score. You're an artist! You could be successful too if you were willing to crowdsource your entire existence. Theoretically, anyone could. But you? You've got principles. And vision. A true voice, and something to say with it... someday... maybe. You need to get on that, for sure. And pay some bills. And probably shower more. *But so what!?!* Whether you're writing the great American novel or crapping out listicles, you're still a thousand times better than her trend-hopping, Neruda-quoting, Summer scarved, Pixies-tattooed, boholier-than-thou, Joan Didion-wannabe poseur ass. *Fuck her!* She wouldn't know an original thought if it gored her fiancée to death in the middle of la Maestranza. She has no idea what it takes to create something meaningful and honest and new. To say something that's never been said. The tenacity and sacrifice and... and...

Your mental stroke-session is kiboshed into photokeratitis as you round a bend and are briefly dazzled by a killer sunset – all Renaissance cyans and eiderdown clouds, limned in heliotrope and creamsicle. The tree line stops like someone took a paper-cutter to the world, and there's nothing in any direction but healthy clover and vibrant wildflowers.

Well, almost nothing...

As your rods and cones repopulate, and you tear yourself away from the supernal majesty overhead, you realize what had seemed like an (admittedly, suspiciously symmetrical) patch of arcadia is, in fact, just a recently clear-cut piece of rural real estate, at the far end of which stands an austere citadel of chrome and plate-glass surrounded by a gratuitously simonized fleet of Honda Accords, Civics, and CR-Vs. Glancing back at the sylvan seclusion from which you just emerged, you see several trees still marked for death with stinging, red, *Fern Gully* X's, and further up ahead, a billboard, shouting out this forthcoming venture in arrant capitalism.

The Promenade lacks the wherewithal to even aspire to its bougee-as-fuck name. It'll be anchored by a Trader Joe's, sure, but will also feature a Beef 'O' Brady's, a Cato Fashions, a 24-hour gym, a Subway, a Verizon store, a Lady Footlocker, and a Dialysis clinic. You're not sure this even qualifies as gentrification, so unlofty are its goals.

Oh, but the lofts will come.

Sooner than later, some executive will look out over this Wyeth-worthy pasture and think "Damn, this'd be a beautiful place for a Wal-Mart," and in the wink of a sunshine-yellow smiley's eye, all the stores that sell one thing will crumble beneath the Always-Low-Priced bootheel of the store that sells everything.

Next, the prefab favelas will sprout, rising above the remaining treetops to beckon rich students and poor faculty alike into lives of sleek, modular functionality. An ultrahip salon with a name like "Faded" or "Dye Happy" or "Kiss Kiss Bangs Bangs" will set up shop. The Cato will fast and cleanse until it's an American Apparel. The Beef 'O' Brady's will cook down into a Laotian gastropub. The Dialysis clinic will lose a foot. The Lady Footlocker will go out of business as a direct result. Fro-yo creep will set in. Before long, some local champion barista will sink his inheritance into a hoity-toity beanery and that'll be that. The Wal-Mart will stick around to keep the lights on – Wal-Marts never die – but the locals will resent it and make snide comments behind its back over fair-trade cappuccinos (even as they occasionally slink next door for a clandestine pair of sweatshop skinny jeans). It's a parfait accompli. Death by a thousand pixie cuts. *The Promenade: Something for Everyone.*

Trickledown tears coagulate at the corners of your eyes, and all at once, your calm caprice is broken. Artemis gets to live in Prague. You haven't written anything of substance in years. Your asshole still feels like it has a parquet floor, and you're at least an hour's walk from the comforts of home and hemp. You try to call an Uber, but find you're without a signal, and so you make your way toward the Honda complex hoping to piggyback off its Wi-Fi. It's there, however, that you are greeted – nay, enthusiastically waylaid – by an astonishing sight.

Gesticulating in the evening air, mouths agape in exuberant glossolalia, there flutter and jive before you no fewer than seven bright-and-beaming AirDancers. An extension-corded choir of purling parishioners welcoming all to their joyous jamboree. Lordy, Lordy, Honda days are here again!

You know immediately what you have to do.

You get a signal, secure a five-minute ETA, and quickly fish into your bag for a pair of scissors you swiped from the GRUNDL supply cabinet. The wraparound windows are clean enough that you can see directly through the showroom to the glowering woods behind, but the place appears deserted save for a custodian half-asleep on a riding floor buffer. You have to be fast though. Timing is everything.

Clenching your blade between your teeth, you steal up to the first oversized, whimsically gyrating windsock like you're Seal Team 6, squeeze your hands around his nylon throat, and cut.

You'd hoped to decapitate him completely, but the slick, parachute material proves more durable than expected. Nevertheless, upon releasing him, you're delighted to see his punctured trunk no longer raising up alongside his charismatic brethren, but rather flopping around like a Bozo Bop Bag that finally met its match. He grovels before you - genuflecting in deference to his wicked new master - renouncing faith, swearing obedience, begging you to spare the rest of his billowy claque. But you remain unmoved. Dispassionately, methodically, you work your way down the line, severing their silken windpipes one by one, and leaving them to contort through their death throes until some kind soul comes along to pull their plugs for good.

About to finish the job, hoping with a little extra effort you might take this final, clownishly drawn head clean off, you hear your ride approaching. The flat, black, oval eyes flash in the headlights, and you feel, if not pity, then at least satiation. Enough was enough. You would let him live, if only as a reminder of what you did to the others. May no one say you are not a benevolent god.

Episode 11

You pack a pristine bowlus ˊand hit for the cycle: one puff, two puffs, three puffs, four. Your mood has lightened considerably in the aftermath of your cathartic, roadside massacre, and with your mind now pacified, you switch on the TV and start maundering up the dial.

Dr. Phil shills for an "organic" douche, a motorcycle zips through an interstate pileup, a Tucson woman buys a vowel, *Dirty Dancing* cuts abruptly to a Maybelline commercial, Skip Bayless and Shannon Sharpe argue across whatshername's rack, Phoenix University offers you a sad fresh start, Leonard and Sheldon have a shrill disagreement about *The Incredible Hulk*, a cheerful voice lists side-effects for a beta-blocker, Anderson Cooper emotes about Waziristan, smooth jazz plays over a weather map, and so on.

Your brain inspissating under the soporific spell of Gander's palmfrond kush, you're three clicks away from just watching whatever's on when...

"Wacky waving inflatable arm-flailing tube man!

Wacky Waving Inflatable Arm-Flailing Tube Man!

WACKY WAVING INFLATABLE ARM-FLAILING TUBE MAN!"

You can't believe it, but there it is, like a gift from the Meliae: *Family Guy*'s first classic Al Harrington cutaway gag! You know it like you know "Who's on First?" or "Nudge Nudge Wink Wink." Like "Naima" or "Nuthin' but a G Thang." You'd know it anywhere, yet it still catches you off guard. What are the odds? That it would just randomly appear at this moment? Just *be on*? Do you matter somehow? Is your chronic paranoia justified? Is TV watching *you*?

It's not the first time you've detected a supernatural, potentially divine connection between the world out there, and your nights in here. In point of fact, you've discovered a striking phenomenon over the years by which once-innocuous jokes, through no fault of their own, become retroactively offensive due to wholly unforeseeable real-world events. When it happens, these MetaFails (™) are rendered so unforgivably, irretrievably, artlessly dark, that they cease to function as jokes at all, morphing instead into grim reminders of the very horrors from which TV is supposed to help us escape.

The quintessential example comes, unsurprisingly, from *Seinfeld* – (S05E09) – in which Elaine, dating a man who shares his name with a fictitious serial killer terrorizing the city, is mortified by an escalating string of mix-ups and jokes at her beau's expense. Encouraging him to choose a new alias, she pulls a few suggestions from a stray *Sports Illustrated,* landing innocently enough, on OJ as her top choice. The episode aired November 18th, 1993, and seven months later, OJ Simpson murdered his estranged wife Nicole Brown Simpson, and her friend Ron Goldman, forever altering this stochastically silly punchline. No one knew. No one could have known. It just happened.

Other examples include *American Dad* S07E07 (wherein a dart-throw gag about Subway spokesman Jared Fogle having been excommunicated, and then recommunicated by the Vatican would, four years later, take on a disturbing second layer of meaning when Fogle was caught with an argosy of child pornography), and *The Cosby Show* S07E03 (centered around Cliff Huxtable's aphrodisiac-spiked BBQ sauce, a plotline so horrifying in light of Cosby's serial rape conviction that it practically qualifies as circumstantial evidence). Without warning, these jokes were suddenly *on us*. Bizarrely prescient as they were, they could never be enjoyed the same way again. Sometimes, the universe trolls us all.

Family Guy, on the other hand, is impervious to such reversals of comedic fortune.

It gets out ahead of the universe by making these kinds of blithely inappropriate jokes every week.

Creator Seth MacFarlane is an equal opportunity troll, and something of a patron saint to the cause. The voice of the titular "Family Guy," Peter Griffin, as well as his sociopathic, infant son Stewie and his fustian, gin-swilling dog Brian, he's created a world in which nothing is off limits. As a reliable barometer of the acceptable lowbrow, he revels in stereotypes, and if a stereotype doesn't exist, he'll happily create it. His show lapped the field in the 21st century's race to the bottom, and has stayed there - thrived there, really - sarcastically slow-clapping while the rest of society catches up.

Vaguely galvanized by this internal hagiography you've begun composing on spec, and with a saucepan of creative resentment still simmering at the base of your brainstem (*fucking Artemis!*), you queue up a binge, grab your laptop, and resolve to write something for your neglected blog.

Family Guy is to the 21st century what *The Simpsons* was — at least initially — to the 20th: a distillation of middle-class American life bleak enough to make us all feel a little bit better, edgy enough to make us all feel a little bit worse, and universal enough to make us all feel a little bit the same. The parallels are blatant, but while *The Simpsons* has sagged into a bloated, saccharine middle age – phoning in their prank calls for so long now they don't even realize most of their fans blocked their number years ago – *Family Guy* continues to reach new heights of nihilistic delirium without even dialing. They just go down to the bar and start kicking people in the nuts. I can't remember the last time *The Simpsons* ended an episode without trying to teach us something, but *Family Guy* understands we already know everything we care to, fuck you very much. Why the Hell else would we be watching *Family Guy*?

This thesis is somehow both combative and dull, and anyone who bothers to read it will tell you as much, probably in all caps, and festooned with poop emoji. You delete, your letters evaporating backward like they've been hacked by F-Society.

And isn't that the very reality *Family Guy* inauspiciously helped to inaugurate? One in which intelligent, honest debate is no longer about who's rightest? Or smartest? Or funniest? But rather about who's loudest? And quickest?

And meanest? One in which we dive like jacked-up jackdaws toward any eyepopping tidbit of information, and sprint to be the first to relay it to our "friends" or our "followers" - who then sprint to be the first to Tweet wise about it too soon. Always too soon. No event - from the smallest dick pic scandal to the largest civilian drone strike - can escape the noxious, pyrocumulus inferno of "too soon." Best doesn't really even exist anymore. Only first.

Ah, Twitter - that great coin-sorter of intellectual capital - the winching mechanism by which discourse was lowered screaming into the abyss - the perfect medium for people with *almost* nothing to say. You didn't want to join, but like Facebook before, it felt inevitable. Twitter saw all the ways internet culture was incentivizing people to give in to their worst impulses, and they made a play. A play to be our voice; to be the platform for our every banal, or banally evil thought; to bring us all into the light, and show us just how little we matter to one another.

In all honesty, you don't even know what people talk about anymore.

Thanks to vertically integrated marketing strategies and the commodification of "cool," true originality has almost ceased to exist.

Individually, we may all be snowflakes, but together, we're a fucking whiteout. We've all read and heard and seen all the same things, and been told what to think about them by our distinctly chosen filters. We've all been there, done that, and tagged the selfie to prove it. Jeans come pre-ripped. Everyone has a tattoo. We've all watched that YouTube documentary. No one cares about anyone else's band. Everybody's working 'round the clock to prove that they understand and appreciate *everything* - that they're not just unique, but that they're the *most* unique. With all the world's information at our 100-WPM fingertips, *seeming* smart has never been easier, but actually *being* smart has never been more difficult. In this environment, what's a true artist to do?

    You pack another bowl and start again.

    Across 15 seasons and counting, *Family Guy* has made 186 rape jokes, 195 pedophilia jokes, 58 suicide jokes, 82 domestic abuse jokes, 182 child abuse jokes, 28 AIDS jokes, 47 cancer jokes, 147 jokes mocking parents who've lost children, 41 jokes mocking children who've lost parents, 648 categorically racist jokes, 81 categorically ageist jokes, 306 categorically ableist jokes, 202 categorically homophobic jokes, and honestly, too many misogynist jokes to count (JK, it's 918). For every bit of tongue-in-cheek social commentary they manage to pull off, there are five more gags spawned from pure, gut-level bigotry, and another five in service of the absolute laziest brand of "oh no they didn't!" shock value. This is a show where slow-witted black men are voiced by snarky, middle-aged white guys, where a terminally dumpy teenage girl is voiced by *Esquire*'s 2012 Sexiest Woman Alive, and where a fat, New England slob is voiced by... alright, that one's fair.

You stop typing, unsure of where this is coming from. You love Seth MacFarlane. You've sent him actual, physical fan mail. On paper. With stamps. He's your guru; your Galt; your Obi Wan. You did that joke count out of respect, during your seventh voyage through the series. You wanted to know who he hated the most (women, natch). Why would you waste those numbers on a hit piece? You delete again.

That said, you've always found the disparity between the voiceover cast and their corresponding characters amusing; like mean-spirited, reverse avatars. Save for poor, frowzy Alex Borstein as Lois, every actor is playing someone less attractive than themselves, and playing them for frumpy fools. While not quite on par with blackface (except, of course, for Mike Henry's Cleveland Brown, which absolutely is on par with blackface) it's certainly reprehensible. Call it Fatface. Or Trashface. A gang of smugly attractive, B-list Hollywood celebs riffing on the pathetic spectacle they perceive as middle-class American life.

Likewise, the fiendish, masquerade soiree of Social Media has taken such willful misrepresentation to its logical antipode: namely, the photoshopping of reality.

Why, any longer, should anyone snap a lonesome selfie at home when, with a curatorial touch, he can create a tableau in which he spends every night out on the town, surrounded by a revolving retinue of fabulous hangers-on? Why would anyone choose a crapulous driver's license photo for their Match.com profile when, with a bit of spot healing and a dab of Gaussian blur filter, she can look like a young Angelina Jolie in perpetuity? How could any restaurant be expected to display their menu items on grease-streaked wrappers under bare, heatlamp bulbs when, with a little threshold and saturation work they can make a Big Mac look like it was plated at Nobu? Why would any tourism board worth its

Himalayan salt pass up the chance to goose its natural terrain with gradient masks and Orton effects until the whole world is booking flights to their high-contrast promised lands? What value is there in being truthful, when everything can suddenly be better than the truth? An active online presence has given everyone a second chance; to stay young; to look hot; to make those colors pop!

Having raised our expectations beyond perfection, the internet has thusly turned every aspect of life into an oversharing, overcompensating, over-getting competition. An inescapable cyclorama of who's the prettiest? Who has the nicest house? The flashiest car? The best-looking kids? Who ate the best meal? Saw the best concert? Took the best vacation? Look at me. Look at my page. Look at my life. Friend me. Follow me. Tag me. Like me. Retweet me. Judge me. Accept me. Love *me*.

While you count *Family Guy* among your best-versed series, it's proving harder to write about than you would've guessed. It's as fan-proof as it is critic-proof; a true "love it or hate it" proposition. Perhaps it's folly to give it any more thought than that, especially when it so clearly aspires to not be thought about at all.

You are, however, beginning one of your all-time favorites.

A masterstroke of comedic countermaneuvering, "Petarded" (S04E06) finds Peter taking an IQ test only to discover that, in the eyes of the medical community, he's so uneducated as to qualify as mentally handicapped. It was an astonishingly ballsy move for MacFarlane, and one I'm still surprised he was allowed to pull off. But pull it off he did, establishing himself as an unrivaled polymath of hatemongering, and revealing his comprehensive contempt for his fellow man via little more than the transitive property (ie – if Peter Griffin = the average American, and Peter Griffin = a DSM-textbook dullard, then by the transitive property, the average American = a DSM-textbook dullard). This gambit also bestowed upon his creation the infrangible and perdurable defense of legitimately not knowing any better. Through Peter's diagnosis, MacFarlane basically wrote himself a hall-pass to "go there," and then used it to find the school laminator. He invented a character who could be the worst in all of us, and get away with it, forever.

You lean back, mildly pleased. This is not bad. You could take it in any number of directions. Media ethics. Hate speech. Artistic freedom. Take your pick. Nope. Not bad Sir. Not bad at all.

You highlight the text block, delete with a single Backspace, and pack another bowl.

You knew all along this would be where you ended up. Your writer's block doesn't actually block you from writing so much as it bores into you the certainty that all writing is completely useless, and after a self-immolating toke that chars your brain Monastically crispy, you set about proving yourself right.

Within minutes, you've found three blogposts unpacking *Family Guy* with an eye to Bazinian objectivism, two more applying Judith Butler to Brian's inter-species sexuality, and another about Stewie's engagement with the Lacanian mirror stage. This leads you to a trove of comp lit dissertations analogizing Peter with everyone from Fallstaff to Ignatius J. Reilly to the Hindu god Ganesh, and a lengthy treatise on Lois and the feminism of Luce Irigaray. By the time you're done, you've skimmed four different articles about the "Petarded" episode - all making your same point better than you could with a MacArthur Genius Grant and a year to research.

Even if you're the only person who's read them, it doesn't matter. You've confirmed your most self-sabotaging suspicions. You are a hack, and everything you have to say has already been said. Everyone will see. Everyone will know. Everyone will point and laugh at you for trying. *How dare you?* they'll ask. *How dare you think you have something to say? Who are you to fucking try?*

You pull another thick choke of potsmoke in behind your vitrified eyes. Your neural pathways are at zero visibility. You'd need a mattock and a rescue Dalmatian to get out of your head now.

You feel a deep unease with all these ways we've turned life into a communal activity; with this seismic self-centering of... *everything*. Nothing matters anymore so much as what *you* think about it. Whether it's Tweeting Britney Spears at 2 A.M. about teabagging her on the Jumbotron at a Lakers game, or unfollowing Colin Kaepernick because we're sick of thinking about Trayvon Martin during kickoff, or posting "back, and to the left" memes at Ted Cruz during Reddit AMA's, it's not really about them anymore. It's about us. Judging public figures makes us feel better - about ourselves; about our accomplishments; or about our decisions to accomplish nothing. And that's the real trick. Social media has turned *everyone* into a public figure. It lets us live every day as both celebrity, and paparazzo, and the sheer scope of that enterprise - the way it snowballed downhill, *Katamari*-ing up everything in its path - has turned us into monsters.

Seventh grade suicide campaigns. Unpoliceable revenge porn. Alt-right eugenicist tirades. Mommy blogs. It's no longer enough to just disagree with someone. We have to dehumanize them; threaten their rapes, and the razing of their homes. We want to bring one another to ruin, and if we get enough likes, sometimes we can. The veil of cyberspace allows every person on Earth to act like they're the only person on Earth; to finally feel important; to attack others for feeling the same. All of our opinions matter, and none of our opinions matter. No one seems real anymore once you put their whole life on a screen.

Somewhere in the middle of your ninth *Family Guy*, Hulu stalled out and you failed to notice. Your dimmed television wants to know if you're still watching, and your dimmed senses don't know what to tell it.

Should you point out that you're always watching? That we all are? That something larger likely is too, laughing at our efforts, stirring the anthill, creating MetaFails (™) and smoking away its troubles with that higher-than-God green we're all trying to get our hands on? That we're all just looking to escape? To watch something entertaining enough, listen to something loud enough, take something strong enough, or fuck someone hot enough - that lets us forget for a moment that absolutely nothing we do matters?

You click "Yes," and empty your pipe into your lungs as Peter forcibly farts on his daughter's face.

You laugh.

You still have to shit.

Defeatedly, you trudge your browser toward your porn site.

The most anyone can hope for is to be heard above the squall for a week, a day, an hour, before the world scrolls over to the next next-big-thing. It's not something you can reverse, this lemniscate, backchannel exchange of ego and id social media provides. It's already in place; ingrained in an entire generation, uploaded from the day they were born to the day they could start uploading themselves. Even your most righteously felt outrage is still part of the outrage machine. At your best, you're just a parallax viewed dinghy, taking potshots at a dreadnought.

And where does that leave you? Screaming on street corners? Building bunkers off the grid?

Stockpiling weapons? Making bombs? Be serious. You'd be dead in a week. The truth is, you don't stand a chance. The internet has you, just like everyone else.

Episode 12

Porn is everywhere.

As someone who vividly remembers a time when it was nearly impossible to get your greased-up palms on it - who dug through the trash for his mother's discarded Victoria's Secret catalogs, or stayed up late to catch *E's Wild On* and *USA Up All Night*, one hand poised on the channel changer, one ear pressed to the door, auscultating for parental footsteps - you know as well as anyone: kids have it too easy these days. You'd stare at vermiculated, colloidal slides of the tinted-green Spice Channel like a horny histologist, fiddling with yourself and the vertical hold for hours on end in hopes of catching a half-second interstice of tits or ass at the exact moment you needed it; the masturbatory equivalent of harnessing a lightning strike into a DeLorean. Getting off was an operation back then. Covert, and precise.

Fast forward to today, and all that windswept smut is as available as oxygen. The candlelit softcore of HBO and Skinemax trickled down those networks' gartered, pay-per-view thighs and splashed its formula all over basic cable. Watch The History Channel for a week, and you're guaranteed to see something peddling itself with leatherbound gravity as *The History of Sex*, or better yet, *Sex and Hitler*. Check out The Food Network, and you'll soon be an expert on arousing edibles. The Learning Channel barely tries to hide it anymore. TLC indeed.

And all that's before you even get to the internet.

Our most trusted sources for information about the Affordable Care Act and the Iranian nuclear program purfle their margins with "nip slips" and "blowjob bootcamps" like they're all underwritten by *Penthouse Forum*. Sports and pop culture sites are even worse, and GRUNDL's no exception. You hate it, but you still look. It pays your bills after all, including the bill that lets you nightly wander the halls of Uporn like Sokurov in the Hermitage.

Pornographic pics and vids are as numerous as the stars in the sky or the sand on the seashore, sorted and cross-referenced by every conceivable seed of metadata for your prurient convenience. Finding what you want is as easy as knowing your search terms. Age (18, barely legal, coed, milf, mature), body type (skinny, petite, athletic, busty, curvy, plumper, fatty), hair color (blonde, brunette, redhead), ethnicity (ebony, Latina, Italian, Brazilian, Czech, Asian, Hentai), locale (bedroom, bathroom, kitchen, car, bangbus, plane, club, beach, office, school, gym), wardrobe (lace, leather, schoolgirl, teacher, nurse, secretary, cheerleader), position (handjob, footjob, blowjob, titfuck, POV, doggystyle, reverse cowgirl, anal, piledriver), population density (threesome, foursome, gangbang, blowbang, orgy), affect (innocent, naughty, dirty, nasty, filthy, slut, whore), fetish (spanking, squirting, creampie, bondage, watersports, cumplay, scat, cucking, incest), and intensity (romantic, erotic, rough, hardcore, pounded, fisted, throatfucked, facefucked, brutalized, destroyed, ruined).

Women, as a species, would be appalled, were they suddenly made privy to all the thoughts that come unbidden to even the most upright of men's minds.

We're oversaturated with silicone and our own secret secretions. Every inch of available ad-space in our day-to-day lives has been colonized by the imagery of fucking. Not love. Not sex. Fucking. Short of building a cabin in the woods (which none of us knows how to do anymore), we couldn't escape it if we wanted to (which honestly, we don't). The first thing we think whenever we see a woman - any woman - is a yes or no proposition. *Would you hit that?* Our glands have been reprogrammed. Our chemicals are imbalanced. We've no more worlds to conquer, save that ass. Or that one. Or *that* one. Of course we're not listening. Of course we're trying to picture you naked. How could we not be? Why would you even entertain the possibility of anything else? Look around! Men control the world, and men know what men want. If you think your guy is different, you're kidding yourself. We're slaves to our dicks, and so are you.

Fishing a fortuitous sock out of your couch cushions, and feeling somewhat ambivalent about sheathing yourself in it, you decide to skip the foreplay and go right for a no-nonsense trollop.

Tori is crazy for big ol' corn-on-the-cob dick. Her plumptious pussy lips engulf Coke-can girth and Titanoboa length until her shotgun barrel snatch pumps out animalistic sprays of orgasmic juices. Where so many lesser performers have perfected their breathy exhortations to the point of internalized collective parody, Tori's ululations of pleasure ring truer than the Biblical word. She's a missionary for every position but; a soaked and squealing Sermon on the Mount; a shining, waxed kitty on a hill.

Stuck in neutral, you search "redhead BDSM" and shift to the Third Reich-crimson locks of Jasmine.

Jasmine has skin like she bathes in the blood of Mouseketeers. Bulging out of a black leather corset in taut, balloon animal shapes, she...

You pause, already bored. As a quantifiable 10, Jasmine never debases herself below what a 7 might acquiesce to on a slow night, and the kind of shit your uncooperative member wants to see is well beneath her bordello-chic wheelhouse. You switch to Sophie, a wild-eyed, carnelian-tressed 6 who thrills to the behaviors of a slovenly, sperm-slurping 2.

Sophie fucks like she was raised by rabbits. She always appears naturally slickened – glistening with an internal, backwoods humidity – and men line up at both ends to ride her like a dirty talkin' slip-n-slide. Her ability to remain adorable amid acts of rabid, multifarious depravity is unparalleled. Her left hand rarely knows what her right is stroking, and she's the only gal in the game who can still smile with two cocks in her mouth. Flutelike, every hole filled makes her squeak a little higher. Anal turns her into a piccolo (it plays "Take the A-Train").

Watching Sophie absorb splooge from six different directions like a happy, soppy, human sponge, you think you might be getting somewhere, but then she giggles her girlish giggle and you resoften. You're not in the mood for playful tonight.

You decide to go off-bookmark and see if you can rustle up a tougher titty at the end of the bar. A real last-call, heartland skank. You search `"nasty-whore + throatfuck."` The cock wants what it wants.

Rachel has a face like a Hooters waitress and a cunt like a cigar cutter. She practices what some might call slight-of-mouth, teasing out endless strands of precum like a magician regurgitating knotted scarves. Where many of her XXX sistren are pressured into such slobbery schlong-swallowing by knobby hands at the backs of their uncertainly shaking heads, Rachel requires no such chaperoning. Slimy stalactites dripping from her defiant chin, she shoves her tobacco-deadened throat further down than any man ever could, stealing every second of screen-time, making sure her cyanotic face is all anyone can see.

Rachel is a rare breed of blowbanging warrior. She earns a dogear in your digital seraglio. But despite everyone's most scurrilous efforts, you keep getting distracted.

Julia's alabaster housewife getting plowed into her kitchen island just makes you question how often countertops are really the exact right height for sex.

Sasha's society bitch fellating an ox-cock in Blahniks and blood diamonds only gets you pondering what else you might convince her to do, were you blessed with equally tremendous equipment.

Would she mow your lawn? you wonder, looking disappointedly down at your semi-hard...

Do your taxes?

standard-issue...

Remodel your house?

garden-variety penis.

(People who claim the brain is the biggest sex organ clearly don't watch much porn. Brains lose out all the time.)

But this is ridiculous.

Enough is enough.

You need a closer.

Eva is a fucking closer.

Eva likes cum on her face, regardless of volume or consistency. Her virtuosic deepthroat technique almost certainly requires circular breathing, and her pronounced lack of a gag reflex may well signify partial brain death, but her true calling is as a cheerfully encouraging focus-object. Happiest on her knees, hair coiled back in a sensible chignon, she spurs men to unburden themselves across her cherubic visage. Be it projectile ribbons connecting her faint freckles into cobwebby constellations, or thick pints of suffocating goo sealing off her orifices like a coat of primer, she is muse, model, and canvas for the penile Pollocks and Picassos of her pornographic generation, eternally licking her lips clean of their masturpieces.

Furiously hoicking your joystick like it's the last level of *Super Punch-Out!!*, you watch three guys baste Eva with baby gravy - her wide, anime eyes beaming proudly upward - and at long last, you too squeeze out a thin strand of jism.

Breathing hard, you lean back and take a toke from your nearby nepenthe. Tonight was concerning. Pornography is your last refuge. If you lose your ability to enjoy even this most isolationist of erogenous activities, what's left? You don't even want to speculate...

Best to get on with the business of ensnaring the real thing.

Δ

On some level you're still kicking yourself for not sticking it in every one of Emma Lee's flopsweat-emolliated pokeholes when you had the chance. What you then rejected as a big, steaming pile of overfed compromise, you now remember as a deliciously chesty specimen, eagerly singing for her piping hot supper. You've thought of her often since the karaoke fracas - standing alone amidst the wreckage; that gorgeous blue vein bulging as she worked to stave off hyperventilation. She was beautiful in that moment, transformed by trauma from Madison's milksop sidekick to the protagonist of her own future. You gave her that. You don't regret it.

Ever since, however, your penis has been exhibiting the erratic behavior of a rogue state within your body politic. You betrayed him, with your high-minded principles and arbitrary ideals, but he's close enough to your ass to know you're full of shit, and he demands retribution.

So too, it appears, do the OKcupid algorithms, as you're now beset on all sides by rabid, ravenous PAWGs. The site is pushin' cushion like a Labor Day mattress sale, larding your homepage with sweet, cookie-dough faces, custardy Titian tits, and moist handfuls of muffin top. Your dick may as well have a cowcatcher attached at the head.

After thinning the herd a bit, your eyes plunk down onto Amberly – a yawning expanse of Berkshire-white cleavage in a lubricious, red halter-top whose racy literary quotations (**Rimbaud, Colette, Anaïs Nin**) suggest both a highbrow ceiling, and a debased floor. You picture her moueing and sucking jam off her thumb in a giant cloth diaper; getting her mallowy ass spanked with a wooden spatula; trussed up with a fudgsicle in her mouth. Alas, she's been inactive for months, likely having met some other low-bar lothario off of whom to lick coulis and remoulades. Moving on.

After several more pages of "before" pictures, you break the porcine cycle with Nicole, a pale "after" in a *Battlestar Galactica* tank-top she's utterly failing to fill out. She offers little personal info, but has maxed out her word limit under favorite books, listing everything from **Isaac Asimov** to **Timothy Zahn** in her attempts to escape sci-fi introversion and find someone to cosplay with. You can easily imagine using her inexperience against her. Employing mild verbal abuse and a little gaslit coaxing, you could probably get her to spend a weekend chained to your radiator subsisting on nothing but black coffee and sperm. With the phrase "So Say We All" lying perfectly flat across her planar chest however, this all seems like more trouble than it's worth. Hard pass.

Your next stop, despite your better judgment, is Isabella - a willowy 8½ with F-holes tattooed down her lissome back. She plays the **cello** professionally, and **tennis** semi-so, and you envision bending her over the net and paddling her with her own catgut until her ass looks like bright pink graph paper. She likes **George Eliot**, making her own **pasta**, and indulging in occasional trips to **Shondaland**.

Every callous fiber of your being is telling you not to bother - to listen to your ruthlessly efficient instincts and return to the flabby arms and confidence gaps you know so well - but for whatever stupid-ass reason, you decide to toss your stupid-ass hat in the stupid-ass ring. Blame your cooing, coddling mother.

"**Hi there**" you type, waiting while she, hopefully, at least skims your profile (a veritable wordcloud of embellishments touting everything from your **McSweeney's**-caliber literary prowess to your **comprehensive Coltrane vinyl collection**). After five minutes, you try again.

"I see you're an accomplished tennis player. Have you read *Infinite Jest*, or any of David Foster Wallace's essays on the sport? His writing on Federer is sublime."

Five more minutes pass - the site's design stretching the mercifully brief monosyllable "no" across an infinity cove of rejective silence - each second ticked off by the cruel blink of the text cursor.

Your every keystroke a self-flagellation, you decide to give her the benefit of the doubt and reach out one more time.

"That's really impressive that you play the cello. I often write about music in my work and have great respect for anyone who's dedicated themselves to an artform. Commitment to craft is not something many people understand. Do you find it difficult, as I do, to meet others who relate to your passion?"

Nothing. Your brain balloons with noxious apoplexy. Why isn't she responding? She sees you! She knows you're there!! Would she ignore someone in real life if they asked her to dance or bought her a drink!?! Is it so hard to just say no!?!? To do you the courtesy of blowing you off!?!? Jesus Christ!!!!! What's this bitch's fucking problem!?!?!?!?

Seething with impotent fury, you type "**I want you to jack me off until you get tennis elbow!!!**" followed closely by "**GO TO HELL CUNT!!!!!**"

You can't believe you let yourself fall into that uppity twat's siren trap. You knew better.

You *know* better. Imagining all the ways you'd like to ruin her pristine, kegel-tightened box, you stop for a surgical hit of the bowl before clicking over to the next trichinosal slab in this Mumbai-scale meat market.

Beth's page shows all the signs of someone recently dumped into insignificant otherness. Several of her pictures feature a disembodied arm around her shoulder – its owner photoshopped into amputeeism – and biographical tidbits she likely intends as flirtatious (**strip aerobics**, *50 Shades*, the ability to fit **nine marshmallow peeps** in her mouth at once) read a little closer to desperate. But she's got a great ass.

"Hey. You seem cool" you type.

"Hi" she types back, not even bothering to scan your page for serial killer red flags.

"I like your pictures. You're crazy hot."

"Awwww, you're sweet. I needed that tonight" she answers with a winking emoji.

"So… wanna come over to my place and get your asshole reamed out like a Jack-O-Lantern?" you ask, your temperamental dick worming around in your boxers at having said something Hellaciously pervy to a complete stranger.

"Fuck you creep!"

"**Your loss**." you type, adding a mischievous wink of your own before scampering away, quite sure this was more in line with what she "needed" tonight (and that she'll love every minute she spends relaying it to her shocked besties tomorrow).

More importantly, with this exchange, and another insulating puff of cerebral gortex, you leave your anger and rejection in the rearview, ready to continue browsing for low-risk tail. It's then you're greeted, once again, by that rarest of birds: the unsought, uncajoled female text bubble.

"**Hey**" types **Claire93iguess**, and your brain falters trying to recall why that screenname looks so familiar. You type "**Hey**" back and click to her page...

Claire! Of course! The grumpy Christmas party picture! You're almost surprised she's a real person, but her profile is far too strange to suggest catfishing - unless of course someone tailored it specifically to catfish you, in which case, well... you'd at least be curious. They went to all that trouble.

You begin typing some benignly clever non sequitur about her Scrooge-faced holiday card, but she beats you to the punch.

"So, sexually deviant art film huh? Did you think that was a smart thing to say to a woman you've never met? Is that, like, your opening line or something?"

Goddammit. Your expectations realign as you sense she may only be here to give you a high-handed scolding.

"I dunno" you type back. **"You're talking to me aren't you?"**

She lets your bravado hang in the air. The eyes of that sullen photo seem to scan you for vulnerabilities. Taking your measure. Deciding if you're for real. It takes everything you have not to amend your churlish comeback with some humorous apologia, but something tells you a single keystroke here would be taken as a sign of weakness; that if this girl is who you think she is, then it's simply not your turn to talk.

"So, what theater?" she finally asks. **"What time?"**

Was she serious? Was it really going to be this easy?

"Wow. Ok. Do you know The Cinespect? Little 2-screen job on the Westside?" you ask, betraying your surprise in service of some self-deprecating comedic effect and instantly regretting it.

"**Yeah**" she replies. "**Do you? You seem a little unsure of yourself.**"

Who *is* this girl?

"**Yeah. I'm sure. They're showing some cool stuff for Halloween. How's Friday at 8:00?**"

"**Fine**" she types. "**See you then.**"

Her matter-of-factness bordering on that of a companionship professional, you sense she's done talking to you, but for whatever reason, you can't leave well enough alone.

"**Wait**" you type. "**Don't you want to chat or anything?**"

"**About what?**"

"**I dunno. I like your profile picture. You look miserable.**"

"**You 'dunno' a lot of things. That's twice now, and I've only asked you four questions.**"

"**...It's more a figure of speech.**"

"**It's fine. Most guys think they know everything. It's refreshing really.**"

"**Thanks?**"

"**Anything else?**" she asks.

You stare at the screen. You're out of moves. You were out of moves three moves ago. You're only playing yourself now, and she's only observing. It's intimidating, and spectacular - like flirting with Dagny Taggart. You decide to bow out, lest you further undermine your bewildering success.

"Nope. I'm good. Seeya Friday" you type, nimbly signing off before her in a final flourish of confidence you both likely recognize as gamesmanship, but also both (hopefully) respect for it.

You are elated. Never in your wildest dreams did you expect to meet such an odd, inveigling creature amidst the mad, barking pageantry of the online dating carnival. But there she was, as forthright as she was mysterious, and at the end of this grueling day, you finally feel yourself start to loosen up.

You grab Blaze Pascal, hurry to the bathroom, and no sooner than you've sat down does a fibrous shaft of stool *lathe* out of your puckered anus like *knurled gunmetal*. You feel an ASMR shiver at the splashdown and light up in celebration. Your vanquished foe is a *knotty wizard's staff* – (*fucking mixed nuts!*) – gnarled as Gandalf the Grey's, and you smile as your mind replays his bellowed decree: "YOU SHALL NOT PASS!"

But pass you did, and exhausted, you flush your victory down the commode – the estocada to the heart of this bullshit-filled day – and head to bed where, with a YouTube Yanni mix lullabying out of your laptop, you drift off to dreams of stoned girls, writhing on dirty mattresses, under cold, red light.

Episode 13

The Cinespect opened two years after your own theatre bit the dust, and has done steady business ever since. The type of tiny, artsy affair that can only maintain two screens, but still runs magisterial, burgundy curtains across both of them - you're filled with resentment every time you come here, forced to agonize over what they could possibly be doing right that you did wrong.

You arrive 20 minutes early to find your mark already waiting for you. Leaning against the brick façade in a long-sleeved, knee-length black dress that matches her yé-yé-bobbed hair, she smokes a cigarette in the pale, film noir light. Pretty but unhealthy, bored but resigned to it, she looks like the kind of girl who was offered motorcycle rides from a very young age. When she pushes away from the wall, you can't help but notice that her shoulder blades protrude further outward than her breasts do, giving her the momentarily unsettling appearance of having her head on backwards.

"Hi," you say.

"Hi," she says back.

Neither of you extends your hand.

"I'm surprised you're here so early. I thought I'd beat you for sure," you say, finding your smokes.

"I don't like to miss the coming attractions" she replies, taking a sumptuous drag that seems almost transportive for her, and blowing a thin jet of exhaust over your shoulder. "What's your excuse?"

You falter for a split-second, impressed by her metastasized disdain. *This girl was alright.*

"...Likewise, actually. I know they're all online now, but it's just not the same."

"Right?" she concurs. "It's a ritual. Seeing them up there, on the big screen."

"Exactly."

She smiles for a moment, more at the ground than at you, but quickly retouches her Kumadori of cool.

"So, which one are we seeing?" she asks, glancing up at the decaying light of the marquee.

Overhead is a Halloween double bill of arthouse horror. For the likes, there's William Friedkin's criminally overrated *The Exorcist*, which should keep this crumbling shrine in business another couple of weeks while also covering the losses on its esoteric undercard: Jan Švankmajer's *Lunacy.*

A film for the competitively un-faint-of-heart, *Lunacy* is an unscrupulous nightmare of sadism and sacrilege; one that molests the senses and skidmarks the soul. Indeed, there begins a sequence around the twenty-minute mark that, for your money, stands among the greatest visions of mass-trolling ever committed to celluloid. You've seen it at least a dozen times.

"I'm down for whatever," you say, "but if it's up to me, I'd go for *Lunacy*."

"Oh thank God!" she exclaims. "*The Exorcist* is such trash."

"It really is!" you agree, "and I much prefer to Jazzercise my demons anyway."

Your joke slips through her defenses like the shuttle Tydirium, and she gives up a laugh in spite of herself.

"So you've seen this *Lunacy* before?" she asks.

"Oh yeah. One of my favorites."

"What's it about?"

"...Blasphemy? It's kind of hard to describe. It's a Švankmajer, if that helps; Czech stop-motion guy?"

"Oh yeah! I've seen his *Alice in Wonderland*. So creepy."

"Nice. This is a little more... challenging. Definitely not for everyone, but I think it's brilliant."

"Sounds good."

You mill around one another as though on a crowded dancefloor despite remaining ostensibly alone, smoking, studying, both sensing a potential connection. People are quick to decry cynicism as the enemy of romance, but when it finds its match, it can be as aphrodisiacal as any pas de deux.

"Well," you venture, meeting her dark, eldritch eyes, "shall we?"

"Lead the way," she says with a mischievous grin, ashing her cigarette to the black sabbath wind.

Δ

The previews are a parade of festival darlings and foreign oddities - a documentary about kombucha, an adaptation of *Mother Courage* set aboard a cruise ship, and an American indie you feel confident ends with the word "fin" despite being entirely in English. As the psychotic parlor music of the title sequence clangs to life, Claire unwraps a contraband Milky Way she muled in in her purse. Glancing around you confirm, you're the only two people in attendance.

You've forgotten how campy the first few scenes are, but Claire is quick to remind you, petulantly dividing her attentions between the subtitles and her cellphone. Raw meat slithers across the screen, and the Marquis flashes a few Luciferous smiles, but your date remains a bundle of childlike sighs and amused-for-all-the-wrong-reasons chuckles. Fortunately, it's around this time that you hit the twenty-minute mark.

Driving nail after hateful nail into a life-size crucifix already urchinal with them, the Marquis, with enthusiastic impunity, mocks, berates, and challenges all that's held sacred by the Christian faith, bellowing vile epithets to the heavens even as he decries their very existence. Deriding both God the Father, and Christ his son, he demands that they, not he, be made to repent for their unforgivable sins against mankind. He is euphoric; a fearless fallen angel cannonballing into the lake of fire only to pop up doing the backstroke and whistling *Family Jams*.

"Jesus," Claire whispers, returning her dilated eyes to the screen. "Sorry about that."

"It's ok," you reply. "It starts a little slow."

Three hollow-eyed, moth-eaten disciples and three somber, bare-breasted nuns devour a rich chocolate cake in the shape of a cross, smearing their faces with frosted decadence at the feet of this mad Hierophant. The men continue their gluttony as the women slip under the table to perform fellatio on them, their mouths still filthy with moist, brown icing. A young maiden lies enchained nearby, rocking and sucking her thumb to no comforting effect, demonstratively losing her sanity as she's forced to watch this desecrative ceremony unfold.

"This is crazy," Claire remarks, taking a gratuitous bite of her candy bar.

The Marquis performs a heretical perversion of the sacraments as his corrupt Whoredonnas kneel before his altar of depravity. As he begins his anuminous ravings once again, daring God to strike him down, his sextet of Sybarites fall into a rapacious heap of thrusting hips and flailing limbs. The captive girl strains against her irons, contorting her body into a possessed crabwalk and taking on, not unamusingly, a credible resemblance to Regan in *The Exorcist*.

You turn to share this clever observation, but your jaw goes irretrievably slack as your eyes adjust to a whole new image feed of debauchery.

Claire has pulled her skirts up around her pale, whalebone waist and, having foregone even the g-stringiest of sartorial underpinnings, is rhythmically penetrating herself with her king-size chocolate bar, her glistening labia contracting around the confection like an aulostomus. Sensing your gaze has shifted to her, but unwilling to look away from the wanton display onscreen, she reaches over the armrest with her free hand and starts pawing at your zipper. Much to your dismay however, your cock has followed your jaw's decidedly unmasculine lead and wilted into a swoon – a state of affairs she susses out quickly and abandons without remorse.

Increasingly aware of the El Dorado-scale opportunity you're missing, you make a fumbling grab for one of her A-cups, pinching her nipple through her gauzy dress. She moans softly in appreciation, and thinking now or never, you lean in for a kiss.

As it turns out, you have misread the situation.

Recoiling as from a drunken uncle, she takes immediate countermeasures, evading your smooch, withdrawing her makeshift dildo with a shudder of dissolute pleasure, cramming the now-personally-marinated viand between your still-puckered lips, and pressing you face-down into her swampy nethers. Flooded with a dizzying goulash of flavors - like salted turtle fudge glazed in vermouth - your circumoral muscles start working to keep from choking.

"You like that?" she whispers.

"Mmhmmth," you strangle out, your mouth too full to open more than a centimeter.

You're essentially just rubbing your face against her vulva for the first minute, but as far as you can tell she's enjoying herself, and eventually you manage to bisect the morass into your cheeks and attend to her more properly. You reposition onto the floor, your jeans bonding with the sticky cement, and glancing upward you find that she's plunged her thumb into her mouth in all-too-convincing mimicry of the Marquis's unraveling conscript.

This girl was not alright.

You keep at it, her contented "ohs" and your constricted "mmms" creating a lusty, co-meditative neume. Just when you think you might be wrapping up, her thighs press inward, Xenia Onatopp-style, and the whole of her 90-pounds-soaking-wet frame begins to seize and convulse. She grabs your hair like she's trying to weed your scalp, and pushes your face so hard into her sopping mound you're afraid she might break your nose. Your hands flail upward, clawing at her scapulae, busting the clasp of her necklace, frantic to break the surface of this fathoms-deep muff slough and taste a molecule of oxygen. Your eyes close. Your tongue cramps and falls limp. You give yourself over to it – this bizarre, unexpected mouthfucking – and finally, as if sensing your submission, Claire erupts, skunk-spraying you full in the face with hot, orgasmic juices; Scarlatti clavichord and indecipherable Czech swirling in the background.

Δ

You return to your seat, and after making a fussy show of straightening her skirts, Claire offers you an unconvincingly coy smile and a woefully inadequate wet wipe, but otherwise says nothing. You suffer through a string of wet sneezes as your nose expels ticklish drops of lady-load. You have no idea what to do next. You feel like you just took a smegma-balloon to the face. You feel like you've been embalmed from the nostrils down. You feel like you just got curbstomped by a vagina.

You feel amazing!

With respect to the Mohs Hardness Scale, your dick just went from talc to diamond in a matter of minutes. You are utterly ensorcelled.

It's all you can do not to go buy her another candy bar.

At a loss, you excuse yourself to the restroom, and even as you sidle past - your bulge all but Eskimo-kissing her - she remains a Moai of detachment. Only as you open the door to the lobby, throwing a slant of light across her slender neck, do you hear her softly call:

"Hurry back."

Δ

The bathroom is a floodlit pagoda of pretension, outfitted with marble sinks, distressed copper faucets, four urinals staggered like Von Trapp children, and four immaculate stalls. It smells of lilacs and queefs (though that may just be how the world smells for you from now on), and you give your mug a good scrubbing in one of the vanity mirrors.

Alright. Confession time. You haven't had sex in ten months - a barely-conscious, New Year's Eve park-n-ride in the GRUNDL lot with a woman who was absolutely employing you, your van, and your dick in some sort of revenge scheme against her wayward boyfriend (and who promptly moved to Seattle before Valentine's Day without ever addressing you again save the occasional go-thither stare). It wasn't exactly a proud moment of conquesting virility, but it counted goddammit.

You're not a great lay. You know this. For all the unseemly fantasies your mind concocts, your actual track record is pretty fucking bleak. Altogether you count seven women, in your entire life, whom you've successfully cozened into giving your average-sized-everything a below-average-duration roll in the hay. You've never pounded anyone's tight little asshole. You've never cum on anyone's pretty little face. Whatever "it" is that drives women to brazenly appeal for such things, you're acutely aware that you don't have it.

So now, after nearly a year spent jacking off to an obsessive-compulsively curated stable of the world's most seasoned sexual thoroughbreds – imagining yourself on the receiving end of every blowjob and the giving end of every cumshot – turning every evening into your own personal POV bacchanalia – *now,* you've arrived, face-to-snatch, with the real goddamned thing; a girl who, based on all available evidence, may be so incurably bored with everything, that she'll do just about anything.

With a sexual Iditarod of ideas racing through your mind, you grab a stall and try to picture your grandmother being disemboweled by a grizzly bear so as to soften your hard-on enough to piss – eventually forcing out an intermittent, double-helix stream through the resistant ache one might associate with Superman bending rebar.

You wonder what she's into; if she owns a sex swing, or a ball gag, or an adult *Madeline* costume; if she always has to be dominant, or if that oral throttling earned you some leeway to take charge and make requests. You wonder if she'd wear your belt as a leash, or take a modestly-sized eggplant up the ass; if she'd call you big poppa, or effect a thick, Minnesota accent. You have a recurring, Caligular fantasy about assigning a woman ten Hail Marys and then trying to prevent her completing them using only your dick (based on her reaction to *Lunacy*, it could well be in play).

You wonder if she likes porn. Is there such a thing as clit-gagging? Squirt-Bukkake? Might she double down and make you wear a nose-dildo while she grinds her sinewy loins into your jawline for another hour? Suddenly fearful, you wonder if she'll even want to continue the evening, having already gotten hers in spades. Fuck, maybe she's already left. You picture her huddled in a post-cunnil cab, Instagramming furtive pics she took of the top of your head while you slavishly attempted to please her. You wonder what she's capable of. You wonder if she's as fucked up as you.

Amidst all this wondering your drained member returns to attention, and you begin literally twiddling your thumbs to keep from masturbating as a smooth, *soft-serve* shit winds its way out of your asshole, followed by two quick pops you find almost stimulating, like *Nerf anal beads*. Upon standing, you behold a thing of beauty: your initial loaf rings the bowl, bestowed as gently as a *flower garland*, and just inside it, *two brown quail eggs* sink slowly into the antibacterial oasis below. That's right. You've effectively shit a *basketball hoop and two made free throws*. Surely, this was a good sign.

Δ

Already antsily playing *Angry Birds* by the time you get back, Claire turns and asks "so, is there anything else like that scene coming up?"

"Um... not really" you reply, wishing you had a better answer. "That's kind of the money scene."

"I'll say."

"I'm glad you liked it. It's definitely something to see."

"You wanna get outta here?" she asks, her seat squishing as she uncrosses her legs.

"Sure! Where to?"

"I could use a drink."

"Oh..." you reply, unable to mask your disappointment, "well, there are some bars down the street, if you want."

"That sounds fine," she says to her phone.

"Or..." you venture.

"Yeah?" she says, barely looking at you; not giving an inch; daring you to ask her what you both know damn well you want to ask her.

"I mean..."

"Yes?"

"It's just... I think I might have some beers at my place... If you want."

"Oh," she replies, letting your feeble invitation hang in the air like a dairy fart before adding, with an inscrutable, *Meshes of the Afternoon* expression, "I don't really like beer."

Your intestines twine around your empty stomach like piano wire. You gulp back a haggis of Hershey's-flavored effluvium. The demented film score swells to concussive volumes, providing non-diegetic accompaniment to your internal threnody. *How? How did this happen!? How could you fuck this up!?!*

"I've got wine and vodka at my place though," she says, shutting her purse. "It's just around the corner."

And without another word, and a ludic spring in her step, she heads for the exit. She's laughing her ass off, and already halfway through another cigarette before you catch up to her outside.

Δ

"I just wish you could've seen your face!" she snickers, unlocking the door to her apartment.

"So you said," you reply, trying not to sound irritable despite having been heckled the entire walk back.

"Awww, don't be like that. I promise I'll make it up to you."

"Yeah?"

"Absolutely. You're a great sport, and that movie was fucking bananas. It's hard to even find *porn* that ballsy!"

"Yeah," you agree. "Pretty crazy."

Her apartment is a Patrick Bateman wet dream of crisp orthogonals. Leather divans corral a low, marble chabudai amidst a field of plush, white carpeting. A lunaria tickles the chins of some authentic Columbina masks hanging beside a black bookshelf filled with Joyce Carol Oates, Inga Muscio, Mary Gaitskill, and Virginia Woolf. The walls are a deep, bloodbank red, and an onyx kitchen island is the only promontory in an otherwise open floorplan. She slips behind it to play bartender with all the subtlety of Mae West.

"So I have to ask," she begins, pouring two shots of startlingly expensive Finnish vodka and spigoting two glasses of startlingly cheap, red box-wine, "what made you think that was a good idea? Showing me that? I mean, you don't really know me at all."

"Well," you say, downing your shot with resurgent nerve, "I saw where you listed your favorite movies as *Sleeping Beauty* and *Romance*, so I figured either we were really, really wrong for each other – in which case it would be hilarious – or else, that you were down for pretty much anything."

"Meaning what exactly?" she asks, dropping her shot into her wineglass and pounding them in tandem like some Carrie Bradshaw-inspired boilermaker.

"Meaning I was pretty sure you were talking about Julia Leigh's *Sleeping Beauty* and

Catherine Breillat's *Romance*, rather than, you know, Disney cartoons and Sandy Bullock."

"Well color me impressed," she says, quickly re-pouring and repeating her dipsomaniacal maneuver. "I've been on that stupid site for years and you're the first person who's ever picked up on that."

"Well," you say, feigning self-importance, "I *do* write for GRUNDL."

"Yeah, and lemme tell ya, that was almost a deal-breaker from the jump."

"Can't say I blame you there."

Looking like she's about to proceed further with this line of questioning, she instead offers only a demure, almost pitying smile. Your job is of no interest to her, and sensing an unwelcome lull in the conversation, you decide to grab the reigns.

"So that was a new and unexpected experience for me back there," you blurt as, without your asking, she shuffleboards another shot across the countertop. You hesitate, but hesitation feels akin to death here, so before you can think about your tolerances (low), or how long it's been since you've eaten (lunch – Panda Express), or whether you even feel entirely safe spending the night with this potential succubus (take my soul, *please!*), you throw it back with a wince, mouthwash a merlot chaser, and retreat to the sitting area, feigning aloof.

"So?" you spit, cottonmouthily.

"So what?" she laughs, still unconvinced you are anything with which to be reckoned.

"So what's your deal? I mean, no offense, but no one's ever facefucked me in an art theatre before."

"Are you saying it's happened somewhere else?"

"Fuck you."

"Good," she says. "I was starting to worry you were just gonna be afraid of me all night. I can't do anything with that, ya know?"

"I guess," you say, still very much afraid of her.

"Well to hear you tell it, that movie was something of a test for me, yes?"

You regard her coolly, sipping your wine and confirming with a curt nod.

"Right. And likewise, so was my dabbling in the old in-out-in-out with Mr. Goodbar."

You raise an eyebrow, but say nothing.

"Most guys run screaming when I pull shit like that. They watch all this porn - acres and acres of porn - and they think it's what they want. But most of them don't actually have the stomach for it. So, in short, I have tests of my own, and so far, you're doing pretty well."

"Ok," you say, willing yourself calm in the face of mounting anticipation. "So have you ever showed a guy one of your profile movies?"

"Nah," she says. "They're not exactly mood setters, ya know?"

"True."

"I love *Romance* because it's so brutally honest about what sex can be like for women" she continues. "More than any American film I've ever seen anyway. Breillat packs so many desires and experiences into Marie, but never allows her the delusions of romantic love. No big kiss. No wedding bells."

"She doesn't believe in it," you offer.

"Right. Marie wants everything - wants to *do* everything - but ultimately, she finds everything wanting. She's so wonderfully cynical, and now more than ever, that's how women have to be. People always say girls mature faster than boys, and it's true, but what they don't really tell you is that it's because we have to."

"What do you mean?"

"What do I mean? Well, adult men started spraining their necks in the street to look at me when I was eleven years old. They started coming on to me, brazenly, without shame, when I was twelve. I'm not sure why exactly. I've never had boobs, and I don't think I'm some great beauty or anything, but there they were. Just looking. Staring. Waiting. I lost my virginity in the back of an ice cream truck that year... to the driver... and his manager. They were a little reluctant at first, but they'd been leering at me all Summer and honestly, I just wanted to get it over with."

"It was your idea?"

"Absolutely it was my idea. And fuck you if you think you can tell me it wasn't."

"No. Of course not. I just... that's young is all."

"I know it is. Sorry. I don't mean to be defensive. I've just had to defend it a lot."

"I'm sure."

"Anyway, it never really let up after that. I wanted it all the time, and I never had a hard time getting it. The sheer volume of men I could put in jail. They'd have to build a new wing. I was a terror, and they fucking loved me for it. I guess I just projected... something. Innocence? Experience? Youth? Maturity? I don't know. But something they wanted. Something they liked."

"And did you like any of them?" you ask. "Did you like being liked?"

"Not really" she says. "It was never about that for me. I just liked feeling things."

She heads back to the bar, finishing her current drink en route to another.

"So what about *Sleeping Beauty*?" you ask. "I found it fascinating, but at the same time, I kinda felt like there was no way a man could even fully understand it."

"That's very astute of you."

"I also don't think I've ever met anyone else who's seen it," you say, eliciting both of yours' haughty laughter. "I've always wanted to hear a female perspective. How do you identify with...?"

"Lucy?"

"Yeah. Lucy. What do you make of her?"

"Well," she says, her words forming beautiful, authoritative calligraphy in your buzzy mind, "I took it as kind of a modern response to *Romance*. Lucy fancies herself a cynic, just like Marie, and she puts herself in the same kinds of dangerous situations. But she's making her decisions from a position of power. However-many years later, she pretty much has the sexual freedom Marie was looking for. She's had it long enough to be bored by it. So bored she chooses to give it up; to make a quick buck, sure, but also, I think, because she wants to know what it's like not to have it. I found that very compelling. In the end though, it's all kind of a wash, ya know? You can read *Jezebel,* and grow your bush out, and vote and protest til the cows come home, but the more shit changes, the more it stays the same. We can't win. Lucy's the endgame of the sexual revolution."

"Intresting," you slur. "You kinda look like her too ya know? The actress? Emily something?"

"Flattery will get you nowhere," she says, pouring yet another cocktail, "but thank you. And it's Browning. Emily Browning."

"That's the one!"

"Anyway. When Lucy breaks down at the end, I think it's because she finally sees what she's given up - what all women have given up - in the name of equality. We may have more choices now - more agency - but all that does is make us more complicit in the same shitty, patriarchal power dynamics. For a female director to turn her lens back on scenes of bought-and-paid-for, roofied bodies, and use them as a kind of canvas for all the ways men treat women as disposable - treat them as bodies only - well, it's as stone-cold an indictment of rape culture as I've ever seen."

"She agreed to everything though," you argue. "She took the roofies, and she took the money. Can you really call it rape if she was in on it from the beginning?"

"It doesn't matter! It's about the disparity buried in the premise. Feminism can fight against it, and try to build over it, but it's still there, in the bedrock. The master's tools, right?"

"I'm not sure I... what do you mean exactly?"

"What I mean is, there may come a day when women truly believe we've achieved equality. Equal rights. Equal pay. Equal representation. Equal everything. It'll be a nice day. I'll celebrate, if I'm still alive. But it won't ever be true. Not really."

"Why not?"

"Because *you* won't believe it."

"Who? *Me?*"

"You, men. Men won't believe it. No matter how much we achieve, no matter what gains we make, men will always find a way to turn it to their advantage, and believe it was by their good graces that it happened at all. Maybe it's my cynicism talking, but there it is. I can't see my way to a future where men see women as equals."

"Wow... I dunno... Doesn't that seem kind of... sexist?"

"What? Against men?"

"Well..."

"Oh please. Spare me."

"We're about to have a woman President!"

"Maybe..."

"Come on. You can't possibly think she's gonna lose?"

"I think I'll believe it when I see it. But even if she does win, it's kind of beside the point. That he's even in the conversation - that it's even remotely close - is all the proof I need."

"I don't know. Men may not all be feminists, but we're not all rapists either. And he's such a fucking joke - even before the *Access Hollywood* stuff. I just can't see it happening."

"Really? Ok. Let's take it back to film then. How many male directors have made cheeky, self-congratulatory movies about what cads you all are - *Roger Dodger* comes screaming to mind, or any character in any Neil LaBute movie ever - that prick - but we're meant to keep them at a remove; be amused by their boys-will-be-boys antics and 'locker room talk.' Trump's success is the point writ large. These kinds of guys - they just play everything off. They're tongue-in-cheek assholes. Straw man stereotypes. They may be jokes, but only until they're not. Meanwhile *Sleeping Beauty* is a female-directed, female-driven narrative that lives in the truth those fuckers just tiptoe around. Boys may be boys, but men are animals."

"Men are animals?!"

"You absolutely are," she says with a redoubtable gleam.

"That seems a little harsh."

"Really?" she asks before launching into what feels like another fairly practiced rebuttal. "Throughout history, women have been the gatekeepers of sex. We were responsible for keeping the mystery alive. Men wanted sex, and we had it. Men were supposed to be bad, and we were supposed to make them good. But as each generation inched closer to equality, fewer and fewer women wanted to play that role, and it got easier and easier for us to just say fuck it and go get ours. Sure, there'd always be uppity bitches snickering behind their double-wide strollers, whisper-campaigning against us while we blew their husbands in bar bathrooms, but the writing's been on the wall for a long time. The Madonnnas lost. It's just more fun being a whore."

"But," you stutter, lost in the toxic beauty of her manifesta, "I still don't see..."

"So," she interrupts you, "when I say men are animals, I say it as a compatriot. I have seen the light. 'If you can't beat 'em, join 'em' is the best we're ever gonna do. Men are at the mercy of their most base, animal urges, and that's never going to change. The best ones declare it with pride. 'I'm old-fashioned,' he'll say, or 'I'm a neanderthal.' I appreciate that kind of honesty. I mean, you poor bastards think about sex every six seconds. How could you *not* be neanderthals? I'm a world-class tramp and even I can't imagine that. It's insane. Men are animals, without question. But don't worry. I'm an animal lover."

"Oh my God!"

"What?" she says, sounding concerned for the first time all night.

"That statistic!" you reply, stumbling toward the kitchen, suddenly desperate for water. "I hate when people quote that fucking statistic like it's voluntary! Like men intentionally think about sex every six seconds! It's not like we *want* to ya know? We can't help it! It's a fucking curse! I wouldn't even be on that fucking dating site if it weren't for those fucking thoughts flying at me every six fucking seconds. Do you know how much more work I'd get done? How much more successful I'd be?! If my dick wasn't flooding my brain with its needy bullshit every! six! seconds?! It's invasive! It's instinctive! It's... it's..."

"Animalistic?"

"...Yeah," you say, disappointed in your failed mansplanation. "I guess so."

"Yeah..." she says, propping you against the counter and tipping a glass against your lips so your hands can continue supporting your slumping upper body. "That's all I meant, and it's not such a bad thing. We're all just fucking animals."

"Sometimes I don't even know why I want sex so much," you answer between grateful gulps. "I literally hate everyone."

"I know honey. I know."

You finish drinking, and are about to shove off back toward the couch when she leans in and kisses you, tenderly at first, and then deeper, sinking the whole of herself into your mouth; planting her flag; daring you not to requite her.

"Is that better?" she asks.

"Yeah," you say, almost bashful now. "Sorry. I don't usually drink like this. More of a weed guy."

"It's alright. Why don't you sit down and let me take care of you?"

"That sounds nice," you say, as she leads you back to your seat.

"So, all that's to say," she continues, "I am not a delicate flower. I've never wanted a pony. I've never tried on a wedding dress. I've never held a baby - not even my infant niece."

She returns to the bar to mix herself another devil's Cosmo.

"I showed up to my senior prom with a purse full of molly and basically orchestrated an orgy in the girls' locker room. They almost didn't let me graduate, but my grades were immaculate. That Fall, in college, I fucked my way through the lacrosse team for sport. They were supposed to go all the way that year. Instead they finished 3-12, and the goalie broke the star midfielder's jaw while I egged them both on. I didn't really care who won the fight. I just didn't want it to stop."

She saunters back to the coffee table; shot glasses dangling from her fingertips like castanets; her other hand choking up on the neck of the vodka bottle. Before you can protest, she's pouring you another, and you're letting it trickle around your numb, prickly tongue.

"My junior year, a professor left his wife and proposed to me in front of his tenure review board because I said that was the only way I'd believe he really loved me. I was just trying to get him off my back. I never thought he'd go through with it. I said no. I was embarrassed for him. He killed himself a few weeks later."

"Thats…" you slur, before she kindly interrupts you.

"I know," she says. "I know exactly what 'that' is. I'm not proud of it, but I don't really feel bad about it either. I mean, who *does* that?"

"I dont know," you say, tugging at your shirt collar, darkened with alcoholic sweat.

"I don't want you to have any illusions about me," she continues, clearly holding her liquor in ways that, even in the wildest nights of your youth, you could never have managed. "I fuck a lot of guys. And some girls. I like fucking. I'm on Tinder. I'm on Grindr. I'm on five other dating sites besides the one where we met. I write my own number on bathroom walls. I like to cast a wide net. I'm not a sex addict, or a nympho. I don't hate my father, though I don't particularly like him either. I'm not looking for a husband, or a boyfriend, or even a second date. I'm just looking for a good time. If that's not ok with you, then I can call you an Uber right now. No hard feelings."

"Thats ok with me," you say, a little more Otis-in-the-Mayberry-drunk-tank than you mean to.

"Do you have any questions for me?"

You consider her for a moment, and then remember: "I still wanna know whats going on in that Christmas party picture."

"Oh that? Sure, I can talk about that. Why though? It's just a picture."

"Its beautiful! The look on your face. I couldn't stop thinking about it."

"You're sweet," she says in a tone that, while sincere, suggests the tiniest bit of reservation. You hope you haven't taken a drunken misstep.

"So there was this guy Dustin. We met at a show. Some sanitized rave club thing. Cashmere Cat maybe? Who fucking remembers? Anyway, he had molly, so I backed my lil thing up, ground him into the dancefloor, and eventually let him follow me home. It was a fun night."

"Ok."

"I gave him my ground rules, and he seemed fine. He lingered a little long the next morning. Wanted to keep playing. Watched me getting dressed with that doofy look you guys get."

"We can be doofy."

"But I mostly ignored him, and after a while he got the hint and got out. He asked for my number, and I gave it to him, while expressly stating it was just in case he could get me drugs. He said that was cool."

"Uh oh."

"Yeah. So before the week's out, he's basically decided he's in love with me. He's calling. Texting. DMs. Facebook. He will not take no for an answer. I tried to be nice at first - still hoping to score some rolls probably - but he just didn't get it. He took it as encouragement. 'Playing hard to get.' Seriously. Do I seem like the kind of girl who plays hard to get?"

"You do not."

"Right. So then I tried being mean. Like, really fucking mean. I made fun of his size. His technique. His stamina. I was actively trying to give the guy a complex. And you know what he did then? He fucking apologized! Cried and begged. Said he'd get on Viagra. Said he'd start jelqing. Said he'd get fucking dick implants! Whatever it took. Whatever I wanted. Anything for a second chance with me."

"Jesus," you say, experiencing a tremulous tarantism in your pants as your dick speculates as to the kind of treatment that could break a man down so thoroughly as this.

"So, it's been like a month of this shit. He's not letting up. He's found where I work. He's sending me flowers. Presents. Still blowing up my phone every day. He's being fucking impossible. So finally, I relent. It's Christmastime. He wants to take me to this office party. He's told all his buddies about this hottie he banged. It's really important to him. So I say I want $400 worth of molly, up front, and I'll go. No promises whatsoever about the rest of the evening. But I'll go."

"Wow."

"Yeah."

"And that's the party from the picture?"

"Yeah. 'For the Gram' he said."

"Yikes."

"So, we're hanging out. I'm getting sloshed on eggnog, having a decent time talking to pretty much everyone except him. He doesn't seem to care so long as he can show me off to his dudebros. He just was *so* not the person I thought he was. It's amazing the douchebags who can get their hands on good drugs these days."

"Fucking EDM."

"Seriously. So anyway, they've hired a Santa, and everyone's kinda encouraging the girls to sit on his lap - doing the whole fratpack mentality thing - and a few hop up and act cutesy with it - show some leg, kiss him on the cheek, whatever - and everyone has a good laugh. And then they start in on me like 'hey Claire, were you a good girl this year?' and 'nah, she's on the naughty list for sure' and just being oh so clever..."

"Classic."

"And Dustin's giving me this desperate 'please don't' look, and it seemed like as good a time as any to get on with the business of destroying him, so I queued up Quad City DJ's 'What You Want For Christmas,' swagged on over to the man in red, and proceeded to give him the nastiest, skankiest, most stocking-coal-worthy lap dance you've ever seen. I stuck my tongue down his chimney, rubbed my milk and cookies in his face, and shook my ass like a bowlful of jelly. I was half-naked by the end; down to an elf hat and my holiday tights. Pretty sure that Santa suit needed dry-cleaning too. All the guys loved it. All the girls left the room. It was awesome. Dustin took a bottle of Rumple Minze to his office and I didn't see him again for the rest of the night. And that's the story of the Christmas party, and also the last time I went on a second date with anyone."

"You're a fucking gangster," you say, raising your glass.

"I like my space," she replies, cheersing back, "and besides, that guy was a grade-F loser. But even if he hadn't been, I just don't have time for other people and their bullshit. I mean, what's the longest relationship you've ever been in?"

"Well," you hiccup, "Ive been watching *South Park* since day one, so..."

"Ha. That's good. Lots of guys get really serious around this point in the evening. They decide they either want to save me, or beat the shit out of me. Humor is good."

"Glad to hear it."

"My point is," she says, standing back up "I don't need to be saved. I don't want Prince Charming. I want Prince. I don't want to make love. I want to fuck all night. No strings. That's my whole deal."

"...Ok."

"If you can get on board with that, you'll find I'm down for pretty much anything."

"Anything?"

"Anything. I am extremely eager to please. I want to be your go-to locker room story. I want to ruin you for porn. Years from now, when you're old and grey, and your wife's lost her figure, and you need pills to get it up, I want this night to be the thing you think about. So... can you get on board with that?"

You stare at her, your cock quietly lubricating itself with bubbly prejac. *This is really happening.*

"Aye aye Captain," you sloppily salute.

"Settle down. You're not that funny."

"Sorry," you say.

"Don't apologize."

"Sorry," you say again, a split-second before you realize what you've done. "Fuck, sorry," you repeat a third time, which, somehow, seems to endear you to her all over again.

She laughs. "You really don't drink much do you?"

"Like I said. More of a weed guy. A total pothead if you wanna know the truth."

"Well, maybe I can help with that too."

You're so close to the night of your life you can taste it. Even after three shots and two glasses of wine, your every concealed burp still smacks of snatch s'mores. You watch as three Claires accordion outward from the central Claire like paper dolls, and six slender arms reach back to unzip their dresses as they glide toward the bedroom. You're about to dredge your besotted limbs from this fermented ocean and try to follow when she peeks back through the doorway, showing off a smidge of bare shoulder, and a completely new smile - one whose warmth and generosity would've been unimaginable up til now.

"Stay put," she says. "I'll be right back."

Δ

You wait nervously, your ballhair velcroing to your leg hair, your dickhead seat-belted into your waistband. You check your breath, and sniff at your armpits, but this reveals nothing except that you're too drunk to smell anything.

Sweating hollow points, you decide to doff your sweater, but one of your shirt buttons snags, leaving you stuck halfway out. Arms raised over your swaddled head, you struggle against what feels like a full-body Chinese finger trap as you hear her feet pad softly back into the room. Panicked, you try ripping through the sweater in a display of Hulked-out virility, but this too fails, and as you feel her hands begin to fiddle with the turncoat button, you slump backward, certain of your impending ouster. *Please. Not now. Not like this.*

Your sweater pulls gently upward, however, and when the bottom hem rises above your sightline, you are greeted not by the frowny face of failure, but instead a belvedere view as lovely as anything in the Southern Sky. Claire's skim milk midriff, a sweeping concavity of unblemished skin, lies nestled between such feathery, nimbus-white underthings as angels might wear when God invites them to bed. Her belly button is pierced with a tasteful ruby - a raspberry drupelet surrounded by delectable whipped cream. She has the toned, Corinthian thighs of a runway model, and though you're already well-acquainted with them, and the dewy, glabrous nirvana to which they lead, seeing it all in the candelabra mood-lighting of this sexpot apartment, showcased in such exquisite lacies, is like seeing her for the first time.

"There now," she giggles as your gaze moves slowly upward. "Isn't that better?"

You nod, grinning like an idiot.

"Now, what can we do for you?"

Before you can answer, she turns around and bends over the coffee table, subtly shaking a tailfeather in your face, her shapely bottom suggesting two perfect scoops of buttercream Ben and Jerry's. You lean forward and take a nibble, as if trying to avoid brainfreeze, and she giggles again, popping up on her toes before turning around to scold you.

"You better be good. Now close your eyes. I have a surprise for you."

You cross your arms contentedly behind your head and do as she says. Cocooned in eigengrau, your consciousness suffused with images of Claire flouncing around in her barely theres, you hardly notice the flick of her lighter.

Even after she climbs on top of you, you keep true, blindly awaiting her gift.

It's only after her delicate fingertips skate down to pip your nose; only after they part your lips into a wide, expectant pout; only after her own mouth seals itself tightly against them in blissful, hermetic coupling, that you realize what she's doing.

Claire blows a shotgun of thick cannabis smoke directly into your mouth.

[You are a hypocaust.]

You open your eyes.

Now even under ideal circumstances, a single, well-executed shotgun is an inordinately powerful method of getting high - one which can subdue even the most seasoned of cannoisseurs for several hours. Combine it with your current intoxication level, and it's enough to take your head clean off. Suppressing an army of pertussal coughs, you feel smoke escaping your nostrils, pouring out your ears, and leaking around your instantly bloodshot corneas. Your lungs are San Pedro cacti Milt Jacksoning your ribcage. Your stomach is a crockpot electrical fire.

"You like that baby?" she asks, oblivious to your agony. You mumble something unintelligible with what you hope is a positive inflection, and retreat to the pinwheeling blackness behind your eyelids.

You are a motherfucking Kush God you silently admonish yourself. You once made a gravity bong out of a keg shell and a trashcan. You've stayed high for an entire Turner Classic Movies Oscar Month. You can handle this. You *have* to handle this.

You feel her unzip your fly and peel your viscid boxers away from your dick which, despite your body's screaming descent into Defcon 1, has somehow remained erect. She lets out a girlish gasp you can't imagine is sincere, but still would've appreciated were you not trying to keep from swallowing your own tongue.

She gives your shaft a teasing, tantric stroke, and you spasm as she pulls back a strand of spiderwebbing.

"Wow" she says, now definitely sincere. "Been a while has it?"

You gurgle in the affirmative.

"That's ok. We've got all night. Why don't I just get this easy one out of the way for you?"

She wastes no time, wrapping her tongue around you like a caduceus before enveloping you whole, savoring you, letting your flavor react to the esters and flecks of caramel undoubtedly still present in her palate. The cloud of mustard gas in your brain, you're pleased to discover, has a silver lining of sexual durability, and after several minutes of the most creatively improvisational head you've ever received, she pulls away, squeegeeing your effusive tip with a voluptuous kiss.

"You're taking longer than I thought you would sir," she says, feigning grumpiness. "I think maybe you tricked me a little."

"Noooooooooo," you moan, wiggling uncomfortably as cool air hits your damp crotch.

"I don't know how much longer I can wait. If you don't cum soon, I might have to just go ahead and fuck you."

"Dhnt stp," you plead, drowning your vowels in saliva.

"Ok," she says. "I'll keep sucking your big, yummy cock. But why don't you open your eyes. I love it when you watch. You can finish anywhere you want."

With some effort, you pry open your rusty lids, and in that first moment, you connect; her wide, devoted eyes looking up at you, enraptured; yours looking back, wishing they were polaroid cameras; wishing they could watch forever. *This*, you think. *This is heaven.*

In the next moment, you swallow a sour, curdled belch.

In the one after that, your vision blurs and swirls like a sitcom flashback.

In the one after that, you are a busted sewer line.

You are a sulfuric, Yellowstone geyser.

You are the Deepwater Horizon of vomit.

It gushes out of you in Kanagawa waves. It congeals her hair into a shower drain mass, and streaks downward in targeted rivulets, stinging her eyes, forking around her aquiline nose, and trickling between her velvet lips. It Niagaras off her shoulders and turns her bra-cups sacciform - like grocery bags filled with chunky beef stew. It rolls down the inward curve of her stomach, soaks into her pantyline, and pools around her in a slowly spreading stain - a forensic outline of her knees and ankles in the ivory carpet. In one fulsome blast, you've turned her into an action painting; a Tachisme of runny sputum. It's on her. It's on you. It's everywhere.

She falls backward onto her unconscionably perfect ass, stunned, and glares at you with helpless rage.

"Im," you say, throwing up a little more on your dick, "Im so sorry."

She remains silent, evoking a Lilithian contempt that far surpasses even her meanest moments before now.

"Let me help you."

"Don't."

"Please. Just let me..."

"No!"

"Here. I can..." you say, rising unsteadily. "...get you a towel or something."

She quails in disgust as you loom over her, dripping viscous fluid like the fucking Swamp Thing, unable to stanch your body's seepage.

"Get the fuck out!!!"

"But..." you stammer, still too fucked up to grasp the severity of her anger, "but we have all night."

"Are you fucking kidding me!?!?!"

"Whats the big deal? Lets hop in the shower."

You paw at your dick, trying to friskily indicate that you're still good to go. Her mouth now agape in horror rather than welcome, she finds her feet, gathers your clothes, and shoves you into the hall, pants still around your ankles.

"Come on baby," you plead, managing to wedge a shoe in the door. "I was so close. Help a brother out."

She turns back. Her eyes – up til now having resembled nothing quite so much as the blazing twin suns of Tatooine – seem to soften. She drifts toward you like a slimy, sensuous Rusalka. Her lips, still glossed and glistening with your regurgitated stomach acid, smile once more. She presses a hand to your sodden chest, closes the other around your dick, snakes her leg around your ankle, leans in close... and pushes you backward as hard as she can.

You go sprawling into the coarse, lake-red hallway carpeting as she slams the door, shouting a muffled "phuck yoo!" from the other side, and only then – staring up at the baroque wallpaper in a stinking, stuporous heap of treacly bile and matted body hair – do you realize: you are cumming all over yourself.

Episode 14

It's 4:00 PM, and you're still hungover.

Having managed to spend $67 you absolutely do not have at a Taco Bell in the redacted space between Claire's hallway and your bed, you awoke this morning to four-alarm heartburn; your heartbeat a middle school drum corps attempting Don Ellis time signatures; your queso-thickened blood globbing through your arteries like a procession of baby hippos being slowly digested by a gluttonous python; pooling in your chest cavity, painting the walls a radioactive orange, and sealing off your atria with the vengeance of a pepperjack-based Montressor.

By the grace of something that was most definitely not God, you staggered to the bathroom and experienced a kind of oral menstruation, shedding the bloody lining of your esophagus into the toilet before hastily mounting the bowl reverse cowgirl, draping yourself across the tank like a piano lounge chanteuse, and spraying the basin, seat, and more of the floor than you're proud of with as painful and omnidirectional an ass blast as you've ever produced – a *Tabasco-based borscht of shredded beef and soggy cornflakes coated in Doritos dust*. This went on for an eternity, this *Tartaran mess* squirting out of your *batholithic anus,* each time with the wet, smacking thpppppth sounds one might associate with *stomach raspberries* or *Sylvester the Cat* – a *succotash of suffering* indeed – after which you passed out in that compromising position for several more hours.

Now, as you're finally able to stand, you almost vomit again at the panoramic view of your recently evicted innards. Your bathroom is a GG Allin-themed sanguinarium. It looks like you chugged a bottle of Drain-O and survived. You feel genuinely lucky to be alive, but also like a massive coronary wouldn't be entirely unwelcome.

Even after a vigorous shower you still feel disgusting. A few somber pulls from Blaze Pascal help yank you back up to functional, but functional is clearly the best you're going to do today. You want nothing more than to slither back under your clammy covers and cry until you sink into the Lethe, but the enzyme stench of humiliation wafting through your house is too much for your battered GI tract to bear. You have to get out of here.

You start walking with no destination in mind, your headphones on but silent as you fear even the breeziest Ben Webster solo would feel barotraumatic. Discomforting questions grate your mind: Why didn't you eat more yesterday? Why did you drink so much? Why did you even mention weed when you were already so drunk? Why did you risk everything when you were so close? Was it self-sabotage? Fear of success? Fear of failure? Are you secretly gay? So far in the closet you don't even realize you're living your life in some hyper-masculine, over-compensatory hetero-Narnia? Or are you – and this one stands out as a little more likely than the rest – just kind of a dumbass?

That has to be it, doesn't it? You were handed a sure thing, on a silver platter, all sewn up with a lacey, white, Victoria's Secret bow, and instead of unwrapping it and letting it adore you like the lick-happy Christmas slut-puppy it so wanted to be, you drowned it in a bathtub of your own chyme. The words pound on repeat like a percussive footwork sample: you. had. all. night. You. Had. All. Night. YOU. HAD. ALL. NIGHT. She said it herself. It was all there for the taking. She wanted to give it to you. And yet here you are, plagued by vespine thoughts of what might have been.

You're so engulfed in self-loathing you don't even notice the Women in Black until you're hip-checking your way between them without so much as a grunt of apology.

"Watch where you're going!" the ringleader yells at your back, likely not expecting to be heard through your elephantine headphones.

"Why don't *you* watch the fuck where I'm going," you bark into the middle distance before turning around. "Or is even that much action anathema to your little club's code of conduct?"

The women stare at you, dumbfounded. In all these years, they've never once heard you speak.

"Seriously," you continue, happy to have a target for your bilious anger, "you three are everything that's wrong with the world today. How many years have you been at this? How many times have I walked past you in this exact spot? How many other people have? Does anyone ever thank you? Does anyone ask how they can help? Would you have anything to say if they did!?!"

Having rendered their protest silence exceedingly awkward, one of them - the one you thought only spoke Farsi - steps forward to respond.

"Today starts vigil for missing girl," she says in a thick, Middle Eastern accent. "We do every year. To give hope to parents. To help."

She points toward a familiar poster tacked to the gate – one which will remain up through January and accrue a flotilla of candles, flowers, and teddy bears along the way courtesy of recently woke college girls who haven't yet learned to tourniquet their bleeding hearts. It depicts a wholesome-looking blonde named **Cassie Abrams** from about the nipples up – Senior yearbook-style – in a sky-blue cowlneck; gold cross resting atop her pillowy bosom. **Missing: 2008 to Present** it reads. **Please Call (555) 237-9847 With Any Information**; below that, a sad, simple **God Bless**.

"You think *this* is helping?" you scoff.

"Probably more than *you've* ever done," the leader shoots back.

"Jesus Christ," you reply, your pupils circling your eye-whites like roulette pills. "First of all, you don't know shit about me, or what I do with my time, whereas I've observed firsthand how you spend yours. At least Malala over there has the excuse of maybe not fully understanding how little you're actually accomplishing with this personal-is-political, subvert-the-dominant-paradigm bullshit – she's probably coming from somewhere even this level of activism can get you lined up in the street and shot – but you two ought to be ashamed of yourselves. Out here in your mass-produced sackcloth and ashes - most of which probably came from sweatshops, by the way - and, I mean, it's just ridiculous, ok? It's fucking enough already. There are craploads of homeless people literally a block behind me. Have you ever done anything for them? Has your silence ever brought them peace? Do you ever even leave this park? Do you have a web presence? A hashtag? Anything!? You have to know better. You just *have* to. And to pull this poor lady into your gossipy little sewing circle under the auspices of 'making a difference'? It makes me sick. But then again, I guess you're teaching her a valuable lesson about this country. There's nothing more fucking American than standing around doing nothing and thinking you're somehow changing the world."

The women continue to stare at you with what feels like fairly profound sadness. You can't tell if they feel bad for you, or for themselves, or for humanity, but you're confident you've made them feel bad, which has made you feel a little bit better. As you head out, the third one - quiet until now - attempts to get the last word, indignantly exclaiming "we have a MySpace page, if you actually care!" and prompting you to duck your head back through the gate. With your face forming a Bergmanesque, cheek-to-cheek stillframe beside poor Cassie Abrams, you reply:

"This girl is dead you know. She's been dead for years."

Δ

Energized by your clash with those self-deluding squawkboxes, you decide to treat yourself to a trip to The Dust Jacket, a shanty-town of rickety, mismatched shelves filled largely with thoughtless airport purchases, dogeared bodice-rippers, and triumphantly discarded University course materials. All the usual suspects of the secondhand market abound – battered Brontës, abandoned Austens, barely-cracked Melvilles and Joyces, and stacks of Dickens and Michener so tall and ossified they've likely become load-bearing structures. It's not a great bookstore, but you find it soothing sifting through such familiar fare, and occasionally nab a gem for next to nothing.

By necessity, this decision leads you to The Village – a five-square-block, faux-metropolitan quadrangle of bars, restaurants, and bar/ restaurants into which the entire student body attempts to squeeze itself every weekend for close-quarters binge drinking, bathroom hookups, and various other youthful indiscretions to be retroactively misremembered as "best night(s) ever." More like a diorama of city life than an actual city, The Village is where training wheels fall off, hard lessons get learned, and year after year the word "epic" is high-fived into meaninglessness; a midsize hadron collider of sex and substance abuse that spits out more problem drinkers than happy couples, but where everyone goes because it's all there is and how else are you ever gonna meet anybody anyway?

Even during school, you always hated The Village and never felt at ease there, throwing back well shots and yelling over 80's pop while trying to glom onto roving "girls' nights" like so much drier lint to a provocatively tight sweater with temporarily lowered standards.

You drank like a stevedore, and danced like a drunken stevedore, but amid all this excess, no matter how much fun you had, you never actually *became* fun, always lapsing back into showy recitations of pop culture minutia and sad sack appeals to pity at last call. After a while, The Dust Jacket - nestled unassumingly between a Hooters franchise and a 24-hour laundromat - became the only place in The Village you wanted to go.

Still reasonably stoned, you are momentarily distracted by the logo for America's favorite breastaurant - in which those perky twin O's somehow represent both an ample pair of hypersymmetrical b**OO**bs, and the wide, lecherous eyes of a cartoon owl presumably ogling same. You've seen this unsubtle graphic hundreds of times, but never before considered the bizarre, Mulveyist implications. Are these primitive breasts staring at you? Do you want to suckle at the pupils of this nocturnal bird of prey? Is the Hooters logo somehow both inviting *and* returning the male gaze?

You stare at the sign for an inappropriately long time, pondering these questions (and getting mildly aroused). You might've continued even longer had The Dust Jacket shopkeeper's bell not disentranced you, drawing your eyes back to the sidewalk, and the exiting frame of its most recent customer.

And what a frame it was.

Long, thick hair the dark scarlet of codeine cough syrup cascades down a snug, turquoise flannel, its bouncy ringlets tapering off just North of the most perfect backside you've ever observed in the wild. Exquisitely adumbrated in sheer, black lycra, playfully joggling up and down, sassily swaying side to side, its two impudently concupiscent halves canoodle with one another - seemingly locked in ongoing and passionate osculation. Rendering words like "butt" and "ass" wholly obsolete, it brands upon your brain in bold, curvaceous, 100-point girlycue font a single, undeniable word:

Hindquarters

This is not the braying, "omigodbecky" behemoth booty popularized by House Kardashian. Nor is it some buns-of-steel glamour muscle honed into hospital corners by hot yoga and soul cycling. No. It is somehow more natural, and more alien than either of those modern extremes. It's a pair of buoyant, baby sea lions frolicking in the arctic surf. It's two ripe, rosy apples, plucked from the Tree of the Knowledge of Good and Evil. It's the convivial heads of two legato semiquavers beckoning you, instructing you, to "follow the bouncing ball."

As it recedes into the distance, getting smaller but no less substantial, you are overcome by an immediate sense of loss, and the sting of last night's imbroglio creeps back in. This vision of posterior pulchritude makes Claire look like a skinny, bugbitten child - chasing boys on the playground and running off knock-kneed to spread lies about how they cried when she kissed them. You scream silently at her - *Slut! Cocktease! Spoiled Selfish Cunt!* - forcing back tears, and watching the mystery girl with the kundalini allure disappear into some future of which you have no part.

You look at The Dust Jacket and consider an afternoon spent mindlessly shelfreading its disintegrating inventory. Then you look at the Hooters and contemplate - a little more seriously - an evening of bottomless wings and the bought-and-paid-for attentions of a bevy of buxom ladies just a little too prudish or uncoordinated to get into stripping. And then, for reasons you could never explain to any friend, authority figure, or jury of your peers - honestly, without really even thinking about it much at all - you start walking after the girl with the perfect bottom.

Δ

You just want to see her face.

Having gifted her more than a block's head start, you hoof it past another half-dozen boutique coffee shops, Asian fusion eateries, and industrial-chic wine bars in hopes of closing the gap on your unwitting eye candy – your urgency further incentivized by your tempestuous stomach, which is giving a damn Ted Talk on the dangers of alcohol abuse and feels like it must be building toward some grandiloquent conclusion – all the while getting closer to the well-kept grounds of your alma mater, an area you generally avoid as one might a known gang neighborhood or the fallout zone surrounding Chernobyl.

Every time you wander back onto campus, you inevitably see at least three women who make you question your entire approach to life thus far. Buzzing around from boy to boy; collecting the nectar of friendship; dispensing the honey of exploratory, nubile love; adorning themselves in the brightest, most eye-catching colors and patterns of the day; each hoping, consciously or not, to attract a mate during this, the freest and most instinctively sensual time in their lives. College coeds are a source of observable wonder, as fleeting and as sempiternal as the changing of the seasons. You wouldn't be caught dead quoting Matthew McConaughey on any subject, under any circumstances, but you sure as Hell know what ol' David Wooderson means when he talks about girls of a certain age.

That's the blessing and the curse of living in a University town. Each year a new batch of younger, prettier people sets up shop, and each year they feel a little further out of reach.

You can't even skirt the intramural fields, where sports bras and soccer shorts frolic, without facing deep-seated regret. They seem so kind from a distance; so open, and warm, and exceedingly gettable. Would it have been so hard? To be a business major? To join a fraternity? To wear polo shirts? To eat right and exercise? To not see the worst in everyone? To not bring up Nietzsche, or abortion, or *The Seventh Continent* at parties? To talk about poetry, or your dreams, or the stars? To not get high every, single day? To care about something? To care about *anything*? Would it really have been so hard, to just act like everyone else? Might things be different now? Might one of those smiling, laughing, fleeting girls have flitted over and landed on you? Might that have made you happy?

Stepping onto the East quad, you've gained some on your claret-tressed pair of sumptuously surfeited leggings, but still can't help noticing all the pretty young things left undone. It's unseasonably warm for November, and the University's female population is taking full advantage. Sunbathers snooze in the fescue.

Skirts lindy hop in the Fall breeze. Flesh is rampant. To your left, a Golden Grain blonde is positively spilling out of her spaghetti straps as she tumbles around with her Irish Setter. On your right passes a waifish Japanese girl in a dress small enough to have been borrowed from a My-Size Barbie. The style of the moment appears to be pulling an exorbitantly large t-shirt on over immodestly short shorts, fostering the "I'll never tell" illusion that one might not be wearing bottoms at all.

You quietly christen this "the walk of shame look," and the deeper you burrow into school grounds, the more it's fucking everywhere, painting the picture of scores of women just crisscrossing their ways home from one-night stands in whatever they could find on some guy's floor in the dark. It's so commonplace it quickly becomes boring – *of course they're all wearing bottoms* – and as you leave the Village-adjacent portion of campus, still tamping down the cheesy-double-beefy-crunchy contents of your insides, you make yourself refocus on the heart-shaped matter at hand.

Now in the cool shade of antebellum administrative buildings, 70's era high-rise dormitories, and gleaming, modern obelisks all claiming a singular status as the "Center" of some field or discipline - not to mention the cinderblock Circus Maximus around which it all somewhat priggishly revolves - you begin to sense a different vibe.

The snatches of freewheeling conversation have all but disappeared, eerily replaced by random, scattered phone alerts. A ding here. A buzz there. Feet tapping to unheard music. An outburst of laughter at a private joke between a man and his earbuds. The nervous movements of people repeatedly taking their phones in and out of their purses, pants, and backpacks - trying for seconds at a time to look at something else - to engage with the world around them - but always succumbing to that interior pull of the tiny, infinite worlds in their pockets.

Your headphones have slipped down around your neck, posing a vague resemblance to the death collars from *Battle Royale*, and in the distance you hear an inclement weather alarm - a long, low tone reminiscent of moody John Carpenter soundtracks - that bends and pitch-shifts as it bounces off the walls of hallowed academia. To your left, a kid zips by on a hoverboard.

Only about 20 feet away now, and oblivious to anything outside her phone, your butterbutt Beatrice has parked her patifolian ass at a bus stop. You still can't see her face, but a peek of taut, plaid-encased side-boob bolsters your flagging resolve, and when she steps through the front door of a northbound bus, you slip in through the back. The rear of the bus is elevated, offering a lurking, buzzard's eye view of the ground floor, and you deftly perch there while shushing your roiling belly, lest its chorus of urps and gurgles give you away.

When you were in school, public transportation fostered a temporary, forced community – short-lived, but unifying – but now, scanning this mobile hotspot, you don't see a soul who isn't connected to an electronic device. Wires wind down out of ear canals into AV ports, turning every passenger into a self-programming, closed-circuit network. Thumbs scroll through acres of illuminated text as retinas read, skim, skip, watch, burn, blear, blink, and repeat, ad infinitum, absorbing more information in the average day than their great-grandparents did in the average month. The object of your infatuation – whose face, in your captive, Stockholm Syndromed imagination, has come to resemble a cross between Monica Bellucci and an actual angel – is still impossible to see.

You lean forward and attempt to apparate her reflection in one of the windows, but only succeed in glimpsing her entertainment in progress. You immediately recognize it as the "Ozymandias" episode of *Breaking Bad*, and slump back in your seat. This was upsetting. How anyone could make it through five seasons of the most soul-battering, color-draining, pulse-deregulating drama of our time, and decide, of her own free will, to watch its devastating culmination - arguably the most perfectly realized episode of television in modern history - on a screen the size of a playing card, is unknowably beyond you. Look upon my works ye mighty and despair indeed.

Though you find her lack of judgment legitimately offensive, it also abolishes all doubt in your mind. Whoever this girl is, she needs you more than you ever could've imagined. With one hand on her remote, and the other firmly cupping her tempur-pedic fanny, you'll show her a better way. You close your eyes, float out of your saturated latrine sponge of a body, and into a brighter future. You see pajama parties; you in pinstriped button-downs; her in stretchy, curve-nuzzling cottons; feeding each other Chinese food with fumbling chopsticks; blowing cannabis smoke into each other's mouths; Making love, and watching Netflix. Always watching Netflix.

The bus reaches the decrepit Science library, and as you come to, it suddenly dawns on you that you've followed this girl all the way across town. You're miles from home. Your high has completely worn off. It's getting dark out. Thunderclouds are gathering overhead. And you still haven't even seen her face. *What the fuck are you doing!?*

You've never been convinced you're anyone's idea of a "good person," regardless of how they define that highly subjective societal designation, but you're most definitely not *this* either. You don't lose yourself in fantasy over strange women you see on the street. You don't stalk people for hours on end. You've never gone near the third-rail territory of assault or rape. Not even close. You can't say what you thought was going to happen if-and-when you caught up to this girl and her spectacular, apparently-mind-altering ass - but they weren't that. Never that.

You decide right then: you'll stay on the bus until it loops back around, walk home, and set your troubles ablaze, putting this bizarre incident as far out of mind as you can. No one ever has to know.

It's at this moment that the girl unfurls from her seat like a centerfold page, and finally turns around.

She is immaculate. A Godsent knockout. An Alberto Vargas vision come to life. Even after all the disturbing personal revelations you just checked down, you can't help but look, and as she walks toward the exit with all the fluid, sensual ease of Aphrodite stepping out of the Adriatic, she looks back.

She freezes; a millisecond – nothing more; a tiny glitch in her otherwise flawless programming. But you see it all the same: a flash of recognition; a moment of pause. She looks away immediately, and you can't be sure, but you think she takes the last three steps off the bus a little quicker. Had she seen you outside the bookstore? Does she realize you've been right behind her this whole time? Riding her bumper? Your doused headlights glued to her high-beam taillights? Is she angry? Horrified? Frightened? *What must she be thinking?!*

The doors are folding inward. In seconds, the heavy gears will skirl, a carminative plume of exhaust will be expelled, and the bus will move forward into that same exclusive future you wanted so desperately to be a part of, putting irreversible distance between you and the extant knowledge that the most beautiful woman you've ever seen likely thinks you're an inept, bumbling, would-be-rapist.

"Wait! WAIT!" you yell, jumping out of your seat.

You see her head whip around as you deboard, and not knowing what else to do, you offer a feeble smile and the kind of shy, motionless wave that suggests a child waiting to be called on in class. She takes it in, this living, breathing postcard from the edge, and then she begins to run.

You run too, reprising your cry of "Wait! WAIT!" but she barrels toward the Science Library, its double doors a finish line, its interior a safe space from which to yell olly-olly-oxen-free until the nearest campus cop or burly, scholarship athlete comes to her aid. She's faster than you would've thought, considering her dimensions, and you are slowed by the imminent threat of a violent upchucking.

Sweaty and out of breath from what barely amounted to a 50-yard dash, you clear the entryway just in time to catch a final snapshot of those supple, salacious, reason-Juicy-sweatpants-were-invented *Hindquarters* undulating with fearful exertion as they propel her into the women's restroom. It's over. If she didn't think you were a rapist before, she sure as shit does now, and once again, you find yourself on the other side of a door from a woman who hates you.

Feeling like you've been walking around all day in a full diaper, you waddle exhausted into the opposing men's room, grab a stall, and finally wretch, dislodging the last stringy holdouts from your half-digested run for the border.

Tacked inside the door is a flier for an insufferable looking punk "collective" called The Anarchist's Lookbook. They're pimping their new album, *Hate Ain't a Crime,* at a nearby coffee shop/ clay studio where customers are forced to make their own mugs before they can purchase any fair-trade, single-origin sludge with which to fill them. It's perhaps the stupidest "green initiative" you've ever encountered, but each year a new generation of counterculture-appropriating, straight-edge freegan-vegans manage to keep the low-wattage lights on. Jesus fucking Christ college is the worst.

Still breathing hard, and sniveling with self-pity, you take a seat and start defacing the band with Alt-Right iconography while weighing your shitty, shitty options.

Ok. So you know, with absolute certainty, that she's right across the hall - as close as she's been all day. There's only one way in, and one way out. If you were to cross that last line of defense - go ahead and say it, *if you were to follow her into the bathroom* - she'd have to listen to you, right? She could lock herself in a stall - Hell, she probably already has - but she'd be trapped. Even if she started screaming immediately, you'd still have a few seconds to make your case. Was that enough time? Could you effectively convey "I saw you - I was transfixed - I just kept walking - It was an accident - I didn't mean to frighten you - I'd never hurt you - I'm so sorry - Please forgive me - Let me buy you a coffee" before some middle-aged librarian put you in a full-nelson and dragged you to the ground?

For that matter, what if she just attacks you herself? She could already be in position, ready to clock you with a paper-towel dispenser she wrenched away from the wall. Self-defense is basically core curriculum for hot coeds these days, and with an ass like that, you doubt you'd be the first guy she's had to knee in the gonads.

What would you do? Could you bring yourself to fight back? To hold her down? To cover her mouth while you explained your side of the story? Do you have that in you? You don't think so, but as you continue brainstorming you allow for the possibility that no one really knows what they're capable of until they do it. And you've always believed you could do anything you put your mind to.

Shit, you think. *Maybe she should be afraid of me.*

You've now given three-quarters of The Anarchist's Lookbook Hitler moustaches and swastika tattoos. You're about to start on the bassist when a voice emerges two doors down.

"You ok bro?"

"Fuck. I thought I was alone in here," you answer, too startled to convey your annoyance.

"Yeah. Sorry. Wasn't sure I should say anything."

"Whatever it's fine I'm fine," you say in a single, unpunctuated grunt, hoping to nip this act of concerned citizenship in the bud.

"...You wanna talk about it?"

"Um... are you serious?"

"Sure man. Why not? We're just two people here. Sounds like you could use a friend."

"Who the fuck even are you?!" you demand, now more than happy to convey your annoyance.

"Whoa. No need to get hostile bro. My name's Schuyler, and I'm an art major. Who're you?"

You pause, adding some Nationalistic touches to the drummer's ear gauges before answering "Joey. Joey Mengele."

"Cool," he replies, completely missing your contemptuous joke. "You in the first stall, Joey?"

"...yeah."

"You see the flier? For the Lookbook?"

"Yeah."

"That's me on the left."

For the first time all day, you smile. You'd done him first. He was the spitting image of der Führer, if der Führer pierced his labret, shaved half his head, and dyed the other half lavender.

"You should come out to our show tonight," he continues as you slip quietly out of your stall. "There's gonna be lots of cool people there, and some killer tunes if I do say so myself. Should be a great place to... mingle-a."

"Yeah?" you reply absentmindedly, casting about for some means by which to abuse him.

"Yeah! Might help turn your day around. Redirect some of that negative energy. You feel me?"

"Well that's mighty white of you friend," you say with demonic sarcasm, miming a forehead smack of joyous discovery as you spot the army surplus bag sitting just inside his stall door.

"What do you mean by that?" he asks, suddenly wary.

"Oh. Well, with your album title, I just figured you guys were, ya know, down with the movement."

"*What* movement?" he asks, edgier still.

"Do I really have to say it?"

"I think you'd better, bro."

"WHITE POWER!"

"Jesus! No! Fuck no! Absolutely not! Dude! Why would you even think that?!"

"Hate ain't a crime?!" you ask incredulously. "Are you serious? I mean, shit, why *wouldn't* I think that?"

"But that's... you see... so punk rock is... we didn't mean..."

You can hear the fixie bike wheels turning in his brain as he realizes his band's "collective" phraseological mistake. To drive the point home, you retrieve the flier and drop it over his stall.

"Oh God!" he shrieks. "These fliers are all over campus! We pressed 300 copies of the CD!

And 50 more on vinyl! Jesus! Fuck! What are we gonna do!?"

"I can't speak to that, friend," you say as he collapses into the same snuffling despair you were experiencing just moments ago, "but you were right about one thing."

"What?" he asks, loudly blowing his nose on toilet paper.

"You have absolutely turned my day around."

And with that, you hook your arm through the strap of his bag and bolt for the exit before he can even protest. You kick open the ladies room door, lob a stentorian "BITCH!" like a flash grenade, and then sprint out of the building into a howling, torrential rain. Shivering with rage and glee, you run until your lungs give out, letting the storm scrub you clean of the last 24 hours. You ditch the purloined satchel in a dumpster without even looking inside. It's not about that. Not this time.

302

SEASON 2

Episode 15

It's Christmas Eve, and you can't find a tree to save your life.

After your disastrous weekend of stymied skirt-chasing, you spent all of November in recovery, staying turbo-blunted and - other than a brief respite to watch that terrifying sonofabitch pull off the greatest electoral upset of your lifetime - ingesting only the most holistic, reliably happifying comedic fare: all seven seasons of *Californication*; the entire Monty Python catalog; an indeterminate amount of vintage *SNL*; whatever felt easy; whatever felt safe.

Meanwhile, you've been a wight at work - trudging through the motions and smoking yourself emphysemic on 5. Your porn habits have gotten darker and less defensible as of late, and you've been adamantly avoiding OKcupid ever since your pyloric misadventure with Claire. Worst of all, after a screaming match with your student loan officer last week, your teetering self-esteem took an Odessa Steps tumble that saw you stress-smoke two ounces of mids you meant to last all the way through the new year. Having finished off Gander's tropical sensimilla yesterday - the last bud you had in the house - you're now closing in on 24 hours without weed, and your systems are malfunctioning accordingly.

Your epidermis is a Whack-a-Mole of subtle irritations as your malware-infected brain seeks outlets for its unclearable cache of nervous energy. Every zit grows to outsized proportions, suggesting horns sprouting from your cranial ridge. You scratch scabs into erythemal craters, pinch bug-bites into purulent volcanoes; skim gooey barnacles from your nostrils, and pluck tickly nose hairs until your eyes water. Once they've outlived their usefulness, you turn your fingernails against each other, shredding off ragged, scimitar slivers until you can no longer effectively scratch an itch.

When your cannabinoid-levels get this low, some part of you begins waging an anxious battle for smooth perfection. You want to strip yourself down to the studs; peel everything away and start over new. A single, perfect cell of skin.

And that's nothing compared to the psychic toll. Your brain is an apiary for weeks – just a desultory swarm of evanescent thoughts and wrought emotionalities – before leveling off into cumbrous dysthymia. What few tools you have for combating negativity dull, rust, and fuse into a jaggedly soldered farrago of sharp points and razor edges. Your favorite things feel distant and mundane. Your least-favorite things feel pervasive and catastrophic.

All you want to do is sleep, but sleeping becomes impossible - a tossing, turning turf war of twisted sheets and putrid nightsweats - and whenever exhaustion does win out, it's reliably accompanied by vivid, seamlessly crafted nightmares the likes of which your subconscious can generate under no other circumstance; ephialtes that expand, and surround, and consume you like the Navidson house; fears so primeval you're barely aware of them until you're in them, and they're happening, and it's already too late.

The last time you coaxed yourself to sleep in this fiendish state, you dreamed you were driving to college - your van stuffed floor-to-ceiling with every valuable you've ever owned - every underlined-and-highlighted book - every rare jazz 78, and prized, Criterion Collection DVD - every childhood toy and favorite t-shirt - mom and dad right behind you; your future stretching out ahead. And then, with that jump-cut instantaneity only dreams can make sense of, a guardrail materialized; and you were careening through it; and off a bridge; and into a lake. Water came drowning in, but with your last available gasp, you escaped. Treading frantic, chattering with cold, you watched your ruined life sink out of sight, and then looked up to see your parents looking down: not dialing 911, not screaming or flagging down help, not diving in to save you; only staring - chilly imagoes of resigned disappointment - shaking their heads, chiding you, practically mocking you as your sodden treasures bobbed to the surface. Their faces said it all. Their son was a loser. This was typical. They never expected more.

Placed beside this harrowing vision, things like unprepped exams and pantsless talent shows seem almost quaint by comparison. Withdrawal dreams don't traffic in such oneiric cliché. They're smarter than that. They know you better. They dismantle you from the inside, and stick with you long after you're out.

These are the thoughts bombinating through your mind as you gorge distraitly on a dinner of stale Nutter Butters and BBQ Pringles and root through your carpet for stray nugs of dank. You don't know how you let this happen. You're usually so careful.

Back when you still talked to people, there were other heads in your orbit whose lives you could weasel your way into - "hey man, long time no hear from. My cable's out. Mind if I come watch the game?" You'd get your fix, and if they made the mistake of leaving their stash unattended, pinch a pocketful of loose leaf their ablated senses never missed. You knew itinerant, wannabe flower children and self-styled shamans whose homes stayed unoccupied for weeks, filled with more verdant delights than they dared transport any one place at any one time; who left windows full of suntea unlatched or keys lazily hidden beneath bast mats, practically inviting you via their peace-and-love naivete to stop by and harvest their bumper crops.

Yeah, you used to know all sorts of people, and begging, borrowing, and stealing weed was no big deal. But you don't know anyone anymore, and dealers are nowhere near as reliable as addicts.

Having exhausted your THC truffle-hunting skills, you prise a nail from your wall and start scraping together a resin ball. As your fingers busy themselves with this method of last resort, your unraveling mind wanders back to those days, so many of which you've worked hard to forget...

Δ

Though your first few years after college were devoted mainly to bong rips and watching all 460 films ever nominated for Best Picture – put that on your resume and smoke it – you also managed to accumulate enough random drug buddies and fellow cinephiles to constitute an imperfect social circle. Some closer than others. None you particularly encouraged. Just an assortment of not-all-who-wander-are-losters who, despite your standoffish posturing, adopted you as their own.

Over time, however, they all succumbed to the insistent dog whistles of adult life. While you carried on playing mortician for various dying media formats, they started applying for different kinds of jobs. The kinds of jobs that lead to careers. The kinds of jobs that require clean urine just to get to a second interview. When they inevitably got those jobs, they moved to bigger cities. Not always far, but far enough that dropping in for a j and some *Planet Earth* reruns wasn't really in the cards anymore. They worked long hours, and spent their evenings inhaling vaporized cocktails in gentrified zip codes; trending feverishly toward upward mobility. Their tastes aggrandized as they burrowed through the next couple income brackets. Occasional nosebleed NBA seats turned to season tickets on the company account. Old school SNES games turned to expensively accessorized MMOs.

Warehouse rap shows turned to festival glamping. And why not? They could afford it now.

You were often invited, at first anyway, and sometimes you made the effort, once scrimping and saving – selling off some sought-after Arkestra records – to join them at the Governor's Ball in New York. Jay-Z was headlining, and you told yourself it would be worth it, but once you got there it just wasn't the same. They drank $12 Moscow Mules from craft distillery tents all weekend while you nursed overpriced PBRs at $6 a pop. They were excited for Hov, but acted uncomfortable, and a little judgey, when you got to grinding on some muzzy, Molly-trashed blonde during "Big Pimpin'". They smoked – almost, it seemed, as a courtesy to you – but not a ton. Not like they used to.

It wasn't that they weren't happy to see you. They just didn't know how to talk to you anymore. You felt like a cautionary tale; like all those days they'd so enjoyed stopping by your place to cheef and chill had also inspired them to get off their asses and not end up in your same sedentary position. You'd always been a loner, but never before had you felt so alone.

It was around this time that you began to experiment with offline trolling.

The arc of history is long, but it bends toward corruption. If the aughts were all about the power of the internet to bring people together, then the 2010s were decidedly about its power to divide them, and you planted yourself firmly on the front lines during that first wave of violent balkanization. For all the blunts you'd passed with those erstwhile bros, none of them had any idea what you really were; of the bloated, saurian monstrosity into which you'd fashioned your cyber self.

They didn't know, for example, that you were behind a widely condemned viral video intercutting Luke's strafing of the Death Star trenches and firing his photon torpedoes with footage of the planes hitting the Twin Towers on September 11th (this sped up to ludicrous speed and set to "Yakety Sax"). They didn't know that you regularly popped into Christian dating sites to bombard virginal would-be helpmeets with images of "Tub Girl" and "Booyaka." They didn't know that you posted paeans to new microbrews on Al-Anon message boards, or embedded epileptic support group threads with GIFs of high-frequency strobing light. They had no fucking idea.

But no matter how many dicks you photoshopped into the mouths of unsuspecting babes, you grew increasingly dissatisfied. These were bargain basement thrills. People might get mad, or "triggered," or hurt - in the epileptics' case, maybe even physically - but you couldn't *see* it. It didn't feel real any-more. *They* didn't feel real.

It started with the little things. The feints at traffic. The stealing. Minor vandalism (you had a particular affinity for rearranging church marquees; Our God He is Alive = ure God is A vile HOe - it was not a perfect science). One night, you broke into the University's beloved butterfly conservatory with a flyswatter in each hand and executed a frenzied, fritillary holocaust. You wanted to do harm, but not too much. You wanted people to care, but not enough. You wanted to see their reactions, or lack thereof; to see what it looked like on the other end of all those thousands of characters of anonymous opprobrium you'd posted over the years; to see it in the flesh, with your own candent, basilisk eyes.

You discovered your love for karaoke, and also started attending open mics for the singular purpose of tearing down those who'd only just mustered the courage to stand up. You heckled would-be comics with razor-sharp persiflage, reduced slam poets to self-pummeling stutterers, and badgered fledgling singer/songwriters into mixolydian messes of flat notes and open tunings until you were dragged bodily from every bar and coffee house within a 50-mile radius, kicking and screaming "Freebird" all the way out. Several places even put your picture up, like some amateur night outlaw, cementing your online gunslinger prowess that much more firmly in the real world.

You bought a thrift store suit and a powerful Bluetooth speaker, and began crashing Sunday church services. You'd affect solemnity, lying in serpentine wait for the most sacrosanct moment, and then drop some vile Slim Shady bars into the vaulted acoustics like a well-enunciated bundle of dynamite. You pulled the same trick at outdoor weddings (like when you interrupted a bride's long-awaited aisle walk with Ludacris's "She's a Ho") and funerals (like when you blared NWA's "One Less Bitch" as a wilted grandmother was lowered into the ground). Occasionally, you'd forego the music and just sprint through some randomly crowded "safe space" screaming obscenities. It's really fun. You'd highly recommend it.

You weren't exactly happy, but you were – in the addict's parlance – stringing together some good days. And it was smack dab in the middle of this personal Imperial Phase of trollery when, one balmy Saturday, there came a knock at your apartment door...

"Who iiiiiis it?" you called in the deranged tone of Jim Carey's *Cable Guy*.

"Hello, sir! My name's Jamie!" replied a nervous contralto.

"What can I do for you Jamie?"

"Well, I'm with the First Baptist Church, and we're out door-knocking today, and I was just wondering if you'd maybe like to talk for a little bit?"

Oh, this was going to be fun.

You remember you took a long, profligate hit off your bong before you responded, deadening your conscience to whatever you might say next. You'd fucked with plenty of Jesus-pushers in your day, but behind this tremulous young voice, you sensed true innocence; an angelic blonde perhaps; 16 or 17, in vestal white; wholly unaware she was witnessing to Nosferatu.

"Alright Jamie," you said, settling in. "What would you like to talk about?"

"Do...do you want to come to the door?" she asked, trying for all the world not to sound impolite.

"No. I'm quite comfortable. Just go ahead and give me your pitch. Don't be shy."

"Ok... Well, like I said, I'm from First Baptist, and we're out spreading the good news today, and..."

"And what good news is that?" you asked, interrupting just to throw her further off her game.

"Why, the good news of Jesus! Tell me sir, have you heard about Jesus Christ? Do you know his love?"

"Sounds familiar. Pray continue."

"Well!" she said with such excitement that you felt certain this was already the furthest she'd gotten with anyone all day - "Jesus was the Son of God. He came to Earth to teach God's love, and to teach people to love each other too."

"Yeah? And how'd that go for him?"

"I...I'm not sure what you..."

"What happened to the guy?" you asked, biting back laughter. "Does he live around here? Does he tour? Is he on Facebook?"

"Oh," she said, laughing a little herself. "No. He's not... He was killed. Crucified. He died so our sins would be forgiven."

"Doesn't really seem fair."

"Well, it wasn't. But that's the point. We're all sinners, but Jesus was without sin. He was perfect. He chose to die, even though it was unfair, so we could live. And now, if we follow his teachings, we get to live with him forever in Heaven."

"Sounds like a pretty good deal. So what are his teachings? What's he all about?"

"Well, you have to accept Him into your heart. Admit you're a sinner, and that you can't not be a sinner, and that only Jesus's love can save you."

"I dunno Jamie. That sounds great and all, but I'm a pretty committed sinner. Do you really think Jesus would forgive me?"

"Pastor Keith says there's nothing so bad Jesus can't forgive us."

"I mean, sure, fine, that's what all pastors say Jamie. But come on. Is that really true? What if I told you I was doing drugs in here, right now, even while we've been talking? Would Jesus forgive me for that?"

"I...I think so sir. As long as you promised to stop."

"And what if I don't?" you asked, taking another puff to add some poetry to the moment.

"Well...I think he'd still forgive you, if you asked. We all make mistakes. We all fall short. That's why we need Jesus in the first place."

"That's a pretty good answer Jamie. I can tell this isn't your first rodeo."

"Sir?"

"I'm just saying you're doing good. I'm interested. Let's keep talking."

"...Ok."

"So, you think Jesus would forgive the drugs. Ok. What if I told you I was gay? And I was in here being gay with my gay boyfriend this whole time? Would I still be welcome at your church? Would Jesus still forgive me?"

"Ummmm...."

"Yeah. That's what I thought."

"Wait, no!"

"Yes?"

"Well...if I'm being honest...no. You probably wouldn't be welcome at my church. People are pretty serious about that stuff there. But if you want to know what I think, then the answer's yes. Jesus would still forgive you."

"Wow. Alright Jamie. I underestimated you. You're not just a sheep, are you? You think about things. Go your own way sometimes. That's commendable."

"I have a friend at school who says she's a lesbian," Jamie replied, further letting her guard down. "She's really nice, and I don't see how she's hurting anyone. If Jesus can forgive thieves and murderers, I think he can forgive her too?"

"That's very open-minded of you Jamie. I'm really impressed."

"...Thanks? I guess? Mister, are you sure you don't want to come to the door? I feel like this would be a lot easier if we could see each other."

"This is working just fine for me Jamie. But please, continue."

"Ok... What else do you want to know?"

"Hmmmm. Let's see. You already took thieves and murderers off the table. That's a pretty big swath of the world's sinning populace."

"You talk funny," Jamie giggled.

"Yeah, I'm a real card. Alright. Here's one for you. This is a thinker."

"Alright."

"A man walks into a church and murders an abortion doctor in cold blood, only to be killed by police while fleeing the scene. Which man goes to Heaven, and which goes to Hell?" you asked, suppressing more malevolent laughter.

Jamie didn't make a sound, but you remember hearing a pocket Bible being furiously flipped through.

"Jaaaaaaaamieeeeeee? You still there?"

"Yes!" she answered, rattled, like you'd walked in on her touching herself (it was around this point you started wondering if she might be of age, and in any way corruptible). "I'm here. I just... That's a really hard question. It's like a riddle or something. Abortion is murder. It just is. I don't know what would happen to either of them. I think only God does."

"I suppose that's fair."

"I'm sorry," she answered, disappointed in herself.

"Don't worry Jamie. I was trying to stump you, and I did. It's nothing to be ashamed of. Even the smartest people at your Church will probably tell you there are some things we just can't know."

"I guess."

"That said, I have to tell you Jamie, I'm still not convinced I can be saved. I'm a really bad person."

"I'm sure that's not true!"

"Oh it is Jamie. It really is."

"Well, what did you do that you think is so bad?"

"Wow. That's kinda personal Jamie."

"I'm sorry... I just thought..."

"No, it's ok. I respect you asking. That took guts."

"..."

"Honestly, it's not any one thing," you told her. "It's a hundred things. A thousand. Maybe even a million. It's a million little bad things that I've done, and continue to do, every day, even though I know they're wrong. Even though I know they hurt people. I do them, these little things, and I enjoy the Hell out of them. They don't make me feel bad at all. They make me feel good. Do you know what I mean Jamie? Does being bad ever make you feel good?"

"...Maybe. Sometimes. At first. But I always feel bad after. I always try not to do it again. Try to do better."

"See, that's the thing Jamie. I don't try to do better. If anything, I try to do worse. To top the last bad thing I did. It's like a game. How much can I get away with? How bad can I be? It's fun. I don't really want to stop. I don't really want to be forgiven. I'm not really sorry. I figure it's just the way God made me, ya know?"

"I don't believe that," Jamie said, fear creeping in.

"Why would I lie?"

"Well, lying is bad. Didn't you just say you like doing bad things?"

"Ah, very clever Jamie. But then, wouldn't that just prove I was telling the truth?"

"..."

You could hear her brain working overtime, straining against new concepts and traps of logical thinking she'd likely never dealt with before. She'd reached for the carrot. Time to give her the stick.

"Ok Jamie, I think maybe we've waded out past your theological depth here. That's alright. I'm a difficult case. Why don't we try a different approach? I still think you can help me."

"Really?"

"Sure. You just got a little off track. Maybe instead of telling me all the good stuff that'll happen if I accept Jesus, you should try telling me about the bad stuff that'll happen if I don't."

"Well..." she said, hesitant but firm, "I guess you'd go to Hell."

"I see. That sounds pretty serious."

"It is," she answered, attempting gravity.

"You think I should be concerned?"

"Well, Pastor Keith always says it comes down to one question: if you die today, will your soul be with Jesus? If the answer's 'no', or if you're not sure, then you need to get right with the Lord."

"Wow. That's heavy stuff Jamie. But I've gotta be honest, I don't have any reason to think I'm gonna die today. Or anytime soon. I lead a pretty dull life. What's to keep me from just carrying on, doing all the terrible things I so enjoy doing, and accepting Jesus at the very end? What's the difference? That's what Charles

Darwin did. And Christopher Hitchens. Probably the two most famous atheists of all time. Seems like a pretty smart move. Have your cake, ya know?"

"Um, I'm not sure about all that, but the Bible says no one knows the day or the hour. You could slip in the shower, or get hit by a bus, or get struck by lightning. You just don't know."

"So I should convert to Christianity just in case? Like an afterlife insurance policy? That's pretty weak Jamie. I think you can do better."

"...Um, ok. What about the end times then? No one knows when that's coming either. It could happen any day. Jesus could come back and take all the saved people to Heaven, and you'd be stuck here until you died and went to Hell. It'd be too late. Just pain and suffering forever."

"Ugh. Ok. That's kind of the same argument conceptually Jamie, but fine. I'll bite. If the apocalypse came tomorrow, it'd be the happiest day of my fucking life."

You recall hearing a muffled gasp at your use of the abhorrent F-word.

"Pardon my language, Jamie. I told you, I'm not a good person. But in all seriousness, and I mean this from the bottom of my heart, the apocalypse is the only cause of death that doesn't scare me even a little. If it happens in my lifetime, I'll welcome it with open arms."

"But... but why!?"

"FOMO, my friend. It's the ultimate FOMO. The only thing that scares me about dying is not knowing what happens next. What'll happen after I'm gone. I hate the thought that shit will just keep on keeping on, getting better, or worse, or more interesting, or less. Life's just a story, and I want to know how it ends. Ergo, if the apocalypse comes, that's it. There won't be an after. There won't be anything to miss out on, so there won't be anything to be afraid of. Maybe it's narcissistic, but if I die, I feel like the rest of the world should be good enough to up and die with me, and realistically, the apocalypse is the only way that happens. Plus, I'm guessing the demons will look badass, and there'll be, like, explosions and shit. Rape and murder all over the place. Just a bloodbath, fuck-fest, free-for-all. I honestly can't wait."

"That's horrible!"

"What'd I tell ya kid?"

"But what about all the people?! Don't you care about anyone?!"

"Fuck 'em."

"Please stop cursing."

"Fuck. Sorry," you said, finally letting a ghoulish cackle slip out.

"It's ok. It's just... to want the whole world to end? I don't understand. Isn't there anyone that matters to you? What about your boyfriend?"

"Oh, I'm not gay. I was just fucking with you. Whoops. Sorry. *Messing* with you. I'm totally straight."

"Ok. A girlfriend then? Don't you want to get married someday?"

"Love doesn't last Jamie. Marriage is just an outdated system people use to pair off, save on their taxes, and spend the rest of their lives reassuring each other they're doing better than the friends they left behind."

"Well... what about kids? Don't you want kids?"

"Nah. Having kids is a purely selfish act. It's a free pass to abandon perspective; a biological do-over. People only have kids once they realize they've given up on their own dreams."

"But don't you want to be happy!?!"

"No one's happy Jamie. Anyone who tells you he is is either lying, or an idiot, and probably both."

You could hear her sniffling through the door now, fighting back fat *Les Misérables* tears.

"Jaaaaamieeee. You still with me?"

"...Yes..."

"I know this is hard honey, but it's the truth. The world is a bad place full of bad people, and I am absolutely one of them. I never had any intention of accepting Jesus, or coming to your church, or even opening my front door. I've been lying to you this entire time. Do you understand?"

"But why?! Why do you want to live like this?! Jesus is real! He is! Please, just open the door. I promise there are good people out there who want to help you!"

"Who wants to help me, Jamie? Your church? Pastor Keith? You?"

"Sure. All of us. Everyone."

"Kid, I hate to break it to you, but religion is nothing more than groups of scared people getting together once or twice a week to pretend like they know what's going on. Pastor Keith doesn't know shit. Your parents don't know shit. You don't know shit. Not about life. Not about death. Not about the fucking apocalypse. And not about me. You don't know a goddamned thing. And what's more, I don't even believe there's any way you could. The very idea of empathy is presumptuous as Hell. Like anyone could ever really understand how anyone else actually *feels* about anything. It's the height of arrogance. Every connection we make, every person we choose to care about, every kindness we attempt - every fucking thing we do Jamie - is just a distraction from the inevitability of death. Even love... Especially love."

There was a moment of silence, like an infant's deep inhale before a tantrum, and then she burst. A wailing wall of sound. The ugly, honking, sobbing, gagging, uncontrollable anguish of a person whose heart has been broken. You'd done it. Some part of her would never recover from this day.

Thinking you might tempt her inside with her first puff of lye, or maybe even soothe her sorrows in the back bedroom, you finally got off the couch. People, you figured, could be extremely open to suggestion when their entire worldview had just been shattered.

When you opened the door, however, you were surprised to discover that Jamie was no barely-legal beauty. He was, in fact, a young boy, no more than 12 or 13, with a mop of brown hair and thick prescription glasses that self-tinted in the Summer sun. Sitting on the ground in cargo shorts and a youth group t-shirt, he was flipping through his Bible - too quickly to read anything, but so intently that he didn't even look up until you said his name again.

"Jamie?"

"What?!"

"Jesus," you said, feeling true remorse. "I'm sorry kid. I thought...well I thought you were someone else."

"Maybe you should've answered the fucking door," he said, stomping the penultimate word like a tent spike, enjoying the power of saying it for what you were sure was the first time.

"You shouldn't say that."

"Why not? You said it like a jillion times."

"It's a bad word. I told you, I'm a bad person."

"Maybe I'm a bad person too."

"Trust me kid. I've been at this a long time. You're pretty clearly not."

"I want to hit people sometimes," he said. "Other kids."

"That doesn't make you a bad person."

"They pick on me."

"That makes *them* bad people."

"Because of my voice."

"Yeah. What's the deal with that anyway? You in the Vienna Boys Choir or something?"

"I have an undescended testicle," he said with the deep sadness of a child whom life had forced to learn the word testicle at much too young an age. "It's genetic."

"That sucks."

"Yeah. All my friends make fun of me. They call me uni-ball."

"Friends are just people you compete with until one of you gets so resentful that he can't be in the same room with the other one anymore," you said, laying another personal truism on the kid, but this time with kinder intentions. "Fuck 'em. You don't need 'em."

He continued flipping pages like he was trying to rotoscope them to life.

"Well, I really am sorry. You were doing such a good job talking, I just assumed you were older."

"And a girl?"

"...yeah."

"Yeah."

"You know, I went to church when I was your age. It's...not all bad."

"That's not what you said before."

"I know. But still."

"My Mom says God's testing me. That if I have faith, everything will be alright someday."

"That's...that's a nice thought," you said.

"Are you a test too?"

"..."

Having hit the back cover, he chucked his Bible angrily against the side of your building, and you both turned and watched it glance off into the weed-choked pocket yard. A moment later he stood up and looked you dead in the eye, as if taking a mental snapshot. He didn't say anything else. He didn't look back. He just turned, and walked away.

Δ

You kept trolling, to some degree, but it was never quite the same after that. You'll still lob the occasional stick of thermite into Breitbart or The Daily Caller, but you've mostly let the online pot-stirring go and resigned yourself to only the most benign acts of public mischief (give or take the occasional karaoke riot). That day, you found the hurt you'd been looking for, and it felt... uncomfortable. You weren't sad, or even particularly repentant. You just didn't see the point. The world didn't need you to create more people like you. It already had plenty. Best to focus on them. Like *Dexter*, or Omar from *The Wire*, a man's got to have a code.

Having accumulated a decent-sized ball of creosotal sludge, you eagerly banish these memories back to the cerebral charnel house from whence they came. After 24 hours without, the toxins are fast-acting and potent. Tomorrow will bring the dreaded withdrawal dreams - there's no avoiding them now - but tonight you'll sleep like a baby. Like a rock. Like a baby that's been hit with a rock.

Sometimes, in these dire hours when you can't get sorted and you're peeling yourself apart by the layer, you fantasize about having something removed, or drained - some subcutaneous thing that, upon resection, would suddenly render you a happier, healthier person. One who doesn't need to stay forever high. One who doesn't traumatize strangers on the internet, or children through his deadbolted door. One who just lives and feels things, the way almost everyone else seems to do without issue. You doubt this is the case - that some malignant body pressing against your pleasure center is, in fact, the source of all your troubles - but it's a nice thought. Almost as nice as the idea of Jesus. A chance at salvation, tucked away, somewhere inside.

Episode 16

You sit alone at a table for eight, picking at your food and watching dozens of well-heeled white people attempt the Harlem Shake en masse. The worst of your detox symptoms have subsided, but you're far from out of the woods. Your fingers tap of their own accord, first to "I Wanna Dance With Somebody," and then "Uptown Funk," and then "Shout," lightening their impact at measured intervals as the Isleys implore everyone to get "just a little bit softer now." Only then, amid this relative quiet, do you hear a sweetly sarcastic voice drift over your shoulder with the slightest of Carolina accents.

"You look like you're having fun."

You turn around to an uncommonly attractive torso cinched into a Midori-green dress with a checked, pink and white ribbon-bow. Your eyes rove across this eye-popping ensemble – lingering a half-second too long on the curvaceous, flip fantasia cantaloupes nestled halfway up – before landing on the Disney princess eyes of a powdered-sugar cherub whose luxurious, flowing river of chestnut hair is giving the chocolate fountain behind her a run for its money.

You are crushed. Without a word, you are certain she paints, and bakes her own bread, and speaks Dutch, and knows the Foxtrot (not that you do, but she'll teach you), and a hundred other things you cannot possibly yet know.

"...Hi..." you say, tongue-tied by even that solitary syllable.

"Are you?" she smiles, well aware of the impact crater she's just made in your brain.

"Am I what?"

"High?"

"Oh. God, I wish. My connect's been dry for weeks. Fuckin' holidays, right?"

"Wow. That was a little more blunt than I was expecting."

"Really? Because it's a little less blunt than I was expecting to have for this Brooklyn roof party of a wedding."

Her eyes somehow find space to widen at this, and then quickly scan the room before inviting you to peek inside her tinselly, silver clutch. There, beside an Eisenhower-era lighter, atop a bed of makeups and ponytail holders, rests a pristine joint - spiral striped with red lipstick to resemble a tiny candy cane.

"I saw a gazebo outside," she says. "I'm going to go smoke a perfectly ordinary, 100%

legal cigarette. Wait five minutes and come find me?"

"I love gazebos!" you reply.

"Yeah. You had that look about you."

At that, she turns toward the door, her delectable, Cinnabon backside wiggling in time with "Apache (Jump On It)." Your tongue a carpet roll, your eyes torpedoing out of your head like a zoot-suited cartoon wolf, you somehow manage to ask, "What's your name?"

"Eleanor," she replies over her shoulder. "Eleanor Jacob. But most people just call me Elle."

"Elllllllllllllllllle," you repeat, elongating the phoneme as though you were learning the twelfth letter of the alphabet for the first time. You open your mouth again, almost certainly to say something redundant or too-clever-by-half, but thankfully, she's already gone.

Δ

It's dark out, but a ring of toadstool lanterns encircles the gazebo, creating a kind of parhelion effect around Elle's vulpine figure. Others dot the circuitous, cobblestone pathways - a Celtic knot of wrought iron garden wickets and thatched lattice pergolas - all leading, in perfect harmony, toward that central point - a chipped white porch swing rendered temporarily effulgent by its radiant occupant. Legs crossed elegantly beneath that Christmas carol of a dress; lips smoking a slender, perfectly legal cigarette; eyes looking up through the Spanish moss at the winter stars; she waits for you.

"Welcome to the afterparty," she says. "Care to sit?"

"Sure," you say, taking your place beside her and pushing off hard to give the pair of you a quality ride.

She lets out an enthusiastic "wheeeeee!" and you both pull your knees up, enjoying the breeze around your corseted and cummerbound bodies. She lights another cigarette and hands it to you. She's smoking Capris, an elongated, anorexically thin brand usually reserved for sorority house mothers.

"I don't usually smoke these," she says. "But one of the other bridesmaids left them in the dressing room, and I was like 'free is free,' ya know?"

"Free is free," you agree.

"So how do you know Artemis?" she asks, ashing into a tulip.

"Shit. Did you see how many people were in there? I just assumed everyone in the tri-state area knew Artemis. I think I saw Lil Wayne by the ice cream bar."

"Actually, Wayne's in Cabo this week. That's his cousin, Medium-Sized Rob. His mixtape drops next week."

"Any good?"

"Oh, it's next level, no doubt."

"I mean, it'd pretty much have to be, right? At least height-wise," you respond, thrilled by the ease with which you've fallen into patter.

"Seriously though?" she asks.

"Seriously? I've known Artemis since high school. I was kind of her... what do you call a beard for a lesbian?"

"You were her heels?!"

"Ha! That's pretty good. Yeah. I was her heels until we graduated. Then it was off to the college pussy buffet. Didn't see her much after that."

Elle snorts and little puffs of smoke escape her button nose. "College is great for that," she agrees. "Real lesbians. College lesbians. Slutty straight girls. Suggestible drunks. It's a wonder guys get laid in their 20s at all."

"We don't really," you reply with what you hope is a rakish, Han Soloesque half-smirk.

"Aww. I'll bet you did alright. If the great Artemis, It-Girl extraordinaire, found you worthy of being her heels..."

"I guess. So... dare I ask how *you* know Artemis?"

"Is that *really* what you want to ask me?"

"...sure."

"We were roommates in grad school. Sarah Lawrence."

"Oh," you say, audibly relieved.

"And then we dated for two years after that," she continues, enjoying bursting your bubble.

"Oh."

"Yeah. I wouldn't go so far as to say I was a college lesbian, but I definitely stayed drunk a lot of the time, and, well, I'm sure you know how persuasive she can be."

"I missed my uncle's funeral for her cat's bat mitzvah, so..."

"I almost went to that!"

"Oh, it was a Hell of thing. I have no regrets. My uncle was an asshole."

"Mazel tov."

"So don't take this the wrong way, but the thought of you and Artemis together is pretty much gonna replace porn for me for the next week."

"Not at all. We were hot."

"That's big of you."

"Yeah. It was great for a while, but as much as I hate to admit it, at the end of the day, I just need some good old-fashioned deep dicking."

"Did you just quote *Chasing Amy*?"

"I did."

"Wow. Marry me."

"Did you just quote *Arrested Development*?"

"Uh... yeah. That's totally what I was doing."

Elle smiles again, a warm, natural smile you can't imagine ever getting tired of. Her openness puts you at ease. She speaks in a spritely soprano bursting with the wholesome, apple-cheeked sincerity of American classical music. Copland, perhaps. Or the *Parks and Recreation* theme song. She reminds you of a simpler time, when the only difference you knew between the sexes was that girls wore dresses and had long, pretty hair.

"So you know your movies then?" she asks.

"I like to think so."

"I wrote reviews for our college paper. Not endorsements so much as, like, weekly elitist irony. Feminist takes on Stallone flicks. Queer undertones in *Toy Story*. Stuff like that."

"I mean, Buzz and Woody? Come on. That practically writes itself."

"Right!?"

"That's cool though. I once wrote an article about Pixar's *Up* as an extended metaphor for the old man's descent into dementia."

"Wow. That's dark."

"Pixar's dark. I'm just the messenger. Did you see *Wall-E*? People think it's just about cute robots saving people from global warming or whatever, but for my money it's the most cynical film of the 21st century."

"Awwww. I think that's overstating things a bit."

"Think about it though. It's essentially a movie whose lesson is to stop watching movies. It teaches kids that if they don't get out of the theater, or off the iPad, or away from whatever terrifying, ocular implants Apple comes up with next year, they'll end up morbidly rotund Weebles and spend their golden years on a perpetual monorail watching, you guessed it, more fucking movies. But you have to watch the whole movie to learn that lesson! And even then, the humans don't save themselves. Robots do! Advanced electronics who are, by the way, also totally smitten with movies. It's supposed to be profound that Wall-E loves an old-timey movie like *Hello Dolly!*, but it's actually completely irrelevant. In *Wall-E*'s future, even the robots need to escape. Honestly, the only lesson I took away is that we're already fucked."

Somewhere during your Pixar jeremiad you stood up and started pacing. Elle seems, if not upset, then at least concerned. She hands you another Capri.

"Sounds like you've given this a lot of thought."

"...Well... You know..."

"Did I ask what you do for a living?"

"I write for GRUNDL. I hate it, but it's criminally easy, it pays the bills, mostly, and it gives me time to work on my own projects."

"What kind of projects?"

"I have a blog for, well, for pop culture polemics like the one I just foisted on you there - sorry about that. The robots are cute. I'm just a crank."

"Anything I might've read?"

"It's pretty under the radar. I haven't posted anything in years."

"Why not?"

"Eh. GRUNDL kinda took all the fun out of it for me. I do have this piece I've been kicking around about *Friends* and the death of individuality, but it's not really there yet."

"I'd read that for sure. What's the site called?"

"*ForDrapersOnly*. It started as a *Mad Men* fan page, once upon a time."

"You're kidding!"

"No. Why?"

"I've read a ton of your stuff then!"

"Really?"

"Yeah! It's been a while, but yeah. Artemis actually turned me on to it. She never mentioned she knew you though."

"Typical."

"So, wow, you really hate Almodóvar huh?"

"Oh God. You're one of those?" you chide, playfully.

"I think he's brilliant! You're so hard on him."

"He's so overrated!"

"How is that his fault?! The man isn't in charge of how he's perceived. Come on. You can do better than that."

"Alright. I guess what really bugs me is the histrionics. He takes warmed over melodrama and treats it with the pathos of real life. He's basically just making telenovelas with nicer camera equipment."

"So?"

"So? That's your response?"

"Yeah. So what if that's what he's doing? Aren't we all looking for a little melodrama in our lives? And aren't soap operas just a concentration of the most interesting things that happen in the average lifespan anyway? Amnesia and evil twins notwithstanding."

"But how is that helpful? What's he adding to the conversation?"

"I think he's adding perspective, like a lot of international filmmakers have, that transcends borders and easy stereotypes. He has a handle on something unique and true about life everywhere. I think he's about... *feeling everything*. A dramatic maximalist. He's trying to speak to, and for, people who experience real tragedy in their day-to-day lives; people for whom tragedy is ever-present. He wants to give the most emotionally shuttered, internally hardened people something that can let them breathe, and cry, and forgive. He wants men to get past their machismo, and women to get past their hysteria, and people to feel pleasure, and pain, and love, and hate in less destructive ways. He attacks life from the extremes and works his way back to the everyday."

You lean back, smiling in spite of yourself. You're not sure you've necessarily lost this argument, but you want to.

"I think you're overselling him a little," you say, playing devil's advocate just to hear her keep talking. "What about *Talk to Her*? What about *The Skin I Live In*?"

"I'm not saying he's perfect. But he's authentic. Even when his films don't quite hang together, he always has something to say. That's more than most filmmakers can claim. I think if he doesn't always play well in America, it's because we have it too easy here. His movies seem overwrought – even silly – because our lives are so much... safer."

"That's... really interesting. I don't know if I like him any better, but you've definitely made me want to revisit some things."

"I'll call that a win."

"So, at the risk of sounding self-involved, have you read anything of mine that you liked?"

"Oh, I liked the Almodóvar stuff. Don't get me wrong. It's thoughtful, and funny. I just didn't agree with it. There's definitely a difference."

"Ok. Anything you agreed with then?"

"Hmm... Well, I loved your dissection of *Gilmore Girls* as Socialist agitprop. Fucking hilarious. But I'm pretty much always excited to meet a man who's engaged with *Gilmore Girls*."

"Yeah. What a weird show."

"Do you write anything else? Anything... personal... or whatever?" she asks, trying not to sound condescending, and mostly succeeding.

"Well," you start, pausing just enough to let her know this isn't something you share with everyone, "I have a screenplay I tinker around with."

"Oh yeah? What's that about?"

"Ummmm... it's like a postmodern meta satire thing. Like Tarantino meets Craig Zahler, with a little Ryan Murphy thrown in. But not in a serious way. I actually kind of hate Ryan Murphy. Well, I love to hate him, if you know what I mean."

"Ok. But what's it *about*?"

"Um... I'm still kind of working that out. It's a lot easier writing about other people's art than it is making your own, ya know? But I'm trying. I'm finding my way with it."

"That's cool," she says, taking a drag from her tiny, doll cigarette. "You don't need to talk away all your ideas. I'm just being nosy."

"No. It's nice of you to ask. People generally don't."

Elle looks at her knees, uncertain; a small caesura in the conversational sonnet you had, until now, been composing in tandem.

"So what about you?" you ask.

"What about me?"

"What do you do?"

"Oh, right. Well, I'm kind of between things, creatively. Right now I work as a PA for this little clothing company - affordable couture stuff. Before that I did layout and wrote some copy for *Cosmo Girl*, but I was actually starting to smell my soul decompose, so I quit."

"Wow. What does decomposing soul smell like?"

"Like soggy money you find in those wooden outhouses by the beach."

"Gross. And, if you don't mind my asking, from whence does decomposing soul smell emanate?"

"I do mind a little," she laughs. "A girl has to have her secrets."

"Come on now. I fully expect my soul is decomposing too. I mean, have you read GRUNDL?"

"I'm ashamed to say I have. I'll read pretty much anything I can get my eyeballs on about the Kardashians."

"Ok. I'm judging you hard right now, but suffice it to say, you know what I'm up against. What if my soul's decomposing and I don't even know it? I'm a guy. I'm probably emanating weird smells all the time. Where do I sniff out rotting soul carcass?"

"Well, it starts in your belly button."

"Really?"

"Yeah. Especially if you have an innie. If you're an outie, you're more likely to smell it through your ears."

"How do you smell your own ears?"

"It's tricky. You might need some bendy straws."

"Well, thank God I'm an innie."

"Me too. Outies are so gross."

"They really are repulsive."

"Agreed."

"Agreed."

You both giggle for what seems like the hundredth time, and you shift ever so slightly within the caress of the swing, preparing to lean in for a kiss. But Elle turns her attentions to her purse, either failing to notice your attempted move, or worse yet, pretending not to, and you decide to hold off. After some poking around she returns with the candy-striped joint.

"So I don't really smoke much," she says, flicking her lighter with Hepburn aplomb. "But I was dreading tonight. Artemis can be so…"

"Exhausting?"

"Exactly. Here. You win the green hit for that."

"Don't mind if I do," you say, sparking up with Bogart alacrity.

"So, what do you write for GRUNDL? Presumably, not the Kardashian stuff."

"No. We have some actual goblins who handle the Kardashian stuff, along with the *Real Housewives*, *The Bachelor*, and all the Royal Weddings.

"God, those hats."

"I know, right? Pippa's fly though."

"Do not get me started on Pippa. I'll throw so much shade you'll think it's a goddamned lunar eclipse."

"Whoa. Alright. Fuck Pippa. She's dead to me."

"Good," she replies, pulling the j from your lips for a victory puff. "Triflin'-ass bitch."

"So yeah," you continue, more than a little turned on by this display of petulance, "I do more highbrow pop culture stuff. Prestige television. Top 10 Oscar snubs. Best Argentinian Flicks You've Never Seen But Should. Crap like that. Also some music here and there. Mostly hip-hop, but only because they won't let me write about jazz."

"I'm not gonna lie," Elle says, "you just hit, like, eight of my cultural erogenous zones. Are you Jesus?"

"I... I don't think so."

"You have to tell me if you are. Jesus and cops. Those are the rules."

"That makes sense. There aren't many things I hate more than Jesus and cops."

She laughs again, and you've heard it so many times now you're starting to pick out the specific notes. It's a tinkly tremolo of a thing - like an Ahmad Jamal piano solo.

"So what's your favorite movie?" she asks, handing the joint back.

"Oh, come on. That's such a huge question. What does 'favorite' even mean? Are you asking what formative movie from my childhood made me first realize how much I love movies? Are you asking what movie I love watching over and over again, anytime, day or night? Or are you asking about, like, greatest artistic achievement? Because I can answer all three, but picking one is nearly impossible. I'd be more comfortable telling you who I voted for last month, or how I lost my virginity. Favorite movie is huge."

"Ok, then let's take it in order. What's the childhood one?"

"*Star Wars*. And don't ask which one. I take the trilogy as a whole, just as George Lucas intended. Every stick in every backyard looked like a lightsaber to me until I was at least 14."

"Ok. What do you watch over and over?"

"*Pulp Fiction*. I hate a lot of what it spawned, but at the time, it felt revolutionary. Like the beginning of a new, cinematic beatnik or gonzo movement. I can practically recite it from memory, but it never gets old. Just talking about it has me thinking I might watch it when I get home."

"Is that an invitation?" she teases, moving on before you can answer. "And what's the artistic one?"

"*La Dolce Vita*" you say, hoping you didn't just miss another opportunity. "I'm not big on Fellini in general. I feel like he hit a few homeruns in a career full of singles and doubles. But *La Dolce Vita* is, I think, the most perfect summation of the human experience ever committed to film."

"I love *La Dolce Vita*!" Elle exclaims. "It's so wonderfully... honest! Ya know? It's like, life is almost 100% bullshit. The most seemingly authoritative institutions, the most brilliant and beautiful people, they're all just looking for something bigger than themselves. And even if they're doing it in ways that seem more interesting or authentic than the rest of us, they're still not finding it. Not really. And Fellini's response to that is to laugh. To just laugh at it all and carry on because what else can you do? Sincerity's just an idea. It only exists in our heads. In practice, I don't know if I believe in it at all."

"Wow... I mean, yeah. Exactly."

"You seem pretty sincere though," she says. "It's kind of freaking me out."

"I dunno," you say, unsure how to take this compliment. "I try, I guess."

Smiling, she hands you the toasted-brown peppermint roach to inhale into embers.

"Alright, your turn," you say, eager to shift focus.

"I suppose you've earned a reprieve."

"Childhood favorite?"

"*Heathers*," she says, giving the swing another push. "I saw it pretty young - 11 or 12 probably - the exact right time, I think. It made navigating all the impending idiocy of high school girldom really easy in some ways, because I already knew exactly what not to worry about. I still reach for my pepper spray whenever I see anyone with Christian Slater hair though."

"Christ, that's awesome. It's a wonder you fell for Artemis."

"Isn't it? Sometimes Christian Slaters hide in places you'd never expect. And she has great hair."

"She does. Ok, so what about your go-to rewatch?"

"You're gonna laugh."

"I promise I won't."

"Really?"

"Cross my heart."

"Ok. Well, I can pretty much do *Roman Holiday* line-for-line."

"Awwww. Why would I laugh at that? *Roman Holiday*'s a goddamned fairytale."

"I guess maybe you didn't seem the type for fairytales."

"I mean, they have to earn it with me, for sure. I'll be the first to eviscerate tripe like *Pretty Woman* or *Love, Actually*, but I've seen *The Princess Bride* more times than I can count. Fairytales are essential. They keep us human."

"Yeah... That's really nice."

"Ok. What about artistry?"

"That's harder for me. I don't always think about movies that way. Maybe something from the French New Wave? *Jules and Jim*? No, *Bande à Part*. Definitely *Bande à Part*."

"They're both great."

"They are, but *Bande à Part* is less distinctly French and more... universal. It's like a different reaction to the same shit we were talking about with the Fellini. Even though his characters realize they're lost, and their lives are aimless, Godard refuses to accept it. He fights it with every frame."

"If sprinting through the Louvre isn't a perfect metaphor for modern life, I don't know what is."

"Right? He rocks his audience's foundations, and genuinely doesn't give a fuck whether they appreciate it or not. He's completely unselfish, and completely uncompromising. It's not about the viewer, or the critics, or even his own artistic vision. It's like he's a conduit - like he's got a line to the muses or something. Ideas just continually spill out of his head, and if he doesn't express them, he'll fall out and fucking die on the spot. I think he may be the most sincere filmmaker who's ever lived."

"I think you may be right. You know, for someone who doesn't always think about movies that way, that was damned eloquent. You want a job at GRUNDL?"

"God no. I'd just end up supplanting the Kardashian goblins, and then where would I be?"

"Yeah. You're too good for that place. Shit, the Kardashians are too good for that place."

"You are too, you know. Don't sell yourself short."

"I guess," you say, looking back toward the hall as people start filing out in little drunken pods of loosened ties and carried heels. The sexual tension hangs in the air between you - subtle as the difference between "goodbye" and "goodnight."

"Looks like this thing is winding down," you say.

"Looks like it."

"I don't know if I can drive," you say, knowing full well that you could. "Maybe I should call an Uber."

"Maybe we should share one," she offers, a gleam in her eye, when suddenly there comes a dynamic shriek across the garden, amplified by top shelf champagne.

"Elle!!! Elllllllllllllllllllllllllllllllllllllllllllle!!!!!!!!!!!"

"Oh God," she says, leaping to her feet.

You try to think of something, anything to keep her from leaving, but you know when Artemis calls, people come running. And when Artemis calls drunkenly on her wedding night?

There was just no way. You could offer Elle a triple-decker platinum yacht with her name on it, a diamond the size of a balance ball, and a night with Ryan Gosling in a navy uniform, and she wouldn't even hear you over the shrill cries of your mutual frenemy.

And then, some-miraculous-how, the universe proves you wrong.

Halfway to the beaming bride without having even said goodbye, Elle turns back, pulls something out of her clutch, fiddles with it for a second, and places it atop one of the toadstool lights.

And then she's gone, every bit the Cinderella exit you would've imagined.

Much higher than you realized (you may not be ok to drive after all), you wobble over to retrieve her favor. It's a cocktail napkin from the wedding, and written in that same candy cane lipstick: "I had a great time tonight. Call me. Sincerely." Her number on the back.

Episode 17

The day wakes you like the dandelion kiss of a Hyrulian princess. Matutinal birdies flirt outside your window as you roll over and preempt your alarm clock, sparing yourself the relentless screech of morning.

You slept deeply – your withdrawal-induced hellscapes having finally given way to kinder visions – and with your mind giddily pouring over last night's conversational enchantments, you hurry to retrieve the napkin from your pocket – its pilly textures cozied up against your sebum-softened suicide note.

It was real. *She* was real. You'd met her. Even charmed her somehow. It seemed utterly impossible, but it had happened. The dream girl. The one you've been waiting for.

You cannot fuck this up.

Kicking aside weeks of rumpled clothing, you queue up the powerful, call-to-arms "Intro" from Killer Mike's *I Pledge Allegiance to the Grind II* before settling your ass into the mulchy carpet.

Your first sit-up in years is a struggle of Procrustean proportions, but with excessive grunting, you manage to do four, along with several valiant, fractional efforts you feel, collectively, probably add up to another six.

Sweating toxins like a Bufo frog, you flip over and attempt some push-ups, maxing out at eight (though your form would surely be deemed feminine by any drill sergeant, personal trainer, or P.E. teacher worth his vituperative coach whistle). Your triceps effectively dissolved into gelignite, you decide to hit the showers lest you risk explosive muscular rupture.

Thanks to Artemis's hearty, grassfed-meat-and-GMO-free-potatoes wedding banquet, you enjoy a long, slow peristalsis – one that causes your eyes to flutter and your cock to perk as you envision a *woman's slender fingers, adorned with gimcrack rings and gewgaw bracelets, gently extracting a lube-slick rubber dildo* from your asshole. Fully erect at the finish, you are unsurprised to find that you've shit a *Toblerone*; a splendidly solid log that braces across the bowl and requires three consecutive flushes to capsize.

Stepping under the energizing blast of your showerhead, you feel your body's dormant systems switch on one by one, like the lights of a sleepy, wartime village as word spreads of a late-night armistice. The fight is over! The day is won! Oyez! Oyez! You jerk off with the jollity of a town crier waving his handbell, but refuse to let yourself think of Elle, instead inviting a parade of pillowtop pornstars to crowd her off her mark at centerstage of your consciousness. Your sordid imagination is no place for a woman of her caliber, and when you jizz between your soapy fingers the lather stings your peehole as if to chastise you for even considering it. She's above that. Above them all. Above you, even. A sinless stylite atop a golden pedestal of your love.

Dressing for work, you take care to find a stain-free shirt, jeans with all their cruciate ligaments intact, and socks that don't already smell like your feet (or your dick). You bypass any number of suppurating takeout containers in favor of a frightened, photosensitive apple in the back of your crisper, and set out without even glancing at the TV.

You know you have to wait three days.

The sun is shining. The birds are singing. The world feels as new. And you have to wait three days. To call. To text. To ask her out. To ask her to marry you. To build a massive, interconnected complex of temples and basilicas and onion domes in honor of her ineffable beauty. To travel the world spreading the gospel of her kind, forgiving eyes, composing canticles to her healing smile, and proclaiming in wild, ekphrastic frenzy the love inscribed immortelle upon her perfect face. To Elle be the glory, great things she hath done.

Yea, for the next three days you'll harrow the frozen shores of Cocytus, bound by the draconian precepts set forth in *The Rules* and *The Bro Code*. But on that third day, you shall be born again. As a new year dawns, you'll rise from these anfractuous depths, float to the firmament atop your own burgeoning afflatus, and pen a text message to erase every pointless moment of your life up until now. In three days, you shall be free. Oyez. Oyez.

Up ahead, you spot Carmen and Scheherazade arguing over an empty softpack of Newport Lights. While part of you wants to duck behind a bush and see if their scantily-clad spat goes full catfight, you instead stroll confidently up like you just spent the night lining their g-strings with Benjamins and bottle service. Proffering a pair of loosies from your own box, you light them both up with ease before bidding adieu with a gentlemanly tip of your headphones.

You get a charge from this encounter you can't quite place. Was it the calm self-assurance with which you'd engaged two women you once watched simultaneously eat bananas out of one another's vaginas like some potassium-rich sex Auryn? Was it that, even as you felt moved to help these callipygous hoydens, you also felt revulsion at the thought of visiting their place of business ever again, lest you bring terrible shame upon your newfound love? Or was it the simple act of motiveless generosity? Maybe when you're so happy there's nothing left, you have to start giving shit away.

You sidle into the Golden Pantry, buy a Grape Swisher Sweet with a $50 bill, and get your change all in ones. With a plyometric spring in your step, you approach a heap of fomitic rags praying over an empty Bustelo can and let a Jackson's worth of Washingtons float down in front of her through the stale, steamgrate air. The woman looks up at you with such gratitude you half-expect her to start washing your feet with her oleaginous, grey hair.

Puffing on your purple cigarillo, you proceed to march through downtown stuffing singles into every outstretched coffee cup, ballcap, and bucket you pass (some of which are promptly overturned to provide rhythmic appreciation). You make eye contact with everyone; offer blessings and encouragements; pat backs, rub shoulders, and lay hands on more than a few faces wracked by rosacea and gin blossoms. A nubile young woman in a provocatively ripped Stryper t-shirt offers you a freebie in the alley – twerking up against you in time with the bucket drummers – but you push

her gently away, wrap her in your own coat, and implore her to call her parents. You're sure they must be worried.

By the time you reach the park you have three dollars left, earmarked for the Women in Black. You've been actively avoiding them since your dustup two months ago, so cowed were you by the rest of that humiliating weekend, but today you feel like extending an olive branch.

Alas, you find their post abandoned, and wonder bemusedly as you step around a pool of token remembrances to Cassie Abrams, if after all these years, they'd somehow completed their mission; if your current bliss is not in fact the result of your falling ass-over-teakettle into googly-eyed love, but rather some mysterious, Saramago-style global euphoria. Maybe, without wavering or tweaking their game plan even once, the Women in Black had finally effected world peace.

Δ

"Good morning!" you shout across your office building's cavernous rotunda, leaving Jennica so startled by the murmuration of starling syllables echoing around her that she swallows her gum.

"Good morning!?" she replies with a peppy interrobang. "You're in a good mood!"

"Very observant Jennica! I *am* in a good mood!"

"Well don't keep me in suspense!"

"I've met the perfect woman!" you blurt, unable to keep it down any longer.

"Awwwwwwww!"

"I know! I can't even describe it. I mean, I do write for a living, so I could, I guess. I have the words. But they don't seem sufficient, ya know? Or, like, there aren't enough of them. She's just... everything!"

"Well, she sounds really special! I'm so happy for you! I don't want to overstep, but you always seem so down when you come through here. Like, pretty much every day. I know we're not super close or anything, but I worry about you sometimes."

"Oh Jennica. Dear, sweet Jennica. So steadfast. So capable. So reliably *nice*, day in and day out, while scores of angry young men file past your little waystation here; their ears feigning interest in your tales of weekend warriordom; their eyes stroking the fabrics of your stylish, mall maven outfits; their mealy mouths fumbling for something interesting to say - that illusive skazat' novoe slovo, as Dostoyevsky called it - that might catch your simple fancy. You know, I'd wager a thousand pickup lines are born every day, in this very room, only to die unspoken on the lips of poltroons. You're a ray of sunshine girl, and can't nobody bottle that up. I'm so sorry for all the times I've brushed past you; all the mornings I've barely acknowledged your indefatigable bonhomie; all the cumulative hours I've spent nodding along to your inane chatter while secretly trying to discern the cut and color of your panties. You're one of the good ones Jen. I hope you know that."

Jennica looks at you as though you might be a Replicant. Normally, her face lives inside an aura of inertly professional pretty, defined by a cute, kid-sister smile that displays only her two front teeth and makes her look a little like Brittany, the hottest Chipette. But now, leaning back, biting her beestung bottom lip, crossing her arms beneath her tastefully boosted B-cups, she's strangely unnerving.

"I'm wearing cheekinis today," she says, breaking a lengthy silence. "Peach-colored ones."

"Oh."

"They're lace. I like them. So does my husband."

"Oh. I didn't know you were..."

"Married?"

"...Yeah."

"Well I am. He's in real estate. He actually owns this building. And the one next door."

"Oh," you say again, wondering how you never knew that.

"I don't really even need to work," she continues. "I just get bored, staying home all day. I like being out. Meeting new people. Talking to strangers."

"Sure."

"You're right though. All the guys who work here suck."

"...yeah," you agree.

"I get whistled at and catcalled every goddamned day, but not one of them is serious. It's always just this loser bro bullshit. Half the time they're not even looking at me. They're looking at their buddy. Trying to get a laugh. Looking for his approval. It's like they're hitting around me instead of on me, ya know? Talking about how funny it would be if they actually had the balls to ask me out. It's sooo lame. I mean fuck, I know I'm pretty. But I'm not unapproachable. I'm just a person. I've worked here seven years and no one's ever talked to me like you did just now."

"Really?" you ask. You've never heard her curse before, and it's positively sublime. It reminds you, for some reason, of that old meme of the kitten with the sniper rifle.

"Really," she says. "I don't know what that Nova Scotia thing you said was, or who that guy is who you said said it, but the rest was really nice."

"Dostoyevsky. He's a writer. Russian."

"Ah," she replies, checking her cuticles. "I don't really care about that. But thanks."

At a loss, you follow her gaze to her immaculately manicured fingernails.

"So how come you don't wear a ring?" you ask.

She shrugs. This question bores her.

"It's just... if you don't want people hitting on you... seems like an easy fix is all."

"Who says I don't want people hitting on me?"

"Um... I thought *you* just did."

"Then you weren't listening."

Jennica sighs, clearly wondering if she's overestimated you, and then with body language that seems to translate as "meh, fine" she grabs a ballpoint, scribbles something on a post-it, and leans over to slide it into your shirt pocket.

"Here's my number," she says. "I don't wear a ring because my husband doesn't own me. I do what I want, and he does what he wants, and we don't really keep tabs on each other outside our house. Give me a call if you wanna hang out sometime. You can tell me more about your Russian writer guy, or I can tell you more about my panties, or whatever. Just don't blab to anyone around here. Seriously. I'll fucking end you. Got it?"

You nod.

"Ok, well, so great talking to you!" she says, switching effortlessly back to her typing pool politesse - making a show of just how easy it is for her to lie. "And congrats again on your new lady. What's her name anyway?"

"Elle," you mumble sheepishly.

"Well she's a lucky girl!"

Δ

Inside the elevator, you pull up your sleeve and pinch yourself. Nothing. You yank a few nosehairs. Nada. Shit. You could be ascending to the observation deck of Freedom Tower and still not have enough floors to process what just happened. You're well aware of the old "when it rains, it pours" adage, but you never could've imagined it would kick in this quickly or... explicitly! Were you a stud now? Was this what it felt like? To be one of *those* guys? Those guys who don't have to *try*? Your day's barely started, and you feel like you've already picked a winning pony, pulled an inside straight, and made out like a trips-cherries one-armed bandit. You've got the hot hand. You're on the roll of your life. Everything's coming up [_____________]*!

Once at your desk, your morning skim of the newsfeeds only sweetens the pot. First and foremost, there's about to be a troll in the White House, and it's going to be a fucking riot (the lunatic is already talking about parading tanks through DC for his inauguration like he's fucking Kim Jong Un); meanwhile *The Celebrity Apprentice* is rebooting with Arnold Schwarzenegger (suck it, Arthur); the last *Star Wars* movie's still in theaters and the next one's already got a release date (*whistles *Star Wars* theme*); the original drummer for Weather Report died (good. fuck fusion); the Falcons are playing absolutely lights out (you're really starting to believe this is their year); Criterion is in talks to finally bring the films of Naomi Kawase to American audiences (about damn time); a Kardashian is going through a nasty divorce (it doesn't matter which one); Rae Sremmurd improbably have the #1 streaming song in America (skrrrrt!); and so on.

---

* Insert your name here.

Hot damn! You could turn out "Top 10 Best Things That Happened Today" without even clicking another link. Taking a satisfyingly crispy bite of your apple, you decide a cup of coffee sounds like just the ticket before you start extolling all this good news to the world.

You strut into the breakroom like you just bought the bar and set about brewing a fresh pot. Seated at one of the Formica tables, Bradley's reading a *Vanity Fair* whose cover winks at you with Vanessa Hudgens's dark, bewitching eyes. You wink back. Today, even she feels within reach.

"Morning Sweats," Bradley says.

"And good morning to you Bradley!" you reply with enough zest to instantly make him wonder if you're making fun of him. "What's the good word?"

"Ummm... I dunno."

"Well, what are you reading about?"

"I...I don't know if I should say. It might make you mad."

"Bradley, let me assure you, nothing in the pages of *Vanity Fair* could possibly make me mad today."

"Well..." he says, weighing his options, perhaps doing some quick mental math regarding his proximity to the door and his chances of reaching it before you.

"...the big news is..."

"Spit it out man. I promise, I'm good."

"Ok... they're remaking *Back to the Future*."

You stop, frozen in the act of rummaging for a mug. The room is silent, save the stillicidal drip of the Cuisinart. You can actually hear Bradley's muscles tense, awaiting your critical tirade.

He wasn't wrong to fear sharing this news. It's the sort of thing you'd normally let ruin your whole day (and everyone else's). The week the loathsome *Phantom Menace* premiered, for example, you nearly got yourself expelled, slugging a high school classmate after he suggested the Podracing scenes were "kinda cool." You're a volatile fan and a vociferous purist when it comes to certain things - the things you loved before you were old enough to care about pussy. You didn't mind the whole lady *Ghostbusters* deal so much personally, but you *got* it.

Today, however, you feel only the briefest wavelet of anger, promptly swallowed up in an ocean of oxytocin, and after taking a beat, you locate a mug and ask, "Who's gonna play Marty?"

Stunned, Bradley lifts his magazine a touch higher, indicating the Disney starlet on the cover. He seems relieved, but also like he's still waiting for the other shoe to come flying at his head.

"Interesting," you say, further assuaging his fragile brand of anxiety. "Vanessa Hudgens is actually pretty funny. She's got this manic energy. It's weird. You don't expect people that hot to be funny, but she totally is."

"Right!?!" he leaps to agree. "I've seen her in three or four things now where she was hilarious! I love Michael J. Fox - that movie's a classic for sure - but I think she'll do a great job."

"Sure," you say. "I guess I just feel like the whole sequel/remake/reboot machine has gotten way out of hand. It just seems lazy. Like, there are so many stories out there that've never been told. Is it really so hard to come up with something new?"

"Oh," Bradley says, the wind in his sails abruptly reduced from a Saffir-Simpson 5 to a drifting dead calm. "Yeah, they're pretty stupid I guess. Sorry."

"Dude, no! Don't do that. It's my issue. And I'm pretty clearly in the minority. I mean, reboots make bank, and that's kinda the point, right? A lotta people must like 'em. I'm just set in my ways, ya know? I don't like change. Shit, I was mad when they remade *Footloose*. You know me. I don't give a shit about *Footloose*! It's just the principle."

"Yeah, I guess," he says.

"You know, I really admire you Bradley," you begin, lying in a pleasant shade of off-white. "You have this boundless capacity to appreciate almost everything. Your writing isn't weighed down by flowery language or showboat-y comparisons to more obscure, less heralded works that only prove to the reader what a smartypants you are. I've never heard you fawn over the Arri Alexa digital camera, or invoke Jean Genet in a recap of *The Vampire Diaries*. You take everything on its own terms. You seem like you still enjoy movies and TV in a way the rest of us just don't anymore; in a way I maybe never have..."

(at this point, you're no longer sure to what degree you're lying)

"...There's a reason your articles get more hits than mine. You have the common touch my friend. I know that sounds pretentious and snooty – and let's be honest, I'm kind of pretentious and snooty – but I swear I mean it as a compliment. I could never do what you do. I honestly believe you could be the next Roger Ebert if you put your mind to it. So don't worry about me, man. Fuck, don't worry about anybody in this fuckin' place. Just keep doin' you. Keep getting psyched about reboots. Keep caring who plays Spider-Man. Keep loving *The Simpsons*. Keep that sense of wonder. The world has enough critics. Entertainment needs people who are still willing to be entertained."

As you end your second interpersonal soliloquy of the day, Bradley begins to weep. He grabs his *Vanity Fair* and holds it aloft (and upside-down), pretending to read to hide his tears as you walk over and put a hand on his shoulder.

"I... I th-thought you h-h-hated me."

"I know, man. I know. And you weren't wrong. The truth is, I kind of hate everyone. Especially here. But I'm working on it. And, for what it's worth, I've always hated you the least."

Bradley looks up from an inverted photospread of the Olsen twins doing cartwheels on the beaches of Majorca (amusing in its juxtapositions, they rather look like they're grasping at sand for fear of falling into the sky). Dabbing his dopey, Neverland Ranch-hand face, he stands and encircles you in an awkward hug, which you return with a couple brotherly raps on the back.

No sooner than he's sat back down do you hear Barry's signature harrumph, and turn to find him pointing a pudgy knuckle in your direction.

"If you two are done playin' grabass in the room where the rest of us eat lunch, I'd like to see you in my office."

Δ

Arthur's already waiting in Barry's office when you arrive, and you offer him the same spirited salutations you've been dishing out all morning. He gives you a look comparable to Bradley's - that of someone trying to figure out exactly how they're being made a fool - but ultimately extends his fin-rotted mackerel of a handshake.

"What's with you today?" Barry asks - you suspect through a hangover - as he squeezes around his cramped desk. "You get laid last night or somethin'?"

"Good one boss!" you reply with exaggerated verve. "But no. Nothing so crass as that. I'm just in a swell mood. Having a run of good luck, you might say. Hey, maybe you should let me set your lineup this week! When do the playoffs start!?" (this last bit of cheek is a straight-up heat check, as you're fully aware Barry missed the cut for his league's playoffs weeks ago).

"I'm going to ignore that, because fuck you," he says. "Honestly, knowing you're in such a good mood almost makes me want to call this whole thing off. But since you're here... I actually have some good news for you two bozos."

"What'd *I* do!?" Arthur asks indignantly.

"Yeah, what'd *he* do?!" you pile on.

"Good Lord, shut up! Both of you," Barry replies, clearly wishing he could clunk your heads together a la the dominant stooge. "Just let me talk for Christ's sake, and then you can go."

Arthur aims a hilarious scowl in your direction, and while you could riff on these two high-strung nincompoops all day - you are the dominant stooge here, whether they know it or not - you straighten up and indicate to Barry that he has your full attention.

"Ok, so, the honchos upstairs have gotten it in their heads we need to shake things up. They're tired of cranking out clickbait. They think it's a dead end. They're probably not wrong. We're doing fine now, but in ten years, no one's gonna read this crap anymore. So they want us to try creating more in-depth content. Stuff that actually has informational value. Stuff with a voice. They're gonna pour some money into design updates, and they think if we put our people in a position to succeed, we could rebrand

and compete with sites like AV Club and The Ringer. They asked me to do sports, and to pick two of my best keyboard monkeys and test the waters. See if we can move the needle. So whaddaya think keyboard monkeys? Wanna try stringing some complete sentences together? Think you got something to say? Anyone? Anyone? Bueller?"

Arthur looks at you in disbelief. You can see his mind racing through his beady, codestrung eyes; validating the countless hours he's spent boring his sulci into slot canyons of worse-than-useless information; outlining his pandect of reality television; envisioning himself as the first true historian of the medium; the man who finally put it all together. He's too excited to speak; too excited to blink. He may, in fact, be physically restraining himself from leaping onto his chair and paraphrasing "O Captain! My Captain!" in deference to Barry, GRUNDL, and the dudes from *Storage Wars*. Sensing a response is needed, you decide to take the lead.

"Well boss, I think we'd both be thrilled to take this on!"

Arthur nods vigorously.

"Greeeeeeat," Barry says, slow and unconvincing, like a tranqued-up Tony the Tiger.

"And can I just add," you continue, "I know GRUNDL probably isn't any of ours' dream job. I mean, sure, there are worse ways to make a living - including every other one I've tried - but I think it's safe to say we all shuffle through these halls most days feeling a certain level of... aggrievement. Like we're better than this place. Like we deserve more. And you know what? We're fucking right! The three of us are halfway decent writers when we want to be. At least as good as those demon gadflies at *Perez Hilton*, Arthur, or those league-sponsored shills at ESPN, Barry. We've languished a longass time together in this wiki hellhole, this memeified necropolis, this Cyberian wasteland of frozen screens and 20-to-life buffer times. But no more! We've got a real chance here. A chance to build something. From the ground up. A site we actually care about. A site we'd actually read! Finally, we can write about anything we... hey Barry, can we write about anything we want?"

"Pretty much."

"Even jazz!?!"

"...Maybe. Don't push it though."

"We can pretty much write about anything we want!" you continue, springing to your feet, fighting the urge to step atop your own chair.

"Starting today, things are gonna be different. We few, we happy few, we…

"Not today," Barry interrupts.

"What?"

"You have to wait til Monday."

"Why?"

"Fuck if I know. Bureaucracy. Outta my hands."

"Oh. Alright then… Starting Monday! Things are gonna be different! We few, we happy few, we band of bloggers, will ride forth into a future of our own design! Into the motherfucking breach! All for one! One for all! Just do it! Shoot your shot! You miss 100% of the ones you don't take, right boss? Let's be like Mike! Do it for Caretaker! Ducks Fly Together! Clear Eyes Full Hearts! RUUUDY! U!S!A! RUUdy! U.S.A. U.S.a. U.s.a. u.s.a…"

The room stares at you blankly. It's so quiet you can hear your coworkers' notification dings and keyboard clackings through the walls.

"…Are you done?" Barry asks.

"…Yeah."

"You sure?"

"Yeah."

"Arthur? Anything you wanna add to… whatever the Hell that was?"

Arthur shakes his head, still a rictus of excitement.

"Alright then. We'll start meeting next week to talk about... all that shit you were just talking about. But like normal people. Sitting down. Over coffee. Probably Wednesdays. I haven't decided yet. But for now, congratulations. This is a real opportunity. You should both be proud."

"You got it boss!" you say, flashing your shit-eating grin with what you hope is a discernible newfound respect.

"Good deal," Barry says, seeming to appreciate the gesture. "Now go say goodbye to the minors, boys. You're gettin' called up to the show."

Δ

You pinch yourself again as you return to your desk, surveying your surroundings for crouched, *Candid Camera* crews waiting to pounce from an empty cubicle and declare you *Punk'd*. But no. This too is real. Maybe the blue pill isn't all it's cracked up to be.

The rest of your workday flies by, a blur of salubrious shits and abbreviated smoke breaks; research and notetaking; outlines and abstracts;

all the long-form pieces you never thought you'd get to write. An examination of Antonioni's Alienation Trilogy and the modern ennui of social media? Absolutely. A gongorist ode to Peter Brötzmann, the most monolithic musical titan the average American's never even heard of? Unquestionably. An open love letter to Hannah Horvath and her take-no-prisoners invagination of the MPDG archetype? Count it. She's the voice of her generation after all, and emblematic of exactly what you look for when trawling OKcupid for adventurous *Girls* (Well, almost. You want a Hannah in a Marnie's body. With a Jessa's ass, as long as you're mix-and-matching).

Of course, you can't think like that anymore. You have Elle now. The complete package.

You wonder if she'd play naked ping-pong with you.

In this moment, anything feels possible.

Δ

Having skipped lunch, you clock out early and set off on an afterwork errand of amor.

Vitalink Video, known for its unbeatable 5 Movies/5 Days/5 Dollars deal, is a long-cherished institution in your town, and represents, for you, the kindest of rewinds. In the days before Netflix, you'd spend hours stravaging these dusty aisles - scanning epitaphs in this analog ossuary - arranging your perfect quintet. You share secrets with this place. You've discovered wonders here. Grindhouse detritus and foreign language opuscula; esoteric museum loops and hand-etched celluloid animations; Robert Bresson and Matthew Barney; New Wave and No Wave; *Happiness, Daisies, Salò, Stroszek, Pink Flamingos, Holy Mountain, Cat Soup, Space is the Place,* and more drowsy Frenchwomen getting sexually woke than even the most voracious viewer could ever hope to consume.

Best of all, behind a motheaten, cambric curtain that isn't fooling anyone, lies an exhaustive "Special Interest" section - an unsanitary sanctum sanctorum of the most enduring, time-honored smut ever made, from *The Opening of Misty Beethoven* (a classic) to *Backyard Cum Fiesta 9* (a modern classic). In those first lean, post-collegiate years when you couldn't yet afford Wi-Fi, this place was your house of worship, and your house of ill repute. Whatever you needed, its doors were always open.

Knowing these shelves like your own home library, you hustle to the Spanish-language section and harvest a cinco-strong cross-section from Almodóvar's copious corpus of work. You want to be fluent the next time you see Elle; to examine through specs newly rose-tinted, a filmmaker you've always found frustrating and self-contradictory, and be proven utterly, inarguably wrong.

"Almodóvar huh?" asks a smirky twenty-something in a Lebowski sweater as you pony up to the checkout counter. "Cool man. Cool. I went through a little Almodóvar phase back in the day."

You can sense this guy's movie buff arrogance instantaneously - it takes one to know one - and while you can't help but wonder what exactly "back in the day" means for someone his age, you resolve not to take the bait. You're in too good a mood.

"You watch a lotta foreign films?" he presses, spoiling for a pissing contest.

"Here and there," you reply to the vintage *A Face in the Crowd* poster over his shoulder.

"Yeah," he persists. "Almodóvar's alright. Kind of a hack compared to the greats though. Do you know Buñuel?"

"Yeah..." you say. "I know Buñuel."

"Cool. Cool," he says scanning at a laborious pace. "He's definitely one of my faves. *Discreet Charm of the Bourgeoisie*? Unbelievable! How relevant it still feels, like, to today's political climate and stuff? It's surreal, man."

"Yeah," you mutter, wishing a hit squad would appear and mow him down in violent homage. "I mean, he is a *surrealist*, but sure."

"Right. I know," he says, maybe finally picking up on your annoyance. "But even **Buñuel** is kinda Foreign Film 101, if you know what I mean. What I'm really into right now is Bergman. Life is meaningless. Death is inescapable. He's the real deal man. And his shot composition! Outta this world. You don't know what black and white cinematography is until you've seen Bergman."

"Mmhmm," you say to the poster. From where you're standing, Andy Griffith appears to be screaming directly into this kid's ear. Lucky bastard.

"Yeah. It's pretty heavy stuff. Definitely not for everyone" he adds.

Dammit…
The balls on this guy…
You're having such a good day…
You just want to go home…
But no…

You have to say something…
This aggression will not stand.

"So what're we talkin' here?" you ask, jumping in with the quick, darting cadence of a bookie working a mark. "You get stoned one weekend and watch *The Seventh Seal* because you saw it on *Animaniacs*?"

"Um... no? What's *Animaniacs*?"

"Ok. What then? You show some girl *The Virgin Spring* because she's into horror movies and you're too elitist for *Last House on the Left*?"

"Dude. No. I'd never show a girl either of those."

"Alright. So maybe you studied the opening sequence from *Sawdust and Tinsel* in, lemme guess, Foreign Film 102? Is that it? Cuckolded clowns your thing?"

"Uhh..."

"Well what then!? Speak up man! If you know so much, please share! Enlighten me to the glories of *Ernst Ingmar Bergman*!"

"Well..." he starts, punching off his back foot in the face of your verbal bull rush, "I really liked *Persona*. Super creepy. And I've seen most of *Wild Strawberries*. I fell asleep, to be honest, but I'm gonna finish it tonight."

"Those are great," you agree, before launching into another didactatribe. "A great start. But if you're really serious about understanding the Bergman ethos, you need to check out *The Trilogy of Faith*. The spider god? The putrescence of belief? The ticking clock we all face, every day, counting down each wasted hour between the moment we're born knowing nothing and the moment we die knowing less? *The Trilogy* is where it's at bro."

"Wow," he says, visibly spun. "So, you know a lot about Bergman then?"

"Half the Bergmans in this place are only here because I put in customer requests," you say, a little too proudly. "Not to mention the **Dušan** Makavejev stuff, the *Guinea Pig* series, and all those Region 2 Peter Greenaways with the warning labels about not working in American DVD players."

"Holy shit, you're *that guy*!?!"

"Uhhhh, yeah," you say uneasily. "That's me."

"Dude, this whole conversation makes so much sense now."

"What do you mean?"

"You're a fucking legend around here man!"

"Is that right?" you ask, puffing up a bit. Liking the sound of that. You had, now that you think about it, had some pretty great chats with

VitaLink employees over the years. You're surprised anyone would remember you, but it's nice to hear you're remembered. Maybe even this insufferable exchange will prove no match for your hot streak in progress. Maybe you've ascended to untouchable, unstoppable, god-mode status. Maybe Elle really has magically changed your entire life for the bett...

"Yeah!" he interrupts. "The older guys here fucking hate you!"

"...oh."

"Don't get me wrong. I dig your tastes. That's the whole reason I know who you are. Every time I rent something you requested they talk about what a pain in the ass you were, always bugging them to order crazy shit no one cared about. I can't believe I'm actually meeting you."

"Oh," you say again, staggered; off-balance.

"I honestly thought you might be made-up. Like they were hazing me or something. Messing with the new kid. Wow. I have so many questions. They say you'd just wander around for hours. Keeping everyone late? Closing the place down?"

"Yeah," you answer quietly.

"Holing up in the adult section?"

"...Mmhmm."

"They said one time you rented five Michael Haneke movies and then, at the last minute, ran back and grabbed the porn parody of *Hannah Montana*. Like you'd been wrestling with the decision, and realized you just had to have it. They started calling you the Grim Creeper after that."

You chuckle mirthlessly.

"Did you really call Andy a philistine for saying he preferred the American version of *Funny Games*?"

"...uh-huh."

"That's nuts! I never believed that story!"

"Mmhmm," you say again.

"I'm not trying to be a dick here, but look," he says, pointing at his computer screen. "You're still the only person who's ever rented those Greenaways. See?"

You read your own name in outdated, DOS-block lettering – the lone account listed beside titles like *The Baby of Macon*, *Drowning By Numbers*, and *Prospero's Books*.

"I mean, I'm not really surprised," you say, attempting to fling some of his own shade back at him. "Greenaway's pretty out there. Definitely not for everyone."

"Sure," he says, a victorious glint in his eye. "Also, they literally *ruin* DVD players, but sure."

You look at each other for what feels like an eternity, him smiling with ease, you trying to force any expression other than abject humiliation. In the end, he throws you a rope, if only to dope you back in for a knockout.

"For what it's worth, *The Pillow Book*'s pretty cool. It even got me laid once. I probably never would've heard of it if it weren't for all the shit they talk about you."

"Thanks," you say, extremely ready to leave.

"And I'll totally check out *The Trilogy of Faith*. It sounds rad."

"Sure."

"So, your total's $47.53. Cash or card?"

"$47.53!?!?! What happened to the five for five deal?!"

"Late fees man. Looks like you rented *Dogtooth* back in 2012 and kept it for over a month. We let 'em slide when people are coming in here on the reg, but it's been a while since we've seen you, so... time to settle up."

You try to get mad, but your heart can't get off the mat. You've lost, and any protestation you make will only further confirm your embarrassing "legend." You hand him your credit card, and watch it slide into overdraft (adding a $30 bank fee to this already-exorbitant transaction). You were so close. If he'd talked about anyone else - Fassbinder, Kurosawa, Tarkovsky - you would've been fine. But no. It had to be Bergman. Leave it to the dour Swede to fuck up your perfect day.

Δ

You spend most of your walk home mentally flogging yourself like Béla Tarr's *Turin Horse* (you'd bet good money that punkass clerk wouldn't get *that* reference), but even with this bad omen drifting wraithlike between your amygdalae, you can't shake a sensation of sapling success. By the time you're relocking your gate with a new jazz birthdate - (Clifford Brown until April) - you're chuckling at your own comeuppance.

Inside, you fix yourself a sensible pasta dish, get cozy, and fire up Almodóvar's *Dark Habits*. Your mind is open. Your heart is full. You're barely jonesing, and more than that even, you genuinely feel you have better things to do than get high. You never thought you'd see the day, but it seems as though the life you've been waiting for - the life you've always wanted - the life that all your reams and reams of self-inflicted edutainment has convinced you you deserve - is finally about to begin. Oyez. Oyez.

Episode 18

It's New Year's Day, and you wake up with words in your head!

You hop out of bed feeling rejuvenated - your entire body a megawatt luminaria of creativity and confidence - overflowing with the urgent, implacable need to write. You push through another onerous round of exercises, shower up, and brew a full pot of jailhouse sludge to further goose your thrumming synapses.

Though you might attribute this unexpected breach of your long-besieged writer's blockade to the ongoing, quasi-mystical influence of your would-be inamorata, perhaps more directly to blame is the absence of THC from your system. Weed makes you feel good, sure, but you can't remember the last time you felt this... *well*.

Staying high all the time is not unlike living life with a low-grade cold. You feel run down, torpid, and more-or-less resigned to sit still and convalesce until you feel better. With committed headdom however, the malady has a way of convincing you it's also the cure, so you just keep smoking, and you never really feel better. Your whole life becomes a convalescence.

As a result, on the rare occasions when you actually manage to clear the decks and reboot your mainframe with nothing but source code, you can come out feeling almost superhuman on the other side. It's like turning the cheats on in a video game. Suddenly, you're faster than the world around you. Lights flare. Processes whirr. Every link is a hyperlink. Every key is a hotkey. Every word is wordperfect.

As has been your new year's tradition since you were a poorly supervised tween, you pop in your VHS of *Pulp Fiction*, and get ready to begin your first piece for the new GRUNDL.

The magnitude of this moment is not lost on you. For years you've played the straight-A pop culture student, viewing all screens as one interconnected, fluxing Lyceum, and yourself as their peripatetic disciple. No matter where you were, or who you were with, if there was a TV on in the room, it invariably won any battle for your attention.   It always had more to teach you. Real life could never compete.

But now, you will be the teacher. You've been given the gift of influence; of pulpit; of branded benefit of the doubt. No longer will you kowtow to the midcult, namedropping celebrities and de-purpling your prose for pageviews. From here on, you write in ultraviolet! Fuck Kimye! Fuck Brangelina! Fuck Donald Trump (*You* have the best words!). Fuck superheroes and *Star Wars* (yeah, you said it) and fuck Michael Bay with Megatron's big fucking robot dick! You are the AllSpark; the be-all, end-all, post-post-everything, final fucking word! The righteous will hear your authoritative first-person voice in their malleable third-person heads and know that you are good! And the wicked will speak your name in whispers and fear your stylus like the flaming sword of Uriel! And in a pyroclastic rain of Vesuvian hot-takes, you'll burn this Twitter nation to the ground!

And first up, declares your crescendoing internal monologue as you start scribbling notes, *is that millennial fucktard at the video store!*

The culture of the video store prick begins and ends with Quentin Tarantino and Kevin Smith. They are the *OG hipsters.* The *encyclopedic know-it-alls made good.* True *troll's trolls.* The first to make memorizing marginalia and speaking analytically about film seem cool, they gave hope to every sleepy-eyed stoner who ever made his popcorn butter working Blockbuster nights. They wrote some of the most *stylized dialogue* Hollywood had seen since Tracy and Hepburn, and swore to anyone who'd listen that it was *"the way real people talked."* With *Reservoir Dogs* and *Clerks*, they effectively shrunk *auteurism* down to the size where you could drown it in a bathtub, so long as that bathtub was an antique clawfoot with some gnarly wallpaper peeling behind it. Above all, they *prized obscurity* – the less something had been seen, the more value it inherently had. Little did they know, they were presaging the very elitist attitudes that would lead to their own *Flanderization*.

Arguably the last two directors to become household names without the widespread aid of the internet, Tarantino and Smith paved the way for a world where *rarity itself is now exceedingly rare.* The abundance of content available today is so unwieldy that *keeping up with the new* has far superseded ferreting out the old or forgotten. With rental houses going South faster than a bespoke bank heist, and streaming sites gobbling up every available property for bitcoins on the dollar (not to mention the diligent efforts of BitTorrent vigilantes like *YIFY* and *FreakyFlicks*) these days, if there's a movie out there you want to see, chances are the internet is your man.

Sure, there's that well-traveled statistic about how *75% of all American silent films are lost to history,* but unless you trip over a perfectly preserved tin of nitrate while exhuming your grandmother's chifforobe, you're unlikely to find anything no one else has seen and/or sold at Sotheby's. Even Smith's student documentary *Mae Day* is now a bonus feature on the Deluxe 10th Anniversary DVD of *Clerks*, and Tarantino's unfinished first film *My Best Friend's Birthday* – at one time as sought-after as the cigarette-singed drive-in curiosities he lionized in his youth – today can be *found and downloaded in the time it took to read this sentence.*

Put another way, Smith and Tarantino gave too much. They sold the things they loved too cheaply. They're the losers who hustled their way into the in-crowd via one big score – *the long Comic-Con,* as it were – and in the process became the vatic impresarios of today's hyper-monetized, Starfleet Insignia tramp-stamped, *Big-Bang-Theory*-chic *nerd culture. Mallrats* and *Pulp Fiction,* their respective sophomore manifestos, remain razor-sharp career aretes. *Chasing Amy* and *Jackie Brown,* their *indulgent third acts,* are fiercely beloved by somewhat diminished, niche audiences. And after that, everything just gets kind of sad.

In *shifting away from art and toward content,* these Gen X iconoclasts chose starkly different roads. Today, Smith aspires to little more than *continually remaking the same two or three movies he's already made* with updated dick- and fart-jokes, while Tarantino got Mia-Wallace-*high on his own supply,* joined the Hollywood elite, and carved out a cushy life on the nod, staging ∞-budget homages to his no-budget first loves. Somewhere in there, he probably even got to *bang Uma Thurman*. You hope not, but probably.

You look up from your choppy notes to enjoy the five-dollar-shakes and fancy footwork of the Jackrabbit Slim's vignette. You've never found Thurman particularly attractive in any other context, but here, in this mode, with that hair, and those restless eyes – one-too-many shirt buttons left undone – one-too-many bad men wrapped around her middle finger – she's the epitome of sexy cool. Of course Marsellus Wallace threw Tony Rocky Horror off that balcony for massaging her feet. This is a woman whose slightest indiscretion demands recompense.

Revenge, incidentally, is what Smith and Tarantino have come to represent for you in the latter halves of their careers. Smith, the revenge of the laconic, husky slacker; Tarantino, the revenge of the ugly, motormouthed nerd. Indeed, on a grander scale, Tarantino has styled himself as a kind of *avenging angel for all underappreciated genres*, and (perhaps less effectively) all *oppressed peoples*, be they women (*Kill Bill, Death Proof*), Jews (*Inglorious Bastards*), or most recently, black people (*Django Unchained, The Hateful Eight* sort of). A megalomaniacal, after-the-fact justice warrior, he delights in carpet N-bombing Americans with their own violent history. *All stories are his story. All struggles are his struggle.*

This is what you, and people like you, really love about Tarantino.

It's not the violence, or the craftsmanship, or the unfettered license to use racial slurs. It's the *grievance*; the absolute, unassailable belief that everything that's happened on Earth up to this point has been fucked up and backward and unfair, and that he, and by extension you, have been every bit as oppressed by it as its actual victims. He doesn't see color. He doesn't see race. He's one of *those* guys. And somehow, over the course of 8½ projects, ideas like *"bad movies are better than good movies"* and *"criminals are cooler than cops"* morphed into *"I am the one person who can right the wrongs of slavery and the Holocaust through the power of film!"*

Tarantino's post-*Pulp Fiction* oeuvre exists in that sweet, sweetback sweet spot between being *too smart for dumb people, and too dumb for smart people.* He courts dunderheaded energy drinkers and half-caf latte sippers; high schoolers and Academy voters; controversy and prestige. His *marketing campaigns* are the real art, the way each of his movies gets billed as a landmark event, Barnum Effecting every citizen of what is, in case you hadn't heard, a *deeply divided country,* into thinking it looks like something that would appeal to his or her particular, and refined personal tastes.

He gathers us all together, under the big-top, for three-hour *alternative history lessons*, forcing us to reckon with his chatterbox, letterbox, black box vision of the American experiment gone awry, and then he sends us all home with a pat on the head and some viciously *cathartic*, wish-fulfillment vengeance we can all agree on. We leave confused, not knowing if we enjoyed it or not - not knowing if it was even *good* or not (whatever that means) - but we all liked when that plantation master's bitch wife got shotgun blasted into the next room, or when that sick-fuck SS officer got scalped with a good old-fashioned American Bowie knife. And that gets us talking. And talking gets us thinking. And that's the power of Tarantino.

You watch John Travolta drive a hypodermic needle through Uma Thurman's breastplate.

In your most secretive alcoves of shelved ambition, these are the kinds of stories you'd like to tell, though you've kept those alcoves under lock-and-key so long now they may well have rusted shut. Ambition is a trap, and what's more, even if you did somehow career ass-backward into some kind of success, the thought of other people enjoying anything that sprung from your toxic psyche - finding it accessible or, God forbid, relatable - makes you physically ill. It's the catch 22 of anhedonia. To paraphrase that old Borscht Belt joke, you'd never want to write for anyone who thought you were worth reading. It's the gravity that keeps you pinned to the sofa and the schedule-1 narcotic air you breathe.

But...

With the way things have been going for you lately, and the way you're crushing this article you don't entirely hate, you feel a twinge of temptation - to take a microfiber wipe and dust off your old screenplay.

It's been years since you even looked at it, but you hear it now, calling out from the recesses of your hard drive: a three-quarters-finished sociopolitical revenge fantasy that, with a little polish and some gratuitously balletic action sequences, could trade bullets and banter with anything old Mr. Brown ever put his name on.

You retrieve your laptop - briefly looking over your shoulder before you open it as though someone might actually be watching you, waiting to laugh at your hopeful folly - and once you're convinced you're safe, avert your eyes, and click...

TITLE CARD: [the PS22 Chorus National Anthem plays] One year ago, 14 schoolchildren and 9 teachers were massacred in Anyton, Kansas by a lone madman with a gun.

TITLE CARD: Recently returned from his 7th tour of duty in Afghanistan, Ox Manbun is trying to start a new life. But the war has followed him home...

FADE-IN: A close-up of the American flag waving in the breeze. Machinegun fire cuts in. The flag contorts wildly. Smoke fills the screen. When it clears, bullet holes spell out the title:

Playground
Zero

Oh yeah. You went there.

In an instant, you're back in your first apartment - a spartan, McNulty-style studio - clacking away on a bug-infested laptop missing its P, V, and F2 keys; making just enough money to smoke all day and work all night.

Reading it now brings an impish grin to your face and runny tears to your eyes. This is it. The last remaining evidence that you ever wanted to be someone different from who you are.

EXT. ELEMENTARY SCHOOL – MORNING

A podium decked out with red, white, and blue bunting in front of the school. Teachers lead lines of children and seat them in rows on the grass. There are folding chairs set up for teachers and parents. Cameras and news crews line the outer edges of the seating arrangement, and protesters are visible in the far background. Everyone's been given an American flag/pencil to wave for the Vice President. The camera lands on two young teachers: a bombshell blonde (TRACY), and a wholesome-looking brunette (ANNABELLE) who's wrangling twice as many students as her coworkers.

                    TRACY
     Oh you poor thing! Is he late again?

                  ANNABELLE
       It's alright. I really don't mind.

                    TRACY
        But still, it's not fair. So
              unprofessional.

                  ANNABELLE
     I know, but he's just been through so
        much. And he's so great with the
                    kids.

TROLL

TRACY
When he bothers to show up!

ANNABELLE
He's done a ton of good for the school too. Those active shooter drills. And the afterschool self-defense program. With everything that's happened, things just feel safer with him around.

TRACY
I know, I know. Gosh, you're so sweet Annabelle. I just don't want to see you get taken advantage of.

ANNABELLE
It's really ok Tracy. I'm happy to lend him a hand until he gets back in the swing of things.

TRACY
I'll bet you are, you naughty girl. So is it true what everyone says? You know, about his? [directs a sly look at her own crotch]. Rumor is you'd need to lend two hands.

ANNABELLE
Tracy!!!

TRACY
What?! I've heard it's like a bazooka.

ANNABELLE
I wouldn't know. We're just friends.

TRACY
Come on! Don't be that way. It's just
us girls here.

ANNABELLE
Sure. And the entire school, and the
local news, and the Vice President.

TRACY
Pleeeease?! I swear I won't tell.

ANNABELLE
There's nothing to tell! He's a very
kind man who's had a hard couple of
years and wants a fresh start. I'm
just helping him readjust to civilian
life. That's all.

TRACY
Whatever. Prude.

ANNABELLE
[Rolls her eyes]

TRACY
I'm just saying, if I were "helping
him readjust to civilian life" I
wouldn't be able to shut up about it.
Those arms. Those abs. My God. I'd
readjust his brains out.

ANNABELLE
Shush! The kids are gonna hear you.

TROLL

<pre>
            TRACY
[Pokes her tongue into her cheek and
simulates oral sex with her American
            flag pencil]

          ANNABELLE
    Stop it! You're so bad!
</pre>

The two share a knowing smile, but they're interrupted as a commotion comes over the crowd. The camera cuts to OX MANBUN being circled by three protesters in Confederate Flag gear. One brandishes a sign that reads "You Can Have My Gun When You Pry It From My Cold Dead Hands." As the men converge, OX expertly evades their attacks, knocking one out with a punch, breaking another's leg with a kick, and pivoting to face the third, who pushes an elderly woman aside as he runs away. OX retrieves the sign from his unconscious attacker's hand, breaks it over his knee, and walks over to TRACY and ANNABELLE.

<pre>
             OX
 Morning ladies. Sorry I'm late.
</pre>

Your nervous system floods with serotonin self-esteem. You'd forgotten how great this feels. Things like architecture and city planning, medicine and genetic engineering, were all obvious nonstarters for you. You were never really that kind of go-getter. Definitely more of a stay-putter and a take-what-comes-er. But as long as you could write, you were mostly ok. It was a way for you to win - to build worlds and make them do exactly what you wanted; to exercise total control. Cities crumble. People die. But stories? Stories are forever.

You skip ahead, past the Vice President's speech - which is moving, if you do say so yourself - and some news footage-style scenes of clashing parents and protesters presented by intrepid local reporter Convivia Nefertiti (more on her at the top of the hour). Back inside, Ox and Annabelle discuss the morning's events. This is where it starts to get good.


```
INT. HALLWAY OUTSIDE OX'S CLASSROOM

                  ANNABELLE
      Ox, there you are. I got your kids
        back to your room, but mine are
       waiting on me. I can't be in two
              places at once.

                    OX
       Sorry Annabelle. Dillhoffer just
     almost fired me for getting into it
            with those protesters.
```

ANNABELLE
What!? That's so unfair! They started
it. You were just defending yourself.

OX
Well...

ANNABELLE
Ox? You *were* just defending yourself,
right?

OX
Yeah! Definitely! ...against the
second and third guys. The first one?
...I might've provoked a little. But
it was his own fault for having that
stupid sign. I mean, what was I
supposed to do? *Not* compare his dick
to a baby carrot and let his wife
squeeze my bicep?

ANNABELLE
Ox! You didn't!?

OX
[Smiles mischievously; winks at
ANNABELLE]

ANNABELLE
Well, if Principal Dillhoffer saw any
of that then I'm impressed
he *didn't* fire you.

OX
Day's still young baby.

OX and ANNABELLE share an awkward silence, drenched in the possibility of unexplored romance.

                    ANNABELLE
So... got any fun plans this weekend?

                       OX
I've got some army buddies in town.
We're planning a jet-ski shark hunt.

                    ANNABELLE
                  Is that...?

                       OX
        Exactly what it sounds like?

                    ANNABELLE
                    Yeah.

                       OX
     Yeah. It's hammerhead season.

                    ANNABELLE
                    Oh...

                       OX
             ...What about you?

                    ANNABELLE
Oh, I'll probably just stay in my PJs
all weekend. Make a big pot of my
famous Cavatini al Annabelle and
binge bad tv. There's an *America's*

TROLL

*Next Top Twerkaerobics
Instructor* marathon on.

OX
Is that...?

ANNABELLE
Exactly what it sounds like?

OX
Yeah.

ANNABELLE
Yeah. I'm totally addicted. And I
figure as long as I'm packing
mozzarella directly onto my ass, I
might as well learn how to use it,
right? [laughs self-consciously]

OX
Makes sense. [Takes a not-so-subtle
peek at ANNABELLE's ass]

[Another awkward silence ensues.]

OX
So Cavatini huh? I haven't had that
since I was a kid. My mom used to
make it whenever I was sick.

ANNABELLE
Awww. That's so sweet. It's
definitely the ultimate comfort food.

                    OX
Absolutely! You can't beat it. I've
mostly been eating Hungry Man dinners
and power bars since I got back. I'd
     kill for a home-cooked meal.

                 ANNABELLE
Well that's easy, silly. I'd be happy
 to share. All you have to do is...
            come and get it.

                    OX
   Maybe I'll take you up on that.

OX's and ANNABELLE's eyes meet. They
appear seconds away from kissing when
gunfire and screams erupt offscreen.

                 ANNABELLE
            What was that!?!

Teachers and children run past in a
panic.

                    OX
  Get to class and lock the door. The
          halls aren't safe.

                 ANNABELLE
         What are you going to do?

                    OX
Looks like today's my day to be hall
               monitor.

You are rock hard.

You can't believe how well this thing has held up. You never got around to mapping out the ensuing hallway fight scene (you've always envisioned a shot-for-shot homage to *Oldboy* with pencils, staplers, etc. replacing the knives and hammers central to that classic bit of ultraviolence), but from there the plot unfolds via the dutiful reportage of woman-on-the-scene Convivia Nefertiti (story at 10). Al Qaeda militants have infiltrated the school, taken the students (adorable moppets all) and teachers (pretty young things to the last) hostage, and holed up in the gymnasium. Ox knows he has to get to that gym, before it's too late.

```
INT. HALLWAY - BATHROOM
```

```
OX picks his way through dead Jihadis
carrying a metal yardstick and a
bloody pair of scissors. Responding
to a scream from the women's
restroom, he finds a TERRORIST in a
headwrap menacing TRACY with a
scimitar. After a close-quarters
swordfight, OX disarms him and
wrestles him into a stall.
```

```
                OX
    If you guys think waterboarding's
    bad, you're gonna hate swirlies.
```

OX shoves the TERRORISTS's head in the toilet and flushes.

                    OX
          Who are you working for!?

                 TERRORIST
                [spluttering]
            Die American pigdog!

OX swirlies the TERRORIST again.

                    OX
       Tell me who you're working for!?!

                 TERRORIST
             I work for Allah!

OX swirlies the TERRORIST again, nearly drowning him.

                    OX
Answer me asshole. I won't ask again.

                 TERRORIST
     Then glory awaits me. 72 virgins.
     Each more beautiful than the last.
     All more pure than your American
          whores [looks at Tracy].

OX, enraged, holds the TERRORISTS's head in the toilet until his body goes slack. OX flushes again, and the suction catches and unravels the

TROLL

TERRORISTS's headwrap, revealing his face.

OX
Oh my God!!!

TRACY
Ox? What is it?

OX
It can't be!

OX drags the TERRORIST out of the stall. Not of Middle Eastern descent, he looks a bit like OX himself, with chiseled features, a crewcut, and a neck tattoo of the Twin Towers that reads "Never Forget."

OX
I know this guy.

TRACY
What?!?

OX
He was in my first battalion. His name's Johnny. Johnny Jackson. But everyone called him Jackoff. We were supposed to go shark hunting this weekend.

TRACY
But Ox, that doesn't make any sense.

OX
Well, he did jack off a lot. Like, all the time actually. And at the weirdest moments too. This one time, we were picking our way through a minefield, and he...

TRACY
No! It doesn't make sense that he was dressed like a terrorist and attacking me! What the Hell is going on!?!

OX
I don't know Tracy. But I'm gonna find out. These kids are counting on me. And I don't care if they're working for Osama or Obama, no one calls hardworking, American teachers whores on my watch. You gals are the real heroes.

TRACY
[swoons]
Oh Ox! What are you gonna do?

OX
I've gotta get to that gym. That's where we'll find our answers.

TRACY
Well that should be easy for you Ox. You clearly know your way around a gym.

TRACY steps over JOHNNY's body, unbuttoning her blouse to reveal a gorgeous pair of Double Ds in a flimsy bra that can barely contain them. She kisses OX hard on the mouth and slides her hand down to his crotch.

                    TRACY
Oh my. I see the rumors are true. You
 got a permit for that thing soldier?
I don't know if it's legal stateside.

They kiss passionately, but OX steps
back.

                    OX
   I wish I could stay but...

                    TRACY
             The kids.

                    OX
        Right. The kids.

                    TRACY
     They do... come first.

                    OX
    Yeah. [Turns to leave]

                    TRACY
             Ox!

DAVE FITZGERALD

The sound of Vincent Vega's gun bursting young Marvin's head open like a Gallagher watermelon startles you back to reality, where you've been absentmindedly stroking your wordplay-boner through your boxers. Eager to reward your syntactical brilliance with a dip into your stockpile of military-themed porn, you skip to the finale.

At this point, Convivia Nefertiti has joined the action, having snuck in with a camera phone to capture the story from the inside. A blackbelt in Krav-Maga, she comes to Ox's aid during a shootout in the science lab, leading to an array of double entendres involving words like "titration" and "astatine," and a brutal moment where she burns a terrorist's face with sulfuric acid and quips "That's for all the women you motherfuckers are keepin' down you jive-ass burqa turkey!" before turning to Ox and adding "no wonder they don't want bitches goin' to school." After another scene of palpable sexual tension, the pair reach the gymnasium.

```
INT: GYM

CONVIVIA ducks down a side hall as OX
enters the gym. Hostages sit on the
floor and in the bleachers. Some roll
sports balls back and forth. Others
cry on their teachers' laps or listen
quietly to stories. Terrorists mill
around, chatting and looking at their
phones. A few even try to make small
talk with the teachers. OX ducks
under the bleachers, emerges out the
other side, and gets the drop on the
leader. Holding his scissors to the
man's jugular, OX uses him as a human
shield while addressing the room.

                  OX
Alright! Nobody move or I'll cut this
       guy's throat like a piece of
          construction paper!

Everyone turns toward OX. Several
terrorists draw their weapons,
```

shouting in broken English with
Arabic accents that don't quite
convince.

                    OX
I swear to God, don't test me. I'm a
          teacher. I will pass.

                 TERRORIST
You fool! Who do you think you are?
Fucking Johnny American Chuck Rambo
McClane? Yippee-Kay-A motherfucker?
You can't possibly take us all by
                yourself?

                    OX
Maybe you're right. Maybe I can't
take all of you. Everybody's gotta
die sometime. Maybe today's my day.
But I can definitely make it to where
you're standing before I go, so I'd
watch my fuckin' mouth asshole.

                   KID
Hehe. Mr. Manbun said a swear.

                 TEACHER
                  Shhh.

                    OX
You know, I dedicated my life to
fighting for this country. Signed up
the day the towers fell. Felt like it
was my duty. I've seen some terrible
things in this world. Done more than
my share too. But I never once

regretted my decision. Not until
today.

CONVIVIA NEFERTITI slips in through a
side door and starts filming.

                    OX
I thought America was the greatest
country in the world. Believed it
with all my heart. I fought side-by-
side with some of the bravest men
I've ever known, and now today, I saw
one of those same men attack a
defenseless woman, dressed in the
garb of our enemies.

Terrorists fidget and murmur. Some
bring their eyes to their gunsights.

                    OX
Now I'm not sure exactly what's going
on here. Maybe some of you are Al
Qaeda. Maybe some of you aren't. I
don't know, and I don't really give a
shit. What I do know is these kids –
and these women who care for them –
they're our future. They're who I
fight for. As far as I'm concerned,
the rest of you can all burn in Hell!

OX presses the scissors harder. His
captive cries out.

                    VIC
Ox! Wait! It's me, Vic! You don't
have to do this!

                    OX
Vic?! You're part of this!?! What the
         fuck is going on?!?!

                   VIC
    This came down from the top, Ox.
  We're just following orders. You know
               how it is.

                    OX
No, Vic. I don't know how it is. I've
killed a lotta fuckin' people today.
I drowned Jackoff in a toilet. These
 scissors have 50 kinds of blood on
 'em. So no. I definitely don't know
 how it is! You wanna tell me how it
                  is?

                   VIC
  Fi... fifty people?! Jackoff!?! My
     God! What have we done?!?

                    OX
That's between you and your God, Vic.
  Whichever one you worship now.

                   VIC
    Ox. Please. This is all a
misunderstanding. No one was supposed
  to get hurt. These are good men.
These guns aren't even real. It's all
              for show!

OX
What?!

VIC
It's a false flag. Stage a standoff.
Fake some dead Hadjis. Get some
cryin' kids on the news. Greenlight
another war. That's all. Just
bullshit politics. I swear Ox. You've
gotta believe me.

OX looks around the gym, his rage
building. On the wall he sees an
American flag hanging above a plaque
memorializing the Anyton school
shooting. The PS22 Chorus "Tears in
Heaven" fades in.

OX
You hear that kids? These men can't
hurt you. Their guns are just toys,
like you play with at home. But you
know what? That doesn't mean they're
not bad men. It doesn't mean they're
not terrorists.

Terrorists look around uneasily.
Teachers and children rise to their
feet.

OX
Does everyone remember what we
learned in our afterschool program?

KIDS AND TEACHERS
Yes Sir Mr. Manbun!

417

DAVE FITZGERALD

                    OX
And is everyone sick and tired of our
  school getting pushed around?

            KIDS AND TEACHERS
            Yes Sir Mr. Manbun!

                    OX
And does everyone want to get the
        heck out of here?

            KIDS AND TEACHERS
            Yes Sir Mr. Manbun!

                    OX
Well kids, let's show 'em what their
   tax dollars paid for! Attack!

With unexpected quickness and
ferocity, the children converge on
the terrorists. The camera moves
through the melee in a virtuosically
choreographed tracking shot,
capturing the following scenes: a
girl fells a terrorist with a
headbutt to the balls, and stomps him
with velcro, *Barbie* tennis-shoes;
four boys surround a terrorist, latch
onto his arms and legs, and pull him
to the ground where a fifth gouges
out his eyes with a plastic
Lunchables spoon; a teacher pulls the
chopsticks from her hairbun and
drives them into a terrorist's neck,
drawing a fountain spray of blood;
several children grab hockey sticks

and baseball bats and whack gleefully at terrorists' ankles, knees, and genitals; a boy shimmies up a climbing rope, leaps onto a terrorist's back, and bites his ear clean off; children and teachers surround a terrorist and stone him unconscious with baseballs and hockey pucks; two girls feign fright, convincing a terrorist to pick them up only to claw his face to ribbons with *Bratz* press-on nails. With terrorists falling left and right, the camera begins following one as he crawls outside the fray, only to come face to face with an adult high-heeled shoe. The camera, embodying the man's POV, pans up a shapely leg, past the hem of a tight, black skirt, across a snug, white blouse, and finally comes to rest on the face of ANNABELLE, who thrusts her American flag pencil down hard into the man's eye socket [simulated by the camera cutting to black]. Meanwhile, OX forces VIC to watch the carnage unfold.

VIC
You'll burn for this Ox. These men were soldiers. They had families. They were just doing what they were told. They deserved better.

                    OX
They knew the risks. So did you. So
does anyone dumb enough to sign up
for this endless, pointless "war on
  terror." It's bullshit Vic. We
haven't been on the right side of a
war since Hitler. No one knows that
            better than us.

                   VIC
[Opens his mouth, but says nothing.]

                    OX
           Any last words?

                   VIC
       ...Support our troops?

OX slits VIC's throat and lets his
body slump to the ground.

                    OX
      Women and children first.

[You are a goddamned Yoni Wand.]

From here, it's just wrap-up: teachers tying up the surviving terrorists with jump ropes; Ox rolling around on the blood-splattered ground while kids dogpile him with hugs; Convivia Nefertiti reporting the truth to the world; Annabelle inviting Ox and Tracy back to her apartment for a pot of comfort cavatini.

In the interest of keeping things MPAA-friendly, the story ends with Tracy stepping aside, giving Ox a long hug, and whispering "we'll always have the little girls' room" before leaving him and Annabelle to consummate their long-simmering tryst. Your vision for the unrated director's cut, however, concludes on a near-pornographic threeway - whatever you can get away with that keeps things NC-17 rather than XXX - which escalates to a fourway when Convivia shows up to find Tracy and Annabelle reciting the "this is my rifle…" mantra from *Full Metal Jacket* as they take turns servicing Ox's giant schlong. You figure it's been a long day. They all deserve to blow off some steam.

About to pop off just thinking about this salacious scene of patriotica, you flip to your cache of pretty Privates in camo panties and release your own homegrown tension into your sticky undershorts; The Lively Ones' "Surf Rider" twanging in the background.

Δ

With the movie over, you relocate to your bedroom to transcribe your notes, but can't help daydreaming about finishing your script.

You've always pictured someone impossibly beefy in the roll of Ox. A real roid-rager. Dwayne Johnson would be your first choice, if only for the guaranteed box office, but if he's unwilling to stake his everyman-growth-hormone persona on such risky material, you'd be open to bringing in Vin Diesel, or even an older, craggier name like Mickey Rourke or Sly Stallone. The female parts you'll just fill out with pornstars. None of them has to do much besides lust shamelessly after Ox anyway, and you imagine they'll be falling all over themselves – and each other, if you tell them to - to be in a real movie for once. You'll hold makeshift, sexual Olympic trials to decide the leads, posting daily, March Madness-style brackets to keep the competitors hungry. Hopefully Elle will recognize all this for the once-in-a-lifetime opportunity it is, and not hold it against you too much.

Additionally, you'll call up every horn-rimmed, midriff-cardiganed, "cool girl" who's ever rejected you, and lure them to the West Coast with promises of a kitten-heeled foot in the door. You're sure they'll come. How could they refuse? It's every little girl's dream: a plum role on the silver screen. You'll even let them audition. You're nothing if not a man of your word. You'll line them up with the pornstars so they understand exactly what's expected – *This is how L.A. works sweetheart. How bad do you want it?* – and give every one of them a Weinsteinian shot at the bigtime.

You'll still hire the pornstars, of course. That's show business. But reducing all those polished "It Girls" to broken-down, disheveled "Its," sobbing on the floor of your trailer, groping around the casting couch for their underwear while you tell them you've "decided to go another way"? Well that would be the greatest revenge of all. Quentin would be proud.

You realize this might be harder for Elle to forgive.

With your movie an international blockbuster, championed by critics and commoners alike, you'll be hailed as the next great American auteur and spend the following year garnering a reputation as the new bad boy of the festival circuit. You'll attend chandelier-lit parties and chandelier-swinging afterparties full of designer labels and designer drugs. You'll talk shop with Tony Kaye and Harmony Korine, shoot pool with James Franco and Ryan Gosling, and hook up with Eva Green, Marion Cotillard, and at least three of the umpteen Emmas running around making a name for herself these days. You'll be one of them – *one with them* – seeing the world through their beautiful, big screen eyes, breaking the fourth wall from the outside, and *Purple Rose of Cairo*-ing yourself into nonstop adventure and excitement. No longer the audience, you'll finally be part of the show.

It'll help that you'll be treating your body like a test kitchen during this time – cliff-diving into K-holes and floating out on wings of DMT – outsmarting ayahuasca with enough MDMA to roll any burdensomely heavy thoughts out of frame – mixing meth and mescaline, cocaine and ibogaine, and sprinting full-tilt through the mirror halls and trapdoors of your consciousness until you either achieve a permanent state of transcendent enlightenment, or leave your Earthly body to find one.

With the planet your playground, you'll trip across Europe, Asia, and the Middle East, becoming an enemy of the people and a citizen of the world through the kaleidoscopic, fisheye lens of psychedelic pharmacopeia. You'll scale the Eiffel Tower like a jungle gym and corkscrew back down the Wadala. You'll treat the Palm Islands of Dubai like a lazy river, tubing naked through trillion-dollar suburbs and pissing in their saltwater infinity pools. You'll Uber from Dachau to the Gulag, posting selfies for the genocidal fallen – throwing up sets and pouring out 40s at every historical marker along the way. You'll get airlifted atop the Kaaba, unfurl a 50-ft. *South Park* Muhammad down the Western wall, jackhammer through the roof, and livestream its ancient secrets from the inside.

You'll Yelp the finest whorehouses from Abu Dhabi to Helsinki; Lisbon to Taipei – fucking the tits off as many women as you can buy. Your bang map will look like Bezier curve string art. They'll call you Casasupernova by the time you're done. At the end of this sexual walkabout (fuckabout?), you'll squire the AVN Best Blowjob Award winner (whoever that lucky lady happens to be) around Cannes on a suede leash, feeding her ecstasy like dog treats and patting her bouffant during red carpet interviews. You'll humblebrag at every opportunity, effecting the perfect mixture of swaggart pomposity and mawkish gratitude, but still you'll lay awake at night, feeling something's missing; wanting something more.

You'll meet the crème-de-la-crème of your field – an astonishingly exclusive brotherhood – and they'll adopt you into their tribe. Coppola will ask you to assistant-direct his long-delayed *Godfather Part IV* (you'll promise to go to the mattresses for him). Herzog will invite you to Madagascar to document the Betsileo Zebu

Rodeo (and later tell *Der Spiegel* you were his greatest on-set inspiration since Klaus Kinski). Von Trier will request your help in finally completing *Wasington*, the abandoned third installment in his Brechtian *USA: Land of Opportunities Trilogy* (but when you arrive at his Zentropa studios in Denmark, he'll reveal he was trolling you, that no such film would ever be made no matter how badly you wanted it, and fuck you for thinking you mattered enough to convince him otherwise. You'll remain lifelong friends).

Come February, you'll receive Oscar nominations for Best Original Screenplay, Director, and Picture, and win all three in a California landslide, using your first acceptance speech to tearfully renounce your well-known exploits in the fields of substance abuse and sexual perversion, your second to defer all credit for your achievements to Elle's inspirational love and support, and your third to propose live on TV. She'll accept, of course. How could she not?

And that would be it. Once you have her, you'll have everything – the last piece of your puzzle – that ineffable Quinta Essentia that finally makes you whole. You'll be married in June, and live happily ev... well, you know. A true Hollywood ending. Inside every Tarantino, there's just a fat, lonely Kevin Smith who wants to be loved.

You feel your stomach rumble and notice the dusk between your blinds. It's already almost dinnertime. You've very nearly made it. A few more Almodóvars tonight, and tomorrow you can call her. Your journey can begin. The first day of the rest of your life.

With your drug-free brain humming away, you flip through your notes and put the finishing touches on your GRUNDL piece.

You may have a conflicted relationship with Tarantino and Smith, but they're likely more responsible for shaping who you are today than any of the arthouse masters you so love trumpeting to the plebs. For a generation of magniloquent movie geeks like yourself, these two were unassailable. You matinee-idolized their *historicity,* their *authenticity*, and their *gumption*, as things you could emulate, no matter how incapable you were of throwing a tight spiral or convincing a female classmate to let you put your hand up her shirt.

Whatever their faults, in their primes they felt like the intentionally terministic, postmodern vanguard – *the last two filmmakers who had anything new to say* - but all they really ended up saying was that there's nothing new to say. They both sold out hard, happy to keep fleecing trustafarian hosers and Reddit dilettantes in lieu of coming up with any fresh ideas, but at a time when virtually everything at the Multiplex is a sequel or a reboot, they still fall on the more original side of the creative spectrum. Sadly, this just further reinforces the stark, inescapable truth: there are no new ideas. *Art imitates art. Life is a whole other thing.*

Episode 19

You call Elle around lunchtime, and she immediately expresses surprise at your "played-out head games," sounding for all the world like three days was plenty of time for her to forget whatever it was she liked about you. *She* had a great time the other night. She *thought* you did too. Your insistence that the three-day embargo was unintentional, and that you'd simply been busy with work (you break the emergency glass on the good news of your promotion, a topic you'd hoped to save for the date proper) is met with skepticism, but after a little more wheedling damage control, you settle on a place and time to meet up for drinks.

Hearing her explain with mild insult that you could've called her the next day - and what's more, that she would've thought better of you for it - hits like a punch to the solar plexus. You somehow backed your way into contention with this girl, and then through transparent, bush-league tactics, promptly played yourself right out again. At best, you'll be starting at square one tonight. Likelier still is that you're already down a few points, and you know you're not built to win from behind.

Everyone complains about first dates, but second dates are the real challenge. Your best moves are already known quantities by the second date, and for a middling, late-round prospect like yourself, sex isn't realistically on the table until the third. She's got a read on you now. She's spent three days studying tape. Any mistake could be crucial.

You arrive just before 8:00 at Thalia's, a half-renovated sheet of flypaper on the West end of The Village - the kind of place where townies and TA's unwind with hand-muddled mojitos and feed quarters to a Seeburg full of Harry Nilsson and Elvis Costello. It bobs lazily in that neritic zone between true shithole status and gentrified grotesquerie, charging ten dollars for drinks served in repurposed pickle jars and occasionally subletting its exposed brickwork to spoken word poetry and acoustic jazz. It never gets terribly crowded, but the intentionality of its atmosphere is stifling. It would not have been your first choice.

You order an overpriced farmhouse ale you can speak somewhat intelligently about, pacing yourself so there's still some brettanomyces to explain when she arrives, but growing nervous as she becomes ten, and then fifteen minutes late.

You're already regretting revealing your GRUNDL news over the phone. You'd hoped to hit her with that as soon as she walked in the door, establishing a mood of celebration that might encourage her to drink beyond her usual threshold. Even though you're feeling things you've only experienced via the music of Teddy Pendergrass and the self-mythologizing of Ted Mosby, you still find yourself trying to predetermine the course of the evening - to plot a winning strategy.

On some level, you know you can't control the night this way, and that you shouldn't even try. But on another level - one much closer to who you are and how you understand the complex pavanes and polonaises of modern courtship - you can't really help it. You're always aware of your intentions. Small talk never feels small. You're forever trying to steer it; to make it lead somewhere. If there's one thing working in Elle's favor, it's that she appears to be the rare presence that lets you forget, at least for a time, just how awful you are.

She walks in right as you finish your conversation piece Saison, with the forced determination of someone who's come straight from the office and wants to give her best, but would much rather be home ordering takeout and browsing Amazon. Her eyes long for a disco nap; her natural aureole dimmered low by aposematic, dress code blacks and greys (a far cry from the emeraldine party calyx she wore at the wedding). That said, her hair is still reminiscent of those dark maids that drove Ted Bundy right up a wall - a rich, silken waterfall of brunette convolutions that positively enhalo her classically beautiful features - features which light up as they find you across the room. This is it. She's here. You're on. Time to begin the precise and delicate work of recapturing lightning in a bottle.

"Hey," you say. "Glad you could make it."

"Yeah, sorry I'm late. I got stuck on a call. Some pissy buyer from Brooklyn. A real Red Hook cunt. I hope you haven't been waiting."

"Just a few minutes. Can I get you a drink?"

"Good God yes," she replies, flagging down the bartender with little more than her eyelashes. "A Manhattan, Dashiell. Straight up. Two cherries."

"You got it Ellie May," the bartender says with noticeable familiarity.

"Come here often?" you ask her, affecting a cheesy, pickup artist baritone.

"Oh, that's just Dashiell," she says, attitudinizing nonchalance. "May's my middle name. He's one of the only people I still let get away with it. We go way back."

"Ah."

"Yeah. I didn't know he'd be here tonight. He tends bar at like four different places right now."

"Small town."

Dashiell returns with Elle's drink and, rather than set it down like a professionally distant member of the service industry, hands it to her directly such that their fingers make light, momentary contact. She's been here less than five minutes, and somehow you've already faltered into second place.

"You can put that on my tab," you say.

"Need another beer?" he replies dismissively, oozing the unspoken bitchiness women think is exclusive to their gender, but which a certain brand of modern man has weaponized to devastating effect.

"No thanks, *Dashiell*. I think I'll follow Elle's lead and switch to the hard stuff. Got a lot to celebrate."

"A Manhattan then?"

"Nah. I'm feeling adventurous. Tell me my thin man, do you know how to make a Nick and Nora Charleston?"

"...Yeah," he says, his eyes lasering into yours like he's trying to correct your astigmatism.

"Capital!" you say, sliding a dollar tip across the bar as he storms off to spit in your brandy.

"He really hates that stuff," Elle informs you through a knowing smirk, directed at neither of you in particular, so much as the spectacle of maleness in general.

"Good thing I didn't ask about the Maltese liquor then," you reply with a grin.

Her smile broadens, and you can feel the unbroken ice starting to cleave. You're doing ok. Off to a decent start. After Dashiell returns with a surprisingly well-realized Charleston, you relocate to a table far removed from his interloping presence, pull out her chair, and take a seat opposite her on a long, upholstered bench that spans the entire back wall. You keep reminding yourself to drink slowly. You need to find the ideal rate of consumption at which you can keep your wits about you, while still spurring her to lose track of hers.

"So, rough day at work?" you ask.

"It really was. This bitch thinks she's the next Rachel Zoe just because her ass was in the Lululemon catalog like three years ago. And I mean that literally. It was only her ass. So now she's got a little boutique with just the stupidest fucking name - The Cat's Knees? The Bee's Pajamas? - I can never remember - and she's all 'you didn't ship the infinity peplums I ordered, and..."

Already three-deep in the "words you don't even *want* to know" department, you zone out and reacquaint yourself with Elle's immaculate design. Under the mellow light of a faux Tiffany fixture, she's every bit as warm and animated as you remembered, and her idée fixe status in your mind these past three days feels wholly justified. Lost in the malachite filigree of her irises, the plosive pressings and partings of her lips, the sumptuous decantation of her Sassoon locks, all the way down to her open top button and its artful suggestion of cleavage - a fashion trick of the eye you gladly fall for - you almost forget she's still talking. It doesn't matter what she's saying anyway. She's perfect. She could be inviting you to a book burning, or a Dianetic audit, or a Jason Mraz concert, and you'd agree without hesitation. It's only by her fortuitous mention of female unmentionables that you're pulled out of your spiral-eyed trance.

"...so, long story short, I told her to go fuck herself in her hand-stitched crotchless panties, and we lost the account. But whatever. I don't want to talk about work. What about your big news!? Tell me everything!" she says, perhaps noticing where your eyes had drifted, and chest-passing the ball back into your court.

"Yeah," you sputter into action. "I'm still kind of in disbelief. It's really exciting."

"Absolutely," she agrees, raising her stemware to clink your Vlasic jar. "So, what are you going to write about first?"

"Actually, I've already written it. I spent all day yesterday. It's centered around Quentin Tarantino and Kevin Smith, but the umbrella thesis is more positing the death of the American auteur."

"Oh... Really?"

"Uhhh, yeah. Why?"

"Oh, I dunno. It just seems a little... obvious. Don't you think?"

"Well, I didn't until just now."

"I mean, sure, they were the last of a generation. Probably the last of *our* generation. But come on. America still produces plenty of auteur filmmakers. What about David Fincher? What about P.T. Anderson? Hell, what about Wes Anderson?"

"Ugh. I hate Wes Anderson."

"I don't see why that should matter. I don't think anyone can deny he's an auteur, and a pretty original one at that. I mean, obviously I haven't read your article, but it sounds like kind of a 'you kids get off my lawn' approach you're taking. Is that really the first impression you want to make?"

"Well, it's not exactly flattering to Smith and Tarantino either," you answer, giving your collar an autonomic tug. "It's more about how, in the age of the internet, and constant content churn, the whole industry's turned into a vapid, IP-obsessed remake-and-sequel factory. Tarantino and Smith are as bad as anybody. I'll give you P.T. Anderson, but everyone else is just making the same movie over and over again. Burnishing their brands. Getting those likes."

"...Ok?"

"What!?" you ask, betraying more frustration than you mean to. You really hadn't expected to be on the defensive so early.

"It's just... you write for the internet. You get that right? I know the idea of 'building a brand' is kind of gross, but if you like your job, then 'things were better before the internet' isn't really a viable take. In fact, it's kind of the same as your weird grudge against *Wall-E*. Why poke your audience in the eye?"

"Because I want to change things!" you insist.

"You mean you want to change things back," she counters.

"If you mean I want talented filmmakers to stop signing on for the 18th *Spider-Man* reboot and start doing original, creative work again, then yeah, I want to change things back. I mean, Christ, they're remaking *Back to the Future* now! Can you even believe that shit!?"

"Sure. Vanessa Hudgens is a cutie."

"Auugh! No! I mean, sure. She's fine. Whatever. That's not the point."

"Then what's the point?"

"The point is, it doesn't matter if she's good or not. It doesn't matter if the *movie* is good or not. The original's a classic. They shouldn't be messing with it at all."

"Oh God," she says - a hint of legitimate fear creeping in. "You're not one of those *Ghostbusters* assholes are you?"

"No. It's not like that. It's not a sexism thing. Some movies should just be off limits. That's all. Come on. You know what I mean, right?"

"I'm not sure I do. The way I see it, at its heart, *Back to the Future* is just about finding common ground. Kids understanding their parents, right? It's universal. It's the same reason we still perform Shakespeare."

"You're comparing *Back to the Future* to Shakespeare?"

"Don't be obtuse. You know that's not what I'm doing. It's maybe not a perfect analogy, but really, why should *Back to the Future* be any different than Shakespeare? Why isn't that a story worth retelling? 1985 is as far away for kids today as 1955 was for us. All a remake does is make a good story more relatable to the next generation. Makes sense to me."

"But, don't you think anything should be off limits?"

"Honestly?" she asks.

"Of course." you insist.

"...Not really."

"Nothing?" you ask again, offering her one last opportunity to recant.

"Nope."

"So a few years ago, when Ben Affleck and J-Lo told everyone they were going to remake *Casablanca*? You were fine with that? You thought that was a great idea?"

"Well I didn't think it was a *great* idea," she says, annoyed at having to continue explaining herself. "But no. I don't think there's anything inherently wrong with remaking *Casablanca*."

"Ok. What if it was your favorite movie then? What'd you say the other night? *Roman Holiday*?"

"That's one I mentioned, yeah," she says, now nakedly frowning.

"Ok. So, some jerkoff decides he's going to remake *Roman Holiday* with, I dunno, Channing Tatum and Scarlett Johansson. What then?"

"It would probably be bad!" she says, fighting exasperation. "I wouldn't see it. But that's not the point, and it's not even what you're arguing. Just because it would be bad doesn't mean it would be wrong. *Roman Holiday* isn't some sacred text. It's not the fucking Talmud. Explain to me what's *wrong* with remaking it?"

"God! Ok. Fine. Then what about Disney? They're cranking out these live-action, CGI remakes of their entire animation catalog! Redoing them, essentially shot-for-shot. With the songs and everything! What in God's name is the point of that?! It's a middle finger to artistic integrity. It's a shameless cash grab. Those movies are sacred. Messing with them is wrong."

"So, you think movies that make money are inherently bad? Because those Disney cartoons made a pile of cash the first time around too."

"No! But..."

"If anything, you're just making my same point better than I did. Those stories are older than our great-great-great-grandparents. Older than Shakespeare in some cases. They've been told a million different times. What's wrong with updating them for kids who've grown up with different standards for animation? Technology improves. Time marches on. So what?"

"But..."

"For that matter," she interrupts, now in a full court press, "what *about* the fucking Talmud? And the Torah, and the Bible? The oldest, most sacred books in the world. Even they just started as stories. Told and retold. Passed around the campfire, down through the oral tradition; written out from memory by a bunch of different people who spoke a bunch of different languages; translated, and retranslated, and re-retranslated; interpreted by wildly different authors with wildly different motivations across thousands of years and hundreds of cultures. Parables adapted into books adapted into plays adapted into movies. Stories we tell even when we don't realize we're telling them. *Ben Hur* to *Cool Hand Luke*, Randall McMurphy to *The Matrix*. You say we're a remake factory now? I say it's all we've ever been. And if Darren Aronofsky - another totally respectable American auteur by the way -

can make a movie about rock monsters helping Noah build the Ark, then I think we can survive a live action *Aristocats* or a Vanessa Hudgens *Back to the Future*. Don't you?"

Mentally exhausted, and ready to cut your short-term losses lest you damage your long-term goals, you stare into her bright, mesmeric eyes and surrender.

"...maybe."

"Wow... Thank you. I wasn't really expecting that."

"What can I say? I know when I'm licked. Guess I'll be doing some revisions tomorrow, if I don't just scrap the whole piece and start over."

"Heh. Yeah. Sorry about that," she says, sounding rather proud of herself, and not particularly sorry. "Guess I got a little worked up there. I did literary society all through college."

"No kidding."

"Yeah. But also, I just don't have anyone in my life right now I can talk to about this kind of stuff. The girls at the store are really sweet, but, well, let's just say I mentioned Fellini in passing once, and was immediately regaled with three different stories about getting drunk in New Orleans."

"No worries," you say as your hand makes a daring, funambulist trip across the table to touch her lightly on the arm. "I actually kind of like losing arguments. Sometimes."

This earns you your biggest smile of the night.

"I have to say," she continues, "I'm a little surprised to hear you defend some of these positions so passionately."

"Oh? Why's that?"

"Well, they just seem kind of conservative, in light of some of the stuff you've written for GRUNDL..."

[You are thrown, as from a horse.]

What was she talking about? What had she seen?! Listicles are short. Three days is an eternity. She could have read them all. Everything you've written for the past five years. Even a screengrab of that *Game of Thrones* rape scenes one is likely still cached somewhere in the cloacal hidey-holes of Reddit or 4chan. Is she here just to watch you squirm? To observe you in a controlled environment with frosty, scientific remove? To strip you of all your affected trappings and intellectual platemail and expose you for the irredeemable creepmonster you are?! What if she hadn't liked you or changed you at all? What if it was all in your head?

"...If those Disney cartoons are so perfect, why were you so hard on them in your piece about stealth sexism? I thought it was really insightful, but now I'm wondering which guy I'm talking to. Couldn't *The Little Mermaid* and *Snow White* stand to be rebooted for reasons that have nothing to do with animation quality, or even art? Couldn't one argue that, as society becomes more enlightened, we just learn to tell certain stories better?"

"Oh..." you say, crushed by relief. "You read that one huh?"

"Yeah. It was great."

"Thanks," you blush, more from the residual shame of panic than the flattery.

"So where'd that come from? I read maybe a half-dozen of your pieces today, just out of curiosity, and that was the only one that felt like it had the weight of conviction behind it. It was analytical, sure, but you clearly had some strong feelings. I liked seeing that."

"Yeah?"

"Yeah. A lot of what you said was spot on. Those Disney movies were a mindfuck. Give up your voice. Do as you're told. Look pretty and wait to be rescued. That's what we grew up seeing. That's the fairytale. There wasn't one proactive Disney Princess until, like, *Mulan*. All those other bitches were just mopping dirt and marking time. Seriously, the sheer amount of mopping Disney Princesses have done over the years. It's insane. No wonder they all started talking to mice and birds and shit. They were losing their fucking minds."

This cracks you up. You're right back in it. You never want her to stop talking.

"I always hated Belle the worst," she continues. "*Beauty and the Beast* is basically just a PR campaign for spousal abuse. 'You can change him honey. Just keep at it. Sure, he locked you in his house and threatened to kill your dad, but he won't be a beast forever, and in the meantime, you can be friends with the teapot.'"

"Right!?!"

"Absolutely. Jasmine sucks too. Like, seriously, how many times can one person get kidnapped? She's basically the *Taken* girl in see-through parachute pants. Take some goddamned responsibility for your shit, Jasmine."

"Totally!" you agree. "Jasmine's mad dumb. But I'd even take it one step further and say the Disney canon was just as harmful to boys as it was to girls."

Elle stalls mid-sip, seemingly for the express purpose of giving you the most rectilinear side-eye you've ever seen.

"Excuse me?" she asks.

"Um... I dunno," you reply. "I just think..."

"Hold that thought," she says, tossing back the rest of her drink like she's slugging Gatorade during a timeout, before motioning a busboy over to your table.

"I'll have another Manhattan. Dashiell knows how I like them."

"And you sir?" the busboy asks.

"Old Fashioned?"

"What a shock," Elle wryly observes before handing the kid a crisp twenty. "I'm gonna run to the ladies'. Round two's on me."

Δ

You can feel Dashiell's mordant stare from across the room. Contrary to your pre-date stratagem, your drink is very strong, while Elle, upon returning and tasting hers, disdainfully requests that the busboy call Dashiell a pussy on her behalf. You know he's stacking the BAC deck against you.

"So," Elle says, sipping her whiskey. "You were saying something stupid about Disney movies?"

"Um..." you reply, nervously drinking your too-strong drink too fast.

"Please. Explain."

"Well... I... so it's like you said. With the whole fantasy thing, right? You grow up watching these stories, and at the time, they seem like really special stories. It wasn't like it is today, with 20 animated movies a year. We got one, if we were lucky. They were events. Magical. You watched them with your whole family. Sometimes over and over. I'm pretty sure I watched *Aladdin* every day the Summer after 4th grade..."

"Uh-huh."

"Right. So, these movies - these magical, fairytale movies - which were also marketed within an inch of their lives - toys, clothes, books, McDonalds - they gained outsized importance. For all of us. Cultural touchstones. Any kid you met anywhere was bound to know at least a couple of these movies. They were, like you said, what we grew up fantasizing about. Playing at. Pretending to be."

"Right..."

"Ok. So you're saying growing up seeing all these Princesses just sitting around, resigning themselves to bad situations - mending rags for mean girl stepsisters, offering free maid service to random midgets, shacking up with emotionally unavailable werewolves or minotaurs or whatever he's supposed to be - was damaging to entire generations of women. That it taught them to be subservient and docile, and that if they were subservient and docile enough, a nice man with good bone structure would ride in on a white horse to rescue them, and if they were lucky, they might even get to keep the horse? Are we on the same page so far?"

Shook, you're working overtime to infuse this thorny subject with some levity, but none of your jokes are landing, or else she's willing herself to ignore them. You feel like Antonius Block. From here on out, any move could be your last.

She takes a drink, appears to consider everything you've just said, and nods for you to continue.

"Ok. So, it's not like I disagree with you. Obviously. I mean, you read my article."

"Listicle," she hisses, practically in Parseltongue.

"Jesus. Ok, my listicle. You read it. We are not in disagreement. All I'm trying to say is, look at it from a guy's point of view. You grow up watching these movies, same as the girls, but what you see is a whole lot of hot, helpless ladies just sitting around waiting to be rescued. *By you.* Jasmine in her see-through pants. Pocahontas in her buckskin minidress. Ariel in her shell-bra. All beautiful. All perfectly proportioned. I mean, the way they're drawn - all tits and eyeballs - it's fucked up. Even the Priest in *Little Mermaid* got a hard-on. Disney Princesses are pretty much sex symbols with training wheels for little boys."

"...Ok," she says. "Let's put a pin in the pervier aspects of... all that, and just say for now I agree with you. The Disney Princess template is sexy. Sexualized, even. Every girl wants to grow up to look like that. Slender waist. Nice rack. Perfect hair forever. Everything you need to wear an empire waisted, buttercup yellow ballgown to your wedding reception and not look like an asshole. They set an impossible standard. But please, for the love of God, how is that as damaging to boys as it is to girls?"

"Well, when you put it that way... but still, I feel like all these images of perfect women just sitting around with no prospects, hoping against hope that with the aid of some magical shoe, or interventionist flying seamstress, or whatever, that somehow, against all odds, someone will choose them, save them, I mean..."

"What?! What do you mean?!"

"That it's not that easy! That it's not really like that when you grow up. No one's waiting to be rescued. Women have more prospects than they know what to do with. They do the choosing now.”

“We sure do,” she says, looking at you almost piteously now, like you just put a winning lottery ticket through the wash.

“Don’t get me wrong. I believe women are 100% equal to men.”

“Thanks. That’s big of you.”

“No. Obviously. It’s just, like, you grow up thinking you’re supposed to be this manly, heroic, protector guy - the knight in shining armor - and when you find a girl you really like, she’ll just be waiting. And that’s not just Disney. That’s the vast majority of mass entertainment. Sitcoms, romcoms, action movies, video games, you name it. But instead, what you find is most women either don’t want that, or else they’ve already committed to the idea that it doesn’t exist. So instead of holding out for Prince Charming, they’re busy trying to fixer-upper the Beast, or Gaston even, and the real hero can’t even get a foot in the door.”

Elle laughs. A scornful, corrosive laugh you haven’t heard until now.

“Wow. So that’s your deal then? The ‘nice guy’ who never got to rescue the Princess?”

“I think that’s a little reductive. I’m not saying women should be Princesses waiting to be rescued. I'm just saying men shouldn't be taught that they are either. That it's harmful to us too. Is that so wrong?"

"I'm sorry," she says, laughing harder. Meaner. Like stickpins. "I'm just imagining you, like, standing in the rain with a boombox right now, and it's kind of priceless."

"Fuck you," you say, less playfully than you intend.

"No, really. I'm not trying to be a bitch. I see your point, I guess. I just don't think you realize how precious you sound right now. I'm also laughing a little at how much you and Dashiell would probably get along if you got to know each other. He's a sad boy too."

You lower your head, wishing for an avenue to backtrack out of this conversation; feeling nothing behind you but solid brick.

Seeing she's maybe taken things too far, Elle attempts to talk you down a bit, apologizing again before adding, "I've certainly dated my share of Gastons."

You look up. Maybe you still have a chance here.

"I just think you have to realize," she continues, "that regardless of the danger of stereotypes in general, the stereotypes boys get growing up are way more empowering than the stereotypes girls have to work with. It's so obvious to me it's hard to even see your argument. It's like, I'm sorry not every girl you ever liked liked you back, but at least you had it in your head to go after the things you wanted. Not one of those princes ever *had* to go save the princess, you know? They *chose* to do it. To strap up, ride hard, slay the dragon, and get the girl. They had the agency to take risks, and they reaped the rewards. That's more than you can say about any Disney princess until almost the turn of the century."

"I guess."

"And just for the sake of argument, let's say men haven't had it easier for the whole of human history. Then what? Surely you can't be arguing that women have?"

"No... I think we're equal... I think there are advantages to both sides, and that those advantages have balanced out, over time, to something as close to equality as we're ever going to get."

"Ok. I'm not sure about all that, but in lieu of getting into equal pay or reproductive rights or a whole host of other touchy, fucked up things - up to and including who just got elected fucking President - if we're already equal, then what's your problem? Do you think we shouldn't be?"

"Of course not. It's just the misrepresentation, I guess. We were sold a bill of goods. The fairytale is a lie."

"Isn't that a good thing though? Isn't the real problem not that the fairytale is presented as truth, but that it's presented as ideal? I mean, fairytales might keep adults human - like you said the other night - but they also keep kids from becoming adults. Call it the soft misogyny of high expectations. What we're taught is the template for romance is actually just an extension of the patriarchy. Even a dumdum like Jasmine could see that. Women aren't prizes to be won. And right now, whether you mean to or not, what you sound like is a member of the most thoroughly *advantaged* demographic on the planet who still just wants to complain about how unfair everything is. It's not a great look."

"But... I mean..."

A fumbling of fermatas and enjambments, you are forced to concede again. A demoralizing second-half blowout. You honestly don't even know what you're arguing about anymore.

"Look," you say, as she checks her phone - scrolling through less taxing conversations she could be having elsewhere. "I think you've got the wrong idea about me here. I'm not this sexist fanboy guy. I'm just someone who maybe spends a little too much time thinking about pop culture. I always have. I take it seriously. I think it says something about us. About society. The lens through which I view the world. If it's made me a little wrongheaded in some areas, I'm open to that. I just... I just really like you is all."

"I like you too..." she says, a phantom "but" seeming to follow like a contrail.

"It's like you said before. I don't really have anyone I can talk to about this stuff. Who cares about it the way I do."

"You work at GRUNDL."

"Yeah, but come on. You've read the site. They're all idiots over there... Drunk on Fellinis, right?"

"Yeah," she says, her smile warm, but sad.

"Can't we just start over? I haven't even had a chance to thank you for turning me around on Almodóvar yet. I revisited after the wedding, and I really enjoyed it. I think I had him all wrong."

"Oh. That's cool. Which one did you watch?"

You rattle off the five films you rented from VitaLink, singling out *Tie Me Up, Tie Me Down* as your favorite. Her face is doing something new now, but you're not quite sure what.

"You... you watched all five of those since the wedding?"

"Yeah! Hey, maybe that's what I should write about."

"Yeah... Maybe."

"Obviously you know his work better than I do. What angle would you take? What do you like about him that maybe hasn't been said?"

If your latent fear that she might've agreed to this date solely to study you on an anthropological level had subsided, it quickly gains new traction under the stern, inquisitive look she's giving you now. You feel like she's undressing you with her eyes, but in no way because she wants to see you naked.

"Actually, if you don't mind, could we maybe talk about something besides movies?"

"Oh... Sure. Sorry."

"It's fine. I'm just a little movied out."

"Ok..."

You both sip your drinks. She starts checking her phone again. You drum your fingers to an unfamiliar Neil Young song. One of the weird, sci-fi ones. You've really grown to hate this bar.

"Feel like a smoke?" you ask.

"Nah. I don't really smoke. Mostly just for nostalgia. You can totally go though."

"Oh," you say, stopping your fingers on a flam. "No, that's ok."

She starts scrolling again. You finish your drink. Neil croons on.

"What about weed?" you ask. "I think my dealer's back in town."

"No thanks," she says. "Same kinda thing. I really just don't much anymore. Weddings and funerals. And Groundhog Day. That's about it."

"Oh," you say again. "Why Groundhog Day?"

She shrugs.

Finally, with nothing left to grab onto, adrift in the real world with a real girl you really want to keep talking to, you utter the only sentence you can think of – the kiss of death for many a date, but better, you hope, than no kiss at all.

"So… do you like music?"

Before she can open her mouth, her phone rings. She answers in an instant – almost like she was anticipating it – and gives you the "just a sec" finger (her ringtone, by the way, is Kitty Pryde's "OKcupid," just in case you needed any further proof that this is a woman after your own heart). Meanwhile, you notice by way of an antique Kit-Cat clock hanging over the jukebox, that it's exactly 10PM.

After a few minutes of conversation breezier than anything you've enjoyed all evening, she says goodbye.

"I love that track," you offer, pointing toward her phone.

"What? Oh yeah, thanks," she says, downing the rest of her drink. "So, look, I'm really sorry, but I kind of have to go. A friend of mine just got into town. I haven't seen her in forever. She's only here for one night. Is... is that ok?"

"Um..." you say, knowing she doesn't really mean 'is it ok if I go?' so much as 'is my leaving going to lead to your suicide?' "...Sure. If you gotta go, you gotta go."

"Thanks," she says.

"I had a really good time," you add, sliding off your bench. "You really know your stuff. That offer still stands if you ever want a job at GRUNDL."

"That's sweet. I had a good time too."

Already three steps away, you get the sense that she's actively trying to prevent you from walking her out, but hustle to catch up anyway, eurostepping around tables and chairs to beat her to the door and clumsily hold it open. Anyone watching you at this point is surely overcome with British *Office* levels of fremdscham.

"So," you say, following her outside. "We should do this again."

"Sure," she says, crossing her arms to indicate that she's chilly and wants to get where she's going. "Text me."

"I will!" you say as she heads off toward the other end of The Village - so quickly she likely doesn't even notice the gingerly step forward you took in hopes of kissing her goodnight. You, in turn, can't help but notice that her arms are swinging freely now, and that it's not really even that cold out.

Episode 20

Despite the catastrophe of your second date, you awake the following day still hopeful you might yet salvage a third. You reach for your phone, thinking you'll play the smitten fool who just can't wait to tell her again what a boffo time he had last night, but the moment you lay hands on it, your alarm clock voices its shattering dissent - a tripwire warning against whatever it was you thought you were about to do. It may have a point. It's still early. Best to wait.

You work your way operose through your new routine - exercises, shower, semi-professional attire, passable breakfast - if only to maintain the illusion that you still feel as enthusiastic about life as you did one day pridian. Day four tends to be the make-or-break day any time you get a notion to start taking better care of yourself. The unfamiliar hormone spikes have worn off, replaced by a host of all-too-familiar realities: sore abdominals still years away from being visibly excavated; a poppyseed bagel that, while not wholly unhealthy, loses what little nutritional value it has under an impasto of jalapeno cream cheese; the nubby, brown hoodie you wear like a non-contact jersey for psychic injury; and worst of all, the hooks of post-post-withdrawal malaise clamping down on your brain like an arcade crane claw machine.

Just as with the agony of withdrawal, the euphoria of post-withdrawal never lasts, and what you're left with is generally recognizable as your true self – shuffling through the banality loops of everyday life – taking slightly deeper breaths – thinking longer, more stressful thoughts – boredly, mundanely drug-free. Nothing is as atrociously bad, or as astonishingly good as it might've seemed this past week; the future is just a low, flat stretch of highway headed toward a noon horizon in the middle distance. How you approach it is entirely up to you.

When you do pick up your phone, you receive confirmation that your primary weed dealer has returned from her jam sojourn, and arrange for a legerdemain transaction in the GRUNDL parking lot. Regardless of what happens between you and Elle, you are in no way yet prepared to bid farewell to the arboraceous lifestyle. It'd take another three months of clean living before you genuinely don't *want* to get high anymore (and all the time) (and forever) and if, during that time, every single thing in your life doesn't go exactly right, well, that's pretty much all the excuse you need to tuck and roll off the wagon, and right back into the weed(s).

Deciding you've been patient long enough, you send out as unobtrusive a flirt text as your mind can assemble:

Hey cutie

You stare at your phone - trying to will a response - but nothing comes. And so, telling yourself there are a billion reasons people don't always text back right away - that she's still asleep (awww), or in the bath (mmmm), or driving responsibly (because of course she would), or in a dead zone (they're everywhere), or out of juice (happens to the best of us), or in another grueling meeting with that gash from Red Hook (which you'll be happy to listen to her complain about for as long as she wants whenever she does respond) - (which she definitely will) - you head off to work.

Quick to start chain smoking again, if only to give your text-thirsty fingers something to do, your route looks (un)remarkably ordinary without satival enhancement. The sky is flat and grey. A tree is just a tree. An oil stain only highlights the imperiled nature of both. Finishing your first cig quickly, you stub out into an anthill and watch its residents scurry topside; mad, microscopic first responders full of futile bravery in the face of sudden, inexplicable disaster.

Reaching for another, you feel your phone vibrate (Yes!) and nearly send your entire pack of Camel lights caravanning into the solenopsist desert as you rush to answer. But no. You were mistaken. A phantom buzz (sigh) – a common symptom amongst your pocket dial generation (what's wrong with us? What is technology doing to our nerves? To our skin?).

You know you should put your phone away (but what if you miss something?). Maybe you'll send her another text (just a quickie). Just in case she didn't see the first one (she's a busy girl). You could be waiting all day for no reason (who knows how often she checks her phone?). A silly mishap (that could easily have been avoided, if only you'd sent that second text)!

About to hit the homeless-heavy portion of your walk, you charge forward, pretending without shame like your cell screen is the only thing in the world. People address you directly (they know your name now), step into your path (you avoid all eye contact), attempt to slow your gait (you push through them like a tackling drill). The Bustelo woman grabs your ankle, and you ash your cigarette onto her gnarled hand. You hear a few working girls (whores) call you an asshole, but they barely register as real people in your current state of mind (fuck 'em all).

By the time you reach the park you're being peppered with boos and maledictions, and throw up a parthian bird out of kayfabe formality (we all have our roles to play). In truth, you couldn't care less, as you've spent this harrying affair drafting (you believe) the text that will turn everything around, ignite a day-long exchange of playful banter, and ultimately precipitate a third date so enchanting it will completely erase the sour memory of the second:

> Had a great time last night.
> How's your morning going?

It's been a long time since you let anyone get this kind of purchase on your psyche, but you're in it now. As helpless to stop thinking about her as you are to quit smoking reefer, or eating Cheetos, or watching *The Simpsons*. What felt, just a few days ago, like the annunciation of some new, divinely bisensuous form of agaperotic love, has since gained the conscriptive weight of cultic mania (you belong to her now). You're not sure how these feelings got so big, so fast, but they've breached your penetralia, and rewritten your mystagogy (she's made a true believer out of you). This separation – this torturous waiting for her to just *fucking text you back already* (!) - feels akin to being cast into outer darkness. But you can't give up (only the fool hath said in his heart, "there is no Elle").

Though the hillock of flowers and candles for Cassie Abrams has only grown (every fucking year), The Women in Black are still nowhere to be seen. Plunging back into paranoia, you wonder: What if they actually *had* effected world peace? (That would certainly explain why Elle hasn't responded to your totally appropriate and chill AF text messages). What if (hear yourself out) sometime during the night, via the reliably dude-free backchannels of Pinterest and Etsy and WNBA Message Boards, the world's female population found the wherewithal to unite and start (girls, girls) running the world? You've always believed, deep down, that women are more connected than men will ever know (or could even comprehend); that things are decided via secret cliterati councils, with encrypted proclamations ferreted through the sub-dark-web (the pink-web?) letting them all in on the plan for overthrowing their worser halves (the unfairer sex). Has there been some tipping point in the gender wars? Human parthenogenesis? Maternal abnegation? Or just a sudden, mass realization, via that low-humming, animist connection they all share (don't try to deny it) through flowers and butterflies and waterfalls and shit, that they just plain don't need dick anymore? (time's up). The chastity bunkers are probably already built. Men are ticking bombs of rage and idiocy. (If women have locked themselves away, we'll all be dead in a month). Their half of the sky will come crashing down in a hail of testosterone-fueled, double-bandoliered, high-capacity-magazine ultraviolence, and even if you survive, the emergent junta will undoubtedly be merciless in exterminating the leftovers (your search history alone would make you a prime candidate for an Atwoodian particicution). Nothing in your file (and they definitely have files) will save you.

Spinning out as you reach the lobby, your fast-mushrooming fear of the coming coup de'twat is put to rest as Jennica greets you with a warm smile (if it was happening, she'd for sure be in on it - one less thing to worry about). You whizz past her into the elevator and turn to see her projectile pouting at you as the doors close. You'll smooth things over later. (Or not). (It doesn't matter). You've still got her number, but you know you'll never dial it. The poor, misunderstood, pretty secretary, and her lackadaisical husband, and her cheekini panties; they mean nothing to you now. It's Elle or bust.

You drop your bag, head to the can, and produce several parched, brittle, *pop-gun* shits that catch on the pilose hairs of your ass crack before blooping into the water below. You count seven of these crustaceous nuggets - you're sure of it - feeling a bit like an *air-mix lotto machine* that just spit out its sequence of ping-pong balls. But unnervingly, you stand to find the basin completely empty - your dumplings vanished into the plumbing pre-flush. Or perhaps, just pungent, voluminous vapor. *Never there at all.*

You return to your desk, and with your Tarantino piece no longer viable, set about scanning the day's headlines.

Carrie Fisher died (goddamn, how'd you miss that!?); *Rick and Morty* remains on indefinite hiatus amid rumors of Dan Harmon's institutionalization (kinda saw that one coming);

Trump's giving Omarosa a job in the White House (they're not here to make friends); the *Back to the Future* reboot has cast Vince Vaughan as Doc Brown (Jesus, really!?!); the Hawks are officially blowing up their most competitive roster in years (fucking Lebron ruins everything!!!) and Charles Barkley had some choice words to say about the decision ("This video has been removed by ESPN"); Mel Gibson is nominated for a Best Director Golden Globe (How!?!); Kim and Kanye have announced they're trying for another addition to their Instagram feed (paraphrasing), and that regardless of sex, the baby will be named "Chicago" (this fucking country); an Elvis/Beatles/Michael Jackson/Nirvana all-hologram tour goes on sale tomorrow (the future (and the past) is now).

This is nightmarish. For the first time all day, you feel some negativity toward Elle (you don't mean it though. She's perfect), both for eighty-sixing your original article, and for continuing to let you twist in the wind with regards to your (now) *two* (!) unacknowledged texts. *What is the fucking holdup?* (Oh God. What if something happened to her?) She's *so* busy she can't take *ten seconds* and punch in a few phonemes? "Hey"? "Not bad"? "How are you"? (a car accident? An aneurysm? Murdered by a jealous Dashiell?) These miniscule niceties are *too much to ask?* (What if she's lying in a hospital bed right now? How would you feel then, asshole?) What are you doing wrong? Why is she finding it so easy to put you off, when you can literally think of nothing else? (You hope she's ok). Should you be more direct? More forceful? Has she misgauged your interest? Does she like a firmer hand? Does she want a Disney prince after all? Does she need to be rescued?

Guided by compulsion, you type a third message:

Hey girl. Having a bitch of a time coming up with a new article after you put me through the wringer last night. Kinda feel like you owe me an apology. Or at least another drink. ;)

It's a little pushy - a little dickish even - but you think the winky face makes it work.

You wait, staring at an analog wall clock until your eyes fill with the specular image; your pupils synchronizing with the second hand, making slow, deliberate trips around your orbital bones as minute after rejective minute ticks by.

After six full revolutions, you snap out of it (still nothing. *Jesus Fucking Christ!*) and angrily start drafting a takedown of the burgeoning hologram concert phenomenon.

Ever since 3-D 2Pac showed up at that fateful Coachella back in 2012, it was only a matter of time before hologram concerts became normalized, and perhaps even the new normal. Holograms don't need tour buses or dressing rooms. They don't have riders full of top-shelf tequilas and pill-pressed painkillers. They can't get sick, or arrested, or OD, or really even miss flights. Just pop 'em on a flash drive and Dropbox 'em to their next tour stop. Presumably you still have to pay them (or their manager, or programmer, or likeness rights holo-pimp) but you're confident the potential for risk reduction will ultimately prove them an unqualified win for the live music industrial complex. As you research the already-tremendous ticket sales for the "Decades of Idols" tour (Good Lord), it dawns on you that they could continue adding dates in perpetuity - not to mention play 100 cities simultaneously, for as many nights as they can sell out - and you're genuinely surprised that it's even taken this long.

While the technology's been restricted thus far to the resurrection of late performers deemed "gone too soon," you have no doubt it will soon be offered to living ones as well (those who can afford it anyway). Why should Taylor Swift (for example) be subjected to the trials and tribulations of life on the road when, with a little greenscreen motion capture, she can record a concert with the same hermetic, studio-bolstered perfection as one of her albums, send it out as her anamorphic ambassador, and kick back while her cut of the gate and merch rolls in? No chance of getting caught in a lip-sync scandal, or rolling her ankle trying to dance like no one's watching in front of 50,000 screaming fans. More time to create and expand her brand. Sure, some people would hate her for it, but whatever she lost in ticket value, she'd make up for in ticket volume (and then some). Sooner or later, hologram sets will be just another way for the internet generation to feel connected (just like streaming television); a way for them to all be at the same concert, regardless of whether they're there on the same night, or even the same continent. They'll still be `seeing the same thing`. Before long, we'll be mix-and-matching dead and living musicians like fantasy football teams (and seeing a superstar live will be akin to scoring tickets to the Super Bowl), lining up to watch Sinatra trade bars with all three Beastie Boys while Flea handles the low end and John Bonham keeps thunderous time. `Punk will see a resurgence` amongst the poor, but the (quote unquote) bucket list band will become a thing of the past. We'll kick our grief down the road, never deal with loss, or worry about the future. There will be time for everything. `Stars will stay young forever. The music really will never die.`

You look over this skeletal outline. It's interesting, but you wonder if it's suffering from the same problems Elle called your first piece out for (you kids get off my lawn!). Is this *really* how you feel, or do you just hate *everything* right now because the woman you're in fucking *LOVE* with won't *fucking TEXT you* the *FUCK BACK* already? *(FUCK!!)*

In a fervor, you rip your phone open and fire off the most passive-aggressive message you can think of that might still pass for louche:

Hey baby. What gives? You're driving me a little crazy with this radio silence. If you don't want to talk to me that's fine, but at least do me the courtesy of saying so.

Damn right you said it. That's how a *man* sends a *goddamned text* (you've played the hopeless romantic enough. You should know better by now)! Confidence! Cockiness! That's what women want! If she doesn't respond (and make it fucking snappy), you may have to take drastic action and actually call her (you don't want to have to do it, but she's forcing your hand). You refuse to be ghosted. Not now. Not like this.

Hey. Sorry. Busy morning. What's up?

(*YES!!!*)

You've made contact. This next message is crucial (don't be a jerk). Pull it back (say something clever). Make her laugh (LOL).

Not much. Just wanted
to say hey. Sup witchu
Pikachu?

[You are a Khmer Rouge mass grave of self-
loathing.]

Not much. Work.

Not great - (not the lolz you were hoping for) - but not nothing. Just keep her talking. Be cool (please, God, let you be cool).

That's cool. I'm at
work too. Obviously.
:)

And before she could possibly have time to put her phone down...

Got any plans tonight?

Again, you wait, nervously tapping your stained-xanthic fingers. One minute. 2. III. 5ive.

T1n (X). Nothing. Fearing cranial hemorrhage, you sprint to the elevator just to get some distance from your phone's cold, silicate gaze. You blow through three cigarettes in five minutes, but start to worry she may have answered right after you stepped away, and that you are (right now) (right this *very second*) making *her* wait, and rush back down. Still nothing.

At a loss, and with scotophilia increasingly your guide, you return to your notes (Barry said he wanted stuff with a voice. No reason to hold back now).

Independent of the obvious grotesqueries inherent to keeping dead entertainers on the books for time immemorial, the `advancement of VR technology` in general has, in recent years, risen pretty high up your personal phobic ranks. Once an appealing prospect to your Indica/in-da-couch sensibilities - that you could one day, conceivably, `stay home forever - your enthusiasm gradually turned to` apprehension. How long, you wonder, before **we** `only interact with one another via the virtual world`? **How long before an** `immersive, indistinguishably accurate digital copy of Earth is` rendered in toto, and made as available to us as Wi-Fi (complete with another fucking utility bill)?

How long until, rather than deal with the hassle and expense of traveling to New York, or Paris, or Timbuktu, or braving the innumerable dangers of climbing Everest or rafting the Amazon, we just do it from our couches? Safely. Comfortably. On our own time? And where will we go from there?

Will we, presumably, also be able to *be* whomever we want within this virtual world - to design our best self (or selves)? Will every woman have big, unwieldy tits and a proscenium ass? Will every man have grenade belt abs and be hung like a Diomedan horse? (*You sure as shit will*). Will pulsating hand-held attachments and electrostimulant sockets - The Nintendo We? The Sony Laystation? The XXX-Box? - actually make sex *feel* better, or just make it *look* better? And how good will the latter have to get before no one cares about the former anymore? (you're nearly there already with just porn and tube socks). And what *about* virtual porn? Will we someday be able to fuck anyone we want, anytime, anywhere? Is that in the cards? Of course, there will still be real people behind all these wandering avatars, but will that matter in a fictional universe where everyone's playing make-believe? Shit. Even if newly complicated rules for dating do take shape in this global cybertopia, for every real woman roaming its hyperrealistic streets, you imagine there will be at least five more 100% `pliable, purchasable, programmable prosthitutes` to be grabbed off the rack and dragged back to your mancave by their (forever perfect) hair. So then the question becomes `not what we` *can* `do, but what we can't do.` Be honest. If you had the capability, in the greased-up palm of your hand, to fuck an `18-year-old Kate Upton` with zero consequences, would you do it? What about 16? What about 14? What about 12? `What will we do, and who will we be, when we're finally given the ability to be and do anything?`

And if we can fuck grade school Kate Upton, then why not `that girl who rejected us`? Why not two or three of her? Why not in front of her boyfriend, or her husband, or her entire extended family? Why not on the floor of the Senate, or the infield at the Kentucky Derby? For thousands of screaming fans? Live on every channel? And as long as you're doing that, why not grow your (already Diggleresque) dick to the size of a baseball bat and beat her to death with it afterwards? It's probably what you wanted to do anyway (that bitch), on some level (thinks she's too good for *me*).

Such casual `violence` may well replace football, video games, and God knows what else as America's `new favorite pastime`, sliding effortlessly into its role as `"just a nice way to unwind after a long day at the office."` Put your feet up, crack open a cold one, and mow down a virtual shopping mall full of virtual bystanders with a virtual AK-47. Who cares? It's just a LARP. You work hard. You've earned this time. And besides, `if it's not real, and everyone's doing it, what does it matter anyway?`

You're breathing heavily. You've wandered so far out into your own future shocked brainstorm that you're starting to fear self-electroporation. Why hasn't she texted you back? *(Jesus, fuck, why)?!* Was the date really *that* bad? (*Did you ruin everything that fast*)? Have you already missed your shot? (*Is this it*)? (*Are you done*)?

You feel another buzz.

Your heart leaps.

A chance.

Hope.

Your hands shaking - reminding you in no uncertain terms that you need to go outside and meet your dealer soon - you slowly open your phone like a Botticelli clamshell, hoping for all the world to find your Venus nestled starkers inside.

> Seasons 1-9 of **Scrubs** now available on Netflix.

(AUUUUUUUUUUUUUUUUUUUUUUUUUUUUUUU UUUUUUUUUUUUUUUUUUGH!!!!!)
   (IT'S NOT EVEN FUCKING HER!)(FUCK!) (FUCKFUCKFUCK!!!)(FUCK ZACH BRAFF!!!) (FUUUUUUUUUUUUUUUUUUUUUUUUUUUUUUUU UUUUUUUUUUUUUUUUUUUUUUUUCK!!!)

That's it. No more Mr. Nice Guy (stop pussyfootin' around)! No more LOLs and emoticons and m'Lady courtly bullshit (time to man up)! (*Show her you mean business*)! (That's what *she* wants)! (That's what they *all* want)!

> Ok. I'm not sure what your problem is, but I don't like being ignored. It's fucking rude.

After five more minutes, panic sets in (*why is she being so fucking difficult!?*). Just as it's been years since you allowed yourself to fixate on anyone in this way, it's been just as long since you felt the nauseating, full-body fistula of true rejection boring through your (already tenderized) core muscles. You hate this feeling. You've built your entire life around not feeling *this feeling*. The anaclitic need for validation is a crutch you have happily done without, primarily by just beating everyone else to the punch; by never giving anyone a chance to not give you one (who the fuck are *they* to validate *you*?). It's easier to always be the smartest guy in the room when you never leave your house. It's easier to be a misunderstood genius when you never explain yourself. It's easier to hate *everyone* than it is to love *anyone*. And you're all about taking the easy way. For almost a decade, you've made it your business to make sure no one could tell you anything, until four days ago, when this dazzling creature teleported into your life from some hot chick Ultima Thule, and before you knew it (before you even thought to try to know it), you were letting her tell you everything. And you were believing her.

You believe her now too. You know exactly what she's trying to tell you in her own heuristic, inter-text-ual way (read between the complete lack of lines). But pride be damned. You will grasp at the hem of her garment. You will cling to these Heavenly clouds. You will *make* her believe in you.

Your only move now (for contact; for anything) is to drop a neutron bomb. (50 Negatons). Make her so mad she *has* to deal with you, and then try to work your way back (the penitent man shall pass). It's that, or it's the end.

You head back to the bathroom.

Wow. Ok. I never thought I'd do this, but I feel a bold move is in order. Lemme know what you think.

This is the caption you attach to your first ever dick pic. The tiny, rudimentary camera on your flip-phone, combined with the dim lavatory lighting, makes for an image severely lacking in resolution quality, but these things can't be helped. You work yourself up to a mizzenmast, snap a pelfie, and set it adrift. You can only hope it looks better (and bigger) on her end. Expelling a travelling circus of baby elephant farts as you wait - pants around ankles, on the edge of your toilet seat - you decide this message is a little vanilla, and look to bring it home with one more cocksure flirt text.

So tell me, I'm curious, how old were you exactly, when you first realized you could get men to do anything you wanted?

At this last provocation, the "Elle is typing" alert appears. This is it...

Dude. You need to stop.

Aww. Come on now. You were playing hard to get. You can't blame a guy for trying.

You're being really aggressive. It's not cool.

I'm sorry. I just wanted to get your attention. It's all in fun. Now come on. How 'bout a peek? I showed you mine.

We went on one date.

Two if you count the wedding.

The wedding was fun, but it wasn't a date.

Well it was the best non-date I've ever been on. You liked me too. I know you did.

It was a nice night. I got really high. That's all.

Come on. Just give me a chance. I really like you.

Look. I'm trying to be nice here. But I'm just not interested.

One drink. I know I can change your mind.

I'm sorry. I think we should just be friends. And if you can't pull it together, then not even that. Goodbye.

Friends.

She wants to be *friends*.

You know what that means.

You shut your phone off without another word, just in case she tries to follow up with some patronizing bullshit. You won't put yourself through that (no one, in the history of mankind, has ever let anyone else down easy).

You return to your computer, but your notes are a madman's pidgin scrawl (prosthitutes? You thought that was clever? *Really?!*). In this moment you feel, profoundly, that you have nothing of value to say (that you maybe never did). That you've crafted your entire persona around something fundamentally stupid. *What was the point?* The so-called Golden Age of television you'd been so keen to historicize? It was already gone – plastered over by the loud, streaming wallpaper of Peak TV (spoiler alert!). This thing you do – *this criticism* – it's unnecessary. It's not a profession. It's barely a hobby. It's parasitic, right up until it becomes saprophytic. It reduces art to numbers (1-10). Ratings (A-F). Formulae, influences, and quotes (This = This + This [with a touch of That thrown in] says So-And-So of *The Website*). This cottage industry of reviewers and recappers? Livetweeters and Top 10 rankers? It's a bubble, like anything else. It may already be bursting. We can only watch so much.

You can feel your utility deteriorating. Sure, you're good with a turn of phrase, and you know a thing or two about Agnès Varda and Antonin Artaud. But so what? You could throw a rock in any terrible bar in The Village and hit someone with a more marketable all-around skillset (that sounds like fun actually). They're coming for you (out with the old). Coming for your content (in with the new). Coming for your likes (no one likes you). And long before we're all banging drag-and-drop deepfakes of pubescent supermodels on our living room holodecks, the entertainment crash will ensure none of us has time to *read* anything anymore - about what we're watching, or anything else. All we'll have time to do is watch (*Wall-E* help us). The past and future will collapse in on the present from both ends, and you'll be left behind - living on the street while the world passes you by in a driverless car (probably while watching Netflix).

It's nearly noon and you haven't turned in so much as an abstract, but with your Youniverse disintegrating around you, you shut down and head for the elevator, giving the finger to the back of Arthur's head, and swiping a framed photo of Cynthia's (Cunthia's) cat off her desk in stride. You don't say goodbye to anyone (*like they'd care*), but you also honestly don't know if you'll be back.

Spurning Jennica again (slut), you meet your dealer outside, purchase your sack, and with one small thing to look forward to firmly in hand, head toward home. Hustling through the park, all you can think about is smoking (you want to get so high you piss yourself and still don't bother to leave the couch. *That's* where you want to be), and upon crossing into downtown you make a savage feint at an obsidian Cadillac, its aggrieved horn blat echoing through the empty streets as it speeds past. In seemingly direct response, a pile of penny-savers and alt-weeklies rises groggily from a nearby bus bench and looks you dead in the eye.

"Don't fuckin' move," says the vagrant, stepping into your path and pulling a knife.

"Are you fucking kidding me?" you ask.

"I saw you the other day, handin' out cash like you was goddamned Ed McMahon. But I didn't get nuthin'."

"Sorry," you say, dripping petulance.

"Well I'ma get it now. Whatever you got. Let's go."

You prepare to turn out your pockets in one final act of submission to this dickpunch of a day, but when your left hand touches Ziploc you realize this will mean giving up your stash, and the prospect of getting blunted on that sticky little quarter-ounce of endo is the only thing standing between you and an evening in the garage, puffing on your van's tailpipe instead. Meanwhile, your right hand brushes against your nubby suicide note, and you decide to go another way.

"No," you say.

"S'cuse me?"

"I said no, asshole. What the fuck do you think you're doing anyway?"

You take a menacing step forward, imbued with every ounce of anger you've ever subsumed behind catfish accounts and Twitter eggs.

"Um...what?" he asks, so surprised he actually seems to consider retreat in the face of even this minor resistance.

"Seriously. Do I look like a good person to mug?"

"Uhh..."

"Look at me!"

"But...the other day..."

"Everything I'm wearing came from Goodwill. I've got a flip-phone if you want. Otherwise it's three bucks and a bunch of maxed out credit cards."

You thrust your wallet at him.

"Here. Take 'em. I'll put 'em all in your name. Have fun payin' 'em off. If you can get a minimum wage job, it should only take about fifteen years."

"But...all that cash...I saw you..."

"I hit a lotto scratcher," you lie. "I was having a good run. Thought I'd pay it forward. And look what it got me. Mugged by your dumb ass in broad daylight on the worst day of my fuckin' life."

"But... I..."

"Fuckin' take it!" you say, drawing up on him two more steps.

He steps back.

"Money's a prison, man," you continue, advancing out of bullyball instinct. "I wish I could live like you. You don't need that shit. You don't need anything. You're fuckin' free. Out here in the world, doin' what you want, grabbin' life by the balls. Freer than I am. Freer than I'll ever be."

"Hey...Ease up. I'm sorry," he says.

"I'm serious. I got nothin' else for you man. This is it. Hand to God."

You throw your wallet at him, but he lets it hit him in the chest and fall to the ground, even taking another step back as though avoiding a poisonous snake or a pile of dogshit.

"You really want to help me out? Why don't you do me a favor and just stab me in the fucking heart right now," you say, puffing your chest and rapping your fist like a righteous Black Panther (if this is how you go out, you'll be luckier than most). "Right here man. Just do it. I'd be fucking grateful."

The bum stares at you for what feels like an eternity - though nothing compared to the space between those texts today - before quietly turning and walking away, leaving you to pick up your wallet and continue home.

Episode 21

All the happiness you've felt since Artemis's wedding twists and deforms in your memory as you stalk across your yard, lashing out at ill-gotten garden gnomes and nicked dog dishes.

That night she showed you her soul, and today she won't even show you her tits?!

You slam the door so hard a shelf of porcelain babies you methodically filched from Marsha's desk comes crashing down, shattering into a jagged Golgotha of neonatal limbs.

Friends? She wants to be friends!? Just because she put you in the friend zone doesn't mean you want to be her fucking friend!!!

Every nascent blossom of humanity you've tended over this laborious fortnight has rotted black on the vine. Your heart is a locust-infested husk. Your mind is a plague of flies. You want to burn yourself down and sow your body with salt. Let the tectonic whims of the Earth swallow you whole and crush your bones to diamond.

That's the only way any woman will ever love you!

You tried. No one can say you didn't try. You put down the pipe. You attempted to better yourself. You *exercised* for Christ's sakes. You did fucking crunches. *Like a chump!* You played nice goddammit! You held the door. You pulled out her chair. You didn't stare at her chest (too much), or anybody else's. You were clever, and smart, and funny. You didn't make veiled come-ons or use cheesy double entendres. You talked. You listened. You cared. *She made you care. And for what?* Nothing. A couple hours at a shitty bar, a handful of texts, and she knew all she needed to know. Swipe left and move on. Your princess is in another castle.

Unable to check yourself, determined to wreck yourself, you bypass Blaze Pascal and head for your closet. Burrowing through piles of dirty clothes, you find her hiding beneath a crusty web of boxer briefs: Dr. Strangelove, Or How I Learned to Stop Worrying and Love the Bong (The Good Doctor for short).

You've gone through more bongs than women in your wrong-side-of-thirty years on this waterlogged hunk of Godshit we call a planet. There was Sydney Greenstreet (lost in a move), Inhale to the Chief (shattered during a bathtub cleaning - she was too big for the sink), and The Lovebong of J. Alfred Prufrock (knocked off your coffee table when you reached for a stray Cheez-it), to name but a few - but this thick hunk of utilitarian hardware is the only one that's stood the test of time – ostensibly retired, but always on call.

You give her a rinse, jam the bowl with misshapen, green wads, and take a hit hard enough to advance yourself toward a CTE diagnosis; deflagrating the entire pile in one go; refusing to let yourself breathe until you're obliterated. Your lungs fill with ash and saliva, your head barking out smoke as the calcination of your brain turns your living room into a turbid iron forge. You lose consciousness for the space of a slow blink, and awake slumped over the arm of your couch. The Good Doctor lays upset on the hardwood, her toxic spillage leaving yet another water stain on a floor already psoriatic with them. Your senses amok, you dodder to the kitchen.

You don't feel thirsty so much as dehydrated. You don't feel hungry so much as empty. Unable to differentiate between desire and impulse, you commence to eating yourself out of house and home. You heft a gallon of milk College-Belushi-style, glugging until your shirtfront's absorbing most of the downpour. You do the same to a gallon box of cheddar Goldfish, chomping with mindless *Pac-Man* mechanics until they're schooling around your mush-filled mouth to the linoleum below.

Your baseline set, you dive into your congealed casserole of leftovers: distressed leather pizza, clotted hot wing viscera, decomposing Szechuan offal, spermicidal potato salad, enchilada entrails, and a cellophane-wrapped plate of thrice-microwaved chicken nuggets emulsified in plasmatic, crime-scene ketchup. You crunch through habanero-flavored gristle. You unearth a Holocene Big Mac preserved in freezerburn and tear into it with primordial ferocity. You wade knee-deep into the loaded nacho everglades and slurp until you feel malarial. You fill yourself up like a Hefty bag – an erratic blitzkrieg of dissociative, pica insanity – and wash it all down with a can of Squirt.

You wonder if Elle is a squirter.

Re-enraged in an instant by this unwelcome thought, you crush the can and chuck it at the framed *Who Framed Roger Rabbit?* poster in your hallway, hitting Jessica square in the tits. You don't feel horny so much as misogynistic, but you immediately know what you want to do next.

Your porn site is a mosaic of freeze-framed carnality, each open-mouthed, gaping-assed screencap inviting you to click inside and watch it in action. A dervish of conflicting desires, you want to see innocence treated roughly, and glamour uglified - to watch women do things their parents would disown them for. That's your way out. That's where *she's* left you. Many of these starlets are as familiar as family photos, while others may as well be jilling off on the backs of milk cartons, but in your current state of spiraling, perspectiveless mania, they all seem strangely present - as if they know you're there; and what you're thinking; and what you are. Taunting you for looking. Daring you to stop.

They can all suck your dick.

You head for your Hentai stash - a realm of grim psychosexuality American smut rarely approaches - where the women are all just a little better than perfect, and the only limits are the radiation-poisoned imaginations of the sole country to ever survive a nuclear assault.

Cuffing your flaccid unit to attention, you watch an animated girl with the face and pussy of a virginal 14-year-old from the suburbs of Saffron City, and the tits and ass of a professionally pneumaticized San Fernando lifer - a true lily of the Uncanny Valley - stare fearfully up at a malevolent mass of suckered hydrostats roughly the size of a Panzer Tank. The bilateral beast proceeds to fill her up like a WWII-era switchboard, inserting tentacle after slimy tentacle into first her mouth, then her nose, eyes, ears, navel, and nipples. Suspended over a swirling ocean vortex, she moans helplessly as two larger, more sentient appendages emerge to drive deep into her vaginal and anal cavities - ripping her apart at the seams, and dragging her drained, lifeless corpse to the bottom of the Yellow Sea.

Barely a wiggle.

The most indefensible clip in your library of licentia has failed you. Your heart wants this shit, but your cock's not in it. Seeking live flesh, you scroll past several real Japanese girls sucking pixelated dick before globetrotting over to your Vatican golconda of vintage, Italian porno. The country shaped like a dominatrix's thigh-high tends to eschew grueling close-ups of testicles slapping taints in favor of a more spliced-and-diced editing approach - perfect for your presently indecisive member.

In the first scene, a solemn prospect at a red, velvet kneeler gives some #blessed Priest a contrite, servant-hearted blowjob through the partition screen of her convent's confessional, ultimately anointing herself with his thick, goopy unction. Meanwhile, in another part of the priory, a no-nonsense Milf-Superior strips a novitiate down to her wimple and dispassionately scalds her virgin thighs with votive candlewax. This transitions to a feisty roadhead session where another would-be-Bride-of-Christ bobs for indulgences while cruising the Tuscan countryside in the actual fucking popemobile. As all parties converge for litorgy, initiates line the pews, presenting their postulate posteriors for judgment. The Pontiff paces the aisles in a breezy humeral, his holy endowment swinging like a censer. Rosary beads are snaked up compliant assholes. Silver-ringed fingers reach back, stroking their sisters' sweaty slits until, in a carillon of orgasmic Pater Nosters - a true cum for Jesus moment - his imminence fucks them all into vows of silence.

Once again, though your brain is enjoying this catechism of depravity, your penis remains in a drowsy torpor. You have to dig deeper.

You close your eyes and enter a forbidden search term, finding the letters by touch - something you've never typed before, but now send out like a prayer to de Sade himself - an offering to the abominable.

i

n

c

e

s

t

You tack on "hot" and "orgy" in hopes of weeding out any edentulous, Appalachian farmgirls slopping their daddies' hogs for meth money, tap Enter, and then… it's just… happening.

A Thanksgiving feast; a corpulent, combed-over patriarch serves moist meat to his blowsy, buxom wife; a spry grandmother guzzles red wine; two blonde, teenage girls - decidedly not twins, but made-up to convince you they could be - fight over a wishbone; a lecherous uncle chases a French maid with a baster of glutinous juices; the scene is set; the wishbone snaps; the losing girl sprawls into her grandmother's lap; shiraz splashes; a food fight erupts; cranberries slather shirtfronts; stuffing flies by the handful; buttons tear; zippers yank; everyone gets a nice, thick glazing of birdfat; the twins start making out; proud papa flops his pecker on a bed of greens; mom and gran take turns nibbling, cleaning his plate; the uncle subdues the maid over a credenza; the room commences to thrusting; a sexual slumgullion of lady-bits and man-stock; all at once, the boisterous brood grows quiet; someone's knocking; the front door opens; "JOHNNY!" the clan welcomes a vascular man in army fatigues; "Y'all started without me!?" Johnny cries; "We couldn't wait," declares a twin, licking redeye gravy off her sister's index finger; a familial game of musical chairs ensues; gran dives under the maid's skirts for a mouthful of avuncular nutsack; Johnny blows his load all over his mother's tawny tummy, a single strand momentarily connecting them like a diaphanous umbilical cord; the twins compete to see who can make the word "daddy" sound the nastiest as their father drenches them in millions of potential siblings never to be born; the clip ends freezeframed on their faces, finally indistinguishable beneath thick cauls of cum.

Nothing.

All that soul-blackening filth, and you remain steadfastly inert, hovering over a pop-up ad for an off-brand Cialis, and considering some very upsetting questions. Was this legit? - *GET BIGGER!* – Would the packaging be discreet? – *STAY HARDER!* – Had you become so loathsome you needed boner pills just to get it up *for yourself?* - *LAST LONGER!* You stare down at your despondent dinger, hanging off your body like wet laundry. *What the fuck has this bitch done to you?*

No. This was not the answer. You'd rather get smacked with Ron Jeremy's dick than succumb to the sexual fearmongering of such mendacious one-eyed-snake-oil salesmen. This is all mental. You just need to focus. That incest shit was so fake. You need something real; something punishing; something barbaric. You need to find the most debased, unrepentant whore on the block, and see her pushed to her limits. You need someone you can hate.

Hunched over your laptop like a maniacally masturbating Quasimodo, you watch an unidentified blonde plant herself on a plastic tarp (always a good sign); her skin taut but supple, like vulcanized babyfat; her eyes flashing defiance. As seven headless, rippling torsos file in from stage left, however - wagging their blunderbuss dongs with haughty disdain - her gameface twitches a skosh, belying a hint of uncertainty. At last, you twitch too, and without further introduction, dicks start flying at her like they're coming out of a JUGS pitcher. *Too late now, bitch.*

Balancing expertly on the balls of her feet, her hands evoke the pulse chambers of a milking machine - squeezing, sliding, and squirming from pole to turgid, purpled pole. Her mouth, smeared shiny with Vaseline, parts compliantly for anything put in front of it, her gullet contracting with every thrust, drawing yards of cock inside her until her lips encircle the base and her gag reflex propels her backward, wheezing and frothing up spume. After ten minutes she's panting from fatigue, but her castmates' intimidating snickers and grunts form an oppressive wall of sound. She knows: this is nowhere near over.

You don't usually watch videos of this length straight through. You get bored easily. You like to skip around. Comparison shop. Porn isn't about finding Miss Right. It's about finding Miss Fuck-My-Ass-Right-Now. But sitting inches from the ochre glow of your flesh-filled computer screen, roughing up your recalcitrant junk like it's late on protection payments, you can sense this girl starting to break. She may yet manage to keep it together - smiling for the camera while beating off wave after wave of marauding, mastodon cocks - but you're beginning to see the cracks; to hear her regret; to feel her shame; to imagine all the decisions that led her to this point, and wonder how many of them she wishes she could take back. You can feel her hurting, and it's working for you.

Her hands still deftly working two membranous schlongs - showing off her Olympic Shake Weighter muscles - she moves to an undoubtedly scotchgarded sofa so as to receive suitors at either end, like a turned-out Bachelorette trying to pack all her contestants into the Fantasy Suite at once. Mimicking the insatiable drinking birdie at a whiplashing pace, she bobs frantically between three staunch units standing guard at her front entrance (each one slap-happily buffeting her about the eyes and face whenever it isn't busy being sucked), while two more invade her from the rear and commence to whipsawing her pliant flanks. Even as joyless, spasmodic sprays of liquid begin to gush from her overtaxed vulva, turning the moisture-resistant surfaces beneath her into puddled swampland, the odd men out keep themselves fluffed on the sidelines, occasionally reaching in to give her breasts a cruel squeeze or tattoo a handprint on her reddening backside. They pepper her with lecherous questions - "You like that baby?" "You want that big cock?" "Are you a dirty little whore?" - knowing full well that the sheer glut of groinmeat she's dealing with renders them rhetorical. It doesn't matter though. They don't care what her answers are anyway.

The situation is still tenuous, but you are now nominally hard. You've been watching this girl get bagpiped for twenty-five solid minutes - her whole body shuddering atop knees locked in self-preservation - prejac and mascara running down her cheeks in inky chiaroscuro - the thin, fibrous wall between her cunt and anus beginning to warp and buckle - and you cannot look away. The level of abuse she's taking has you legitimately questioning her agency. Was she tricked or cajoled in some way; led to believe this was a path to more legitimate stardom? Did she owe someone a large sum of money? Was she a junkie at the end of her rope? Obliged to do anything in exchange for whatever drug best allows her to forget what she's done for it? Is this what she signed up for? Is this what she wanted? Or is this something else?

You don't care. You hope she needs an epidural by the time they're done.

As if responding to a shift-whistle, all seven of her girthy tormentors withdraw from her various jacks and ports and form a semicircular firing squad as she collapses, gasping and trembling, into a demure side-seiza. At this point it must be all she can do not to keel over and succumb to dropsy, and yet she expresses a strange contentment which, now jacking off so fast you're afraid you might tear your rotator cuff, you are quick to dismiss as post-traumatic shock. Still febrile with cock-addled arousal, she furiously rubs her clit while jism rains down in viscous, ivory waterspouts. The men are segregation-era riot hoses. She is a stadium spermtrough. They stagger their blasts perfectly, essentially waterboarding her with cum.

You're so close.

Their Comstock loads blown, your onscreen surrogates taper off, and the camera zooms in on the spunk-smothered girl who, for reasons you can ascribe only to certifiable mental illness, is still vehemently pleasuring herself, laughing and sighing through a succession of giddy climaxes before wiping her eyes and addressing you, the viewer.

"Hi!" she says in a familiar accent you surely would've recognized earlier, if only she hadn't had her mouth full. "I'm Aletta, and I hope you enjoyed my birthday gangbang as much as I did!"

Fuck!

Your imminent orgasm recedes into grim bathos at the Hungarian porn goddess giggling onscreen. Her hair's usually darker, but still, you can't believe you didn't recognize her. She's one of your favorites.

You redouble your efforts as she mugs for the camera, her tongue snowplowing splooge off her lips to gargle, savor, and dribble back down onto her epic, prizewinning tits. This kind of lascivious excess is usually irresistible to your ejaculatory muscles - you literally couldn't stop if you wanted to - but now that you know she's not some innocent neophyte, but a fanatical deviant - one who likely enjoyed creating that last half-hour even more than you enjoyed watching it - you might as well be looking at Nancy Reagan. Aletta's no victim. She's an artist. A doyenne of her field. She probably hand-picked all seven of those guys, and they probably thanked her for the opportunity. Hell, she probably lit the room and did the blocking. You have no doubt. She was in control the whole time.

Infuriatingly, you now find yourself all worked up with nowhere to go. There are, of course, worse things happening to women on the internet every day if you know where to look - (and you do) - but you've reached your limit. Porn has turned on you. Your harem is revolting. You begin to wonder if, through THC overexposure and deep self-loathing, you've accidentally effected one of those 4-plus-hour emergency room boners the Viagra commercials are always warning about. Soon, Elle worms her way back into your thoughts, and with her, a touch of fear. *You brought this thing forth* you think, staring at your angry, chaffed hard-on. *Now how are you going to get rid of it?*

Δ

Doppelbangher.com allows users to upload images of women – be they movie stars, Instagram models, high school sweethearts, much-despised exes, or just that random friend-of-a-Facebook-friend who posted those hot pictures from Fort Lauderdale that one time – and then employs facial recognition software to pinpoint the adult film actress who bears the strongest resemblance. Hello, brave new world. You've never patronized the site personally, always telling yourself there were some lines you couldn't, or at least shouldn't cross... but fuck it.

You find Elle's Facebook and, after scrolling through a torturous cache of images, select a close-cropped headshot that perfectly captures her warm, open, life-affirming, life-ruining beauty. You copy/paste, and the site spits out Josie, a Junoesque brunette with piercing, chrysoprase eyes who, while a little too young, and a little too tall, has several pages-worth of X-rated content available to help you dry those tears and quietly accept your limitations as a man.

Thumbing through screencaps of your consolation prize, all you can see are her shortcomings. Her overstyled hair is a wenge-colored cup of Ovaltine compared to Elle's rollicking, frontier flumes of Godiva syrup, and her ass and Elle's ass are both asses like Stone Mountain and Mount Everest are both mountains. She is, however, stacked to the fucking rafters, and if you squint, and take another hard puff of dro, you might could make this work. You start a 42-minute "cumpilation" video and hobble back to your closet.

Searching for your bong earlier, you stumbled across another long-forgotten objet d'arousal - an inflatable companion named Blow-Up Wanda whom, as the designated driver for the only bachelor party you've ever attended, you were forced to schlep from bar to bar to strip club to IHOP to strip club to bar, and subsequently remanded home with you under the guise of "wanting something to remember this awesome night by!" You don't know if your fellow groomsmen bought that line, but you also don't particularly care. RealDolls ain't cheap -

you can get a used Mercedes for less - and while Blow-Up Wanda is nowhere near that level of agalmatophilic craftsmanship, she does retail for about $200, and comes with silicone orifices in all the right places.

While half-watching Josie effect a one-woman, Busby Berkeley parade of facials, you drag Wanda's deflated body onto your mattress like a *Flatland* hooker, blow her up, flip her facedown, and start railing on the single hole that doubles as both her downstairs entrances - her vaganus, if you will.

Within minutes, you despise Josie, and try to close your eyes and picture Elle instead - stepping out of a ruffly, polka-dot bikini; pressing a detachable showerhead between her soapy thighs; pulling apart a front-clasp bra for a buttery pearl necklace - but your sativa-torched imagination is too scattered to hold still, and even if it could, massive amounts of porn consumption long ago rendered your spank bank insolvent. You've spoiled yourself rotten. You barely remember what real sex feels like anymore.

You've never been one to talk to your sex doll - again, there are lines - but in your current state of increasingly painful priapism, you're starting to think some of your personal rules were made to be broken. Sure, a man's got to have a code, but if a tree does some disturbed, reprehensible shit in the forest and no one's around to hear it...?

"You like that bitch?" you ask Blow-Up Wanda. The back of her head - drawn in thick, ratty tangles of CMYK process yellow hair - has no response.

"Yeah," you continue, fighting internalized embarrassment, "you like that big cock in your ass, slut?"

Still, of course, nothing.

"You don't have to answer," you tell her. "I know what you like. You're nasty. You're a baaaaad girl."

But it's no use. Drawing out the "a" in "bad" as though playfully addressing a mate, rather than demeaning an inanimate fetish object, you feel utterly ridiculous, and indescribably sad.

Another half-hour has passed since you brought Wanda and Josie into the picture, and the latter's thirsty highlight reel is nearing the last of its sticky-faced segments. Trying to think of someone, anyone, in your assiduously organized backlog of faces, tits, and asses who could stand in for the woman you actually want, you land on the futile realization that, among the smut world, she is peerless. The things that attracted you to her are the very things that make it true. There's no such thing as hopeful porn.

As Josie takes a 9-man bukkake bath, you notice Elle's Facebook is still open in a minimized window. Despite all the long-held principles you've abandoned tonight, you still balk at this idea. Even if she did spurn your totally sweet, not-at-all creepy advances; even if she did ignore your clever, well-composed flirt texts; even if she starts screening your calls, or blocking your chats, or somewhere down the line states in adamant, plain-as-day terms that she doesn't want to see or hear from you ever again (and let's be honest, that's probably where this is headed); even if all that comes to pass, you're still not sure this is a line you want to cross. It feels significant. It feels wrong.

You limp back to your desk and maximize the window so Elle fills your screen – not having decided anything – just to consider the possibilities...

[You are a self-fracking strip mine.]

With zero restraint, your ill-defined bicep starts pumping like Rick Allen on the *Hysteria* tour, savagely attacking the rigid bone spur protruding from your pelvis. You are both appalled and empowered by how easily you've come to this point. But there it is. You don't love this woman. You don't even know her. Not really. She's just another disappointment. Just another empty, self-involved cunt who thinks she's too fucking good for you. And she's right. She doesn't even know how right she is. Her only sin was convincing you, for a few short days, that you might be worth saving.

Your mind gives way to a blur of sickening, self-destructive ideas, and you move to print a copy of Elle's picture which, on standard 8.5x11 paper, should be close to life-size. You'll adhere it to Blow-Up Wanda's face and ream the absolute shit out of her. Maybe you'll cut a hole in the mouth and facefuck her too; cum down her stupid, beautiful throat while your shaft gets shredded by papercuts. Maybe you'll...

```
The printer is out of paper.
Load Tray 1 and try again.
```

"Fuck!"

Continuing to pummel your quisling dick, you awkwardly load the compartment one-handed and hit print again.

```
The printer is low on toner.
Change cartridge or select B&W and
try again.
```

"God DAMMIT!"

After a crazed ink-hunting expedition you come up empty, and fuming at your mutinous electronics, you select B&W, hit print again, and finally elicit the crunching, insectoid skirtches and skarls of success. An unstoppable force, slowly wearing down its physically adjoined immovable object, you watch with fiendish elation as the aesthetically flawless image makes its way out of the printer, and into your waiting ha...

Paper jam. Open tray, remove, and try again.

"GODFUCKINGMOTHERFUCKINGSHIT-FUCKINGDAMMIT!!!!!!"

Elle is about a third of the way out. Though her nose and mouth remain trapped in a matrix of shoddily maintained Hewlett Packard belts and gears, her bright, comely eyes gaze up at you in Arbusian monochrome, asking you why you're doing this, and forgiving you for it at the same time. Absolving you. Diminishing you. Pitying you.

Irate, you grab Blow-Up Wanda by the throat and throw her violently to the floor (though her flimsy, lightweight construction makes this less satisfying than you'd hoped), put your full weight on her slightly conical tits, and with your eyes fixed on your laptop, start demolishing her vaganus like a breeding bull. There's nothing but solid concrete under your 40-year-old carpet, and the harder surface is providing great traction. You stab into her with vengeful, murderous intent, slapping her mouth-hole and jamming in your middle finger. You mutter slut-shaming insults and spit on her cartoon face. You try to imagine that Elle, in addition to filling your computer screen, is also watching you through your webcam; seeing the kind of powerhouse, Viking shag you could've thrown into her if she'd only given you a chance; regretting the way she rejected you; maybe even touching herself a little; maybe…

"F U A A A U U U U U U G H H C K ! ! ! ! ! FUCKFUCKOWFUCKOWOWFUCKOWFUCK!!!!!"

You cry out in agony as Blow-Up Wanda pops under your relentless plowing, causing you to fall about nine inches straight down and land directly on your dick (which remains hard enough to nearly impale you). Your wind knocked out, tears wet your face.

You've reached a state of full-on penihilism. Your organ is rejecting your body. You have flayed yourself raw, locked in a battle of wills with your fiercely intransigent member. You're no longer seeking release; only control. You want to fuck broken glass. You want to be buried up to your meatus in a fire ant hill. You want to give yourself a Prince Albert with a three-ring binder and go to work on your shaft with a pair of rusty toenail clippers; crush your balls in a table vice and take a butane lighter to your limp, oozing scrotum. You don't care anymore. Whatever it takes. Open up a pudendal vein and bleed yourself dry. Just let this be over. You are phallicidal.

With quiet resignation, you get up, lower your laptop onto your desk chair, and angle the screen as far back as it will go. Your hands feel macerated and arthritic. Your cock feels ancient and evil. As you lurch over your computer, jacking off like a pre-lingual, cro-magnon troglodyte and openly weeping, Elle looks up at you with that kind smile, and those forgiving eyes, for what you know will be the last time.

You explode in disgustingly spectacular fashion, and let out an otherworldly, basso profundo groan. You look down at yourself jettisoning rivers of jizz, but the end result is like an out-of-body experience. You thought you'd achieve such relief - that you could maybe get over, if you could just get off - but you feel disconnected from every splash of cum hitting Elle square in the face, sliding down the nacreous glass, streaking her further and further into obscurity. You can barely make her out by the time you're finished; no longer a photo so much as a rippling reflection, viewed in a cloudy pool, amidst a hazy dream.

Episode 22

These people are not your *Friends*.

At age 8, you started watching 6 hours of television a day. 9 on Saturdays and during Summer vacation. After high school, those numbers jumped to 8 and 12, respectively, as there were no longer parental patrol units around to regulate your bedtime or relegate portions of your weekends to "playing outside." You weren't a great University student, but you got by. Depending on your menial job du jour, these figures have fluctuated since college - rising as high as 14 hours per day; never again dipping below 8. All told, you calculate you've watched roughly 99,502 hours of TV in your lifetime - if you went back and accounted for Christmases and Spring Breaks, you could probably get it up to an even 100K - the equivalent of 4,145 full days - nearly 11½ uninterrupted years - of watching.

But there will always be more. There will never be enough.

These people are not your *Friends*.

You haven't left your house in two weeks. Barricaded in a scratchy Ticonderoga of blankets and couch cushions, smoking your brainpan into a charred Chicxulub crater, you finish your third consecutive lap through the defining sitcom of the 1990s.

You watch as Rachel, for the third time, gets off the plane, abandons her dream job, and races back into the smothering, blubbering arms of Ross – arguably the most rebarbative leading man in television history – who in exchange, pledges his lifelong fealty to her every want and whim. You watch as the Friends, for the third time, all return their keys to Monica's deluxe apartment in the lavender skies of a magical, alternate timeline Manhattan where, despite living a mere mile-and-a-half from the Twin Towers, nothing particularly bad ever seems to happen. And you watch as the credits, for the third time, roll over that joyous fountain splash fight, where the eternally young, eternally beautiful, eternally terribly-coiffed season-one versions of these interdependent, self-involved monstrosities invite you to run the whole thing back and live vicariously through them again and again and again. The fountain splash fight is life. The fountain splash fight is love, and youth, and togetherness. The fountain splash fight never ends.

You watch all this, for the third time – the capstone to a 360-hour ultra-marathon during which you've subsisted solely on your stockpile of frozen appetizers, and managed only shallow, fitful fistfights with sleep (all of which featured bizarrely immersive dreams about the Friends). Your unwashed hair is as brittle as Ross's gel helmet. Your house smells of barnyard fowl and lab monkey. You're starting to suspect the laugh track is laughing *at* you. And still you watch. You watch, and you know this will be the last first sentence you ever write.

These people are not your *Friends*.

You're working from the wizened desktop you keep connected to your television for streaming. You considered pulling out the antique typewriter Artemis gave you for your 21st birthday, but even in this darkest hour you can't abide such well-trodden pretense. You've never been that kind of writer, and you see no reason to start now. Back in your bedroom, Blow-Up Wanda still lies punctured on the floor like a chalk outline of your humanity. Elle's face still fills your laptop beneath a pirouetting, spirographic screensaver, and a film of crusted-dry ejaculate, just waiting for the slightest touch of the mousepad to reappear and remind you of what you've become, and can never again not be. Your penis is basically a vestigial organ. After what you put it through that night, it wants nothing more to do with you. You've taken to stripping from the waist down and pissing in the bathtub, just so you won't have to touch yourself.

Netflix respawns back to the pilot, and that searing, sustained organ note that cuts through the earliest version of the theme song harpoons your temples like an Aztec yāōmītl shaft. They must be stopped. If it's the only thing you ever do with your weed-wasted, idiot-boxed life - if it's the last thing you do - they must be stopped.

These people are not your *Friends*.

Chandler
or
"It's always better to lie than to
have the awkward conversation."

Chandler was gay to begin with. There can be no doubt whatsoever about that. I think it's important to start any conversation about the character with this in mind, not because I particularly care, but because *he* obviously cares a great deal. A pathologically sarcastic, emotionally stunted misanthrope for the first half of the series, and a paunchy, third place trophy-husband for the second, Chandler is defined almost entirely by his lack of agency - a clear outgrowth of his inability to come out to his judgmental, ad hoc family of "Friends," or perhaps even to himself. *They* wouldn't be ok with it. *He* wouldn't be ok with it. And the show, speaking from the meta, would also have not been ok with it.

An archetypal beta male, Chandler was constantly flummoxed by women – always fixating on flaws (S02E03) or mindlessly self-sabotaging his successes (S01E06, S04E13). While Joey – the physical alpha of the group – has an out-the-door-and-around-the-corner line of ladies waiting to take a number at his sexual lunchmeat counter, and Ross – the intellectual alpha – can't seem to stumble out of bed in the morning without tripping over a new uxorial candidate, Chandler flounders hopelessly from one unhealthy, untenable entanglement to the next, desperate to pass for normal, lost in a version of the world where what he is barely seems to exist.

The *Friends* writing staff might've all shared hearty back-pats for their brave, progressive-minded championing of attractive, upper-class lesbians back in the bad old days of 1996 (S02E11), but their contribution to the LGBT cause pretty much begins and ends with that elegantly fascinatored affair. Indeed, by the sheer, joke-volume numbers, being a gay man on *Friends* was basically the second-worst thing someone could be (more on this later).

The "Chandler is gay" riffing starts early (S01E08), with the show depicting homosexuality and femininity as two sides of the same undesirable three-dollar bill (an outdated and offensive thesis expressed nowhere better than in Phoebe's brother Frank's exuberantly repeated cries of "Chandler's a girl! Chandler's a girl!" [S05E03]). By the end of the series, it's revealed that every one of the Friends thought Chandler was gay upon first meeting him, that Chandler has a gay, trans father of whom he's deeply ashamed (*Friends* was appallingly transphobic long before our Nationally politicized bathroom panic), and that Chandler is functionally impotent – unable to fulfill the heteronormative dreams of his baby-crazed wife Monica (he actually experiences erectile dysfunction – *for the first time in his life* – moments after Monica accepts his marriage proposal [S07E01]).

Add to this a litany of nudge-nudge-wink-winks like his finely-honed skill with tweezers and emery boards (S09E13), his love of the *Annie* soundtrack (S08E17) *Miss Congeniality* (S10E01), and Dr. Phil

(S10E08) – to name but a few – and you start to see Chandler for what he is: a brokeback homunculus of a man who is not, and can never be, his true self.

For their part, the Friends give him no quarter. In their capacity as a self-sustaining panopticon of yuppie decorum, they won't even let the poor guy have a cigarette, much less smoke a bone. Amidst a pervasive groundfog of casual homophobia, a few examples stand out. When Chandler inadvertently develops an effeminate affect from listening to a female self-help whisperer (the utterly ridiculous S03E18), the others are quick to deride the change as unacceptable. When Ross reveals that Chandler once mistakenly kissed a trans woman in a bar, "You kissed a guy!" becomes a rallying cry with which to shame-bludgeon him for the rest of the episode (S07E04). Perhaps most disturbingly, when Ross photoshops Chandler into a number of gay porn stills and uploads them to their college alumni website (S09E17) he makes it clear that homosexuality is disgusting to him, and should be humiliating to Chandler as well.

As a result of all this, Chandler has clearly internalized his shame and fear of ostracism to a paralytic degree, unable to make decisions or deal with conflict. He remains a shifty, untrustworthy cipher throughout the entire series, betraying secrets to curry favor within the group, chaining himself to mundane jobs while his Friends chase their dreams, cracking jokes from the back of the classroom and hoping no one notices he's got nothing else to say. By the time he and Monica get together, it feels like a kindness – as though, after witnessing all his struggles, she finally takes pity on the sad, stray puppy dog that peed on her leg all those years ago (S04E01). That she effectively chemically castrates him with cleaning supplies and needlepoint neurotics is the most relief he can hope for. He's passing, and his Friends are letting him pass. Could he *be* more tragic?

Monica
or
"Be yourself, but not too much."

If being gay is the second-worst thing someone can be in the Bright-Kauffman-Crane vision of New York, then being fat is the worst by a country mile, and no one in sitcom history has ever been fatter than Monica Geller. Despite Courtney Cox weighing in at a sumptuous 115 pounds (est.), the bulbous shadow of her formerly-fat self hovers over every episode, menacing her petite Jewish frame like a Nazi Zeppelin. By the same token, the tightfisted control she exercises over herself – and everyone around her - draws the Friends to her apartment as though it were constructed of her own made-from-scratch gingerbread. She's a chef who can't eat, a neat-freak who can't be alone, a hypercompetitive born loser, "a mother, without a baby" (S10E09), and for every hole in her obsessive-compulsive heart she can no longer fill with gooily-frosted carbohydrates, she shoves a cookie in someone else's mouth and bosses them while they're chewing.

While the women of *Friends* were all fairly promiscuous, Monica always bore the brunt of the show's existential slut-shame. Somehow, despite their all being perfectly-proportioned, attired, and made-up at all times, Rachel was the effortlessly pretty one who had men falling all over themselves to sniff her Ralph Lauren panties, and Phoebe was the carefree, bohemian one who enjoyed sex on her own terms, be it with men, women, or the entire membership of Jethro Tull (S10E06), leaving Monica – in this writer's opinion, the most classically beautiful of the three – to play the almost offensively against-type role of the "hot mess."

Casting Cox as the everywoman set an impossible standard, and to make it work, the writers saddled her with every conceivable sexual misstep they could think up for Monica's needy little snizz. Within the first few seasons, she sleeps with a sleazy coworker on the first date (S01E01), and a 12th grader (S01E22), gets involved with a family friend 21 years her senior (S02E15), and later flirts with the idea of banging his son (S04E08). She's a thirsty conscript of both the Wedding and Baby Industrial Complexes, desperately flailing through a field of dicks in search of a white dress and some motile sperm until, exhausted, she finally collapses onto the BarcaLounger across the hall with a semi-erect Matthew Perry attached to it and says "fine, you'll do."

The show identifies Chandler as the clear winner in this coupling, and the Friends often joke that Monica could've "done better," but given her array of psychoses, it's at least arguable that she's the lucky one. This is a woman who once washed seven strangers' cars on the street just because "they were dirty" (S06E05); who did thousands of dollars-worth of damage to a New York City apartment trying to discover the purpose of a mysteriously inert lightswitch (S04E15); who separates her towels into 11 distinct categories (S04E12), and numbers the bottoms of all her coffee mugs (S03E19); and who willfully misrepresented her identity while seriously considering stealing an unborn child (S10E09). All of which is to say, she may be crazy hot, but she's still fucking crazy.

And all that's before we even get to the fat suit. Good Lord, the fat suit. It was rare for *Friends* to go even one episode without making reference to Monica's rotund past with a gravity usually reserved for recovering meth addicts or cancer patients in remission, but the fat suit was the ultimate concern-troll. The show hit its creative and sociological nadir in a two-part, brutally ugly take on the *It's a Wonderful Life* formula in which we see what Monica's world might look like if she'd never lost all that weight (S06E15&16). The end tag of this hour-long travesty is just 20 seconds of fat suit Monica dancing until she gets tuckered out. This "joke" was supposed to be so inherently hilarious it could play on the walls of the Lascaux Caves. *Fat girl tired*. No further explanation necessary.

In the end, Monica gets everything she ever wanted, give or take a few biological children. She's thin. She's successful. She's a wife. She's a mother. She's forever clean. I'm not sure why exactly, but she's always been my favorite. She's a lunatic so the others don't have to be. She's painfully self-aware, but also limited in her ability to change, if only by virtue of how far she's already come. While the others are finding themselves, she's just waiting for them to catch up, dragging them along with baked goods and hard, sodium pentothal truths. She's the uncentered center around which they all revolve. She's the only reason anyone even *knows* Phoebe. She's a real person – or maybe six or seven real people - crammed into a painstakingly calculated persona. But it's not her fault. The world made her this way. The others made her this way. She's doing her best. She's got real problems man. She used to be fat.

Joey
or
"Female Roommate Wanted: Non-Smoker, Non-Ugly."

Joey Tribbiani isn't a character so much as a sentient pickup line. Though all the Friends had their signature catch-phrases, Joey's was the only one that mutated into a lifestyle. He's a frat guy without a college education; a misogynist who doesn't know the word; a proto-bro. And while the rise of more subversive TV cads like *HIMYM*'s Barney Stinson and *Always Sunny*'s Dennis Reynolds could reasonably be traced back to him, he never possessed even a pinch of their self-deprecating irony or, dare I say, feminist table-turning. The joke is on them often enough that they rarely seem like heroes, and we rarely feel obliged to root for them. But Joey? Joey's the biggest hero *Friends* had to offer.

Matt LeBlanc was the greenest performer of the six when *Friends* started, and it showed. Whoever thought to make his character a struggling, comically untalented actor did him an indelible favor, but even through the lens of "he's supposed to be bad," the writers could only cover so much for his deer-in-the-klieg-lights mugging. It was out of that real and fictional striving to "suck less," however, that our love for Joey was born. While the other Friends were all marginally successful, Joey was perpetually broke, often facing bad reviews, and blithely oblivious to his foundering reality. But we knew if Matt LeBlanc could make it, then

Joey could too. He was the starry-eyed dreamer in all of us. And he sure did get laid a lot, so how bad could things really be?

That the show asked us to condone Joey's Hefnerian misadventures in unrepentant horndogging did a disservice to every woman whose name he forgot by the next morning and cowardly decided to "just stop calling" (S01E05). Sure, he had his share of above-board one-night-stands – you don't get to be the literal poster boy for VD (S01E09) without churning your share of no-strings, clarified butter - but make no mistake: Joey was an inveterate liar, and a stone-cold bastard. He looked deep into women's eyes and told them exactly what they wanted to hear. Let's go to the tape.

In S03E20, Joey fucks a starstruck understudy in a naked attempt to make another woman jealous. In S02E12, he has multiple sexual encounters with a woman who's clearly mentally ill, and believes him to be Dr. Drake Ramoray, his character on *Days of Our Lives*. In S06E03, he conducts borderline-rapey interviews with potential female roommates (his questions would likely get him maced in our #MeToo times). In S03E14, he recounts accidentally incinerating a sleeping lover's artificial leg, only to abandon her, monopeded, in a remote cabin. Taken individually, these are lapses in judgment ranging from unfortunate to heinous, but taken as a whole, they're the actions of a sociopath; a feckless man-whore without scruples or valor. And yet...

By Season 8, LeBlanc had mostly caught up to his castmates talent-wise, and the writers rewarded him with a smidgeon of character growth. He even managed to imbue a Season 10 love affair with Jennifer Aniston's Rachel with more crackling chemistry than ever existed between her and David Schwimmer's Ross. This, we were inexpressly told, was Joey's redemption. This, somehow, made all the vile chauvinism and pussyhound manipulation worth it. This was what he, and by association *we*, had been waiting for. The finished product. The polished turd. The *real* Joey Tribbiani. That he was, by the end, the most popular character and the only one offered a spinoff (the execrable *Joey)* was an indictment not just of the audience's tastes, but of their basic decency. Somehow, against all odds, Joey Tribbiani was the hero America wanted, and consequently, the hero she deserved.

TROLL

Phoebe
or
"All I can think about is how I don't have that lamp!"

Phoebe Buffay would absolutely *not* be Friends with these people. Her Season 1 iteration is the show's crowning achievement, and her Panglossian city-sprite backstory – doled out in delightful non sequiturs only to be dismissed by her square pals' frumpled rejoinders of "...ok then" and "anywaaaaaay..." – includes an undisclosed amount of time spent in Prague (S04E10), an estimable propensity toward recreational drug use (S02E09), the sometime availment of parked cars as permanent housing (S04E01), a stint as a phone sex operator (S07E13), and maybe even actual prostitution (a pimp did spit in her mouth once [S09E07]). Tack on her well-chronicled "mugging days" (S09E15), and it's a wonder she's not pulling a dime out on Rikers. Even behind bars though, Phoebe would still be free in ways the others could only dream of, which makes her insidious descent into vapid materialism all the more heartbreaking to observe.

In the beginning, Phoebe was so outside the group as to function almost like a Greek Chorus – complete with acoustic accompaniment –

commenting on her Friends' lives while remaining blissfully apart. She dressed differently from them. She lived separately from them. She spoke as though carrying on an internal conversation with herself, to which they were only partially privy. Joey is nominally Catholic, and Ross and Monica both feel some discreet allegiance to their Judaic roots, but Phoebe is the only Friend ever depicted as having an active spiritual life, albeit, one defined not by scripture or heritage so much as a general bent toward altruism and faith in humanity. The Friends mock her, but in a gentle, almost probing way, as though searching for a door into her mystically contented mind. Through their constant hole-poking and thread-pulling, however, they succeed only in dragging her down into the shallow muck with the rest of them.

This begins in earnest in S05E04, when Joey and Phoebe make a Book-of-Job wager over the inherent nature of kindness. Joey posits that there's no such thing as a selfless good deed, and a resolute Phoebe sets out to prove him wrong. Though *Friends* stays far from the heady philosophical waters roiling just beneath the surface of this exercise, Phoebe's ultimate loss of the bet feels like the show planting a black flag directly in her golden heart. "People are shallow and driven by self-interest" it might read; "Get on board!" The seed of doubt sown, her world is a little less bright. She was changing. The group, and all its inward social policing, was changing her. From that day forward, one could write a whole book on the gentrification of Phoebe Buffay, but in the interest of brevity, I'll stick to the bullet points:

- (S05E06) Phoebe - committed vegetarian and animal rights activist - falls into forbidden love with a fur coat.
- (S05E07) Phoebe - champion of the working class - repeatedly encourages her health inspector boyfriend to shut down restaurants full of working people, getting off on his institutional power.
- (S05E16) Phoebe - reformed criminal and erstwhile political revolutionary - dates a cop, enjoying the vicarious thrill of being with a man who "shoots badguys."
- (S06E11) Phoebe - anti-materialist - abandons her long-held embargo against Pottery Barn for a must-have, mass-produced lamp.

And jumping ahead a bit...

- (S08E06) Phoebe - fully at peace with using her once-goodly powers for nefarious ends - assumes a false identity and infiltrates the home of the (categorically uncool) popstar Sting in a shameless quest for concert tickets (what would Jethro Tull think?!).

This was the episode where even casual fans had to realize that whatever they thought they knew about Phoebe was up for debate (or else wonder if she and her evil twin Ursula had pulled a switcheroo, and the real Phoebe was off waiting tables on *Mad About You*). By the time we get a scene of her chattering extemporaneously about how she wants to be a Volvo-driving Connecticut soccer mom (S09E16), it just feels like the topper on her forthcoming 7-tiered wedding cake.

From there, truly reprehensible episodes in which she sells out to a corporate massage chain (S09E21), donates her wedding fund to a children's charity only to later demand it back (S10E07), and enters Rachel's infant daughter in a child beauty pageant (S10E08) - play as little more than cruel jokes at the bamboozled viewer's expense. Whether the writers hated Lisa Kudrow, hated Phoebe, or hated the whole of their audience, they clearly had no more time for the humble hippie singing about her odoriferous familiar back in 1994. In trying to imbue her high-strung, self-obsessed "Friends" with a little zest for the unknown – with a little thought for something outside themselves – she became a reluctant, but ultimately willing Galatea, dismantled and reassembled after their own J Crew catalog image. No good deed...

Rachel
or
"Honey, you have principles and I so admire that. I don't have any!"

I have always believed that there are certain kinds of people whom the world will meet halfway: attractive people, rich people, extraordinarily lucky people. I have never been one of these people. But Rachel Green is. Boy and howdy.

While Monica and Phoebe read more as haphazard collections of signifiers than real, recognizable humans, I feel safe in asserting that we have all known a Rachel Green. The kind of girl who received a pony on her eighth birthday, busted her hymen riding it by her ninth, and grew utterly bored with it by her tenth. The kind of woman who aspires to carry a small dog around in a purse that cost more money than it could reasonably hold. The kind of indifferent, entitled, "woke up this way" beauty who's had everything handed to her on a Limoges porcelain platter, and can't even begin to fathom why anyone else might think that unfair. Make no mistake dear readers, though we all know Ross ultimately comes out the "winner" in the great Rachel Green pussy sweepstakes, the truth is, Rachel always wins.

Her story begins only too aptly, when she runs out on a $40,000 wedding (S01E01), soliciting comfort in the arms of five "Friends" whom she didn't bother inviting. They take her in (because of course they do), patiently endure her relentless self-involvement, and basically drop everything to offer shelter, employment assistance, and unqualified encouragement as she, at the tender age of 26, cuts up "daddy's" credit cards and attempts to learn how to make and pour coffee at a semiprofessional level. She does all this while nurturing dreams of breaking into the fashion industry, despite having never worked a day in her life. The implication is she wants a job that will afford her discounts at department stores. That's it. That's her whole deal.

In less than two years, Rachel is hired on at Bloomingdales (because of course she is), and soon comes to believe that she not only *deserves* everything she wants, but that she has now somehow *earned* it too. She manifests an almost supernatural capacity to make herself the center of attention, be it grabbing the mic for some impromptu self-actualization at her ex-fiancé's wedding (S02E24), regaling a Central Perk full of strangers with life lessons she's learned while serving them the wrong lattes (S03E10), or throughout any number of egregiously bitchy efforts to sabotage Ross's attempts at finding happiness with other women (S03E25, S04E16, and God knows how many others).

This pattern of destructive behavior comes to a head in S04E24 when, overcome with jealousy, Rachel flies to England to break up Ross's wedding. She stops short, and the show is quick to absolve her of this ruthless act of romantic brinksmanship, but in perhaps the most famous moment in all of *Friends* lore, Ross says Rachel's name at the altar instead of his fiancée, Emily's, and just by showing up, her victory is secured. The bride, for her part, repays him with a forearm shiver and a defenestratory bathroom escape while Rachel stays prowling around the margins, in one scene laying out Ross's lifelong "obsession" with her point by point like Henry Gondorff recounting a long con. The degree to which she's kept him in the back pocket of her skintight hip-huggers is staggering, and by the time she "accidentally" runs into him at the airport and gets herself invited on his aborted honeymoon, it's difficult to see him as anything but a doomed mark. Rachel always wins.

Bright and bubbly on the approach with girl-next-door-to-a-pilates-gym appeal, Rachel repeats this cycle of manipulation time and again, be it with her handsome neighbor Danny (S05E10), the kind, stoic widower Paul (S06E23), or her college friend Melissa (S07E20) – (lest you think her evil ways extend only to the menfolk). I won't even try to catalogue here all her offenses against her supposed "best friend" Monica (though disingenuously rekindling her romance with Ross the same night Monica gets engaged [S07E01], announcing her own pregnancy at Monica's wedding [S08E01], and annexing "Emma," the baby name Monica's had picked out since she was 14 [S08E24] feels like a reasonable summation) – but the overall point remains the same. Rachel takes no responsibility for her actions, lazing through life with the all-consuming vanity of *Snow White*'s Evil Queen, never *asking* "who's the fairest in the land?" so much as just demanding that everyone agree it's her and always will be (here seems as good a place as any to note that, if you work out the math, Rachel actually ages at a rate two years slower than the rest of the Friends).

In closing, Rachel Green is every girl who ever ignored me at a high school football game, only to call me for a ride when the quarterback ditched her at Steak 'n Shake. She's every girl who enlisted me to lug her mattress up three flights of stairs, but never invited me to lie down on it after. She's every girl who told me I was her best friend – elected me "mayor of the friend zone" – and then in the next breath, explained why that wasn't enough. Only a shameless, sniveling weasel like Ross, with his endless capacity to keep crawling back – keep pushing his Sisyphean way up those eternally perky tits – could ever end up with, as Kanye put it, "a woman so heartless." She may get off the plane, but there's no way in Hell she stays there. I guaran-goddamn-tee it.

Either she uproots Ross and drags him back to Paris, or she leaves him behind, four-times divorced, alone at a shitty bar he didn't even want to go to in the first place. Rachel always wins.

Ross
or
"What if she goes down there and sleeps with a bunch of guys!?!?!"

And that, dear readers, brings us to Ross Geller. The role model that brought the manliest minds of my generation to their groveling, sensitivity-trained knees. I don't know about you, but I've come to hold David Schwimmer personally responsible for my own formative misunderstanding of modern masculinity. His Ross was a creation birthed in the minds of sad, lonely, male writers and held up as an exemplar of what modern women wanted, when all he actually typified was what sad, lonely, male writers *wanted* modern women to want. He was a pied pipe-layer; a leading man to nowhere. His sulky, whiny, neurotic, possessive, paternalistic slap-shtick only intensified over the course of ten years, and yet somehow, the seemingly unattainable Rachel Green ultimately decided she couldn't live without him. To Hell with Watergate. This was the greatest lie ever perpetrated against the American people.

Ross begins the show in crisis, recently divorced from Carol, a fledgling lesbian he inopportunely impregnated on her way to the other side of the playing field. Unable to grasp his predicament, he buries his wholly justifiable anger and resentment under a shroud of "nice guy" behaviors, always doing "the right thing" by his bitch ex-wife, her cuckolding, ur-bitch life partner, and Rachel, the girl he's pined for since puberty. He's an alpha male cut down to beta stature in harrowing fashion, but his demotion is portrayed as a net positive. He may have lost his balls (now floating in separate jars of sandalwood-scented essential oils under Carol's and Rachel's bathroom sinks), but he gained the compassion and understanding essential to modern manhood.

Or so *Friends* would have you believe...

In practice, Ross's ongoing attempts to subvert his dominant nature result in repeated, ugly incidents of rage filtering through his façade of femmepath enlightenment. A matzo ball of suppressed impulses with a PHD in being markedly smarter than everyone else, he regularly winds up yelling like a maniac just to make what should be simple, obvious points (S03E02) or committing physical violence against inanimate objects to release his pent-up frustration (S05E12). He displays a dark, predatory perversity which leads him to corner women on the subway (S04E10), send hatemail filled with bird feces to an ex (S05E12), masquerade as a masseur to get a woman to undress in his apartment (S07E02), and even make an aggressive move on his own cousin (S07E19), all in lieu of just throwing Rachel down on that iconic orange loveseat and taking what's rightfully his (it would have been a much shorter show, but I'm telling you, she would've loved him for it).

Unable to control his own life, Ross becomes demoniacally controlling, first of Rachel whenever their exhausting, on-again/off-again tryst happens to switch on-again (S03E15, and countless others), and later toward many other girlfriends (S04E18, S06E18, etc.). Between Carol's betrayal and Rachel's careless gameplaying, by the time he finds a good match (poor, poor Emily), he's already too unraveled to respool. More than any other member of the Friends' unbroken circle-jerk of neuroses, Ross was a reasonable, intelligent, and strikingly mature adult who was methodically broken down and stripped of his dignity by the shrill demands of an ever-mounting hoard of women. He fought tooth and nail from the day of his bar mitzvah to become a red-blooded, American man, but those cunts just wouldn't let him have it.

For his efforts, he endures two more divorces, is forced to take a leave of absence from work and submit to both psychiatric counseling and neuroleptic medication (S05E09), and is saddled with yet another illegitimate child, this time by Rachel, who – just in case he was getting his hopes up – makes it clear she still wants to keep her options open (S08E09, S09E12, S09E23, etc.). He becomes such a muddled, addled, overtaxed mess he starts actively ruining his own life just trying to keep up with his obligations to that stuck-up slut. The thought of her ending up with anyone else drives him to the brink of madness.

This, my friends, is what I had to work with. These were the methods I saw held up as right and true. When I should have been reading Mailer and Hemingway, I was watching Must See TV, and so Ross Geller became, to my young, impressionable mind, the pinnacle of modern manhood. The guy who walked a thousand miles so the girl of his dreams would take one step (off an airplane). I thought if I was nice enough, romantic enough, *good* enough - that if I tried hardest, and held on tightest - that if I learned to think with my heart instead of my dick - that one day, I'd get my dream girl. My Rachel. That *she* would choose *me*. But guess what folks. That's not how the world works. That's just TV. Just the movies. The stories we write when our stories don't work out how we planned.

It's not that I don't believe in love - quite the opposite in fact. If anything, I believe too much - in the perfect, life-altering, neverending storybook love espoused by every piece of popular literature, music, film, and television that's been hucked at humanity for the past 100 years. I believe in it to such a specific and willfully naïve degree that I'll absolutely never find it. I couldn't possibly. And even if I did, I couldn't help but fuck it up. I've waited too long now. Built it up too much in my mind. It's a sunk cost I refuse to see as fallacy; an ideal I'll cling to forever, despite overwhelming evidence against my hopeless case.

I've just completed my third circuit through Friends in just over two weeks, and like any other drug, bingeing has raised my tolerances. The Friends' codependence is toxic. Their willful disinterest in art, literature, history, and science (and their mob mockery of Ross when he tries to educate them) is repulsive. Their balcony voyeurism and grotesque fixation on their sex lives is symptomatic of their unremittingly judgmental worldviews. They weed out dissent, squelch individuality, deny each other even a shred of privacy, and trundle gaily onward like Siamese sextuplets joined at the hip, reassuring themselves that their bland, cloistered world is all there is or need be.

I used to think I wanted this kind of familial social circle. That it could form naturally under the right circumstances. I never thought *Friends* was real, mind you - I want to be clear about that - but I did think it was realistic(ish). Perhaps you'll think that my hamartia, but these people led lives that seemed achievable to me. *Likely*, even. They were all such dumpster fires emotionally, but they made it work. I didn't have half their problems growing up. My parents loved me. I wasn't fat, or hideously unattractive. I got good grades. Went on dates. Worked on the school paper.

Nothing out of the ordinary. Not really.

But somewhere along the way, the world just got too big for me. What few friends I had left me behind, off to see that world and learn how it works, while I stayed put, idly complaining about all the ways in which it doesn't. I never (to use the parlance of our times) "found my tribe." I watched TV expecting real life to live up to its standards, and myself to somehow live into them. I thought it would just happen. That one day I'd wake up, go meet my makeshift family of friends at the coffee shop, and start talking about our fabulous, offscreen lives. But it never did. I watched and watched. Listened. Studied. Tried. Rewatched. Wrote. Dissected. Explicated. And watched some more. But it never happened for me. I couldn't make it happen.

This article marks a new chapter here at GRUNDL - one of which I'm truly proud. We'll be attempting to create original, discursive content a cut above the Top 10 listicles you're used to from us; long-form criticism like the article you just read. I hope you've enjoyed this one. I hope you'll keep reading. But I'm here to tell you, this will be my first and last.

    I thought it was what I wanted. My place in the conversation. My Parisian dream job. But just as there's no way Ross made Rachel happy after that fateful deplaning, or vice versa, I too can never be. My life, and their love, will remain circling, snarling, Hegelian dialectics until we're all dead and gone. There are no happy endings. No one will be *there for you*.

    So I'm out. I won't be part of it anymore. I can't. TV lied to us, dear readers, just like rock n' roll lied to our parents, and the internet is lying to our kids right now. Right this fucking minute. Everyone makes up their own story as they go along, and no one ever gets what they really want, even when they do.

    These people are not your *Friends*.

You sit back and take a long look around your living room full of multimedia. 99,502 hours. 4,145 days. 11½ years. And this is it. The shining diffusion of all you've learned. A lifetime of watching.

You finished it. That's what matters. It may not be much, but it's the first thing you've finished in ages. You smile weakly through sticky teeth, post directly to GRUNDL, assemble an outfit that will allow you to pump gas without attracting too much attention, and drift out into the night.

You know, on some migratory, sea turtle-type level, exactly where you want to go, but there's one more thing you want to do before you leave this Hellmouth of a town. A farewell address. One last fuck you. A trolling for the ages.

You drive all the way to the park with your lights doused, and find the North gate's rococo scrollwork and Cassie Abrams' moonpie face all looking oddly sinister in the flicker of memorial candlelight.

Giving your can of aerosol corundum a couple of rattly shakes, you begin vandalizing her Hallmark cenotaph with a message crueler than any hate speech - a fatal blow to whatever hope these simpering fools might have left regarding her cold case salvation. Name calling and fearmongering aren't enough this time. You want to do real damage. To not just ruin peoples' days, but ruin their lives. To replace their faith with despair. To offer them a different kind of closure; one uglier, and harder to live with. Something that will sit in the pits of their stomachs and eat away at them from the inside out. Something to convince them that evil has won.

You spray in a gruesome, red scrawl that leaves the sea of mementos mori looking more like a satanic blood rite than a holy votive, and your eyes flare in the delicate flame as you step back and admire the second piece of writing you've finished today:

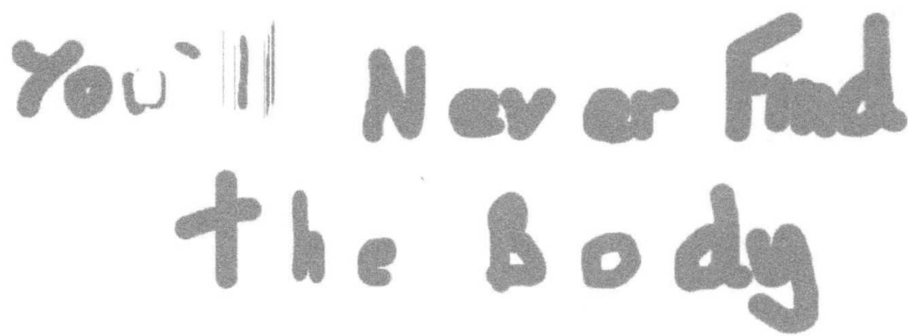

You have to say, you're on a roll.

You laugh lycanthropic, wipe the spray paint can for prints, toss it in a bush, and light a smoke off one of the candles. You know it's risky to linger, but for the first time in days you feel some small measure of power; some regaining of control. In this moment, nothing can touch you. Not withdrawal. Not writer's block. Not Claire, or Artemis, or Elle. Even if a cop wandered up right now, you could claim you were just out for a late-night constitutional. You could even play the hero if you wanted ("Thank God you're here officer, I was just about to call someone. Do you think it was really the killer? Who else would do something so horrible!?"). They couldn't prove

547

shit. No one would ever know. They'd just have to wonder. Forever.

You flick your cig, its tip still rutilant, toward the Women in Black's long-vacated post, and in the flash of its aerobatic cartwheel, your eyes sketch the outline of a figure against the wall. Your breath catches, and you swallow a yelp as some unknown presence grinds your gasper to cinders and steps forward into the wavy, paraffin light.

"You are bad man," says the Middle Eastern Woman in Black - her burqa as good as a ghillie suit at this umbral hour. Who knows how long she'd been back? It could've been days. Weeks even. How would you know? You've been watching fucking *Friends*! She could've been standing there the whole time; hiding a stadium buddy under her ascetic, cloak-and-dagger garments; patiently awaiting your return; refusing to be cowed by your cynicism; ready to clap back; ready to take you down.

"Very bad man," she says again, her *Homeland*-villainess accent growing more adamant as she approaches like floating death, preparing to send you to Jahannam with one bony touch.

You're frozen; your brain bolting toward full-on panic; your test pattern life flashing before your cathode ray eyes. Knowing you must flee now or face real, state-sanctioned justice, social ostracism, and maybe even incarcerated ass-pounding when all's said and done, you lunge forward, push the encroaching wall of black fabric to the ground, and run.

You hear her cry out in pain as you trip over crosses, kick through candles, and scatter flower arrangements to seed, but you sprint all the way to your van without looking back. You slide across the hood like a Duke Boy, dive in, and peel out. Westward ho. A decade after graduation, you're finally getting out of this go-nowhere town.

Finale

You've been driving for days. Your windshield is pockmarked with dead bugs and sports a bindi of birdshit impervious to your wipers' swipings. Your back seat is a veritable Carcosa of crushed energy drinks, grease-slathered jerky sleeves, mangled chip bags, and fragged cigarette stubs (you've grown too paranoid about All Points Bulletin surveillance to toss a single butt out the window, which has resulted in your burning a thousand points of darkness into your upholstery and drenching your interior in acrid, ashen reek).

You can smell yourself, even through the cigarette smoke, but no roadside shower facility could provide the level of security you need right now. Your hands, knees, and ankles all burn from stasis. Your mouth tastes like a gas chamber. Your eyes leak rheum at random, and regardless of whatever slurred trap rhymes or scorching bebop runs you use to fill the silence, all music defers to the motorik beat of your running-scared heart.

Your grandparents have been dead for 20 years, bidding farewell to light and oxygen within 180 minutes of each other after spending their entire star-crossed lives in the same rusty little town right on the border between the Midwest and the West. You spent many a long car trip here, sitting in the backseat, engrossed in the boxed-and-bubbled exploits of various mutant X-teams while your parents counted fenceposts and dead armadillos. Sometimes antelope would bound alongside their station wagon, momentarily drawing your attention away from Wolverine's claws or Psylocke's ass, and out into the endless vistas. You'd marvel at how much of America remained wholly uninhabitable, even amidst the futurist utopian gleam of the 1980s. These bleak swaths of land impressed upon you at a very young age the brutality and heroism inherent in the initial exploration of this evilest of empires.

The way you remember it, the town was only about four streets wide, and defined by the distressed lumber and faded paint of a bygone era, before such things became intentional and trendy; a time when they just were. Smokestacks burped plumes of black lung into the biggest of big skies and rather than decry their contribution to our now-apocalyptic climate crisis, folk breathed deep, relishing the smell of hard work done by rough hands. The drugstore too was aromatic, with the intermingled scents of since-banned disinfectants, baking soda tooth polishes, and nickel ice cream cones spun thick with malt powder. The sidewalks were wood, not cement.

The roads were dirt, not asphalt. It was a prelapsarian world – one not yet falling apart – and more than that even, the last place you remember feeling like a real person.

Exhaustedly scanning the road for state troopers, you pass a grandly opening Starbucks (where once stood an old-timey filling station). Around it runs a line of obese fucks – all glued to their phones – waiting to be among the lucky first few to purchase the country's most readily available cup of coffee. You pull on your cigarette until you throw up a little in your mouth.

Your own phone started blowing up around Bismarck – (don't ask how you ended up in Bismarck) (it was a wholly unintentional detour) (*you* try going on the lam without GPS) (see where *you* end up) – and upon discovering you had 22 missed calls, several from numbers you didn't recognize but felt comfortable assigning to police detectives, bounty hunters, and the aggrieved friends and family of Cassie Abrams, you removed the battery, and the Sim Card, and deposited all three pieces in three different trashcans at three different 7-Elevens.

You don't know what's going on back home – if your face is plastered on telephone poles – if local news has eyes in the sky – if there's a price on your head, or a thrill-kill mob hatcheting through your privacy fence – but your imagination is supremely active. You need to know what you're running from, and how far you have to go to get away.

You peel your eyes for the Public Library, always your favorite part of those childhood trips, but nothing looks familiar anymore amidst an avalanche of retail furniture warehouses and chain buffet restaurants. What had become of this place? With few exceptions, it looks just like the place you left, and every other place in between.

Having reached the spot where you vaguely remember the library having been, you take a few deep breaths into a Doritos bag and turn into the bumper-to-bumper sprawl of a Super Walmart.

Is this the state of the world now? Will the outdoors, someday soon, cease to be habitable? Will the planet become one vast, interconnected matrix of Walmarts through which we walk, drive, and shop our way to whichever Walmart we call home? Walmarts as far as the eye can see? Walmarts all the way down?

You step out into what looks like a splatter of semi-dried vomit littered with chicken bones and, deciding not to speculate on how this gruesome still life came to be painted, hurry inside. There, an aggressively wrinkly woman in a blue polyester vest greets you with a frigorific cough, followed by a croaky, "Welcome to Walmart." You force yourself to smile, and speaking as slowly and deliberately as you can, inquire about the library.

"Oh, the old library?" she asks.

"Yes Ma'am."

"I used to work at the old library. It was so lovely. People don't read anymore."

"Yes Ma'am, I know."

"You young people, with your phones."

"Yes Ma'am. But that's not me. I'd really like to find the library."

"Why don't you just use your phone?"

"I don't have a phone Ma'am."

"You don't? But you're so young."

"It's a long story Ma'am."

"You should try the electronics section."

"I'd really just like to find the library!"

"Well, you've found it!"

"What do you mean?!" you ask, losing patience. "This is a Walmart!"

The woman points a psychopomp finger toward the back of the store, smiles, and repeats her opening line. "Welcome to Walmart."

Already feeling overexposed, you throw up your hands and start walking, the endless repeating aisles of America's favorite big-box retailer only heightening your paranoid disorientation. Laundry DDT to the left. Stuffed endangered animals to the right. Gallon jars of thrombotic pickles. Tiny shoes made for children, by children. Chloroform-ready dishtowels. Torture-ready drill bits. Barbed fishing lures. Blunt wine bottles. Boardgames -*Life*, *Risk*, *Sorry*. Getaway tires. Empty greeting cards. Lingerie. $1 DVDs. Coffee. Lightbulbs. Toilet paper. And on and on. Your head is swimming in low, low prices. What was that dotty old biddy talking about? There's not a book in this whole goddamned store!

And then you see it: the entryway - built right into the wall - a gold plaque hanging beside it, declaring the old public library a historical landmark, and Walmart its faithful steward. In the fine print, you learn that the Walton family bought the land back in 2006, but were barred from tearing down the institution proper because Truman once made a whistle stop there or something, so they just absorbed it like they would a local nail salon or a Subway franchise. Your whole body feels like a cluster headache. The fluorescent lighting and insidious pop radio; the maculated tile and pestiferous, industrial air conditioning; the racks on racks on racks of...

just...fucking...*stuff!* It all bleeds together for a moment, and you have to grip the doorframe and count to thirty before pushing yourself inside.

The room is completely unattended, the walls lined with shelves of face-out, hardback ubiquity; your James Pattersons, your Nora Robertses, your Stephen Kings. The stacks have been allocated, to the last, to movies (wither Blockbuster) which look to outnumber the books ten-to-one. A sign on the wall explains that the lending of any title is free with a Walmart purchase of $5 or more, and to be handled by a "Team Member" at checkout. There are two computer terminals, both so old you're pretty sure they were here the last time you visited, and that's about it. The various annexes – the children's nook, the YA section, the calligraphy and ESL classrooms, the little theater where they'd show nature documentaries – are all padlocked; repurposed as layaway storage.

Fighting the pyromaniacal impulse to run to Automotive for a gas can and Kitchenware for a match and burn this whole fucking building to the ground, you log onto a computer to check your local picayune for reports of your ongoing fugitivity, only to find a different crime plastered across the homepage.

You stare in disbelief at Gander's blood-plashed futon. His three fearsome guard dogs lay in a forlorn heap of simplex, animal grief. His gun, now unholstered, is visible on the table behind them. You can even make out a bit of his ceiling's découpage de décolletage in the top of the frame, beneath the lurid headline *"Threeway Incest Massacre Rocks Local Trailer Park!"* The article proceeds to explain that, as far as police can tell, Gander and his Aunt Sheila were (allegedly) coitus interrupted last night by Sheila's husband Teddy, who (allegedly) opened fire, (allegedly) killing Sheila before being overpowered by Gander's dogs. Enraged, Gander then (allegedly) grabbed his gun and executed his uncle with a point-blank headshot before turning the piece on himself.

No one, it seems, lives in a vacuum.

Your ballooning grab-bag of physical and psychological stressors finally splits its seams, and you vomit into a small, metal trashcan, filling it nearly halfway before you can breathe again. The walls of beach reads and book club selections are closing in. Your mind is a blistering Frank Wright cacophony. Determined to not let things end here in the belly of the smiley-faced beast – to not go gentle into that Blue Light – you bolt for the exit, charging back through the disorganized salmagundi of food and tools; clothes and toys – back past the cryogenic old woman, her third robotic "Welcome to Walmart" cutting you like a deep-discounted three-pack of disposable razors – and back out the automatic doors. All hail dear low-price leader.

You roar onto the main drag, overwhelmed by thoughts of Gander's last moments, and whether your irresponsibly tossed-off advice played a part in his grisly familicide. You still don't know who's after you, or what they're after you for. You haven't slept in days, and cigarettes are doing you more harm than good. You need some kind of release. You consider jerking off while driving, but your dick still hasn't forgiven you, and shrinks from your touch.

Just find the house.

A few miles into the farmland, you spot some imposing stonework bearing the words "Yesteryear Estates" at the entrance to your grandparents' neighborhood. You turn in, past the old mill – now converted into luxury condos. You drive by the home of Connie Barstow, who gave you your first kiss on the low branches of a crabapple tree – since cut down to make room for tennis courts. You steel yourself as you round the final bend, but it's not enough.

The McMansion looming before you, at first glance, appears to be an entirely new structure, dropped atop your grandparents' classic farmhouse Wicked Witch of the West-style. But looking closer, you realize it's even worse than that. Tiny portions of the old house can still be seen – the oaken front door; the breakfast nook at the far-right corner; the circular Rapunzel window in the attic – but the majority, just like the Walmart library, has been subsumed. A three-car garage extends out over what used to be your grandmother's vegetable garden. A DirecTV satellite juts like a middle finger from a brand new terracotta roof.

One foot out the door before you even secure the parking brake, you're ready to grab your tire iron and let it all end here, with you, whoever the fuck is inside that house, and a murder-suicide to call your very own (*God, Gander, why!?*) when a small boy and girl come tearing around the side yard wrapped in towels (surely from some travesty-sized pool out back). Walking slowly behind are a sturdy, bald-headed man and a graying, thin-but-not-frail woman, both in their late 60's. The kids circle back, and the man and woman pick them up and hug them all the way inside. Through the bay window, you see them playing on individual, blue and pink iPads at the table while the woman makes them Keurig hot chocolate. The man watches golf on a 50" flatscreen in the den.

You stop.

You blow your nose on your sleeve.

You look up at the sky, and around at the trees and the other houses and lawns.

You look back at the kids and their grandparents.

You don't know what you're angry about.

You don't know what you're doing here.

Whatever it was you were looking for in this place, it's long gone.

Δ

Back on the highway and nearing neural collapse, your system flooded with caffeine and nicotine, you spill out of your vehicle and stagger into a rest stop near the state line. The walls are splattered with vagrant excretions, and a gang of horseflies menacingly circle the trashcan. You take the last in a long line of empty stalls, grateful for the isolation, and the silence. Dangerously dehydrated, you feel a tremendous pressure in the ball-peen head of your penis, and your tepid stream is so weak you actually piss a little on your own scrotum.

You attempt to force a bowel movement, but your guts have turned to wet concrete, and the harder you push, the more you can practically feel them setting inside you. You press your elbows into your thighs until your knees blanch. You see tracers inching through the foul air. A fly lands on your bare ass, looking for a farm-to-table meal. You notice the toilet paper roll is empty, save a ragged, white isosceles of single-ply surrender. Above it is a generously-proportioned gloryhole, and above that, etched in jagged penknife: "Abandon all hope, ye who enter here."

Taking a few lamaze breaths, you brace for another push when you hear an authoritative voice call out your first and last name.

"I know yer in here," the voice says. "Saw yer car out front."

You freeze, desperately scanning your surroundings for an escape route you know doesn't exist.

"Come on now. There's a lotta people lookin' fer you son."

As though acting out a script, you quietly climb atop the toilet seat, staying low with a foot on each side, not even daring to pull up your pants, lest a telltale rustle give you away.

"Don't make this any harder'n it has ta be."

You can hear his nightstick methodically rapping on, and then pushing open each squeaky door, slowly making its way down the line. You've seen this scenario play out a hundred times, on screens of every size. It's an impossible cliché, and it's about to be your life.

You're sweating washtubs.

You feel a blackout rolling over your mind.

Your left eye twitches strabismal, and for a few seconds, all you see is yawning, dead static.

. . .

. . .

. . .

"*Pbbbth*"

. . .

What?

What's this?

You start back.

You can't believe it.

For once, your body has come to your aid.

Still in your defensive squat atop the commode, your organs snap into place and... *plop*. A single, smooth, velvety turd slides out of your asshole like a mud-puppy - like a golden egg - *like a goddamn baby* - and with barely a ripple, slips into the water below.

A rush of clarity hits you square on the bridge of your nose, and a childlike sense of invincibility takes hold. You hear the cop snicker at your fart and mutter "gotcha now boy" as you reach down between your legs and grasp your perfect offspring.

You feel the wall rattle between your stall and the next one over as the second-to-last door swings open, and the cop's buffed belt-buckle swaggers in front of the gloryhole.

"One more to go" he announces, his field-hand drawl bouncing off the tile.

You keep your eye trained on the hole, watching the buckle disappear below the lower lip as he crouches down.

"Wherever is he hiding?"

You see his badge flash as his chest comes level, and then his mouth working on a plug of chaw as he lowers his head.

"Where oh where can that little boy be?"

And then his eye. His big, brown, bloodshot eye stares straight at you through the wall – this wall that's seen so many encounters between hard men; tricks and johns; curious deviants and professional lowlifes; working stiffs and loathsome criminals; hitchhikers, nomads, and vagabond strangers of every walk and stripe – and you take your shot, shoving hot, rancid shit straight on through to the other side.

The cop screams at a higher pitch than his speaking voice would have suggested was possible as you sprint past him outside, already finagling your keys from your half-zipped pants. You see him stumble out and draw his gun as your engine unleashes a leonine roar, but with a Rockwellian family picnicking nearby, and his depth-perception undoubtedly compromised by the patty of humanure smeared down his face, he can't bring himself to fire. You get, at most, a 30-second head start before a chorus of banshee sirens appears in your rearview.

In a bit of kismet, your MP3 player shuffles onto 2Pac's "When We Ride," all but putting a sideways pistol to your temple and ordering you to step on it. Police cars materialize out of the trees. Motorcycles emerge from behind billboards and beneath overpasses. Blue and red lights illuminate the dusky landscape, creating discordant, disco shadows in the surrounding foliage and clashing with the brilliant, natural pastels of the sunset ahead. An armored prison truck takes up the rear like a charging elephant driving a stampede.

Along this road, there is a notoriously unfinished bridge, partially spanning a large, man-made ditch. Long planned as a reservoir for the town's outlying farm communities, the project was abandoned amid budget cuts, blight, and drought; condemned to permanent eyesore-dom; soon a breeding ground for all kinds of unsavory activities, from meth sales, to runaway rapes, and even the occasional body dump. On city maps, it's just labeled "The Gulch," and often marked, at the behest of some self-amused cartographer, with an X and a primitive skull.

As a child, your Grandmother would read you *The Three Billy Goats Gruff* and insist the bridge over The Gulch was the very same one from the story. As teenagers, your cousins would dare each other to spend the night there on Halloween, but you never heard of anyone venturing past the tabby-striped barricades a mile out.

You can see them now. Rushing up to meet you. Growing larger by the second.

Are there things you'd do differently if you could? Absolutely. Things you'd change about yourself? About the way you've lived your life? No question. Would any of it matter in the end? You feel certain the answer there is a resounding no. This world is a sliding scale of shit, and you've finally slid clear off the end of it. You're ready for whatever comes next - even if it's nothing.

You're right up on the Road Closed barriers now. And then you're crashing through them like so much tangerine kindling. And then you're all alone. In a bit of cosmic timing so ludicrous you laugh out loud – as if some higher power is pulling strings and manning soundboards from above – your MP3 player dies in the middle of Kadafi's verse, and your soundsystem switches over to the radio, and The Hollies' "The Air That I Breathe."

This is it, you think as you hit 110 mph. Your artsy, slow-mo, film school-directed, incongruously-soundtracked finale. Your big finish. The end of the line.

If I could make a wish…

The sun is a runny egg yolk before you.

I think I'd pass…

A sky clear of telephone lines stretches out ahead.

Can't think of anything I need…

The trees are shapeless rivers of grass clippings.

No cigarettes, no sleep…

The clouds are pillowy and pixelated, as though plucked from a Sarasaland sky.

No light…No sound…

Your red and blue persecutors congeal into a bleary, Christlike purple.

Nothing to eat, no books to read…

The world turns to Ralph Steadman pencil scrawls as you hit 120.

You meet the bridge with a violent bounce. Your tires squeal, swerve, and redouble their efforts. You're climbing toward the middle, where you hope your speed will send you soaring over the lightning-edged crack in the center - a gap of about 18 feet. Your toes have gone numb against the gas pedal. You can still feel your own excrement squish between your fingers, and you breathe deep, savoring your personal stench one last time. Your eyes narrow into focused, Eastwoodian slits. You knead the well-worn scrap of paper in your pocket between your thumb and forefinger - its hand-scrawled message little more than a smudge now - and without thinking, let it flutter out the window as the song's epic, titular chorus rains down on you in beautiful, four-part harmony.

You know you can make this jump. You believe you can make this jump. You have to make this jump. With twenty yards left, you begin murmuring softly:

"Just like in the movies."

"Just like in the movies."

"Just like in the movies . . .

You thought that was the end...

But it wasn't...

Stinger

The day wakes you with the sound of your own arrhythmia as interpreted by a Minimoog synthesizer.

You try to turn and peer at the screen, but find your head, and indeed your sum total allotment of appendages, not currently at your disposal. Straining your ganglia toward their peripheral limits, you see your **electrocardiogram** plunging and spiking at precipitous and wholly entropic intervals, and behind that an even more unsettling sight: your parents, slumped dozing in vinyl chairs beneath a boxy, 30" television mounted high in the corner. While Alex Trebek calmly reads answers at a volume just North of mute, your mind screams a million questions, and your eyes recenter on the smoldering landscape of your body.

Your chest is covered by a paper hospital gown, and your arms and legs are individually mummified - encased in a near-panoply of plaster and suspended in traction at cubist angles reminiscent of the flailing figure from the "Slippery When Wet" sign. You are naked from the waist down, your junk covered by a terrycloth towel, your ass pressing into the cold, beveled edges of a stainless steel bedpan. Your jaw is wired shut.

Attempting to test various points of interest, you only manage to light yourself up like Cavity Sam. Your legs are rotting driftwood, rife with industrious maggots. Your ribs are a tangled bale of concertina wire threatening your jiffypop-lungs with every breath. Your arms feel like they shattered, only to be smushed back together with Play-Doh (you imagine your casts would rattle like puzzle boxes had you the abductoral power to shake their contents), and your fingers have been splinted into gauzy penguin flippers. Your tongue seems somehow diminished inside your condemned oral cavity, but is still pliable enough to confirm that you've misplaced close to half your teeth. Your head, needless to say, is throbbing, and even involuntary maxillofacial functions like swallowing and blinking are increasing in pain by the second.

You can see you have a morphine drip, but lack the motor function to operate it, and so, coming to terms with your sole, inescapable option, you start eking out the only sound you're capable of making - a high, embarrassingly pitiful whine that lands somewhere between pinched Evan Parker solo and raped alley cat. Your parents stir - first your father, whose searing disappointment cuts through your dressings like a bandsaw, and then your mother, who rushes to your side and presses the call button amidst weeping declarations of love for you, and gratitude to Jesus Christ.

A strikingly handsome – dare you say, Draperesque? – doctor appears, gives you a few clicks of morphine that fog your brain while barely moving the needle pain-wise, and informs you that you're lucky to be alive in a tone that rather suggests the opposite. He tells you you've been in a coma for two weeks after being hit by an SUV (wait, what?). He tells you what day it is (Monday), what city you're in (your own), and that no one else was hurt due to your accident (the driver said you came sliding across the hood of your van and right into traffic like you were "playing James Bond or something"). He explains that your body was so relaxed, due to extreme THC consumption, that you survived being tossed some 30 feet through the air, and into the side of a Shoney's restaurant (what the fuck is happening!?!).

He emphasizes again, a little more sincerely, that you are extremely lucky to be alive. Then, with all the bedside manner of an NFL "Jacked Up" video, he tells you about your injuries: Broken left foot, broken right tibia, fractures in both patellae and extensive tearing of various knee ligaments, broken right femur, crushed left testicle, lacerated spleen, seven cracked ribs, punctured right lung, compound fractures in both ulnae, cracked right olecranon, nine broken fingers, cracked clavicle, three fractured vertebrae, broken jaw, partially severed tongue, eleven broken teeth, perforated left eardrum, and severe concussion. He explains that you've already undergone two surgeries, and will need at least two more, as well as extensive physical therapy if you ever hope to walk again (and that it will be over a year before you can even try). He says your health insurance through GRUNDL will offset the costs to a degree, but that this will be a staggeringly expensive ordeal. He tells you to get used to this hospital room, as it will be your home for the duration. He tells you a third time that you are extraordinarily, historically, faith-in-God-restoringly lucky to be alive. He then shakes your father's hand, endures an uncomfortably long hug from your mother, and leaves.

Your mother continues through a whole gamut of histrionics while your father just stares at you, searching for something - anything - he might hold on to and understand about this situation. After what feels like an eternity, he tells you through gritted teeth that he's glad you're ok. He says your mother's been worried sick, desperately trying to reach you since your last article posted to GRUNDL (they still read everything you write, without fail). He adds that they've both delayed their impending retirements to help defray the costs of your recovery, as well as any legal fees you might end up owing.

From there he explains with careful tact, but no discernible sympathy, that he's put into motion the sale of your house, and virtually everything of value inside it, mentioning the TVs and the computers, but stopping short of any further itemization. Your mother looks down at you as well now, calming her sobs and blowing her nose on a handful of well-traveled tissues. You can see fear in them both, silently wanting to ask you a thousand questions you won't be able to answer for months, and simultaneously dreading the day that you can.

Your father pauses to let all this sink in, and your eyes naturally drift to the TV, which transitioned at some point from *Jeopardy* to the nightly news, where a story about the crowd size at Trump's inauguration is wrapping up. What appears next sets your nerve endings ashiver with the sensation of a stock-still double take, but even as your vision has blurred noticeably since the doctor upped your dosage, there's still no mistaking what you're seeing: the park - *your* park - packed to the hedges with people of every color and creed - a crowd at least as large as that pictured in the previous segment - engaging in a massive singalong of "All You Need is Love." And at the center of it all, holding up her weather-beaten, posterboard sign like goddamned Norma Rae, is the Middle Eastern "Woman in Black." A newscaster recounts how she was discovered two weeks ago, in the wee hours of the morning, on hands and knees, assiduously scrubbing graffiti off the sidewalk and scraping red paint from candles and toys left in memory of a long-missing girl. Unable or unwilling to identify the vandal to police, the woman described seeing him stumble through the defaced mementos while fleeing, effectively destroying his own message before anyone could read it. Beyond that, she didn't even want her name mentioned. She only wanted to help.

In the weeks since, the community has rallied around her and her small band of peace activists, helping bring National attention to their cause and create a viral movement from her simple act of kindness. The newscaster seems genuinely touched.

Your daring getaway.

It never happened.

No one was after you.

No one saw you.

No one knew a goddamned thing.

While your mouth is ill equipped to form a smile, your eyes must be expressing some semblance of relief, as the sad, bewildered faces of your parents both seem to register a flash of recognition. They'll never know the truth – will likely never even bring themselves to ask – but some part of them will always wonder if there was a connection, between their recidivist fuck-up son, and the bizarre events that transpired mere feet from the site of his horrible accident. They'll wonder, and that wondering alone will be enough to irrevocably break their hearts.

Even now, as the anchors explain there's still an open investigation surrounding the events of that evening, your father becomes emotional and turns away from your listless stare. Your mother, grabbing the baton, changes the channel and continues catching you up on the logistics of your recovery, explaining with borderline-inappropriate excitement how she's already begun fixing up their basement for when you're stable enough to be moved back home. Clearly torn between her fierce, maternal instincts, her love for your father, and in a distant third, perhaps some concern for her own psychological well-being, she still seems happy that she'll soon be spending a great deal of time taking care of you, her precious baby boy.

Seeing your father is spent, and copping to being fairly well exhausted herself, she asks if there's anything else they can do for you before they go, and realizing the televised company you're about to be stuck with, you direct all your remaining strength into another squeamish whine while ommatophoring your eyeballs at the TV, hoping to God she'll change the channel again, or simply turn it off.

Misunderstanding, she raises the volume, gives you a gentle kiss on the head that still feels rough enough to reopen your fontanel, and compels your father to do the same. They promise to come back tomorrow, and shuffle out the door, leaving you finally and decidedly alone, an indeterminate number of episodes into one of the FX network's annual "Every *Simpsons* Ever" marathons.

You feel hot, furious tears streak your cheeks as the clouds part over the sunny, zany, primary colors of Springfield, Wherever-the-Fuck - and then you feel something else. Your anus emits a squelchy, Hershey Kiss fart - a lone canary, cheeping out from your wracked coalmine - and your sphincter clenches, lurches painfully outward, and begins loosing a long, sticky rope of confectionary shit. It slithers out of you like a tapeworm, creating a whole palette of slucking, splurting, gooshing sounds as it coats the walls of your bedpan. It goes on forever - this mortal coil of defecation - leaving slime trails on your buttcrack as it turns to liquid for a time, before resolidifying and continuing to unwind itself, unabated, out and down, round and round. Every contraction is excruciating, as is your seal-breaking first piss into the catheter you didn't quite realize you were plugged into. When your evacuatory functions finally exhaust themselves, you feel desiccated to the point of nausea.

You can feel the top of your homecooked dung heap grazing your asshair, and for the first time in your life, your own shit smells repugnant to you - more like something that would come out of a sick animal than a well human. You're not sure if you're being monitored somehow, or if the smell is so putrid it wafts all the way to the nurses' station down the hall, but as if on cue, a young woman enters to stamp an exclamation point on your unfathomable humiliation.

Her carmine-red hair pulled back in a resplendent French plait. Her plump, glossy lips painted an eye-popping shade to match. Too voluptuous to hide her curves, her white scrubs snuggle her big, soft tits like expertly swaddled twin baby bottoms. She's spectacular, and while your doctor did mention the words "mild hallucinations" earlier - during something about temporary cognitive impairment you didn't quite grasp, and something about temporary memory loss you don't quite recall - there's no getting around it: your assigned caregiver bears a striking resemblance to Joan from *Mad Men*.

You feel your penis quiver for a split-second, but any attempt it might make to rise to this titillating occasion is immediately rebuffed by shockwaves of urethral agony. No. There will be no restorative nurse porn field-tested here today - no hero's welcomes or *Johnny Got His Gun* pity handjobs for you. Instead, you lie motionless and silent as she dons latex gloves and a surgical mask, gently hefts your buttocks like she's guessing hog weights at the fair, and dutifully removes and empties your bedpan. She then gives you a sexless, professional wipe with a moist towelette, plies you with a few more pumps of morphine, and sprays the room with what you feel is an insulting amount of disinfectant air freshener. There is one, brief moment when she bends over to adjust your monitor - the faintest tip of blue vein peeking up from her modest

neckline - that you think the tender, doughy flesh of her comely bosom might graze your cheek or the tip of your mirifically unbroken nose. Even the slightest touch would leave you forever grateful, and suggest some slim hope for a brighter day beyond these institutional, beige walls.

But no such serendipity befalls you. Her spatial awareness regarding her own divine proportions is never in doubt, and regardless of who you are, how you ended up here, and whatever she may or may not know about it, you're sure it's the furthest thing from her mind. She's just a woman, doing a job. To her, you're just another asshole.

Fin

DAVE FITZGERALD

582

ACKNOWLEDGEMENTS

First and foremost, always and forever, thanks to my beautiful, brilliant, and unfailingly supportive wife Jeanette, who gave me the kick in the butt I needed to start this book, and the time, space, encouragement, and love I needed to finish it. I owe it all to you bunny. You are the best one.

Secondly, thanks to Miette Gillette and Whiskey Tit, who took a chance on an unknown author shopping a book that was, essentially by design, guaranteed to rub some people the wrong way. Whatever I do from here on out, I will remain forever grateful to you, your press, and your fearless literary mission. You are the real deal.

Third, a mountain of thanks to Preston Fassel, who first plucked *Troll* off the submission pile three publishers and twenty-some-odd edits ago, championed it through thick and thin, and displayed endless kindness, patience, and integrity as I learned my way into the world of indie publishing. *Troll* owes its life to you, and in you I found both a trusted colleague, and a true friend.

I'd also very much like to thank my dear friends Sean Lincoln, Crystal "Evil" Lee, Ryan Crenshaw, Ryan Hague, and Robbie Steinbruegge, who are, in addition to Jeanette and Preston, the only people who ever read the certifiably insane, nearly-twice-as-long original draft of this book. Your enthusiasm and early insights meant the world to me, and proved invaluable in shaping this challenging character and his deeply unpleasant voice.

Heartfelt thanks to Ryan Smith, for all the chats, cheerleading, and vicariously shared joy and frustration throughout this process. I never expected to find such a good friend so late in the game.

Thanks to Chicago's coolest socialist bookseller/literary publicist/all-around badass Mandy Medley for all the great advice over the past few years. You planted the small press seed that day in Minneapolis, and at long last it's born some fruit. You are the God's honest bomb.

Thanks to Michael Seidlinger, David Leo Rice, Jason Teal, Brian Alan Ellis, Jess Hagemann, Darren Doyle, John Trefry, Lindsay Lerman, Shane Jesse Christmass, Gary Shipley, Chris

Kelso, Debra Di Blasi, David Scott Hay, Matthew Burnside, Tom Kendall, and Charlene Elsby for all your kind words about my words. Each one of you, in your way, made me feel not just welcomed into the small press community, but like I'd finally found my long-elusive tribe. I can't wait to read all your next books.

Thanks to E.W. Harris, Ryan White, Chris Nelms, Caleb Beckwith, Jason Matherly, and every other weirdo who ever darkened the doors of the Cunny Isle Bemusement Park. You all showed me, in one way or another, what it looks like to take your art seriously, and just how far I had to go. Sorry I was such a poseur.

Finally, thanks to my parents, who have always loved me unconditionally, supported my dreams, and believed in me even when I gave them very little justification for doing so; who have never once suggested that I "get a real job" or that writing might be "better as just a hobby;" and who I sincerely hope never, ever read this book.

DAVE FITZGERALD

586

ABOUT THE AUTHOR

Dave Fitzgerald is a writer living and working in the dank and balmy South. He has previously written for *Flagpole Magazine* and the (now-defunct) film website *Cinespect*, and currently contributes to *Heavy Feather Review*, *Daily Grindhouse* and *Cinedump*. He tweets @DFitzgerraldo. *Troll* is his first novel.

ABOUT THE PUBLISHER

WHISKEY TIT attempts to restore degradation and degeneracy to the literary arts. We are unwilling to sacrifice intellectual rigor, unrelenting playfulness, and visual beauty, putting forth texts that would otherwise be abandoned in a homogenized literary landscape.

In a world gone mad, our refusal to make this sacrifice is an act of civil service and civil disobedience alike, and our work reflects this. We welcome like-minded readers and writers.

ABOUT THE AUTHOR

Dave Fitzgerald is a writer living and working in the dank and balmy South. He has previously written for *Flagpole Magazine* and the (now-defunct) film website *Cinespect*, and currently contributes to *Heavy Feather Review*, *Daily Grindhouse* and *Cinedump*. He tweets @DFitzgerraldo. *Troll* is his first novel.

ABOUT THE PUBLISHER

WHISKEY TIT attempts to restore degradation and degeneracy to the literary arts. We are unwilling to sacrifice intellectual rigor, unrelenting playfulness, and visual beauty, putting forth texts that would otherwise be abandoned in a homogenized literary landscape.

In a world gone mad, our refusal to make this sacrifice is an act of civil service and civil disobedience alike, and our work reflects this. We welcome like-minded readers and writers.